BETH URICH

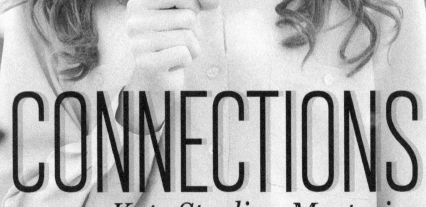

CONNECTIONS

Kate Starling Mysteries
Book Two

Connections

Kate Starling Mysteries
Book Two

Beth Urich

ZIMBELL HOUSE
PUBLISHING
UNION LAKE, MICHIGAN

For permission requests, write to the publisher
"Attention: Permissions Coordinator"
Zimbell House Publishing
PO Box 1172
Union Lake, Michigan 48387
mail to: info@zimbellhousepublishing.com

Published in the United States by Zimbell House Publishing
http://www.ZimbellHousePublishing.com
All Rights Reserved

Hardcover ISBN: 978-1-64390-211-1
Trade Paper ISBN: 978-1-64390-212-8
.mobi ISBN: 978-1-64390-213-5
ePub ISBN: 978-1-64390-214-2
Library of Congress Control Number: 2021908985

First Edition: July 2021
10 9 8 7 6 5 4 3 2 1

ZIMBELL HOUSE PUBLISHING
UNION LAKE

Dedication

To my mother, Eva, who inspired and supported me in so many ways. I wish she could have shared this milestone with me, but she is here in spirit.

Acknowledgements

Many thanks to forensic anthropologist, Frederick Snow, PhD, and Taney County Coroner, Kevin Tweedy, EMPT-P, CCEMTP, who each graciously provided answers to technical questions for this novel.

Chapter One

The flashing lights filled Kate's rearview mirror seconds before the speeding police car passed her on Main Street. Adrenalin electrified her muscles despite the lack of sirens. Dark splatter from the rain-soaked pavement arched across her windshield. She gripped the wheel as the aroma of a breaking news story filled her nostrils.

The officer eased through the four-way stop at the bottom of the hill before gliding left onto Commercial Street. She tapped her brake and checked for cross-traffic as she approached the intersection before making the turn herself.

With a glance at her dash clock, Kate realized her plan to beat her boss to the office would be scuttled by the detour. But postponing the—no doubt—well-earned reprimand could not be avoided. The young officer was on a mission and now so was Kate.

She slowed to a discreet distance as the patrol car proceeded over the railroad tracks and crossed St. Limas Street. The driver immediately turned left onto the large corner lot bordered on the west and north by woods along Roark Creek as it merged with Lake Taneycomo. He parked close to two half-ton pickups where St. Limas dead-ended at the creek.

As the young officer emerged from his car, he pulled on a jacket and hat against the persistent rainfall. The six-foot-six burly frame could belong to only one of Branson's finest—Patrolman Harold "Skip" Rogers. As a city-beat reporter, Kate interviewed Skip last year for an article on police recruits. His polite "yes ma'am" responses made her thirty-two years feel old at the time, but she hoped for the same courteous treatment this morning.

He treaded carefully around three pieces of heavy clearing machinery now abandoned on the muddy acreage. Two of a four-man crew met him halfway from where two others were hunkered down next to a massive uprooted tree stump on the far-side of the property.

Kate approached slowly and parked her car next to a flatbed logging truck situated along Commercial Street. The stack of twenty-foot trunk sections—and the renewed downpour—would conceal her Ford Escort from Skip and the others, if only temporarily. She waited as he listened to the first two men. When the three headed toward the stump, she grabbed the Silver Dollar City rain poncho from the back seat and eased the door open.

The ground, sodden with a week's worth of autumn rainstorms, was treacherous with tree limbs and branches, but she didn't hesitate to follow. Her hiking boots were tucked away in her closet at home, so her bargain-store tennis shoes would have to do. Kate prepared a speech in her mind, knowing Skip would spot her at any moment.

"Wait here," Skip said, signaling the men to stop. Taking a position still a dozen feet away, he surveyed the area on the root-end of the stump. Staring briefly, he lowered his chin to his chest for a moment and then unhooked the microphone attached to his uniform. "Dispatch, Rogers," he said, still facing away from Kate's position.

The female voice on the radio crackled, "Go ahead, Skip. Over."

"Yeah, I'm down by Roark Creek, north of the railroad tracks on Commercial. Looks like these boys found something the detectives will want to see. Over."

"Ten four."

Kate, hoping to eyeball the location before being noticed, eased closer to the group, but her view of the scene remained blocked.

Without warning, Skip spun around and took a stride in her direction. His widened eyes and gasp preceded a disgusted frown. "Jeez, Kate, what are you doing?"

She smiled and cocked her head slightly, meeting his steely glare with her soft blue eyes. "Hey, Skip. What's happening? I saw you rushing down the hill."

He took her elbow and rotated her toward the street. The gentle touch belied his large stature, but his intent was clear.

"I don't believe this," he mumbled. "You have to go."

"Not yet," she said, securing the poncho hood in place and planting her feet in the mud.

He pushed her elbow forward as if it were a throttle, but she shook off his grip.

"Tell me what they found. You know I'll find out sooner or later."

"I'm sure you will. But not from me."

Applying more force, he grasped her arm and accelerated the pace. Closer to the flatbed his hold relaxed somewhat. She pulled away and slogged back toward the stump, the poncho hood trailing in the wind with her now drenched mane of auburn hair.

"Hey," Skip whined. Then he mumbled something she was glad she couldn't understand, followed by a bellowed "Stop!"

She glanced over her shoulder and yelled, "Don't worry. I'll be right back," before crashing into the four men, who apparently felt obligated to help her follow Skip's command. In a matter of seconds, the officer joined the group.

"Look, Kate, you know the drill. You were asked politely, if I must say so myself, to leave the premises of a potential crime scene."

"Crime scene?"

Skip directed his attention over Kate's head and said, "Good morning, detective. Sorry, sir, we have a bit of a situation."

"I can see you have your hands full," Tom Collingwood said.

"Yes, sir."

"I'll take care of this, Skip, and join you in a minute."

Kate froze, somewhere between glad to recognize Tom's voice and disappointed with his timely arrival. His new partner, Sid Green, would have been easier to deal with. Charming a man with whom you became friends in first grade, dated in high school, broke up during college, and resumed a relationship not quite fifteen months ago would be next to impossible.

"Okay, Katie. You know better than to try to intimidate your way into a police investigation."

"How do you know I was trying...? Oh, never mind. I can explain," Kate said.

"I look forward to discussing it. But right now, you need to resume whatever you were doing before you took this side-trip."

"But I was just—"

"I know. But you need to leave."

"Okay. I'm going," she said. Halfway to her car, she turned back and shouted, "Can't you tell me what's by the stump?"

Tom raised his arm, index finger extended toward the street.

Not easily dismissed, Kate retraced her steps, standing about a foot from her on-again-off-again sweetheart and gazed sweetly into his eyes. "I'll make a deal with you."

"That is so considerate."

"Seriously. I'll leave, but you have to promise to give me a heads up before any public announcement about the body they found."

"What body?"

"I get it, Tom. You can't say anything. We've discussed this before. But can't you give me the hometown advantage on your news release?"

"Playing the hometown-advantage card?"

"I'd use the best-friend-forever card if I thought it would help."

"I bet you would," he said, walking away.

In a few steps, he stopped and turned, resuming eye contact with Kate. "I will *try* to alert you before we make a public announcement."

"That's good enough for me," she said, hurrying to her car as fast as the mud would allow. "You have my pager number, right?"

Kate shook off the remnants of mud clinging to her shoes before entering the newspaper office. It was quarter to eight and her boss was talking to a couple of the Branson-beat reporters at the front counter. Helen glanced at Kate and nodded, then finished her instructions to the others.

"I'm sorry I'm late, but I ran into a story," Kate said, following Helen to her office at the back of the building. Two chairs were positioned in front of the manager's gray army surplus desk, which sat in the center of the room. The two women stood eye-to-eye for a few seconds before Helen gestured for Kate to sit, positioning the other chair for herself close to Kate's.

Ten years to the day Kate's senior, Helen Saint James had taken the fledgling reporter under her wing about nine years ago. After college, Kate worked part-time at first, helping her father at his motel most of the time. She didn't become an official, albeit on-call, reporter until five years later. By then, Helen was in a full-time staff position but remained a generous advisor.

Three summers ago, when the incumbent moved to Arizona for his health, Helen accepted a promotion to Managing Editor. She changed her hair from a long brown straight non-style to a blond highlighted shoulder-length body-wave. Her wardrobe went from casual slacks and jeans to young executive suits and tailored dresses.

Helen's attitude changed with her upgrade and a tension developed between Kate and her mentor. The former chose not to analyze it too much and blamed the alienation on Helen's increased workload and responsibilities.

"I'm not sure how to begin," Helen said.

"Say what's on your mind, Helen. How hard can that be?"

"For you? It may be easy. But I don't want to—"

"Tell me what I did wrong. I promise I'll fix it."

Helen took a deep breath. "I wish it was one thing, but it's everything."

"That could be harder to fix," Kate muttered.

Helen paced the width of the room, stopping a few feet from Kate. She held her hands in front of her as if serving from a tray. "We're a small newspaper in a small town that's growing fast. The few of us on the news staff must work together. No stars or egos here. We don't manipulate individuals to get information. We don't manipulate the information itself. We write a factual and professionally prepared article based on our assignments."

"And I'm not doing that?"

"Are you?"

Kate fidgeted in her chair. "I do my job in a professional manner."

"Do you feel you're part of a team?"

"Yes," Kate said with conviction, but Helen's incredulous gaze reflected her own doubt. "Okay, so I work better alone."

The Managing Editor's eyes softened. "This isn't a contest, Kate."

"If I get a lead for a story, I want to follow it. Right now, I have a lead. Something was found on that lot they've been clearing down by the lake."

"Something?"

"I couldn't get by the responding patrolman. Then Tom ran me off. I'm sure it's a body."

"Kate, you are not supposed to *get by* the police. You can't assume that what they found is a body, no matter how logical that may seem. This attitude of yours is what I'm talking about."

"Sometimes you have to work harder to get the information."

"But is that worth alienating the police?"

Kate ignored the allegation. "If I don't do the story someone else will."

"And that would be okay. But my job includes making sure articles are completed in a timely and professional manner. If I give you an assignment, I expect it to be done."

"I see now."

"You see what?"

"You're mad because I haven't done the feature on that woman."

"Henrietta Stupholds," Helen said. "Your article was due two days ago. And *that woman* is responsible for starting an annual activity that brings thousands of tourists to this little town."

Kate stared at her boss, not knowing how to respond.

Helen said, "The article I assigned may not be about a dead body on a vacant lot, but in this town the crafts fair is news and the Stupholds piece belongs in the anniversary series."

"I haven't been able to get an interview."

"You're telling me the bloodhound of *Tri-Lakes Newspapers* failed?"

"I called, but Mrs. Stupholds didn't answer."

"Okay, Kate," Helen said, moving toward the door. "Get the interview. We need to run the first article in this weekend's edition."

"But—"

Helen held up her hand as if stopping traffic. "Don't worry, if that something on the lot becomes news we'll talk about an assignment."

Chapter Two

The morning showers all but forgotten, Kate walked the distance from her office to Connarde Realty, a narrow storefront office on Commercial Street across and down the street from the paper. Marge Connarde, an active member of the Branson Chamber of Commerce, had been chairman of the annual crafts festival for the past fifteen years. A table in her storeroom served as headquarters for the organizers.

Marge struggled with a display easel on the sidewalk in front of the door. Brochures, posters and other paraphernalia were stacked nearby under the awning. Her tailored business suit flattered her petite figure while lending an air of authority uncommon for such a small woman. Amazingly, the red ensemble complimented, rather than clashed with, her strawberry blond Farrah Fawcett styled hair. Somewhere in her mid-fifties, Marge's attitude, dress, and actions were those of a woman fifteen years younger.

"Well, Katie Starling. How are you? How's your dad? Still as feisty as ever?"

"We're fine," Kate said when the woman took a breath. "Can I help with that?" Kate held the back legs steady as Marge adjusted the front, snapping two narrow shelves into place.

"Thanks. You know, I missed Roger at church Sunday. Nothing wrong, I hope."

"Touch of a cold, probably."

"I'll take him some of my chicken soup."

"That would be nice," Kate said.

The woman, twelve-thirteen years his junior, had been infatuated with Roger for as long as Kate could remember, maybe even before Kate's mother died. Definitely before Marge's husband ran off with his secretary almost twelve years ago. The realtor squared two posters and several bundles of brochures on the display, then stepped back to inspect her work.

"Perfect. What do you think?"

In the larger poster, three-man kiosks of canvas, wood, and colorful fabric lined Commercial Street from Main Street to the post office. People—presumably paying tourists—crowded the streets and browsed at each crafts display.

"I don't remember as many booths last year. Nor as many visitors."

"This is an artist's concept, dear. You know what that means. Nothing ever quite turns out the way one conceives, does it?" She collected the extra brochures and savored one final review of the display.

Kate followed Marge into the office and greeted the three women working around the table in the back room. None of them was old enough to be the lady who began the Branson Crafts Fair forty years ago.

"I'm Kate Starling with *Tri-Lakes News*. Will Henrietta Stupholds be in today?"

"Etta," one of the volunteers corrected.

Another lady quickly added, "She prefers to be called Etta."

After a brief pause, the third member of the group said, "Etta's ride had something to do in Springfield. Doesn't own a car herself anymore. Gave it up two years ago. Remember Marge? It was right after that little accident the day of her eighty-fourth birthday party."

The four women laughed as if sharing a delectable secret.

"Guess I'll try her at home," Kate said, turning to leave.

"Tell your father I'll be over later," Marge yelled from the other side of the office.

"I'll tell him." Kate said, imagining Marge and her father slurping soup together.

Henrietta Stupholds lived about two miles north and west of downtown Branson. According to Kate's father, who had worked for Stupholds as a boy, the octogenarian had resided in the house most of her life.

The steel shell for Branson's newest shopping strip loomed several hundred feet back on the left, far from State Highway 248's edge and about halfway to the turn off. Behind and above it, on the ridge, construction was almost complete for the new elementary school. From that point, however, properties were vacant or modestly occupied. Now that Branson city limits encompassed some of the area, empty spaces along the soon-to-be-widened road would be consumed quickly, Kate mused.

Giant oaks and cedars surrounded a robin-egg blue ranch-style house centered neatly on several acres of land. Upon closer inspection, the various additions to the structure were obvious. The roof on the central, possibly original, portion was slightly higher than either side roof. A veranda tied it all together, spanning the full length of the building.

A garage, too narrow for modern cars, stood— albeit barely—at the end of the long gravel drive. Kate parked between it and the house in the shade of an ancient sugar maple.

The white banister hit the older woman slightly above the waist as she stopped the rocker and came to her feet. She seemed small and fragile, even more so engulfed by the broad porch. Her silver hair was pulled away from her face and gathered in the back. She wore dark slacks and a Kelly-green sweatshirt, across which was written, "My soul is six feet tall."

"Welcome! I didn't expect you so soon."

"Called from the phone in my car."

Her blue eyes twinkled. "Isn't that something? Never cease to marvel at today's technology." She extended a hand toward Kate. "Good to meet you. I've read your articles. You've got moxie."

"Thanks," Kate said, embarrassed she knew so little about the subject of her interview.

"Let's go in. Seems a trifle cool this morning." A silver braid trailed to the center of her back, above the words, "Great things come in small packages."

An archway separated the entry hall and the living room where the sunlight filtered through a single double-hung window. The faint musty odor reminded Kate of her grandmother's house. She settled onto a sofa across from a well-worn and faded blue recliner. An old console television snuggled in the corner. Built-in shelves ran the length of one wall, and a narrow fireplace and hearth were centered on another. A walnut end table next to the sofa and a small round lamp table next to the recliner were the remaining pieces of furniture in the crowded room.

"I appreciate your letting me come to your home, Mrs. Stupholds," Kate said.

"Please, call me Etta. Haven't answered to anything else for as long as I can remember. Would you like some coffee? Or something else to drink?"

"No, thanks," Kate said, eager to get back to the mystery on the lot.

Etta eased onto the recliner, swinging her braid forward so it rested on her chest.

Photographs cluttered the walls, shelves, and mantel above the fireplace. Most were black and whites and very old. A vast collection of decorated boxes and miniature cedar chests were scattered among the pictures.

"Your house is so ..."

"Snug?" Etta said when Kate hesitated.

"Cozy," the reporter countered with a smile.

"This is the part my husband Clay built in 1932. We'd been married eight years. We started with this room, the kitchen, and our bedroom, which is smaller than this, if you can imagine. Use it for a walk-in closet now."

Kate chuckled. "Did he add the other rooms right away?"

"Some, but I finished the last of it in 1957."

Kate studied a handcrafted cedar box on the table next to the sofa. A brass clasp, shaped like a key, secured the lid in place.

"I bet each one has a story."

Etta shrugged. "Maybe, but I don't remember any of them. Some I've had since I was a little girl. Sarah refuses to dust any of them."

"Sarah?"

"She's the fine soul who takes care of this old woman."

Kate bet the old woman could take care of herself. Even in the few minutes she'd known her, Etta seemed quite capable and physically able despite her age.

"I took care of Sarah when she was young. She's married with grown children now. She helps around the house, buys my groceries, and hauls me around town. I don't drive anymore, you know. Safer for everyone on the road."

"You're fortunate to have someone close you can trust."

"Yes. I guess so. Tend to take it for granted, don't we?"

The reporter held up a small tape recorder. "Do you mind if I use this, Etta? I'll make notes, but I like to have direct quotes too."

"Won't bother me a bit. But I'm not sure I've done anything worth writing about."

Kate tended to agree. Still, a good feature article, especially one of a personal nature, appealed to readers. And this woman had no doubt lived an interesting and active life.

"People in this area and even visitors to Branson are interested in how things started and evolved to today's world. The paper is doing a special insert for the fortieth anniversary of the crafts fair. My editor wants to include something about the person who started it."

"I had an idea, that's all. My friends and I had fun exchanging our homemade items. I wanted to expand our little gathering to include the tourists who came to fish each fall. I hoped we could make a little money to last through the winter."

"That may be how it started. But what was once the Branson Crafts Fair and has become the Annual Ozark Mountain Crafts Festival is far from a little gathering. With all the theaters and outlet stores on the Strip, the festival is a way to bring people back to old downtown."

"You've been talking to Margie, I see."

"I agree with her," Kate said, picturing the realtor's poster.

"You're very kind. But I can't take credit for all that. The theaters out on West 76 weren't yet imagined when I suggested the crafts fair. Later, once Silver Dollar City opened, we grew quite a bit and relished in the competition."

Etta's modesty seemed genuine. And why not? After all the woman didn't bring peace to Northern Ireland, she merely suggested holding a little get-together. But the festival lures thousands of visitors into downtown stores each fall and that was important to Branson.

"Have you lived in the area all your life?"

"I ventured all the way to St. Louis once. Went to school here through the eighth grade. Got married here in 1924. Buried my husband here. And grew old here. That's the whole story."

Her eyes sparkled with her grin.

"Was your husband involved in the festival?"

"No, Clay died in forty-two."

"I'm sorry," Kate said. "You were so young. You didn't remarry?"

She bristled and straightened her back. "Never got around to it."

This is going nowhere. Kate glanced at her watch. She didn't want to miss a call from Tom. Her time on that lot and with Helen—and now this interview—had kept her from preparing properly for a planning commission briefing to be held later today or tomorrow morning. She wanted to ask the right questions and be able to discern the wrong answers.

"Told you my life wasn't worth writing about," Etta said, clearly uncomfortable with Kate's silence. "You'd probably prefer to be investigating corruption in city politics."

"Should I be looking into something?" Kate asked with renewed interest.

Etta chuckled. "Well, not that I know of. I've been away from all that for a while. But it's the natural thing for an intelligent, ambitious, young reporter to want to do."

"I enjoy learning about Branson's history," Kate said, unsure why she felt the need to defend herself.

"But today you'd rather be somewhere else."

Kate scooted to the edge of the sofa and moved the recorder from one side of the narrow end table to the other. "Tell me about the first crafts fair."

The octogenarian closed her eyes and rested her head against the chair back. Her eyes fluttered open and she said, "I haven't thought about it in so long."

"Where did you set up?"

"In front of the mercantile, on Commercial Street. We had two or three tables."

"And you displayed handmade items? Quilts? Woodwork?"

"Yes. Bird houses. Bird feeders. Many of the things you see today. When we'd sell something, we'd get another and fill the space on the table."

"So, you sold several items?"

"The first year it was more like a few. Still we could see the wives, abandoned by fishermen spouses, were interested."

"Of the women who helped you, are any−?"

"−still alive?" She shook her head.

"I could list them in the article."

"Wait a minute," she said. She blasted from her chair and examined the collection of photos on one shelf. Mumbling to herself she checked a table and the mantel. "Hold on," she said, standing in the middle of the room, fists on hips, glancing from shelf to shelf. Finally, she picked out a faded black photo album, thick with pages, and handed it to Kate. "I know I have at least one of that first year. A customer had a camera. His wife insisted he take a picture. They sent me a blow up, I'm sure."

Etta sat on the arm of the sofa and leaned over Kate's shoulder. The first sheets contained shots of Etta and Clay when they had just married. She explained each one, her words softening to a whisper. Her voice reflected a gentleness, without melancholy, as she told what the young couple was doing, when the photo was taken, and by whom.

"Listen to me go on. You're not interested in my life story, frame-by-frame," she said as she nudged Kate over and took the album. She glanced at Kate and winked. "Let's fast-forward."

She ran her finger down the photos, shaking her head and turning pages. Occasionally the old woman paused as if lost in a memory.

Kate tapped the crystal of her watch. She'd be late for deadline on the article if she didn't leave soon. *Why can't things happen in an orderly, convenient fashion?*

Etta stopped turning. The book was open to an 8x10 inch posed portrait. Three men stood behind three seated ladies, each beaming with the hint of a shared secret.

Kate said, "You're in the middle, right? The man behind you must be Clay."

Etta stared at the photo, touching each image as if reaching back in time to caress her husband and friends.

The reporter waited a moment—instinctively respecting the woman's reverie—then said, "This would be great to go with the article."

Etta tilted her head back slightly and closed her eyes momentarily. "This was way before the crafts fair. We were on a lark in St. Louis. Left Branson without telling a soul. Clay and I were celebrating our fourth anniversary. Our friends hadn't been married even that long."

"I assume the six of you were good friends," Kate said.

"Jack, Lex, and I had known each other since we were toddlers. Clay was a couple years older. He came to my graduation dance with his younger sister. I was thirteen, pretty naïve, and he swept me right off my feet."

"What happened? Obviously, you had the portrait made."

"I don't remember how we paid for everything. When we passed by the photo studio, I begged everyone to go in not even considering how much it would cost. No one was at the desk by the window. The walls were covered with newspaper clippings about the owners, two sisters. Portraits they had done, some from the 1904 World's Fair, were everywhere in the studio. At first we were fascinated, going from photo to photo. Then someone said we better get out." Etta smiled, the memory clearly running in her mind.

"But you didn't leave," Kate said.

"What is it the kids say nowadays? We were busted. One of the sisters came from a room in the back. She asked us if we wanted a portrait.

Jack spoke up. He told her we'd changed our minds. The rest of us nodded agreement and turned to go. But the nice lady said they had a special rate for one day only. She suggested we do a group portrait."

Kate asked, "What did she charge you?"

"Twenty-five cents," Etta said. She slid her hand slowly across the portrait once more, then turned the page.

Kate glanced again at her watch. "I'm sorry. I didn't know how late it was. I need to get this first article submitted for the next edition, but I'd like to do more. Can I come back?"

Etta wasn't listening as she continued her search through the album.

"This is it. The lady on the end holding the afghan. Her husband took the picture."

More than a dozen women stood behind a crafts display. Kate pointed to the shortest woman of the three and said, "This is you."

Etta laughed. "You'd make quite a detective."

"Could I borrow this to run with the article?"

"You bet. Let me write the names down for you. At least the ones I remember. And you can come back any time. Don't know what else we'll talk about, but you're welcome."

Chapter Three

Tom held up his fist signaling Sid to wait by the vehicles. "Better change into our boots. The lot's muddy and full of debris," he said approaching his partner. "Did you call the coroner?"

"On his way," Sid said, popping the trunk. "I saw Kate heading across the tracks. You might know she'd be the first reporter on scene."

"She's a bird dog, all right," Tom said.

"Sounds like she might have nipped at you a bit."

"You know, partner, I really don't want to talk about Kate right now."

"Hey, don't take my head off because you can't manage your love life."

"There is no love life."

"Exactly."

Tom finished lacing his boots in silence, then headed back to the stump. "Let's get to this. I'm guessing it will take a while."

Skip joined the detectives as they approached. "I got preliminary statements from the crew and sent them home."

Tom said, "Give us the *Reader's Digest* version."

"They felled this big oak late yesterday. They sectioned the trunk and did some trimming but decided to finish with it this morning. Came back about sunrise and loaded the sections on the flatbed. They were trying to figure out how to handle the big stump, which, as you can see, is still attached to the ground. That's when they saw the blanket and the partially exposed skeleton."

The two detectives crouched about ten feet from what appeared to be human remains.

Tom said, "The cloth is worn but basically intact. When they tried to pull up the stump, the entire bundle, including much of the surrounding ground, was attached to the roots."

"If the roots weren't holding that blanket together, we'd have a big mess," Sid said.

"Funny, I hadn't noticed the odor before," Tom said.

Skip said, "You mean moldy blanket?"

Sid said, "More like something rotten, but not real pungent. I've smelled a few dead bodies and this isn't close."

Tom shrugged and stood up as he motioned to Skip. "Did you take photos?"

"A few, but I was concentrating on the statements."

"We'll need shots of the entire area from all angles, but don't move anything."

"Yes, sir."

"We'll wait for the coroner, but get shots as it lays," Sid said. "And get close-ups of that covering. Looks like an old army blanket."

"Yes, sir," the young man repeated as he documented details of the scene.

Tom slipped on some latex gloves and handed a pair to Sid. "Let's go over the area in a thirty-foot perimeter around the tree. Not much left of any evidence after this crew plowed it up, but we can take a pass."

Twenty minutes later, they had bagged a few items and were standing by their vehicles making log entries when Artie Richards parked his van on St. Limas. The coroner grabbed a satchel and joined the detectives. Tom figured him to be in his fifties. He'd been in the mortuary business with his family for decades before running for coroner earlier this year.

Sid said, "Thanks for coming so quickly. We've taken photos of the scene and searched the area for evidence. Could be more under the bundle. The cover is in good shape. No telling how long this has been buried. As you can see, it's pretty much intertwined by the tree roots."

"Couple hundred-year oak from the looks of the rings," Artie said. He put his satchel down a good distance from the stump. Before grabbing his camera case, he slipped on a pair of latex gloves.

Tom and his partner hadn't worked with this coroner since the election. Suspicious deaths—let alone murders—were rare in Branson. Still the man's reputation was solid, within the bounds of his training and experience.

Artie approached the scene carefully, taking photos from several perspectives. He zoomed in on the stump, roots, and finally the skeleton bundle itself. After several minutes of shooting, he returned to his satchel and removed a plastic bag.

"Help me with this sheet," he said, tearing open the bag and removing an oversized cloth.

The three men spread the twelve-foot square piece of fabric on the ground next to the skeleton, then carefully approached the object. Artie gently pulled a corner of the blanket toward him, exposing the skull and upper torso bones.

"Definitely human," Artie said, taking some close-up pictures before replacing the cover. "I'm sure you know I'm way out of my league with this. We'll need help beyond our usual support team. Let me make some calls. I don't want to disturb anything until I talk to a forensic anthropologist."

"We'll help you secure the scene," Tom said.

Tom and Skip strung the yellow police crime scene tape in a large circle around the skeleton and stump while Artie and Sid retrieved a roll of plastic and some stakes from the van.

Artie said, "We need to cover as much as possible. Can you arrange for round-the-clock patrolmen to watch the area?"

"No problem," Tom said. "We'll make sure no one noses around."

"I'll make those calls and get back to you as soon as I can."

It was after noon before Tom and Sid finished at the scene and returned to their office in City Hall. They gulped down the last bites of fast-food burgers and worked on their report.

"How long do you suppose the skeleton's been out there?" Sid asked.

"I wouldn't even guess," Tom said. "First thing we need to do is check any open missing person cases."

"Nothing's pending since I made detective a few months ago."

"Probationary detective eleven months," Tom clarified, "with the promotion to Detective Sergeant just two months ago."

"Thanks for the clarification, partner."

"In any case," Tom said, "we'll be examining decades' worth of cases."

"Hey, almost forgot that I saw the lieutenant at the coffee pot. He wants to see us."

"Nice of you to remember that," Tom said. "Any idea why?"

"Nope," Sid said, tapping his knuckle on Lieutenant Dan Palmer's door.

"Come on in," Palmer said as he hung up his phone.

"Almost finished with the skeleton discovery report," Tom said.

"Good. But I've got something else for you."

The Lieutenant shuffled through a stack of files on the right side of his desk, removed one from the middle and handed it to the senior detective.

"The whole thing may amount to nothing. Unfortunately, we can't ignore the complaint. The information, although limited, is enough to warrant further investigation."

"This is a complaint against the city of Branson," Tom said.

"Yes, and a related complaint was issued to the Missouri Board for Architects and Professional Engineers."

"Hey, am I the only person who wonders if this guy made this up?" Tom asked. "He isn't exactly in love with our city government."

"Yes, that occurred to me, but we do not have the option of ignoring him. Besides, if he's right about any part of this, we have a serious problem. For now, he's given us a heads up. If we don't take action, he will escalate."

"What does that mean exactly?" Sid asked.

"Nothing good, I imagine."

"What's the time frame?" Tom asked.

"According to the lawyer he hired, three weeks."

"Sounds like we better get started," Tom said. "I might add, discerning who can be trusted will make our job more difficult."

"You're detectives, aren't you? And make this your number one priority for now."

"Okay, but we'll need to follow up on the skeleton case."

"From what you told me earlier, sounds like that's in the coroner's hands right now."

"I had a couple ideas to check out. Okay if I do it on a low priority?"

"That's fine, but we need to address this complaint pretty quickly. Bryan Porter intends to pursue this as far as necessary to get justice. Those were his exact words."

When Tom returned to his desk, he found a message from Kate. "She didn't leave a number," Tom mumbled.

"You don't have her number?" Sid said.

"Yeah. I've got it all right."

"Are you back together?"

"Not exactly. We've tried a couple of times, but something keeps getting in the way."

"Like Kate, you mean." Sid snickered.

Tom picked up the phone and punched in the number to Kate's mobile phone. When Kate answered, he turned his back to his co-worker.

"Hey, Katie. You called?" he whispered.

"Is this sweet young patrolman guarding whatever is in the hole?"

"You're at the scene?"

"I go where the news is."

"Do you see the crime scene tape?"

"Can't miss it. And the big plastic tent is also rather obvious."

"Do you know why police put crime tape around a scene?"

"Because there was a crime?"

"To keep unauthorized people, such as yourself, out of the area."

"Does that mean you aren't going to tell me anything?"

"At this time, we have nothing of interest to report. When we do, we will issue a statement."

"Okay. Guess I'll talk to you later."

"Hey, maybe we could meet for coffee," Tom said.

Silence.

"Katie?" Tom said, hanging up after another moment.

Sid offered, "That went smoothly."

"Oh, yeah. I'm on a roll."

Chapter Four

Ben Leatherman, Planning/Building Department Manager, stepped up to the podium and pulled the microphone down to his level. "Okay, ladies and gentlemen. Let's get started." In white shirt and khaki trousers, tie but no jacket, he represented Ozarks white-collar mid-level management well, despite his short and somewhat stocky physique.

"White knuckle time," Kate whispered in Bernie Sailor's ear.

The TV newsman smirked but did not take his eyes off the speaker.

Leatherman, hired about two years ago when the previous man took a better job, had been overwhelmed ever since. He had the misfortune of arriving with the "Branson Boom"—as the press tagged it—following the 60 *Minutes* segment which introduced the town to the world. A rash of new country music theaters, hotels, and restaurants sprouted up along the city's main drag. The affectionately nicknamed "Strip" stretched from downtown Branson westward toward Silver Dollar City, its neon lighting reminiscent of the Las Vegas Strip.

His attempts to deal with the growth met strong resistance from city government. According to the unofficial grapevine, he grew more and more frustrated with the "I've lived here all my life and you don't know shit" attitude of local politicians and citizens.

Leatherman cleared his throat. "This is going to be brief. We want to set the record straight so as not to cause undue embarrassment for anyone. The Missouri Board of Architects and Engineers has asked the city of Branson to provide certain records for certain construction projects currently ongoing in Branson. We are cooperating fully. So far no red flags have been raised. Once they finish the review and submit a report with their recommendations, we will inform the public. City staff is confident that all construction inspected by our team is safe and has been completed to code. Any questions?"

Bernie raised his hand and said, "You say, Mr. Leatherman, no red flags so far. Has Missouri started its review?"

As if cued, the group chuckled in unison, then silently turned their eyes on Leatherman.

"The state has provided my office a list of projects. We're collating the records to be turned over to the bureau staff as soon as possible."

"So, nothing has happened so far?" A reporter from the *Harrison Daily Times* asked.

Leatherman glanced in her direction, said, "No," then pointed to Kate, one of many with a raised hand.

"You say inspected construction is safe. But you've also gone on record recently that your department is understaffed. How can you keep up with the demand of current projects?"

Leatherman sneered. "Lots of overtime."

"But," Kate said, determined not to let him brush off the question, "isn't it true your *team* consists of two inspectors after the third quit last week? And we have over thirty active projects in the city, not including residential construction? And don't those same inspectors review all plans submitted as part of the permitting process?"

"Yes, to all your questions. However, we're actively trying to replace our third man."

"And then you'll have three," another reporter said, with a tinge of sarcasm.

City Administrator Mark Orchard eased between Leatherman and the podium, bending his six-foot frame to speak into the mic. "That'll be it for today, folks. When we have more concrete information about the audit, we'll let you know. Until then, please keep your media theories to a minimum."

A man's voice blurted from the back of the overfilled room. "When are you going to discuss what Fortune Enterprises gets away with?"

Bryan Porter stood with his arms folded across his chest, his naturally ruddy complexion flushed a deep pink, his ears beet red. He walked to the center of the crowd, stopping not far from Kate and Bernie.

"Well, Mr. Leatherman? Are you going to tell these folks about Fortune Enterprises starting construction before they had a permit, an apparent exemption from this code of yours?"

"Who's that?" Bernie said, his words barely audible.

"Bryan Porter," Kate whispered.

"Who's Bryan Porter?"

"Until recently, the town joke, but his status may be elevated."

"What's he talking about?" Bernie said.

Kate leaned closer to the newsman. "Larry Allen is property development manager at Fortune Enterprises. He's the grandson of one of the founders."

Bernie mouthed, "Holy shit," his eyes wide with excitement. "He was elected to city council this last April, right? Very heated contest as I recall, especially for a city council post."

Kate nodded, amused by Leatherman's distressed glance toward his boss.

"If you're referring to the Fortune Plaza Office Complex—"

"I am."

"—that project is not yet within city limits," Leatherman said.

"But it will be soon. Isn't that true?" Porter asked.

"On next week's agenda."

Porter forced his way closer to the podium, planted his feet firmly, and sunk his hands into his pants pockets. "Isn't it also true your department is responsible for inspecting projects within a mile of city limits? And, certainly, ones about to enter city boundaries?"

Orchard shook his head and scowled. "That's all we're going to say today. Thank you."

The city administrator eyeballed Leatherman, who quickly took the side door. Orchard pushed his way through the crowd to the lobby exit, closer to his own office.

"What's the answer, Mr. Orchard?" Kate shouted.

Orchard stopped at the double swinging doors, pivoting around to face the media. "Yes, we have an agreement with the county to inspect those projects about to enter the city. Now, if you'll excuse me. I have work to do."

For a few seconds everyone stared in the direction of Orchard's departure, as if expecting his return. Porter broke the silence with a muffled, but breathy, "Humph," followed by a more subdued, "Predictable," as he started to leave.

"Excuse me, Mr. Porter," Kate said, blocking his exit.

Deep lines appeared across his brow. She'd seen Porter around town but hadn't realized how short he was until she stood directly in front of him eye-to-eye.

"I'm Kate Starling, *Tri-Lakes News*. Could I ask you a few questions?"

Again, the room became quiet, all eyes on the man who had disrupted the news conference.

"I'm sorry, Miss Starling. I'm not ready to talk about this until I get my own answers."

Undaunted, Kate said, "Do you know for a fact Fortune Enterprises doesn't have a building permit for the new office plaza?"

"They have one now. Question is when did they get it? By my calculations, they had steel up for all five stories, before they even had a foundation permit. Hell! The thing was almost completed, before the building permit was approved."

"And you're saying nothing was done because Councilman Allen is a project manager at the company?" Kate asked.

A low-level buzz traveled around the room.

"I'd say it seems like a hell of a coincidence. Wouldn't you? Like inspection reports changing before being filed. Lots of coincidences."

Porter stormed out before Kate or anyone else could ask a follow-up.

Bernie said to his cameraman, "Come on. Orchard promised a sound bite. Let's see what he has to say about Porter's comments. Want to come along, Kate?"

She started to follow Bernie but changed her mind when she saw Leatherman come out of his office and head for the men's room. "No thanks, I've heard the drill," she said.

As the chamber emptied, Kate hurried through the witness room to the neighboring office suite. Five small offices and a central bullpen provided limited space for the Building and Engineering Departments. An eight-foot round conference table claimed the center of the overcrowded room. It and a nearby customer counter were piled high with papers, rolled up building plans, and three-ring binders. At least a dozen file cabinets lined the limited wall space.

Kate spoke briefly to an engineering department road inspector, a guy she'd known since high school, then waited at the counter as the secretary finished speaking to a customer. The woman, who seemed to be only a few years older than Kate, started her job less than three weeks ago. With any luck she hadn't been briefed on the reporter's reputation as a city hall pest.

"Okay," the woman began, walking toward Kate, "how can I help you?"

Hoping to put the woman at ease, Kate introduced herself and provided her credentials.

"Nice to meet you. My name's Claire," the secretary said.

"I know you started your job recently. Are you new to Branson too?"

"We came in a couple years ago from Des Moines. Apparently, we were among the many. I've had a few part-time jobs but was thrilled to see this one in the paper."

"Yeah, the boom brought a lot of new folks to town. I'm glad you got the job. I've lived in Branson all my life and worked at the paper for quite a while, so let me know if you want the real scoop on anyone in town."

Claire smiled. "I'll keep that in mind."

"Seriously, we can have lunch sometime."

"That would be nice."

"One thing's for sure, you folks will be needing a bigger office."

"They tell me it was a lot worse before the Health Department moved downstairs."

"That's true," Kate agreed.

"How can I help you today?"

Kate summoned her most nonchalant demeanor. "I'd like to see the file on the Fortune Plaza office project."

"The entire file?" Claire asked, the whites of her eyes expanding noticeably.

"Is there a problem?"

"I'm not sure. I mean, as you said, I'm new. The other secretary is on vacation and I'm not sure what the procedure is to see a file."

"They're public record, right?"

"Yes, I suppose," the woman said, nervously twirling a long brown strand of hair.

"And I'm part of the public."

"I'm sorry. I'll have to speak to Mr. Leatherman."

"Okay, but I ask to see city records all the time," Kate said, not bothering to elaborate how often her requests were granted.

Claire glanced toward the door and relaxed.

Kate craned her neck, following the woman's line-of-sight as Ben Leatherman crossed the threshold and hurried past the counter without acknowledging either woman.

"Excuse me, Mr. Leatherman?" the secretary said as he entered his office.

"Not now, Claire." He closed the door behind him.

The secretary shrugged and said, "Sorry."

Kate considered pushing the point but decided against it. Instead, she made an appointment to meet with Leatherman later in the afternoon. She had one thing to do before leaving City Hall and opportunity presented itself immediately.

Tom Collingwood and his boss, Detective Lieutenant Dan Palmer, emerged from the offices across the upper lobby as Kate crossed the building department threshold. Tom acknowledged

Kate with a halfhearted salute, then turned to resume his discussion with Palmer.

First, he gives her his official stance about whatever was found down by the lake. Then, he fails to let her know about the subsequent press release, as he promised he would. Now, he brushes her off without a word. How can they be friends, let alone something more? She stormed across the lobby and out the exit.

The upper lot and street were empty. "Damn," she said, remembering she'd parked on the lower level. Normally, she would have taken the shorter route, across the lobby and down the stairs to the police department entrance, but Tom and Dan blocked that approach. "Get a grip," she whispered, before silently counting to ten. She took a deep breath, then set out around the building to the Adams Street parking area.

"Katie, wait up."

She glanced over her shoulder but kept walking.

Tom jogged toward her and shouted, "Katie?"

She waited for him to catch up. "I'm in a hurry."

"Okay. All I wanted to—"

She resumed walking toward her car, but he stepped in front of her.

"Hey, where's the fire?"

She detoured around him.

"I get it. You're mad at me. It's been a while, but I remember this routine."

"Why would I be mad?"

"I'm not sure. Why don't you tell me? It'll save a lot of time."

"I'm so glad you're amused," she said, risking a sideways glance. *Why are we acting like teenagers?* Her emotions and behavior resembled someone not quite as mature as she would prefer to be. She stopped, slowly turning to face him.

"Go ahead. I'm ready. Blast me," he said.

"Why would I do that?"

"Who knows?"

"If you're going to make fun of me, we have nothing to discuss."

"I'm sorry. Tell me why you're upset." He brushed her hand, then held it until she withdrew. His blue eyes had always had a calming effect on her.

She tilted her head to one side blocking the rising sun with one hand. "You promised to let me know what was found on the lot."

"But I did. We sent a press release this morning."

She rolled her eyes. "To begin with, the press release said nothing. Furthermore, I expected advance notice from an old friend."

"I did. I mean, I tried. I left a message on your car phone and I paged you."

"You did not."

"Several times."

Her anger returned. "That's not possible!"

He squeezed his lips together and hesitated a moment before lowering his voice. "Have you checked your voicemail? Your pager?"

"My pager is fine." She reached into the outside pocket of her portfolio, grasped the square object, and waved it in front of his face. "See?"

"Yeah, fine but off."

She examined the switch, then remembered muting it to ignore Helen's repeated calls. "I'm sorry," she said.

He grinned and said, "Guess I should've sent a patrol car to track you down."

"That would have been more efficient. You should have known when I didn't return your call something was wrong."

"What? This is my fault? What do you want from me, Katherine Margaret Starling?"

She took a step closer, and then stared directly into his eyes.

"Uh-oh," he whispered.

"I want you to tell me everything you know about the skeleton you found yesterday."

"Everything is in the press release. I swear. The coroner is trying to find an expert to help us. We probably won't know anything for weeks. Besides, you know I can't tell you anything until we make an official statement."

"Yes. You've mentioned that once or twice."

She pivoted around and headed for the parking lot before Tom could say more.

Kate's frustration had not abated by the time she entered the restaurant. Shirley Barrens, her best friend since kindergarten, was already sitting in a booth toward the middle of the room. Kate scooted across the bench, tossing her purse to the far side.

"Are we a bit huffy?" Shirley asked.

"Not at all," Kate replied.

"I've known you a long time. Remember?"

Kate shrugged as she drummed the table with her index and middle fingers.

Shirley pointed toward the noise. "See. Dead giveaway. Tapping does not lie."

"Okay, I had a little disagreement with *His Exalted Detectiveness*."

Shirley's amusement was palpable.

"And what did Tom do to offend your sensibilities this time?"

"I'm not sure I like your implication."

"Shoe fits, does it?"

"Let's order. I have an appointment in about ninety minutes with Leatherman."

"Already ordered," Shirley said. "Don't be so surprised. You know you always have the same thing."

"Did you call your friend in Forsyth?"

"Let's talk about you and Tom."

"We can't get past his stubbornness."

"*His* stubbornness?"

Kate stared at her friend. "Okay, I can't separate my boyfriend from the detective."

"I'm sure the relationship is difficult, especially when you deal with him professionally," Shirley said. "But you need to talk about it. You and I are best friends, Katie."

"I know."

"Why then, have we never discussed your breakup with Tom all those years ago?"

Kate squirmed in the seat and glared at her friend. "I don't discuss that day," she said.

"You need to," Shirley said.

"It was an impetuous mistake. There. Are you satisfied?"

"Not really."

"I regretted our argument. I regretted it even more when he started dating Linda, but not nearly as much as when they married and moved to Kansas City two years later."

"I'm guessing you and Tom haven't discussed this."

"Did you call your friend in Forsyth?" Kate asked, changing the subject.

"Okay, but we're not finished with this."

"Understood, but let's move on right now."

"The property was purchased by Clay and Henrietta Stupholds in 1929."

"You're kidding," Kate said.

Shirley continued, "A superseding deed was filed in favor of Riverside Mercantile on October 23, 1942, and another on April 22, 1945. The last deed added Randall John Brighton and Henrietta Stupholds as co-owners."

"That means that Fortune Enterprises must have a stake in it somehow."

"You interrupted me."

"Sorry," Kate said, gesturing for Shirley to continue.

"Fortune Enterprises, incorporated in 1971, began paying taxes in 1973."

"But no new deed?"

"Nothing since 1945."

"Very interesting."

"It makes sense given what I found out. The company has three officers listed with Missouri: Randall John Brighton, President; Henrietta

Stupholds, Vice President; and Randall John Brighton Jr., Secretary/Treasurer."

"You know what else?" Kate tapped her index finger on Shirley's hand.

"Don't keep me in suspense."

"I'm not sure about the sequence of events, but I'm guessing the original mercantile was on that land. Nothing's been there since I can remember. Maybe Etta can help with an interesting angle for the series."

"Hey, if there's an angle, you'll find it."

"Thanks for your confidence."

Chapter Five

Leatherman's secretary acknowledged Kate's presence immediately as she grabbed an envelope from her desk and came to the counter. "I checked with Mr. Leatherman. He said to copy what's in the file for you."

"I appreciate it," Kate said, weighing the envelope with both hands. "Seems a bit light."

"I copied everything."

"I'm sure you did. And I hope you take up my offer for lunch," Kate said.

"I guess that would be okay."

"How about I check with you in a few days. This week is crazy with all the stuff happening in town."

"No problem. I usually go right at noon."

Kate nodded. "I wonder if I could ask for the file on one more location."

"Sure. What's the address?"

"The lot at Commercial and St. Limas, not far from the lake."

"Where the skeleton was found."

"Yes. That's the one," Kate said, hoping that would not make a difference.

"Let me check." Claire checked her computer then walked across the room to the line of file cabinets. She took out a folder and fingered through it as she returned to the counter. "Not much in the file," she said, placing the folder in front of Kate.

"Can I get a copy of everything for my background file?"

"Be back in a sec." Claire took the folder and disappeared to the area between the suite and the courtroom returning in a few minutes.

Kate added the newly copied pages to the envelope and headed to Etta's house. She learned long ago showing up is the best way to schedule a meeting.

Etta was in her rocker on the front porch when Kate parked. She waved from her car, and then met Etta at the top of the steps.

"Hope this isn't a bad time. I have a few follow-up questions for the next article."

"Come on up. Let's sit outside. Such a beautiful fall day."

Kate sat in one of the large wicker chairs and savored the panorama. "This is very much like the view from our back porch," she said.

"You're married?"

"No. I live with my father in the house behind his hotel."

"Where you grew up?"

"Yes. I moved back a couple years ago, after–"

Etta interrupted, "I'm sorry. You'll have to forgive this old woman. I forgot all about the trouble with your dad. He was such a nice boy when he worked for Clay."

"You remember him?"

"Absolutely. He had quite a crush on me, you know. He was a hard worker. I knew he couldn't have killed that man. I was real relieved when they dropped the charges."

"Thanks. I'm glad everything worked out too." Kate handed Etta the latest issue of *Branson Daily News*. "I brought this for you. Your first article is in it."

"Already have a copy," Etta said proudly. "Sarah dropped it by for me. You did a good job. Made it sound like an interesting life. Of course, I've noticed things sound a lot better in retrospect, especially if you leave out the gruesome details."

"Well, we can put those in this next article," Kate said with a smile. "Still okay to use this?" she asked as she turned on her small recorder.

"You bet. What do you want to know?"

Kate didn't skip a beat. "About the lot you own downtown. The one across the railroad tracks on Commercial, not far from Lake Taneycomo."

Etta furrowed her brow and stared toward the woods.

"Do you know where I mean?" Kate asked after a few moments.

"Sorry, brings back some memories, I guess. Clay and I, we built our store on that lot. We'd been married a few years, lived with my folks at first. We had to move in with Clay's parents when his older brother left home. We stayed with them a while, but Clay decided it would be good to get our own place. Even though Clay helped with his family farm, he had a job in town too. I brought in a little money selling my crafts and tending kids and such. We were able to buy that old lot with some help from a friend. Clay's father said if we moved out, we'd be on our own. By then, that was fine with us."

"When did you move out?"

"It was twenty-nine when we bought it, not long before all hell broke loose in the East. Clay built a small shack for us and we moved in that summer. He built the store in front of the shack with help from friends. They all knew about the situation between Clay and his father. You won't put all this in the article, will you?"

Kate shook her head. "Not if you don't want me to. How long did you live behind the store?"

"For a year or so. Business was good. We weren't far from the lake and the railroad station. We had a little money saved when Clay fell into a deal with some other folks to buy quite a bit of acreage out here. It was a long way from town then."

"What was the store called?" Kate said, glancing at her notes.

Etta rocked out of the chair and walked toward the stairs. "Clay put a big sign over the front entrance. Mercantile," Etta said, gesturing with her hands above her head, "but everyone called it the Riverside Mercantile. I called it Clay's store."

"What happened to the store when your husband died in 1942?"

Etta turned to face Kate. "I guess you might say I merged my business with our friend Jack's store. I took our inventory and the name and moved higher to the building at Commercial and Main Streets."

"Where the Fortune Enterprises flagship store is today?"

"That's the place," Etta said. "All those pictures in the album were of our Riverside Mercantile, not Clay's."

"You're speaking of Jack Brighton, your friend Jack?"

"We grew up together, my best friend next to Clay," Etta said.

"Did Jack's wife work there as well?"

"Neither Lillian, Jack's wife, nor Lex's wife Tory worked at the store. Just Lex, Jack and I ran Riverside. Of course, Jack's son Randy and Lex's boy Bryan helped out, but they were young kids."

"The Bryan Porter who owns the big flea market on the west end of town?"

Etta nodded. "Bryan worked for a year or so after we merged until his father quit to start his own business. That's probably why Bryan left, but he wasn't particularly interested in hard work. He seemed to have a bit of a chip on his shoulder all the time."

"But Randy stayed with the store," Kate said.

"No, he joined the army during World War II. He served through the Korean Conflict, as they called it. He'd had some issues in high school, but the army straightened him out. Got out and got a college degree. Jack was so proud of him. When he left the service, he tried making his own way for a while in St. Louis but came back to help Jack run the business."

"I knew you were a good source. You have lots of stories to tell."

Etta gazed directly into Kate's eyes. "Something else you need to know. Maybe you already do, but I need to be sure."

"Okay," Kate said, still processing the Bryan Porter link.

Etta leaned back against the column beside the stairs and said, "Clay killed himself. Had his reasons, I suppose. The note didn't make much sense, but I know he was having a bad time with things. Personal demons, I guess." She pushed to a standing position. "I don't talk about this. I sure don't want to read about it in the paper. But you needed to find out from me."

"I appreciate your telling me. I promise I won't say or write anything about it."

Etta said, "I know we didn't talk about the crafts fair, but I need to go in and lie down."

"I'll come back some other time, if that's okay. You've been a big help with my questions. I hope I didn't upset you, bringing up memories about your husband."

"Only one bad memory about Clay. But you couldn't have known. I do better in the mornings. I usually go down to the realty office to help Marge. Maybe you can come down some day before noon."

"It's a date. Thanks Etta," Kate said, stifling an impulse to hug the octogenarian.

Chapter Six

Tom checked the tables close to the entrance, then scanned the bar stools for his friend Gary Wyler, the other half of the most value players duo for the Branson Pirates football team two years running—albeit many years ago. As usual, Marvin Selman, another school chum, was tending bar.

"He's in the back, Tom. Bring you a cool one?"

Tom nodded and grabbed a bowl of pretzels on his way to a table in the dimly lit corner by the emergency exit. Gary Wyler raised his beer bottle and shook it upside down.

"Better make that a round," Tom called back over his shoulder.

Gary stood up and pulled a chair out for his former quarterback. "How the hell are you, buddy? Long time no see."

"You're looking good. Getting lots of fresh air and exercise, I bet."

"I'll say. We're turning jobs away every day. So much construction going on in town. It's like San Francisco after an earthquake."

Tom smiled. *Gary could never resist the strange-but-true analogies.*

"Fredo, my man," Gary said as the bartender put the two beers on the table. He took one and held it up to toast and Tom did the same.

"I've never understood why you call him that."

"Too long ago to remember, but here's to old friends." He clinked his bottle against Tom's and took a long pull. "So, what's up? I haven't heard from you in months. Let's see it was that Saturday you and Katie came for dinner."

"Yeah, I guess it was," Tom said, remembering the uncomfortable evening.

Gary said, "Hard to believe that was almost six months ago. She was sure mad at you about something. Bet you had to make up for whatever it was big time."

"We haven't been out since. We don't speak except professionally and even that is low-grade civil."

"Whoa, I'm sorry. Haven't been able to rekindle that old flame, huh?"

"We were okay for a while after I came back to Branson. Unfortunately, our professional lives seem to interfere."

"She's pretty stubborn."

"Hell, she may still be mad I got married and moved away after she dumped me."

"Go figure." Gary grinned and took another drink.

Tom let the comment go with a shrug.

"You know ... talk about a coincidence ... Katie called me yesterday. If I knew you were having problems, I'd have put in a good word."

"Not sure that would help. Why'd she call?"

"Sorry, buddy. Wasn't about you. She had some questions about the construction business in Branson. Said she was doing a story."

"What kind of questions?"

"Believe it or not, I don't remember exactly. We spoke for a while. She asked general things about current business, inspections, stuff like that. Does it matter?"

"No big deal. Never know what she might be cooking up."

"Yeah, I've read some of her articles in the paper. She has quite an imagination."

"No kidding," Tom said before changing the subject. "Seen any of the guys lately?"

"Not many of the boys around anymore. Always good to see your smiling face."

"That goes both ways."

"We don't get together like we used to." Gary went on at length about the rest of the team, how they'd been inseparable the first year or so after high school, then drifted into separate lives. After several minutes, Tom eased the conversation in a different direction.

"Hard to make friends at work when you're the big cheese."

"Ain't that the truth? Who'd ever guess I'd be the boss man one day."

"Not Coach Parstons. That's for sure."

"Yeah. He used to scowl at me, shake his head, and say ..."

Tom joined his friend in the quote. "... once an end always an end."

"Wouldn't he be surprised?" Gary snickered.

"So, how's it going? You're working on the new office complex, right?"

Gary scrutinized the room, before saying, "You know, I've been with the company for ten years, worked my way up. I've done every job at a construction site. And I'm damn good at all of them." He motioned to Marvin for another round. "We've been the general contractor on two major theaters and four hotels, and I've worked on most of those. But I'll be damned if I understand what's up with all the hurdles we're jumping over for this piddling office building."

"Pressure from the city?" Tom asked.

"Yeah, we were going along fine, but now they're all nervous about this audit the state is doing. I mean, it's a small office building."

"Not so small by Branson standards. Most of the office space in town is part of a strip mall. Sounds like this one is different."

"But they're driving me to drink over it."

Tom took another swallow of his beer. "Who's driving?"

"My boss, Bob Clanton, is super. The building owner's grandson, who happens to be best buddies with the architect, likes to pretend he's the job superintendent."

"Ouch."

"And how!"

"Not much you can do," Tom said. "Whoever holds the purse strings, holds the reins."

"Hey, I can get behind that. But, when you don't know what the hell you're doing, you ought to stay out of the way of those who do."

Tom offered, "Just because you can pay for a building, doesn't mean you know how to construct it."

Gary spun the empty bottle and said, "Damn right. Hell, he can't even do *his* job."

"You're talking about Larry Allen, right?"

"Yeah, he's doing everything from ordering materials to scheduling my men. Even Clanton's getting pissed."

"Why doesn't your boss withdraw your company from the job?"

"We're in it too deep. Besides, you don't want the reputation as a general contractor that blows the scene when the going gets tough, especially where Fortune Enterprises is involved. We'll be finished soon, in any case."

"But I heard the permit was only approved last week."

Gary lowered his voice and leaned closer to his friend. "That's one of the things Allen bungled but somehow managed to straighten out. Course, the fat lady hasn't done her solo yet."

"So, you worked without the permit?"

"I was told to keep on keeping on. The plans were under review and the permit would be issued any day. Or so they kept saying."

"How long did that go on?"

"Long. You know, it wasn't many years ago, I would have accepted this little issue ... if you get my drift. But nowadays things are different, people are watching, and the city is more serious about code. Even Taney County is getting stricter about the rule book."

"Allen's position on the city council and running project development for Fortune Enterprises should keep him plenty busy. Strange he'd take special interest in one contract."

"Be my opinion."

"Maybe he's like this on every project," Tom offered.

"Who knows? I figure he needs a girlfriend to take up some of his spare time."

"He's married, isn't he?" Tom asked.

"I rest my case."

Tom sipped some beer and leaned forward slightly. "Did the city try to stop construction? Isn't it difficult to do inspections without an approved plan?"

"Inspection reports are Allen's specialty. He and his crew can bully an approval out of anyone. I consider the city's new building inspectors professional, but they can take only so much shit from someone."

"Do the inspectors change the reports?"

Gary squinted and whispered, "That's a very complicated question. Not sure I can answer that one."

Tom was caught in his friend's gaze for a moment and decided not to pursue the topic for now. He checked his watch. "Better get going or I'll be late for a meeting." He tossed a ten-dollar bill on the table.

"Hey, it was good to see you," Gary said, shaking Tom's hand while pulling him close to a hug. As they walked toward the door, he added,

"Don't make it so long next time, especially if you're going to pick up the tab."

"I'm pretty sure the phone lines go both ways, Bubba," Tom said, getting into his car.

The ride to City Hall took several minutes, time enough for Tom to digest Gary's comments and consider how they applied to the overall Branson construction boom.

The small table in the center of the staff room next to the detectives' office had been set up for the meeting.

"Sorry, fellas. I got hung up with an old friend," Tom said, settling into the chair next to Sid. "Did I miss anything?"

Sid glanced at the coroner, seated on the opposite side. "No problem, I was catching Artie up on the Tom and Kate saga," he said.

"Short conversation," Tom remarked, furrowing his brow in Sid's direction. He pulled up to the table. "Good to see you, Artie. What do you have for us?"

Artie opened the manila file situated in front of the detectives. "Here are my notes, a copy of my photos, and a preliminary report on the remains. Also, I called both the University of Arkansas and Missouri forensic anthropology departments. Neither had anyone who could help right now. Missouri recommended a private contractor who they've used in the past. Arkansas hadn't worked with him, but they were familiar with his reputation and concurred."

Sid said, "He's like a scientist for hire."

"Precisely," Artie said. "I made calls to check his references and determine what else we might need. Then I called him to check availability. The man, Dr. Charles Fredericks, has been doing this for many years. His bio and resumé are in the file. Most of his experience has been in larger projects to identify victims of mass killings."

Tom took out the bio and scanned the list of projects. "Very impressive. Why would he want to help us?"

"He didn't even hesitate. He's available right now and he can see we need his expertise. He'll fly in tonight. I'll pick him up in the morning and meet you at the site."

"We'll be there," Tom said.

"Have you found any pertinent cold cases?" Artie asked.

"Not yet," Tom said. "I've had a chance to review from 1982 to present, the years in our automated system. I haven't pulled records before then. Records for earlier years are in the archives, which I'm still trying to pin down."

Artie glanced in Tom's direction. "I guess you lost the toss."

"How'd you know? I should have gone with seniority," Tom said.

Artie pushed away from the table. "I'm sure we're going to need whatever you can find. We'll learn more from Dr. Fredericks tomorrow."

As soon as the coroner was gone, Sid said, "Guess we better grab a quick bite before the thing starts tonight."

"Thing? You mean the Branson Citizens Police Academy?"

"Fancy title."

"Yeah. I can't wait either," Tom said, heading for the door.

Two six-foot folding tables were positioned against the wall on the left side of the police department meeting room. Handouts and student badges were lined up on either side of a poster displaying the PD organization chart, including external associations. About twenty folding chairs were situated in the center of the room to accommodate the citizen students, many of whom were already seated. Four empty folding chairs on either side of a podium in the front of the room faced the student bull pen. Tom and Sid proceeded to the front table where their boss stood checking his watch.

"Good evening, Lieutenant," Tom said, adding, "Sorry we're late."

"You're good," Dan Palmer said. "We've been waiting for the last attendees to show. How'd it go with the coroner?"

"Not much yet. The forensic anthropologist will arrive tomorrow."

Dan said, "I would guess this one could take a while. Any progress on the old cases?"

Tom shook his head. "Not much to report on the Porter complaint issue either. Between Sid and me we've questioned bosses and workers in several construction companies doing work in Branson. A good friend of mine is the foreman with the general contractor on the big office complex job."

Sid said, "No one has described anything illegal going on."

"Lots of the usual you-scratch-my-back stuff that goes on everywhere." Tom said. "We addressed specific issues, per the complaint. Some innuendo but no specific proof yet. Porter named every project in town, so it was hard to take it too seriously."

"Have you spoken to anyone with the Building Department?"

"Not yet," Tom said. "We have an appointment for both of us to speak to Leatherman tomorrow. His responses are predictable, but we need to hear his perspective."

Sid said, "I'm not holding my breath for a confession, but we've let it be known we'll pay a reward for information on questionable activity. Everything would be confidential."

"Sounds good," Dan said. "Okay. I guess we better take our seats."

"I hate to say this," Tom began, "but participating in a Citizens Police Academy is not my idea of a good way to end this day. I need some time away from City Hall and the crime business."

"Understood," Dan said. "But tonight, you can leave when Chief Daniels completes the overview."

It wasn't until Tom pulled his chair up to the speaker's table that he saw Kate smiling at him from the audience. He returned the greeting then leaned toward Dan and whispered, "Did we authorize press coverage?"

Dan shook his head. "Kate Starling will be one of the attendees. I'm sure she'll use the information wisely."

"Yeah, me too," Tom said still watching Kate. He wasn't sure if her being part of the citizens academy was good or bad, but he knew it would make the classes more interesting.

Forty-five minutes later, Leonard Daniels finished the introductions and overview by saying, "We'll take a break now. Meet Sergeant Munroe in the hallway in fifteen minutes. He'll take you to Dispatch for your next session."

Once the students vacated the room, Chief Daniels spoke briefly to the police personnel before ending with a reminder "to be prepared and on time for your portion of this academy. This class is important for community relations."

As the detectives walked to the Adams Street entrance, Sid said, "I'm going to take off, partner. See you in the morning."

"Okay," Tom said. "I, uh, need to check on something before heading out."

"Right. Good luck with that."

"Seriously, I left something in the office."

Sid peeked over Tom's shoulder. "I think something is by the bulletin board."

"What do you mean?" Tom asked, following Sid's line of sight to Kate. He took a deep breath and made his way across the lobby, surprised to feel the tingles on his neck.

"Anything interesting?" he asked, still a few paces away.

She turned and smiled. "Just killing time."

Tom said, "I didn't expect to see you in the class."

"Why? I'm a citizen."

"Yes, you are. But you already know how the department works."

"I figured it was time for a refresher course. I couldn't pass up the opportunity, especially when Helen suggested I attend."

"Ah. Truth at last."

"I'm sure it will be interesting, but it's still an assignment, a feature article with the blessing of the city's PR rep."

Tom stared into Kate's eyes, not sure how to move forward.

"I better get to the meeting spot," she said, starting up the hallway. "I'd hate to have to stay after school.

"Uh, Katie, I was wondering ..."

She turned to face him. "About?"

"We haven't been out to dinner in quite a while."

"Several months. Did you want to know exactly? I can check my calendar."

Tom shook his head. "You know, I'd forgotten how mean you are."

Kate whispered, "I would love to have dinner with you."

"You would? I mean, that's great. I'll call you tomorrow."

Chapter Seven

The sign hanging on the motel office door was older than Kate. The hands on the tattered cardboard clock indicated someone would return in fifteen minutes. Either the night desk clerk went the way of the others her father had hired or a motel guest called for his assistance. She made a mental note to buy a new sign.

Dried leaves churned by the crisp autumn breeze fluttered across the dimly lighted parking lot. The house seemed forlorn, almost eerie in the shadows, no lights in the windows facing the motel, no trace of her dad or his vehicle.

Along the north side of the house weeds and crabgrass gnarled the garden, once her mother's pride and joy. As a little girl, Kate had marveled at the variety of flowers and plants, which miraculously changed with each season. Later she helped her mother tirelessly replace the tulips with marigolds and mums, trim the iris leaves, and thin out the day lilies in preparation for the next season. She missed her mother's sense of calm and her unconditional love. The garden missed her too. And so did Kate's father.

Even after all these years, Margaret Carson Starling's place in their lives had not been filled.

The view from the back porch, once trees and hills as far as the eye could see, revealed signs of construction on a not-too-distant ridge. No doubt the site of another theater or motel, the newly cleared acreage was conspicuous even in the light of the newly waning moon.

She settled onto the glider, closed her eyes, and summoned memories of the way Branson had been not too long ago, before the boom. Additional businesses brought jobs and a flourishing economy to the area, but at what price? Trees, water, land, and air had all been affected.

"Mighty serious frown, Katie," her father said, letting the screen door slam shut.

She sighed. "I was remembering a different time."

"When your mother was alive?"

"Yes, and before the changes."

"Not all for the good, I'm afraid."

"Not all bad. At least the motel is doing better now."

"Considering its owner was accused of murder."

"That's over. You were totally cleared."

Roger Starling nodded and leaned his back against the railing, crossing his arms across his chest. The paunch, so prevalent in men his age, had never appeared. Thanks to hard work and good genes he seemed much younger than his sixty-five years.

"What brings you home?"

"I live here."

"I haven't seen you for weeks."

"That's not true. We have breakfast every Monday."

"Usually downtown after you've already been at work for two hours. Seriously, Katie, you work too much. Usually, you go directly to your room and I don't see hide nor hair of you."

"You think you're smart, don't you?"

"I know my daughter."

She took his hand, pulling him down to sit next to her. "Where were you?"

"Had to go out."

"Had to?"

"Someone came by. We went for a quick supper. That's all. No big deal."

"Could this someone be female?"

"Could be."

"Marge Connarde?"

His face flushed. "Nothing wrong with Margie. She's a very nice lady."

"I agree. She's a *foxy* lady."

"Not sure foxy is what I need in my life."

"Trust me, you could use a little foxy. You're too young to be alone. If you're comfortable with Marge, I mean Margie, go for it."

"I appreciate the advice of one so experienced."

"Hey. I read a lot."

He cupped her hands in his and set the glider in motion. The associated bitonal to-and-fro creaks blended easily with the symphony of tree frogs and crickets in the Ozarks night.

After several minutes, Roger said, "How's it going with Tom?"

"Why is everyone concerned about me and Tom?"

"Shirley been on you too?"

"How'd you guess?"

"So, how are the two of you getting along?"

"Fine, I guess. Most of the time."

"Must not be too bad, if you're talking."

She twisted around and glared. "Did Tom call you?"

"What if he did? We're old fishing buddies, you know."

"What did he say?"

"Nothing about you."

"Did he say we were speaking again?"

"I got that impression, but we mostly discussed how the trout were biting."

"You'll be pleased to know we're going to have dinner."

"Halleluiah. I thought he'd never ask."

"I'm happy it makes you happy," she said.

"Are you going to tell me why you waited for me on the glider?"

"I need your help with an article I'm doing. You've seen the features on Etta Stupholds and the crafts fair."

"Yes. Reading those brought back some memories."

"Great. I need your memories."

"Okay, but why?"

"Helen wants me to do a series on Branson's history. She wanted Etta and the crafts fair to be the focus, but Etta is running out of steam. She may not put up with me much longer."

"But I will?"

"You can tell me what you remember about this area in the forties, fifties, sixties. You know, the good old days. Maybe you can give me leads on who else I can talk to. I've read the newspapers from the period, but nothing really juicy was ever published."

"You want the juicy stuff, huh? You know I was a young boy in the forties. I'm not sure how much juice I can scare up."

"Do you remember Etta? I know you worked for her husband."

"Had my first paying job sweeping floors at Clay's store. Used to go every day after school. I'd sweep the inside, then the porch, then the storeroom. Whether they needed it or not, every day I'd sweep. Clay ... I called him Mr. Stupholds ... said he would give me a dime if I did a good job. Never failed to earn that dime."

"What was he like?"

Roger tilted his head back and squinted. "Isn't that funny. Can't say I remember much about him. He was pretty quiet. Couldn't have been too tall; he didn't tower over me much and I was sort of a runt until my teens. His face is a blur. Must not have made much of an impression."

"Oh," Kate said, disappointment shaping her tone.

"Remember *her* though. I'll admit to a little crush on Etta. I was ten when I started my job. Guess she must have been around thirty."

"To be precise, when you were ten, she was thirty-one," Kate said.

"Actually, age was not an issue," Roger said, winking.

"So, she worked with Clay in the store?"

"She did *most* of the work. Sales, displays, the books. He did the ordering, but she probably told him what to order."

"How was business?"

"Okay, I suppose. They'd been open for several years. Seems like they had a good share of customers."

"That's odd."

"Why? Did Etta say it wasn't good? She'd know better than I."

"No, but Clay apparently–"

"–killed himself? Yeah, we knew he did it. Hard to keep that sort of thing quiet in a small town. Not that anyone said anything to Etta. I remember hearing her tell your grandma and other ladies about Clay's bad heart. Hell, he couldn't have been much over thirty-five when he died. But whoever she was talking to would say poor Clay, so young for a heart attack."

"She was in denial."

"Well, she seemed brave to me. She was protecting the honor of her pitiful coward of a husband. I'd say that's when my crush turned to love."

"Did you do anything about it?"

"My crush? Lord no. An almost-fourteen-year-old didn't have a chance with a sophisticated gal like Etta Stupholds. Not that I even considered trying."

Kate eased off the glider and moved to the banister. "I can't believe you've never told me this."

"I didn't know father's told daughters about childhood crushes."

"But I've written three articles on Etta. And you didn't even say you knew her."

"Crazy as it seems, I didn't even remember my sweeping job at the store until you asked me about Etta tonight. Anyway, it wasn't long after Clay's death that Etta closed the store and merged with Jack Brighton's. I lost my job and my first love in the same afternoon."

"Why didn't you go to work at the new mercantile?"

"I tried, but no luck. Already had two kids sweeping floors and running errands."

"Etta didn't put in a good word?"

"She may have, but one of the kids was Randy Brighton."

"Jack's son."

"Yeah. The other kid had a connection, too. And, so, with my first exposure to nepotism, I was unemployed."

"That other kid was Bryan Porter," Kate said.

"You're probably right," Roger said, shaking his head. "Small world, huh?"

"It is in Branson."

"I didn't know Bryan in school. He was several years younger than us. Knew Randy though. He was a real hot shot. Even had a girlfriend."

"Were you friends?"

"He was a year behind me. I knew him but we weren't friendly. He had a hot temper. Stayed in trouble a lot. Your grandma wouldn't let me associate with him."

"And you didn't care enough to disobey her."

"More like she had me scared, but my stepdad was worse. No way would I cross either one of them."

"Did Randy make it through school?"

"Joined the army at the beginning of his junior year. Surprised a lot of folks. Gave *me* an idea though."

"A way to get away from your stepfather?"

"The war was over, but they were still calling for recruits. Made it easy to get away. Your grandma was unhappy about it, but she understood."

"Did you ever visit Etta at the new store?"

"No, I guess I got over that pretty quickly. Went to work for the lumber company. It was a lot harder but paid better. Worked until the day before I joined the Army six months after graduating from high school."

"Why didn't Bryan stay with the mercantile?"

"His father quit, opened his own business. It was a year or so after the merger. I considered applying at the mercantile then, but I was doing okay at the lumber yard. Not sure what happened or when, but by the time I returned from the army Porter's store was closed."

"Was it located where Bryan's flea market is today?"

"Wow, you are relentless."

Kate shrugged.

"Frankly, I'm not sure I gave Bryan or his father much thought. I remember hearing about the opening, that's about it. But the store was closer to town. Nothing was way out west back then."

"Do you know what Bryan has against Fortune Enterprises?"

"Jealous of their success, I imagine. He's not a good businessman."

"His vendetta seems more personal."

"I know what you mean. He used to make lots of noise at the planning and zoning meetings when I was on the committee. Most of his objections were about Jack Brighton's requests. And he made some good points. But Jack usually got his way. I wouldn't want to say he was a bully, but he had a way to sway the votes."

"Maybe that's where Randy's temper came from."

"Could be. But Randy's not nearly as hot-headed now. I'd say the service and years away from home calmed him down a good bit."

"But not completely?"

"Everyone has a temper, Katie. Some do a better job hiding it than others. But I don't know of any personal issue between Porter and either Brighton. Of course, I was away in the army for several years."

"Maybe, you'll remember more. If you do, let me know."

"I do remember going to the mercantile when I was leaving to enlist."

"To say good-bye to Etta?"

"Yeah. I lied about being over her. Anyway, she said Randy was happy in the service and she hoped I would be too."

"She remembers you ... said you were a hard worker. She knew about the crush."

"Well, with that bit of news, I'm going to bed."

"Me, too. I've got an early appointment in town." Kate hugged her father's neck. "Let's do this conversation thing again real soon."

Chapter Eight

Kate opened her eyes and wondered why her father was shaking her shoulder. The building department files rested precariously on her lap and her feet were propped on her father's ottoman.

She raised her head slowly off the arm of the sofa. "Guess I didn't make it to bed."

"That was my impression."

"What time is it?"

"Eight thirty. You didn't stop by the office to say goodbye, so I came to check on you."

"I've got to get going." She started toward her room but stopped abruptly and hugged her father. "Thanks again for the talk last night. It was illuminating."

"I'll bet it was."

Kate pulled into the city hall lot at precisely nine-fifteen and headed to Leatherman's office suite. Claire was sitting at her desk, staring intently at her computer screen and mumbling to a sheet of paper on the copy holder next to the monitor.

Ben Leatherman's office door was shut, but Kate could hear voices. She couldn't quite make out the conversation. A period of silence was followed by the door swinging opened and slamming against the inside wall. Claire raised her head and stared at the two emerging men.

Bryan Porter—his cheeks, ears, and forehead red with anger—shook his finger. "Mark my words, Mr. Leatherman, this is slander only if what I'm saying isn't true. Now, take my advice and flush this good-old-boy network out of the city or I'll do it," he said.

Leatherman shook his head but made no comment as Porter left the area and walked across the lobby to the building exit.

Kate cleared her throat loudly and placed her purse heavily on the counter.

Both Claire and Leatherman turned toward the noise.

Kate said, "This may not be a good time, but I'd like to speak to you, Mr. Leatherman."

"Come on in," he said straining a smile.

"I appreciate your seeing me," Kate said as she scooted into the chair in front of his desk. "I couldn't help overhearing Bryan Porter's threat."

"Bryan didn't threaten me. He was merely stating his intentions."

"Point taken, Mr. Leatherman."

"How can I help you, Ms. Starling?"

"I have some questions about the files Claire copied for me."

"I'll try to help."

Kate turned on her recorder. "Do you mind?"

"Not at all," Leatherman said.

Kate took the files from her large handbag and placed them on Leatherman's desk. She opened the top one so he could read it.

He glanced at the three sheets of paper in the file, then back to her.

"This concerns the lot where the skeleton was recently found," she said, pointing to a letter-sized sheet. "Can you tell me why this warning was issued? It was the first item placed in the file."

"How about I explain what's happened with that lot over the last few years. I'll touch on each of these inspection reports and the warning."

"That would be great," she said.

"Clearly, you're aware the property is owned indirectly by Fortune Enterprises, by way of Jack Brighton and Henrietta Stupholds. The actual lot goes back from Commercial at St. Limas to the Roark Creek arm of the lake. The original buildings along the two streets were used off and on for thirty years or so after Henrietta merged her store with Brighton's. In the late 1970s, the buildings were torn down at the city's request. They had been unoccupied for about four years and were eyesores, if not safety hazards."

"Excuse me for interrupting, but none of that is in the file."

"Right. I'm getting to that," Leatherman said, with familiar impatience in his tone. "When the buildings were razed, that portion of the lot was cleaned up, but the woods behind them remained. About two years ago, a crew hired by the owner started clearing the lot of trees. I had been on the job for a few months. The city of

Branson was in the midst of the construction crisis. The environmentalists were pushing the city to preserve the natural beauty of the Ozarks, namely the trees."

"I remember," Kate said. "You were hired, in part, to make sure it happened."

"That's what I was told," he said.

"So, the warning was issued because the company did not have a clearing permit."

"Correct. Allen was unaware of the requirement for a permit." Leatherman stared at Kate perhaps checking for a reaction. "In any case, they stopped clearing and replaced the three trees taken before they received the warning. Nothing else was done with the lot, until the clearing permit was requested and issued last month. The clearing plan and the two inspections which have taken place are filed with the permit."

"Thank you for being so thorough," Kate said.

"Any other questions?"

"Not about the St. Limas lot." She opened the other file and spread the sheets across Leatherman's desk. "Maybe you can give me the same sequence of events on this Fortune Enterprises Office Complex project."

"I won't be able to do that."

"You know historical details of a relatively small lot, which has gone unused for decades, but you can't explain the department file contents for a major new construction job?"

"First, the property is not within city limits. Second, the project is on the list of those being audited by the state. If you have specific questions, I'll try to answer them."

"Okay. Twelve of the sheets of paper in the file are warnings to the owner or architect or both regarding the lack of proper permitting to proceed with the project. In fact, the oldest issue dates are on three of those warnings. Seventeen inspection reports were issued before the date on the footing permit. Neither a clearing permit nor a building permit is in the file. But three dozen additional inspection reports were issued after the date on the footing permit. Some of the inspection reports appear to be altered to indicate approval."

Kate studied Leatherman and waited for his response.

"Do you have a question?" he asked.

"I don't know much about construction. But it seems logical that the permit structure is in place for a reason. A permit is issued for each phase of a project, presumably before the work begins for that phase. Is that correct?"

"That's the intention."

"Why didn't that sequence happen on this project? And before you use the excuse of it being outside the city, I know that does not apply due to the city's agreement with Taney County. Why was Fortune Enterprises allowed to move forward without proper review and permitting by your department?"

"Unfortunately, Ms. Starling, Branson is going through some serious growing pains. Ways of doing business for decades are not going to change overnight. And those changes must be supported on up the chain."

"You're saying someone other than you or your staff authorized the go-ahead?"

Leatherman came to his feet and walked to the door.

"You aren't going to answer my question."

"If you'll excuse me, Ms. Starling, I have a meeting across the hall."

Kate shook her head in disbelief, remaining in the chair for a few seconds after his departure and securing her copies in the envelope.

"Is everything okay?" Claire asked, peaking into Leatherman's office.

"Peachy," Kate responded, then quickly added. "I'm sorry, I should be used to being dismissed by city staff. It happens a lot."

Kate was ready for her next meeting by the time she parked in the newspaper's lot and walked the block or so to the old Riverside Mercantile Building. The side door opened to a stairway as narrow as the hallway at the top. All but one of the wooden doors along the hall had *Authorized Personnel Only* signs. A modest placard on the single exception stated "Fortune Enterprises" in bold letters.

A lone desk sat in the center of the oval reception area, which could have fit two of her father's living rooms. Three doors broke the perimeter—one on her left not far from a cluster of uncomfortable looking metal and cloth chairs, one on the right directly opposite the entrance, and the third positioned about halfway between the other two.

Kate placed her business card in front of the young woman sitting behind the receptionist plaque and said, "I'd like to speak to Mr. Jack Brighton."

The receptionist pushed a long blond tress behind her ear as she picked up the receiver and pressed a button. "Kate Starling with *Branson Daily News* is here to see Jack Brighton." She glanced up at Kate. "Okay," she said with a shrug and hung up.

Before Kate could remember the title of the song playing from the overhead speaker, Larry Allen emerged from the door on the right. She met him halfway across the room. His light green polo shirt complimented his eyes, which were somewhere between olive and Kelly green. But his vacant stare definitely did not match the smile pasted on his face.

"Kate, always a pleasure," he said extending his hand. "I must say your articles lend a breath of fresh air to an often-boring newspaper."

"Thank you," she said, adding, "I think."

"I meant it as a compliment."

Quite the charmer, she mused.

"Sorry, Jack's not available, but perhaps I can help."

"I want to interview him for a Branson history series we're running," she lied.

"Let me try to help," Allen said, leading Kate to his office. "Granddad will be out of town for a few days. Have a seat," he said, pointing to a padded armchair in the center of the office. He sat and swiveled in his desk chair to face Kate, and then rolled a blueprint covering his desk and placed it on a shelf behind him. "First question?"

She shook off her schoolgirl reaction to his charisma, remembering the councilman's harsher side witnessed in previous encounters. He had a way of ignoring questions he didn't want to answer. If pressed, he could turn the tables between heart beats and make a reporter wish he, or she, hadn't asked.

"I appreciate your seeing me, Larry. I know you're busy." She took out her recorder and switched it on. "Makes it easier for quotes," she said.

"Not a problem. But any facts about Branson's history before 1970 will have to be saved for my uncle or grandfather."

"I also have questions about the current projects, specifically, the new office complex."

"I run the day-to-day for that job."

"Then you'd be the one to explain why the building is almost complete but the building permit has yet to be issued."

"It was issued last week."

"Even so, the structure itself is almost finished," she said, wondering why Leatherman hadn't told her.

"What's your point?"

"Shouldn't you have waited for the permits to be issued before beginning each phase of the construction?

"We had waivers."

"Were they in writing?"

"A handshake is a legal agreement." He stood and walked to the window overlooking Commercial Street.

"Are you saying you had *unofficial* permission to start construction?"

"That's how it works."

"For all projects? Or for those run by a city councilman?"

He turned around quickly. "In the Ozarks, Kate. That's how it works." He took a step toward her. "Tell me, Kate. Have you examined records for other projects? Have you compared actual construction start dates to permit issuance on all of them?"

"I'm concerned with this project at the moment," she said.

"Do you think this one is unique?"

"Do you?"

"Are you suggesting Ben Leatherman or his staff did me a favor?"

"Are you suggesting they didn't? The fact is construction started before permits were issued, including the footing and foundation permit. Correct?"

"This project is outside city limits," he said.

"So I've heard. But it is within the jurisdiction of the city of Branson Building Department according to the agreement with Taney County."

"I'm not sure what you want me to say."

"I'm asking you to comment on these discrepancies. I'm giving you a chance to explain, before I run the article."

"Okay. I've made my comments. Now, I need to get back to the site. I'm sure a smart girl like you can find your way out."

The bile was still churning in her throat when she returned to the newspaper office. It took Kate forty-five minutes to finish the article she'd already blocked out on the newspaper's article management system. She marked it ready for Helen's review and made a few phone calls before heading to her boss's office. Helen motioned for Kate to wait before speaking as she finished reading the item on her screen.

"I read the article you uploaded. I have some issues."

"But it was full of information and to the point."

"To begin with, it was supposed to be a follow-up on the crafts fair, specifically, the creator of the crafts fair, Etta Stupholds."

Helen closed the door and motioned for Kate to sit down.

"Etta's in the article. I don't know why you're so upset."

"That is precisely why I'm upset. You don't know why."

"Everything I wrote is true. I used direct quotes. I have backup on everything," Kate said, pushing down on the table with her index finger. "You told me you wanted more Branson history in the pieces."

Helen took a deep breath. "I apparently did not make myself clear. I meant to add background on Etta, not to libel Fortune Enterprises and the city of Branson Building Department."

"Allen as much as admitted he made deals with city staff to get his project completed. He was rude and defensive. I put in his words verbatim."

"Rude and defensive is how you leave many people. I'm not sure we can stretch that to prove Allen's guilt in any way."

Kate stared at Helen, realizing how mad—maybe even how right—her boss was.

"Tell me you have no argument," Helen snickered.

"I guess I don't know what to say. I see what you're getting at, but I didn't make any of this up. The evidence is in the file."

"Here's what I want you to do, Kate. I want you to reread your article word by word. I want you to place the emphasis on Etta and the crafts fair. Leave in what is absolutely necessary about the company. Tone down ... better yet *remove* ... all your implications. Leave the exposé for a different article on a different day, preferably when you have more proof than suggestions."

Helen took another deep breath and folded her hands in front of her on the table. "When you've done that, run it by me again and we'll see if it's ready for publication."

Chapter Nine

Tom pulled up to the lot as Artie and his passenger exited the coroner's van. Dr. Fredericks seemed to be about Artie's age, maybe a bit younger. His salt-and-pepper-every-hair-in-place appearance reminded Tom of the government types he worked with in Kansas City.

"Detective Sargent Tom Collingwood," Artie began, "this is Dr. Charles Fredericks. He says he responds best to Chuck."

"Welcome to Branson, Chuck," Tom said, extending his hand.

"Thanks. I've heard great things about your city. Too bad this is a professional visit."

"Shall we get started?" Artie said.

"Looks like the ground is drying out," Tom said. "No rain predicted for today. What will you need from me and my partner?"

"Artie and I will do most of the work. Once I survey the area, I'll know more."

Artie added, "I've made arrangements for lab space in Springfield. Chuck and I will transport the remains in my van and preserve the chain of custody. I'll assist him, be his gofer."

"You underestimate your contribution," Chuck said with a smile.

"I know my limits," Artie corrected.

As the group approached the police perimeter, Tom struggled to remember the name of the new recruit who had pulled the two nightshifts.

"Morning, Sargent Collingwood," the young man said.

"Morning, Patrolman Sims," Tom said, proud of his timely recall. "Anything to report?"

"No, sir. Nothing but deer and squirrel out this morning."

"You can take off. Thanks for pulling the extra shifts."

Artie and Chuck were already on the far side of the stump, crouched next to the skeleton.

"Glad to see so much of the blanket is intact," Chuck said. "It will be easier to gather the bones and preserve any evidence wrapped inside."

Artie examined the stump end of the root interweaving the blanket and skeleton torso. "We'll need a power saw, Tom, to cut this root cleanly."

"Shovels, too," Chuck said, adding, "I brought my hand tools, but no large shovels."

"I have shovels, clippers, flashlights, body bags, evidence bags, and markers in the van," Artie said.

Tom pulled his radio off his belt, "Sid Green, come in. Sid, do you read?"

Sid's voice crackled over the radio, "Tom, Sid. Sorry, I got hung up with a call on the complaint case. I'm almost to the site."

"Good. Turn around and find a power saw. And bring extra gas."

"Ten four. See you in a few."

The three men returned to the coroner's van. Chuck and Artie slipped on white jumpsuits to cover their street clothes, then selected the supplies and tools they would need. They added the smaller items to Artie's satchel and placed everything next to the vehicle.

"This will get us started," Chuck said, as he and Artie each grabbed a shovel and a bag. "Tom, can you bring the clippers and stretcher from the van?"

Tom complied then caught up quickly to Artie who had stopped several yards distance from the stump.

Chuck walked around the area several times, making notes and sketches. After several minutes, he stooped down beside the skeleton bundle itself. "I've not seen this precise phenomenon before. The bundle is resting on the tree roots that persistently hold the stump to the ground."

Artie added, "From this angle, it seems like the blanket is anchored to the skeleton by those roots that worked their way around the wrapping."

"Good observation," Chuck said, coming to his feet. As he approached the other men, he added, "We'll need to cut both ends of those roots first thing. We'll want to preserve the relationship to the body. The actual grave lies toward the end of one bunch of roots. I'd say the body was initially buried several yards from the tree toward the creek. The root system continued to grow for many years."

"Any idea how many?" Tom asked.

Chuck reviewed the scene as if making a mental calculation. "Thirty, maybe fifty."

"Great," Tom said, contemplating the number of cases he'd have to read.

"Where do you want the saw?" Sid said, approaching the trio and introducing himself.

Chuck said, "Artie, can you please assist me with that? Please leave the gas can there, Sid."

The two men examined the stump side of the roots and Chuck showed Artie his notebook. Artie started the saw and positioned it to make the first cut. Chuck kneeled next to the remains and slid his gloved hands under the roots below the skeleton, then nodded toward Artie. After several cuts the roots were free of the stump.

"These connections into the ground can be severed with the clippers, Tom," Chuck said as he came to his feet.

Tom grabbed the heavy-duty clippers and said, "Tell me where."

Chuck held out his notebook and pointed to a sketch. "About six inches from the bundle."

Tom complied and then stepped back.

"Artie, we'll need a large body bag. And Tom, the stretcher, please."

The men carefully lifted and secured the bundle, including the root system, into the body bag and then positioned and secured the bag on the stretcher. Artie held a large evidence bag as Dr. Fredericks shoveled dirt from the grave floor and dumped it into the bag. He then handed Artie a second large bag and added soil from the area close to the tree where the bundle had landed. The coroner marked the bags accordingly.

"Artie, if you and Sid will take our friend to the van, Tom and I will begin investigating the scene."

Chuck turned to a new page in his notebook and sketched the grave, clearly visible now unobstructed by roots and occupant. "If we consider this a rectangular box, I'd say the head was toward this end."

"I agree, based on the body's position after extraction. From what the crew told us, the earthmover skimmed off the top layer of dirt as they pushed the stump over. It was only partially out of the ground, so they pulled from the other side to upend it completely."

The forensic anthropologist retrieved his camera and a tape measure from his valise. He took several shots of the inside of the box, and then measured the depth of the hole at the center point of each side and several points down the middle. With each measurement, he made a note on the evolving sketch.

Chuck handed one end of the tape to Tom and said, "Let's get several measurements length and width." He added the numbers to his sketch as they moved around the perimeter. "The grave is roughly three feet deep, but this end is slightly deeper and narrower, suggesting two diggers."

"Or one who became tired as he dug," Tom commented.

Chuck smiled, his focus remaining on the inside of the grave. "Artie and I will have to examine more carefully, but it looks like there might have been different tools used as well."

"Three feet is pretty deep for a quick grave even with two men," Tom said. "The ground is filled with rocks in this area."

"They took their time. I'd say they weren't concerned about being seen."

"Maybe they were stupid," Tom countered.

"No doubt," Chuck said, walking back to his tool kit. "I want to get some soil samples and see if anything is buried deeper. You and Sid don't have to stick around. Artie and I will take everything to the lab and have a preliminary report for you as soon as possible."

"Okay," Tom said, somewhat disappointed.

"Don't forget you have homework to do. It will be difficult to identify the deceased without some notion of who he or she was."

"Over thirty years ago."

"That guess is based on the tree. We'll have more to go on when we examine the bones and blanket. Won't be much clothing left. Your open cases will be our best starting point."

"I hope someone cared enough about this person to report him, or her, missing. And I hope they reported it in Branson."

"Hold that thought. And you might also hope that your victim has a viable candidate still living to confirm the identification," Chuck said, motioning for Artie to join him by the grave.

⤜⋯⤛

Sid was already sipping coffee when Tom got back to the office. He grabbed a cup for himself and dropped into his chair. "Tell me about the latest informant. I hope he said more than the other fifty whiners who've called in."

"Afraid not," Sid said. "Lots of words, no substance. I made notes, but it boils down to what everyone else says ... you scratch my back, I'll scratch yours. No hint of bribery or fraud, nothing close. Maybe a wee bit more *good old boy* than we'd like, but who's to say."

"It's occurred to me Porter is mad because he's not part of that in-crowd. He's missing out on the deal."

"Could be," Sid agreed. "Frankly, I wouldn't blame him. The system is unfair and selective. Speaking of which, I set up a meeting for tomorrow afternoon with Leatherman. He'll have his inspectors attend if possible. Maybe he has some idea why Porter is suing the city of Branson and why he issued a complaint with the state."

"Maybe the old boy simply wants to rattle someone's cage and considers anything more than that a bonus."

"Except he seems to be particularly interested in Fortune Enterprises."

"Biggest game in town," Tom commented as Lieutenant Palmer entered the room.

"Who's the biggest game in town?" Dan asked.

"Fortune Enterprises. Sid was saying Porter seems to be directing most of his attention their way."

"Strange coincidence," Dan said.

Tom asked, "Why so?"

"Fifteen minutes ago, Larry Allen called me ... for the second time. He spent the next ten minutes chewing my ear off. Bottom line, he wants to get back on his lot and finish the clearing. Do we know when that might be possible?"

"If he's going to be pushy, probably another week or two, maybe longer," Tom said. "We'll have to consult our consultant."

"By all means, let's do. But try to release the lot before the next phone call," Dan said, adding on his way out, "Get me a date ASAP. The Brighton family, including Allen, have a lot of sway in this town. I can't hold them off much longer."

Tom waited until the lieutenant crossed the common room to his office, and then turned to Sid. "I'm afraid ASAP will have to wait. We have a date with the archives."

"We?" Sid moaned. "That's your thing."

"It was until I realized how long ago and how many years would have to be searched. Besides, that room is dark, dank, and dusty. I need some company, partner."

"Where is this mausoleum?"

"Grab a couple of flashlights and follow me. You're going to enjoy this."

Tom knocked on the counter separating the city admin group from the upper lobby. A young woman, apparently fresh from college, walked to the counter.

"Is Cindy around?" he asked.

"I'm Cindy. You must be Sergeants Tom Collingwood and Sid Green. Nice to meet you both. Ready for the tour?"

The men followed the young woman into the courtroom area next to the lobby.

Sid whispered to Tom, "We don't have to do this alone?"

"She's going to show us where everything is. Then we're on our own."

"I want to tell you a couple of things before we go into the archives," Cindy said, stopping at the back of the room next to the podium.

"Don't worry," Tom said, "we're armed with flashlights and our service revolvers."

"Hopefully you won't need the latter. But keep in mind the records are not very organized. I was hired to figure out what records are in the various department stashes and to organize them for posterity."

Sid said, "Part of the new and improved management concept."

"Right. So, you are obviously searching for police records. Most of the more current files, primarily since the 70s, are in the basement room under the police department suite."

"Basement?" Sid asked.

"A well-kept secret," Tom said.

"Anyway, the earlier file boxes, if they exist, will be behind the courtroom with the building and engineering department records. The public works barn contains some records, but hopefully you'll find what you want in City Hall somewhere."

"That's reassuring," Tom said.

"Sorry. This has never been centralized beyond the department level. We have a five-year plan to organize the records in a special, *large*, controlled room in the city hall extension, but that's a few years out."

"Unfortunately, we can't wait," Sid said.

"Okay, let's get started," Cindy said. She crossed through the small witness room and entered the building department suite, then continued beyond a copier and several file cabinets to a door marked authorized personnel only. She unlocked the door and reached inside and flicked on an overhead light. Looking over her shoulder, she said, "No turning back now."

As it opened, the door brushed the end of a row of floor-to-ceiling metal shelf units on the right side of the room. A small table sat to the left of the entrance abutting the second row of metal shelves on the left side of the room. Each shelving unit was about five feet wide and three feet deep with four shelf levels. A narrow path, less than five feet wide and about twenty-five feet long, spanned the middle of the room, a step stool stood ready for use at the far end of the room.

"Whoa! I'd forgotten about all these boxes," Tom said. "Who'd believe this is behind the courtroom."

"I know what you mean," Cindy said. "Sorry about this overhead lighting. The bulbs here and in the center of the room are it, and they aren't very bright."

"Good thing we brought these flashlights," Sid said.

Tom said, "Not very bright could describe us. Any suggestions how to proceed?"

"I've already checked the boxes. Some have content lists, but they can be vague. I have a comprehensive inventory, but it may be easier for you to examine each box, which I've also coded for department and year. Presumably every call or case was recorded. The journals are here on this table by the door."

"They'll help us get started," Tom said.

"Once you see a box you want to explore, you'll have to get it off the shelf and take it outside. The witness room won't be in use until next week, so you can occupy it during the day. Unfortunately, you'll have to return everything to the storage area each night."

"You mean, if we leave each night," Sid said. "I'm all for doing a marathon search and getting it over."

Cindy said, "Sorry, I leave at four-thirty each day and the room has to be secured by me at that time. You'll have an access key during the day."

"What if we want a particular file? How do we check it out?"

"Go ahead and pull the file. Checkout marker cards are on that small table as well. Slip one in the box where the file was and stack the files in the aisle for the night. If the whole box is needed, leave the card on the shelf and put the box in the aisle for the night. I'll check them out to you officially each night when we close the room. Once files are out of a box, I'll have to put them back. But they'll have to be stacked in the storage room each night. When you get to a point you need copies, let me know. I'm sorry this area is so tight, but at least you can work in the witness room during the day."

"Good enough," Tom said. "What about the basement?"

"From what you said you're looking for, I would bet the files are up here. If not, we'll move on to the next stash."

"Thanks for your help," Sid said, accepting the key from Cindy.

"You know where to find me," she said, closing the door behind her.

Tom said, "Okay, partner. Pick your poison. We need to review all 1960s and earlier missing person cases, solved or not."

Sid said, "Going back to when?"

"Let's say the thirties for now. You take even decades and I'll take odd. I'm not sure how much help the logs will be, but we can grab one for whatever year we're *exploring*, as Cindy put it."

"So be it," Sid said. "See you in the witness room."

Chapter Ten

Kate walked out of Helen's office and exited the newspaper building. She needed a break from editing her article and hoped a short walk and some fresh air would help. She understood Helen's instructions, but she didn't agree with them. The proof of the article was in the facts provided in the backup. Why didn't her boss see that?

Kate started down Commercial Street and then cut down the alleys toward the skeleton lot a few blocks away. Maybe she could speak to Tom about the case. She didn't expect him to tell her anything, but she always took the opportunity to inquire.

Unfortunately, the coroner's van sat alone on the empty lot. Two men were working the scene, which was still encircled by police tape. She recognized Artie Richards but didn't know the other man. Crossing the street, she not-so-discreetly circled the van. The windows were tinted, to prevent media snooping, no doubt. Never dissuaded, she eased the handle down on the rear door hoping to silently unlatch it.

"Can I help you, Kate?" Artie asked, as he emerged from the side of the van.

"Artie, hi. Uh, I've never seen inside one of these things. You know how curious we reporters are."

"I'm sure you concluded that we're conducting official business. Right? Maybe you noticed the crime scene tape and the tent?"

"Yes, I do now," Kate said, staring over his shoulder. "Hey, who's your friend?"

"He's an expert we called for this case."

"Tom told me you were calling a specialist. What kind is he?"

"Sergeant Collingwood?"

Kate smiled and said, "We're old friends."

"I see," Artie said, a tinge of doubt in his voice.

"We went to high school together, but we've also dated since he came back to Branson."

Artie's forehead wrinkled with concern.

Ignoring the silent rebuff, she asked, "Is this man a forensic expert?"

"Forensic Anthropologist."

"Sounds impressive. What's his name?"

"Kate, you really should leave. I have to get back to work."

"Is his name a secret?"

"Charles Fredericks."

"See, that wasn't so hard. So, what are you guys doing? I'd love to see a forensic anthropologist in action. Must be tedious work."

The furrows in Artie's brow took on more depth. "You know, I've never seen you in action. Heard some good stories though. I didn't believe them until now."

"Is that a compliment?"

"I'll let you decide," he said.

When she stood her ground, he shrugged and walked away but stopped and turned back toward the reporter who had not budged.

"Kate, uh ... so you know ... the van is locked."

"Makes sense. Thanks for the info, Artie."

Kate pulled the article to her screen and reread the first sentence several times, unsure what changes would please Helen. She printed the four pages and walked down the hall to the front desk, hoping to find Cassie Yeats, the eighteen-year-old high school senior who had interned at the newspaper office for a couple of school terms.

"Hey, Cassie, I'm glad you're still here," Kate said, stopping at the customer counter.

"Until the last person leaves," the young girl said.

"Great. I want you to read something for me."

"No problem. Do you want me to copy edit?"

"That would be okay, but I basically want your opinion."

"Okay, I can do that." Cassie began reading the first sheet, then glanced at Kate.

"I'll go to my office," the reporter said. "Be back in a few minutes."

Kate returned to her office, packed her portfolio in preparation to leave for the evening, rinsed and dried her coffee mug, and sat down at her desk. The clock on the bookshelf indicated it had been only five minutes, so she read through her article once again, straightened each pile of papers on her desk and filled her stapler for good measure.

Cassie was hanging up the phone when Kate returned to the newspaper customer service desk. "Did you get a chance to read the article?"

"Yes. I've enjoyed all the stories about Etta and the crafts fair. My cousin is the receptionist at the Riverside Mercantile building."

"Young woman with long blond hair, who works upstairs in the Brighton office suite?"

"Yeah, that's Ellen. She's a few years older than me, but we've always been close."

"That's good to know. But about my new article. Did you like the different angle I used?"

Cassie spread the four sheets down on the counter. "Can I be honest?"

"Let me have it ... so to speak."

"The introductory paragraph is great. So is the rest of the first page and the top section of page two."

"But?"

"I read it several times. Forgive me, but it's like you lost the point of the article. You sort of changed the subject. I kept expecting you to come back with a tie-in for the miscellaneous information."

"Miscellaneous information?"

"Several statements don't tie in together or with the crafts fair. It's like they belong in another article."

Cassie's final words echoed Helen's earlier censure. The reporter took a deep breath and collected the four sheets.

"Thanks. I know how to fix it now."

"I'm sorry," the young girl said.

"Don't be sorry for being honest," Kate said, walking down the hall.

As Kate reread the article objectively, the extraneous material became more obvious. She replaced everything from the middle of page two to the end, consulting her notes from her interviews with Etta. She dropped the skeleton lot tie-in but reserved the text for later use. By the time she reread the finished piece, her anger—with Allen, with Tom, with Helen—was gone.

She tagged the file for Helen's review and then reached for her rolodex.

"Time to find out about Dr. Charles Fredericks," she said aloud as she placed a call to a contact at the University of Missouri.

"Columbia Missourian, Anne North speaking," the familiar voice said.

"Hey, Anne. Katie Starling here. How goes it at Mizzou?"

"Not too bad. I'm glad I came back to Columbia and the University."

"Are you still on faculty too?"

"Yes, you should try it."

"I'm not in your league."

"You could finish your master's degree."

"Maybe someday. But I'm a long way from your PhD status."

"What's up?"

"I need some help finding background on a Charles Fredericks, PhD. He's an expert in the field of forensic anthropology. Any ideas?"

"Have you called the anthropology department?"

"Not yet. I guess I wanted to say hello to an old friend first. This has been a low self-esteem day. Any suggestions on who to talk to in anthro?"

"Ask for any expert or interested professor in forensic anthropology. I'm sure they have a professional organization somewhere. Have you tried the internet?"

"I'm not sure the internet has reached Branson yet."

"Sure it has. Isn't your paper connected?"

"And what might I find on this incredibly cool internet?"

"We use AltaVista for searches. It's new and limited, but worth a try if you have access."

"I'll stick with good, old fashioned, long-distance information."

"Good luck with your research, Katie. Don't be a stranger."

"Thanks, Anne."

Forty minutes later Kate had the number for the American Academy of Forensic Sciences, the American Board of Forensic Anthropology, and several other long-named organizations. None of them would provide information—if they had it, which they wouldn't admit to—for Charles Fredericks, PhD. But the contact for one of the groups directed her to another professional certification society. After being forwarded to three different departments and back to the first, she repeated her name and credentials.

"Hi, Kate, my name is Sherry. How can we help you?"

"I'm trying to find information on a Charles Fredericks."

"One moment, please."

Kate assumed she was being forwarded again and was about to hang up.

"Okay, are you still there?"

"Yes. Do you know a Charles Fredericks?"

"We have two Charles Fredericks. Both hold a PhD in anthropology. Do you want me to send you their bios?"

"That would be terrific," Kate said. "Let me give you our fax number."

"I'll get these right to you," Sherry promised.

When Kate went up front to retrieve the fax, Tom was coming in the front door. Her tummy took a little tumble relishing the surprise arrival.

"Working overtime?" he asked.

"I'm not sure," she said, taken off-guard by his smile. "I didn't know it was this late."

Kate took the fax sheets from Cassie and then motioned for Tom to follow her.

"Sorry I didn't call first. I saw your car in the lot and took a chance we could have dinner tonight. I mean, if you're free."

"Dinner?"

"You agreed last night, we could have dinner."

"Did we say tonight?"

"No. I took a chance."

"So you said. Uh, I'm trying to get Helen's approval on an article for tomorrow. I submitted it a few minutes ago. She's left for the day, but she'll dial in to check for it soon."

"Maybe I could read it while we wait. Sort of a preview for an old friend."

"That's very funny. But I have no problem letting you read it. Come around."

Tom sat in her chair and scrolled the screen as he read. "This is good, Katie. Even better than the last one. Who knew the crafts fair could be so interesting?"

"Are you being sarcastic?"

"No. Not at all."

"I hope Helen agrees."

"Why wouldn't she?"

"She hated the first version."

"Let me guess. You threw in a few zingers for some unlucky victim?"

Again, his smile disarmed her, and she couldn't conceal one of her own. "You do know me well."

"Hey, I've been one of those victims."

"That was in junior high school. And it was true. Contrary to some people's opinion I do not make this stuff up."

"Truth, maybe, but stinging nonetheless."

The computer screen cleared, and a small box appeared in the center. Tom read aloud, "Much better, Kate. It will be in tomorrow's edition. Helen."

Kate stepped behind him and leaned over his shoulder. "Let's have dinner and celebrate."

Cassie met them in the hallway. "Is it okay if I lock up behind you and go home?"

"No problem, Cassie. And thanks again for your input."

"You're welcome," the intern said. "Here's the last fax sheet on that Fredericks guy."

Kate took the sheet and stuffed it into her purse as she opened the front door.

Tom said, "Charles Fredericks? Wouldn't be a forensic anthropologist, would he?"

She closed the door and said, "That's the one."

"How do you know about him?"

"Did you forget that I have excellent sources?"

The detective chuckled and said, "Italian or barbeque?"

The waitress set the pizza between the couple and asked if they wanted more beer. Tom eyed his date with an unspoken question. Kate nodded and he turned to the waitress, who had already headed for the bar.

"I hope this is as good as it smells," he said.

Kate served each of them a slice. She sipped her beer then took a bite of pizza. With her next bite, she realized Tom was staring at her.

"Sorry, am I eating like I'm starving to death?"

"No. I'm happy to be with you. I've missed it."

"It?"

"Our relationship, the real one, not the cop-reporter thing."

"Yeah. That one can be a real downer."

"Seems to me, two reasonably mature adults who try hard can find a way to make this dual relationship work out."

Kate recognized the sincerity in Tom's voice and eyes. She focused on the remaining pizza slices wondering how to respond.

"Okay. I'm officially worried. I have rendered you speechless," he said.

"You know, maturity and reasonableness should automatically arrive as one ages."

The lines between Tom's eyebrows deepened. "Hey, I didn't mean for this to be a serious conversation."

"I've had a long day and my biorhythms are out of whack. Helen's putting pressure on me to change my approach to reporting. She says I offend people with my articles."

"All managers are driven by outside influence, even Lieutenant Palmer. Normally, whatever Sid and I do is fine, but let some citizen call with a complaint and he's all over us."

"I can't imagine anyone questioning your professionalism," Kate said.

"Thanks. Mostly they want us to move faster. For example, how long have I been working the skeleton case?"

"Two, maybe three days."

"Exactly, and yet the owner thinks now that we've moved the remains, we can release the lot. He's called the lieutenant twice already. Says he'll go to the mayor if necessary."

"Jack Brighton?"

"No, Larry Allen."

"The councilman doesn't own the lot," Kate said.

"Why am I not surprised you know who owns the lot?"

"Allen is the project development manager for Fortune Enterprises. Brighton and Etta own the lot. He works for his grandfather."

"See. It pays to be best friends with the press, they know everything."

"All of that was in the draft of the article. Helen said it wasn't relevant to the crafts fair."

"Apparently you made her happy with the rewrite," Tom said.

"Until the next time. I'm beginning to question my qualifications for this job."

"Whoa. Your rhythms are whacky!"

Kate chuckled.

"That's better," Tom said with a grin. "Not all the way to laughter, but close enough."

They finished the pizza, exchanging updates on mutual friends and Kate's dad, who Tom saw more often than Kate did. "Why is that?" she asked.

"I like Roger," Tom replied. "You may remember I've known him a long time. We hit it off from the start. Hard to explain why relationships click."

"Definitely inexplicable," Kate agreed.

Tom took out his wallet and pulled enough cash to cover the tip. He paused then placed his hand on Kate's. "I've had a good time tonight."

"Me too," she said, placing her free hand on his.

They walked silently to the register to pay the bill, and then across the lot to their cars. Kate leaned back against her driver's door, relaxed for the first time in days.

Tom stepped closer. "We'll have to do pizza again soon."

"I agree," she said, instinctively reaching for his hands.

He leaned forward and kissed her gently on the lips. A warm, tingle started in her lips and rippled through her body. She moved closer and kissed him back. Her heartbeat echoed in her temples as he took her in his arms and kissed her again. A familiar—if somewhat distant—feeling of belonging washed over her until the static squeak from Tom's radio broke the spell.

"D-1, Dispatch, come in please."

"I knew I shouldn't turn this thing on yet."

"Make a note for future reference," Kate said with a smile.

He rolled his eyes as he keyed the radio. "Dispatch, this is D-1, over."

"Detective, patrol officers request your assistance. Over."

"Stand by, Dispatch." He turned toward Kate. "I have to take this. Can I call you tomorrow?"

"You better."

Chapter Eleven

Despite the grainy photos included on the fax sheets, Kate recognized the older Charles Fredericks as Artie's companion. Although no specific birthdate or academic dates were provided his credentials suggested he was in his mid-fifties. Recognized by several professional groups, he'd been on numerous large search, exhume, and identify projects involving mass graves. He offered consulting forensic anthropology services in addition to workshops and seminars on the subject. Several impressive reviews accompanied a list of organizations he had served. Kate highlighted key points on the sheets and stuck them in a file for use in a future skeleton lot article. Then she called a few local hotels until she found him.

"Charles Fredericks," the male voice said after the fourth ring.

"Hello, Dr. Fredericks, my name is Kate Starling. I'm a reporter for *Tri-Lakes Newspapers* in Branson, Missouri."

"That's quite amazing," he said.

"That Branson Missouri has a newspaper or that I'm a reporter?"

"I'm sorry, Ms. Starling. I arrived in Branson yesterday and I've met five people, including the maid and desk clerk at my hotel. I'm *amazed* that you found me."

"I saw you at the crime scene by the lake yesterday. Artie said you were busy, so I thought I'd call today and see how the project's going."

"I hate to disappoint you, Ms. Starling, but–"

"Please, call me Kate."

"Kate, we are in the middle of an official police investigation. I won't be able to tell you anything about the work I'm doing."

"Yes, I understand. When might you know when the skeleton was buried?"

"You are persistent, aren't you?"

"My specialty, Dr. Fredericks."

"I'll have to refer you to Detective Tom Collingwood of the Branson Police Department. He's the official contact on the case."

"Can I ask how much a consultant like yourself charges a city for services rendered?"

"Goodbye, Ms. Starling," he said, and the line went dead.

"Nothing ventured, nothing gained," Kate said, clipping her sketchy notes to the fax.

She opened the skeleton lot file from the Building Department, hoping she'd missed something. Only the old citation regarding unpermitted removal of vegetation and the most recently issued clearing permit and inspections were in the folder. No justification for the work was provided beyond "future commercial development of lot." A visit to City Hall was in order.

The Engineering Department secretary greeted Kate as she entered the office with a familiar, "Hi, Kate. How can we help you?"

"Hey, Libby. You're back from vacation."

"Yes, and I had a great time. What's up?"

"I want to check pending development permits," Kate said.

Libby pointed to her office mate and said, "Claire, have you met Kate Starling yet?"

"Yes, a few days ago. One of my first challenges."

"You handled my requests very professionally."

"Thanks. What can I help you with today?"

"You must have a way to keep track of ongoing projects in town."

"Yes, we have a log. When a new permit request comes in, the project is added to the log and the log is updated as progress is made."

"Like a spreadsheet?"

"Exactly like a spreadsheet," Claire said.

"Great. I'd like a copy of the current ongoing log," Kate said matter-of-factly.

Claire glanced at Libby, now busy with a customer, and then back to Kate.

"Have I challenged you again?"

"I'm afraid so. I want to be sure of our procedure. Unfortunately, Mr. Leatherman is in a meeting. Can you call or come back sometime after lunch?"

"Sure. But first tell me if any new activity has been logged for the skeleton lot."

Claire walked to her desk and checked a file on her computer then a pile of paper next to the monitor. "It would have to be a new request that hasn't made it through my backlog, and I don't see anything."

"Thanks. I'll see you later this afternoon."

Kate parked in the newspaper lot and walked up the street to the Riverside Mercantile Building. "I have an appointment with Jack Brighton," she told the receptionist.

"Have a seat," the young woman said, pointing to the waiting area. She poked a button on her phone and spoke quietly into the mouthpiece then hung up.

"Your name is Ellen, right?" Kate asked.

The girl nodded.

"Your cousin Cassie interns at the paper. She mentioned you worked here."

Before Ellen could respond, a woman—probably in her early forties—opened the middle door and motioned for Kate to follow. She introduced herself as Judy Stark, administrative assistant to both Brightons.

Judy led the way down a gloomy narrow hallway away from Allen's office. Several feet beyond a door marked storage, the hall opened into an ample-sized area with a desk, credenza, and three file cabinets. The plaque on the desk indicated it belonged to Judy. Across from her desk and beyond the file cabinets another, much shorter, hall led to a door labeled "Randy Brighton."

"We'll be going *this* way," Judy said, her tone indicating a bit of annoyance.

Another hallway, to the left of Judy's desk, led to an arched entryway leading to a large triangular office. Kate guessed the door to her left led to the hallway outside the suite—a private entrance for its chief executives perhaps. The door on her right most likely adjoined Randy's office. One wall of Jack's office was completely covered with framed photos of family and past projects. Four large windows looking out over downtown Branson comprised the final wall.

The man seated at the oversized executive desk in the center of the room stood and came toward Kate. He appeared older than his file photo but still younger than the eighty-six years reflected in his bio—still trim and fit, with a full head of neatly groomed light gray hair. His casual trousers and sports coat communicated an unassuming air.

"My pleasure, Ms. Starling. I've enjoyed your articles about Etta. Brought back fond memories."

"Thank you, Mr. Brighton. Please call me Kate."

"Then you must call me Jack," he said, motioning for her to sit on the sofa next to the window. He eased into a matching chair close by, then glanced toward the still-waiting Judy who quickly exited down the hall.

"I know you're a busy man, Jack, so I'll get to the point of my visit."

"I'd expect nothing less of the professional young woman Etta has told me about."

"First, I want to thank you for meeting with me. I regret it took an assignment from my editor to awaken my interest in Branson's history and to meet one of its most influential long-term residents."

"One of the old timers," he said with a disarming smile.

"According to Etta, you've lived in Branson your entire life. Although you've traveled more than she, you're a true native son."

"Did she tell you about our adventure in St. Louis?"

"Yes, and a few other things. But I'd like to hear some of your stories too. I'll be doing a series of articles on Branson history-makers as a follow-up to the crafts fair articles. I would like to spend some time interviewing you, at a time of your convenience."

"That's flattering, Kate. I'd be delighted. Set up some times with my secretary when you leave. But I suspect there's another reason you stopped by today."

"You're right. I do have some specific questions about current issues." She took her recorder from her portfolio. "Do you mind if I record our talk?"

"Not at all. Fire away," he said, relaxing back in his chair.

"With all the development going on in Branson ... and I know Fortune Enterprises is a leader in the pack ... citizens are eager to know what's happening. People say we have enough theaters and hotels and strip malls. Are there more in Branson's future?"

"That's a good question. I agree we may be approaching our quota of theaters and hotels. Don't get me wrong, the folks who come for the crafts and Silver Dollar City and for the music are great. But, in my opinion, we need to attract a new crowd, do bigger things."

"I've heard rumblings about a convention center. Isn't that a little ambitious?"

"Maybe so, but we can't let Kansas City and St. Louis, or even Springfield, hold all the corporate meetings."

"Will Fortune Enterprises step out on that limb?" she asked.

The glare in Jack's eyes, the ingratiating smirk as he paused before responding, reminded Kate of Larry—perhaps the political façade was a family trait.

"More like a rocky crag," he said, his tone relishing the irony of his comparison. "We don't want to be known as the town that gets all the overflow business."

"Does your company have any specific plans?"

"First of all, ours is a development company. We put together projects initiated and invested by others."

"That's what you've done so far. What about in the future?"

"I wouldn't rule anything out. I didn't get where I am today by saying no one's ever done that before let's not risk it."

"But nothing specific to tell me about."

"My grandson, Larry Allen, is our project development manager. I know you've met him. He'd be the person with details, as they become available for publication. You should get in the loop with him."

"I'm not sure he would welcome me in that loop."

"Nonsense, I'll tell him to call you," Jack said.

"I appreciate your help."

"Okay. Next topic," he said.

Kate flipped the page in her notepad.

"I'd like to talk about the lot where Clay and Etta's original store stood."

Jack squinted his eyes as his brow creased. He seemed to be searching his memories. In a moment he said, "The lot by Roark Creek?"

"Yes, close to North Beach Park."

"I haven't been down there in years, maybe decades."

"The recent articles in the paper were brief."

"Why would that lot be in the news?"

"I'm sorry. I assumed your grandson told you that human remains were found while he was clearing the lot."

Jack grasped the arms of his chair and pushed himself forward, striding around the sofa toward the window. He gazed in the direction of Etta's lot, but the view was probably blocked by several buildings. "Randy, my son, and I were out of town all last week, didn't get in until late last night."

Jack walked slowly to his desk and then moved a fountain pen from the desk pad to a pencil holder next to the phone. He straightened his spine and returned the friendly smile to his lips as he walked back toward Kate.

For some reason she stood up, feeling an urge to leave.

"Obviously, this is news to me. I'm not sure what's been found. I'm not even sure why the lots being cleared. We promised Etta to leave the lot intact. We tore down the original buildings because the city demanded it. Etta insisted I rebuild them exactly as Clay had constructed them but with modern materials. Even stranger, several years ago I seriously considered proceeding with that project."

"Sorry to interrupt, Granddad," Allen said, barreling from the hallway. "I found out five minutes ago that Ms. Starling was interviewing you."

Jack turned and met Larry mid-room, ignoring Kate and cutting her out of the conversation.

"Imagine what I found out five minutes ago, Larry."

"I'm not sure." Larry's tone was uncommonly reserved. He glanced at Kate, then again at his grandfather.

"Kate shared with me about Etta's lot being cleared. Why I heard this news from a reporter as opposed to my grandson whom I trust to run my business truly befuddles me."

Larry swallowed hard. "We should discuss this privately."

Jack stared briefly at Larry, uttering barely audible words drenched in an angry tone. After another moment, Jack turned with a slight bow toward Kate.

"My apologies. We'll have to bring this interview to a close."

The reporter—who had remained by the sofa, trying to be invisible—quickly picked up her things. She extended her hand toward Jack. "Thank you so much for seeing me on such short

notice. I'll call to set up the other interviews."
Entering the hallway, she couldn't resist adding,
"Nice to see you again, Mr. Allen."

Kate nearly ran back to her car at the
newspaper, hoping to get to Etta's before anyone
could call her and quash her access. She wasn't
sure why that might be a problem, but she didn't
want to take any chances.

Etta was nowhere in sight when Kate drove
up and parked next to the small garage, but the
truck in front of the house resembled the one
belonging to Bryan Porter. As soon as Kate got
out of her car, she heard their voices, clearly
arguing about something. She couldn't
distinguish the words until she eased up the
porch stairs and approached the front door.

"Etta, I simply want what I'm due. I know you
have the proof. You owe me that much," Porter
shouted.

Her voice much calmer, Etta said, "Bryan, you
must know I would help, if I could. We were
close, remember?"

His tone lower, more measured, he said, "I do
remember. I remember a young woman who was
generous and giving and caring to a young boy.
She helped me through a difficult time. I'm
asking her to help me now."

"Even if I had this proof, what would it settle?
Nothing can change the past. Nothing can make
things happen differently."

"Think it over. I'll be back."

Porter banged the screen door against the
porch wall and tore across the veranda. He
charged past Kate without acknowledging her

presence. When the truck's tailgate disappeared around the bend, Kate knocked.

Etta was noticeably shaken, but her voice still calm. "Kate. Did we have an appointment?"

"No, I stopped by to ask a couple questions. Are you okay? I'm sorry, but I couldn't help overhearing the loud voices when I drove up."

"Bryan is a troubled man. He was a troubled boy. I wish I could help him."

Once they were settled in the living room, the reporter said, "He thinks you have some kind of proof that he needs."

"He is searching for a solution to his problems."

"May I ask what kind of solution?"

Etta abruptly rose and went to the small front window. "Someone's coming up the drive."

"Do you think Bryan has come back?" Kate asked, following her hostess, who was already halfway to the hallway.

The older woman stopped short of the entryway and turned to face Kate. "I'll take care of this. You wait here."

Kate complied but remained ready, afraid to imagine what the desperate man might do.

Chapter Twelve

"Take the next right. Etta's house is at the end," Tom said. "And tell me that wasn't Bryan Porter pulling onto the highway from her road."

"Looked like his truck," Sid said. "Maybe we should follow him and have a little chat about his lawsuit against the city."

"Let's speak to Etta first. We can always find Porter."

"I didn't know you were on a first name basis with Mrs. Stupholds."

"Haven't you read Kate's articles?" Tom asked as they made the final curve.

"I'm afraid I'm not a devoted reader of *the Kate.* That's your thing. And speaking of the notorious reporter, isn't that her little Escort?"

Tom said. "Better let me handle this."

"You read my mind."

As they crossed the veranda Sid dropped behind Tom who reached up to knock, but the door opened and the woman—shorter than he expected at less than five-foot-tall—stepped squarely into the doorway behind the screen door. She started to say something, but stopped, apparently taken back by her visitors.

Tom introduced himself and his partner before confirming the woman's identity. "We have a few questions about property you own in Branson," he added.

"Can it wait? I'm busy right now."

Tom was about to suggest a later time when Kate came into the hallway.

"Hi, Tom."

"Katie," he said with a nod.

Etta said, "Do you know these men?"

"I've known Tom since grade school. Sid, not so long, but they're both okay."

"Then I guess you can come in. Would you be interested in some tea?"

"No, ma'am. Thanks, but we'll get right to our questions and be on our way," Tom said, staring at Kate.

"Oh," she said, apparently recognizing her cue to leave. "Etta, I'll come back later. I have some things I can do." As she passed Tom in the doorway, she whispered, "You play nice with my good friend Etta."

Tom grinned and said, "Yes ma'am."

As the men followed Etta into the living room, Sid asked, "Was that a threat?"

"For at least one of us it was."

"Make yourselves comfortable, officers," Etta said as she settled into her chair.

Tom said, "We're interest in your lot on St. Limas Street."

The woman's previously warm expression transformed into one of confusion.

"Do you know the location?" Tom asked.

Etta said, "Yes, I know where you mean. But it seems odd."

"Odd in what way?" Sid asked.

"Kate asking about that acreage, doing her articles and all, is one thing. But why would the police care about it?"

"You discussed the lot with Kate Starling?" Sid asked, scooting forward on the sofa.

"A couple days ago."

"Did Kate say why she was interested?" Tom asked.

Etta frowned as if trying to recall the conversation. "I don't remember her giving a reason. But she recorded the whole thing. I'm sure she'd let you listen to it."

"Maybe you could summarize what you discussed about the lot," Tom said.

"My husband and I built a store on the lot and lived behind the store for a while before building this house."

"And the store?"

"We worked it until my husband passed away in 1942. I accepted an offer from an old friend to merge with his mercantile a few months later."

"Jack Brighton?"

"Yes."

"And what happened to the lot?"

"Nothing. We moved everything up to Jack's location on Commercial. The buildings were rented out a couple times, but eventually stood vacant."

"Do you remember the name of any renters?"

"Jack would have the records."

"But you ... specifically you and Jack Brighton ... still own the land?" Sid said.

"It belongs to the business."

"And you are part of the business."

"I suppose."

"And the city of Branson asked you to tear down the buildings on the lot when they became unsafe," Tom said.

"Correct, but that's been almost twenty years ago. Jack said he'd rebuild them for me to honor Clay."

Tom said, "Did Kate tell you what happened several days ago at the property?"

"No, we only discussed when Clay and I were first married and building the store."

"I'm sorry, Etta. I assumed you were aware that while a crew was clearing the lot they unearthed human remains."

"I'm not sure what you mean by *clearing the lot*," she said.

Thrown for a moment by her greater concern with the clearing than the discovery, Tom said, "They were in the process of removing all the trees."

"That's not possible," she said. "Jack promised to leave it as it was."

Sid said, "Maybe they're clearing to rebuild your husband's store?"

"They wouldn't have to remove all the trees," Etta said as she moved from her chair to the mantle. She touched a photo of a young couple, then turned to face the detectives. "I'm sorry, I'm not sure how I can help you."

Tom said, "Would you have any idea how someone came to be buried on your lot or who it might be?"

"I can't imagine. Where was it?"

"Beyond the tree line towards Roark Creek," Sid said.

"Clay and I didn't build beyond the southeast corner. I remember trees covered the lot and adjacent properties clear down to the water. I don't know more about it."

Tom stood up and took a card from his jacket pocket. "Thanks for your time, Etta. If you remember anything that might help us with the investigation, please give us a call."

Etta took the card, then followed the detectives to the door. "Maybe Jack can remember something."

"Thanks again," Sid said as they left the porch.

Tom waved to Etta and closed the passenger door.

"Quite a feisty lady," Sid said as he turned onto the highway. "She seemed genuinely surprised. Struck me she is more concerned that someone was clearing the lot."

"I agree. In any case, she denied knowing about the burial or who it might be."

"So, either she doesn't know, has forgotten, or is lying," Sid said.

"Good summary, detective."

"Thanks. By the way I confirmed Brighton will be at his office this afternoon. Should we head over now?"

"Why not, we're on a roll."

The receptionist showed the policemen into a small conference room next to the waiting area. Mercifully, the soft music playing in the oval room didn't follow them.

"Mr. Brighton will meet you in here," she said closing the door on her way out.

A large window overlooking Commercial Street dominated the outside wall. The other walls were covered with mostly old black and white pictures. Tom recognized Etta and both Jack and Randy Brighton in several shots. The detective was finishing the gallery tour when the door at the opposite end of the room opened.

Jack Brighton was dressed in jeans, a work shirt, and heavy boots.

"Sorry to keep you waiting, Gentlemen, I was at the construction site."

He shook each officer's hand and introduced himself.

Tom said, "Detective Sergeant Tom Collingwood and this is my partner Detective Sergeant Sid Green. Thanks for making time for us."

Jack took a seat at the table. "Am I in trouble?"

"We've come to discuss your lot on St. Limas Street. Are you aware of the recent discovery?" Tom asked, wanting to avoid any surprises.

"Yes. In fact, a reporter filled me in this morning."

"Kate Starling?" Sid asked.

"Yes. While she was interviewing me about Fortune Enterprises, she asked about Etta's lot. I'd been out of town for several days. As I told Ms. Starling, I haven't been on the lot since 1975 when the city of Branson complained about the dilapidated buildings and we razed them."

"Why are you clearing the land now, Mr. Brighton?" Sid asked.

"Technically, I'm not. My grandson runs the project development for my company. He requested the clearing permit."

"Without your knowledge?"

"That's correct."

"Was he unaware of your promise to Etta Stupholds?"

"You've spoken to Etta. I haven't had a chance to discuss it with her. I would guess she was angry when she found out."

Tom said, "I'd say more confused and surprised."

"Larry was unaware of the importance of the lot to Etta or my promise to her. He is trying to prepare it for a future development deal."

"But he said nothing to you?"

"He's in charge of such things. Frankly, I'd forgotten about the promise until Kate brought it up this morning."

"You didn't take the promise seriously?"

"Quite the contrary. If you know Etta, you know I took the promise seriously. But I suppose you could say I hadn't got around to keeping it."

Tom said, "Sorry, we have to ask. Do you have any idea who was buried on the lot?"

"Absolutely not. Etta vacated the property when Clay died in 1942. We rented the buildings to a few tenants for several years, but then the lot sat unattended."

"Would you have a list of the tenants?"

"I'll have my secretary get you the names. It might take a bit of research in our old files, so be patient."

"Archives can be a challenge," Sid agreed.

Tom handed him a card. "Your secretary can call when the list is ready. If you think of anything pertinent to the investigation, please give us a call."

"Absolutely," Jack said, but Tom was skeptical.

Cindy waved on her way to the administrative area counter. "My newest best friends," she said, handing Tom the key to the archive room.

Tom said, "We've been busy all morning, but we were hoping to get back to it."

Sid elbowed Tom and whispered, "Don't forget to ask her."

Cindy said, "Ask her what?"

"Can we check out some of the boxes and take them to our offices to work on as time permits?" Tom said.

"I'm sorry, it goes against policy."

"You can't make an exception for two trust-worthy loyal policemen?" Sid asked with a grin. "We promise to lock them up at night."

Tom chimed in, "After-all, the building is secure. Right?"

"I'm not allowed to make an exception. And ... FYI ... the building is not secure in the truest sense of the word. It is locked and it is unlikely someone would break in. It is even less likely someone would consider stealing these records.

And the final ... and my personal favorite ... we've operated this long without control, why now?"

"Okay, we get it. But you said you are not allowed to make an exception. Who can?"

"City Clerk or Mayor. I suppose the City Council, but that would be a longer process."

Sid said, "None of those are good options."

Tom shrugged and nudged Sid. "Time for our little chat with the Building Department."

"You need to get Palmer to talk to the Mayor," Sid said as the men crossed the lobby. "The witness room is too small to deal with the ongoing investigation, especially on a restricted time basis. And copying the records is not practical."

"Passing the buck, works for me," Tom said, tapping on the manager's office door frame.

"Come on in," Leatherman said. "I'm afraid this may be brief. I've spoken to Bryan Porter several times about his suit against Branson and his complaint to the state. Unfortunately, he didn't provide anything beyond the documents themselves. In his mind, they made his case."

"Fortune Enterprises is called out in both filings," Tom said.

"He singled them in the majority of the allegations. Other companies are included as well, but most of the named architects worked on Fortune projects."

"What is *your* opinion of Porter?" Tom asked.

"He seems like a very frustrated man. My inspectors tell me he's been making idle allegations for years."

"Did something happen to escalate his idle threats to formal claims?" Sid asked.

"Not to my knowledge. When I try to get him to be more specific ... offer witness corroboration or other proof ... he won't or can't. I'm not sure which. All he's done is bring up valid points about the timing issues in the permit process."

"Completing a building as large as the new office complex before the permit is issued is a bit more than a timing problem."

"I wish it were as clear cut as that."

"Explain, please," Tom said.

Leatherman sighed and shook his head. "I've already explained all this to the City Attorney. He's addressing every point in his brief for the judge."

"Please, give us the rundown. We're trying to help you *and* the City Attorney."

"I guess I'm frustrated by this issue taking up so much of my time."

"We understand."

Leatherman continued, "Specifically, on the office complex, the permit itself was late. But the plans were in the review process and, for the most part, work was approved to begin, albeit verbally, after review of specific areas. Inspections were performed properly and work approved before the crew proceeded to the next task."

"None of these verbal approvals were documented."

"Only by inference with the inspection reports. But, for what it's worth, this is how this department has worked for decades. The county isn't even *this* organized. Both governments are taking steps to improve the process and to be within accepted building codes. If we're going to do as much construction as larger cities, we must embrace their procedures."

"And the state's investigation?"

"In the beginning steps. Upon completion, they'll have recommendations. If they find that an architect or engineer merits censure, they will take an appropriate action. Neither the suit against the city nor the complaint with Missouri is a criminal indictment."

Tom said, "I guess it's our job to see if criminal charges should be filed. Thanks for your time. Please keep us posted."

Once in the lobby, Sid asked, "Do we know anything we didn't know before we had that meeting?"

"Did we expect to learn anything?"

"Good point. Back to the witness room."

Chapter Thirteen

Shirley struggled to fasten her seatbelt as Kate pulled away from the hospital and drove the short distance to the merger with US 65 North, "What's the rush?"

"No rush. I have things to do," Kate responded.

"You're welcome by the way."

"For what? Oh, right. Thanks for coming with me on such short notice."

"Not a problem, but why did you want me to go with you? I'm sure you can find your way to the courthouse and maybe even to the recorder's office."

"I appreciate your confidence," Kate said, matching Shirley's sarcasm. "I knew you were off early this afternoon and we haven't seen each other in a while."

"We had lunch two days ago."

"You know, childhood friends can be extremely irritating," Kate said, glancing at Shirley.

"I had noticed that myself," Shirley sniped.

Kate turned onto F Highway and didn't speak again until the turn toward Forsyth. She glanced at Shirley and said, "Tom and I had dinner last night."

"That's great."

"Maybe."

Shirley laughed. "Aha. You brought me along today so I'd tell you everything will be okay between you two ... like it used to be or better."

"That would be a great relief. Can you issue a guarantee with the prediction?"

"Afraid not, Katie. Life doesn't come with guarantees. But you can't *not* do something because you're afraid to fail. Consider how you approach your job. The thought of failure never enters your mind."

"But he kissed me."

"And that terrifies you."

"What *terrifies* me is that I kissed him back."

"All you can do is go with the flow. Enjoy the moment. Worry about now, not when."

"Three clichés without taking a breath. That's a record for you."

"Seriously, it will be fine. You two were a great couple."

"In high school."

"So?"

"What about all that's happened?"

"Are you telling me you two still haven't discussed your breakup and his marriage?"

Kate shook her head.

Shirley laid her head against the seat rest and groaned. "You two need to communicate."

"What happened to worry about now, enjoy the moment?"

"Katie, you can't start fresh if you're both holding back. That's probably what's doomed your other reconciliation attempts."

"I know you're right, but your relationship record is no better, Miss Divorced-after-four-years-of-marriage."

"First of all, that's not fair. Our situations are different. Second, we are not discussing me. We are discussing you and Tom. Third, I didn't say relationships were easy or that I knew how to make one work."

"Maybe I'll wait until you figure it out, then you can help me with mine."

"I would guess you have a long wait."

They pulled into a spot at the courthouse, and the two old friends walked silently to the entrance. Kate turned left toward the recorder's office. "Where are you going?" Kate said when Shirley turned in the opposite direction.

"You'll be okay. I'm going to visit some friends. You don't know them."

"Why does my best friend since kindergarten have friends who I haven't even met?"

"You know, Katie, you think too much. See you right here in thirty minutes."

The entrance door revealed a large red arrow pointing to a take-a-number station and leading to a short hallway all of which facilitated the line of customers Kate found waiting around the corner. She retraced her steps and took the next number. In a few minutes, one of the three on-duty clerks waved her forward. She gave him her business card as she checked his nametag.

"Hi, Evan, my name is Kate Starling. I'm a reporter for *Tri-Lakes Newspapers*. I'm doing research for an article about new developments in Taney County, particularly how the Branson boom has affected real estate activity this decade."

Evan leaned on the counter, an incredulous expression on his face. "You may want to narrow that search period a bit. We've been a bit busy the last couple of years."

"Let's start with the last two or three years, since the 60 *Minutes* piece," Kate said.

"How about I give you a copy of the logbook for this year. All liens, lien releases, and deeds are recorded. You can look it over and ask for details on projects of interest."

"That would be great," Kate said, happy to get whatever she could.

"We charge an admin fee for the copies."

"No problem."

Evan returned to the counter several minutes later and handed Kate thirty pages. "That will be seven-fifty."

"Seems like a lot of pages for less than a full year."

"As I said, we've been busy."

Kate's wallet contained two one-dollar bills. "I'll be right back."

"They all say that," Evan chuckled.

Good as her word, Shirley was waiting in the hall by the entrance to the building. Even better, she had the cash Kate needed for the copies.

"Here you are," the reporter said, handing Evan the required fee. She smiled sweetly. "Can I call you to get more info on particular projects?"

"You bet," he said. "When you call, ask for Evan."

Passing Shirley in the hall, Kate said, "Ready to go?"

"Apparently."

"Thanks for the cash. I'll buy lunch next week."

"Next week? Can't we have lunch today?"

"It's almost three in the afternoon."

"I forgot the 'no lunch after twelve' rule."

"I have things to do before the day ends. You can enjoy the rest of your day off."

Kate stopped in front of Shirley's house and said, "I appreciate your going with me."

"You're welcome, I'm sure. When we have lunch next week, I'll want a full report on your discussion with Tom."

Kate shook her head and grimaced, and then drove away without comment. She wanted to pick up the permit log from Claire before they closed. She thanked the secretary and confirmed their lunch date for the following week. *Never hurts to cultivate your sources*, Kate mused.

Instead of going next to Etta's, as she had planned, she decided to visit Larry Allen at the new office complex site. The project trailer sat about a hundred feet from the main building on an island of bare ground. In preparation for paving, the remainder of what would be the parking area had been leveled and graveled. Although the site lacked landscaping, the building exteriors appeared to be finished. Judging from numerous contracting vans dispersed on the lot and the flurry of men carrying tools and materials in and out of the building, the interiors of the five-story central structure and two-story wings were works-in-progress.

Kate found Allen, alone, in a makeshift office in the mid-section of the cramped trailer. He braced himself against the wall with one hand as his other traced over a blueprint covering a small worktable. A light-yellow polo shirt stretched across his well-developed shoulder and back muscles and disappeared neatly into his navy-blue slacks.

He shook his head, shifted his weight onto the other foot and bent closer to the plan, every dark wavy hair in place. An architect's lamp clamped to the table edge cast shadows on his profile, revealing chiseled features she hadn't noticed before. She waited in the passageway, but his concentration held fast, so she tapped the wall with one knuckle.

"Excuse me," she said.

He turned toward her and stretched to his full height, his frown somewhere between startled and annoyed. His politician's greeting materialized, displaying perfect white teeth set evenly over a square jaw. But the reflex action disappeared quickly when he recognized his visitor.

"Sorry to come unannounced, but I had some questions for you. Is this a good time?"

The phone rang and he swiveled on one hip to reach across the desk. He pressed the hands-free button to answer. "Allen."

"Yo, Larry. We need to talk," the man's voice on the speaker shouted.

Allen picked up the receiver. "Later. Yes, that's right." He punched the disconnect key and turned toward Kate. "Sorry. Go ahead with your questions."

Kate stepped to the window and peeked through the dirty glass. "Quite a project. Five stories seems a bit ambitious for Branson."

"You'll be pleased to know we have 70 percent of it leased."

"How much is for Fortune Enterprises?"

He studied her eyes, his hands pressed against the table. "Can we get to the real questions? They're waiting for me inside."

She consulted her steno pad—although it wasn't necessary—then returned Allen's stare. "I'm working on an article about the rapid growth of Branson since the 60 *Minutes* piece almost three years ago."

"Wow, that's original."

His sarcasm did not impress or slow her down.

"As one of the major players in construction projects in Taney County, Fortune Enterprises will no doubt lead the way in future developments. Can you share with me what you have planned going forward?"

"We have five current projects besides this one. Two of them are just beginning and are almost as ambitious as this office complex. We'll be busy this and next year."

"Yes, I'm aware of those projects since they've been discussed by the Planning and Zoning Commission. What do you have in mind for the future, say five or ten years from now?"

"I haven't planned that far ahead," he said, betraying his smile with his eyes.

"Somehow I doubt that. Your grandfather said the company was ready for bigger projects, even as big as a convention center."

"Jack Brighton sees no boundaries, but nothing is happening at this time."

"He did say he'd ask you to keep me in the loop for any future announcements."

"Be assured, when the time is right, we'll inform the press."

"Do you have something working in the preconstruction stage?"

"Perhaps Granddad said something you misunderstood."

"I assumed since you're clearing that lot by the lake that you must have something in mind for development."

He scrutinized the reporter's face through a squint, folding his arms across his chest. After a moment, he said, "Perhaps I do have something in mind."

"But nothing is on the record regarding future plans for the lot. You have to admit that's unusual."

"If you must know, clearing the lot was a mistake," he said, walking around his work desk and then shuffling through some papers. "I was under the impression my grandfather wanted to replace the buildings on the lot, so I arranged for the clearing. As it turns out, I was a bit premature."

"I'm sorry if I caused a problem between you two."

"No harm done. It was a misunderstanding. We're fine. But I must excuse myself and get back to work." He reprised his politician's façade and accompanied the reporter outside.

Kate couldn't shake the image of Allen's face as they parted. She didn't expect him to give her his business plan, but she didn't expect him to lie to her either. Not that she knew which portion was a lie, but something in his final expression screamed *don't trust me.*

It was after four when Kate walked across the veranda and Etta opened the screen door.

"I hope it's not too late," Kate said. "I wanted to finish our discussion."

"You're always welcome. Come in. I made a fresh pitcher of tea." Etta poured a glass and handed it to Kate.

"I hope everything went smoothly with Tom and Sid."

"They were very nice, as you instructed them," Etta said.

"I didn't know you heard me."

Etta smiled and said, "I'll admit I was taken aback when they asked about the St. Limas lot that you and I discussed the other day."

"Etta, I'm sorry. I didn't know what to say after all you told me. I intended to get back to you sooner, but–"

"No need for an apology."

"Jack Brighton seemed as bewildered as you that the lot was being cleared. And he recalled his promise about restoring the buildings."

"I haven't had a chance to speak to him, but I have no doubt he remembered the promise. He's a man of his word."

"According to Larry Allen, the lot was cleared by mistake."

"Did he say who made the mistake?"

"He believed his grandfather was ready to restore the buildings so Larry had the lot cleared."

"Hmm," Etta said, but offered no other comment.

"Jack agreed to help me with the Branson history articles. But I'd like to do another piece about the more recent changes in the area, including all the construction, and any future plans for development."

"I'm sure that would be interesting."

"As an officer of Fortune Enterprises, you must have an opinion about its future. Jack mentioned stepping up to more ambitious projects. Would you have anything to add to that?"

"Gracious, I'd forgotten I was vice president of the company, mostly an honorary position. I attend a meeting now and then, but Jack and Randy run the business."

"And his grandson?"

"Larry may act like he's in charge, but my money is on Jack, regardless of his age. And Randy always has Jack's back."

"Allen seems quite the confident executive," Kate offered.

"You mean he's cocksure of himself."

"He's the youngest alderman ever elected in Ward 1, which is overwhelmingly *old guard*."

"I'm not saying he shouldn't be proud of what he's accomplished. I'm saying he can be a little much for this old woman to take sometimes. If you know what I mean."

Kate nodded. "I've gone a couple rounds with the man myself."

"Now that would be worth the price of admission."

Kate chuckled. "But you don't know of any big plans? Something they might have discussed at the last meeting?"

"Nothing specific. Jack's always talking about reaching for the stars, doing something different and bigger. That's how he's gotten the company where it is today. He doesn't accept the impossible. If it hasn't been done, it means he hasn't tried it yet."

"Sounds like quite a man."

"And a good friend."

"What about you, Etta? What would you like to see in Branson?"

"I'm with Jack. The sky's the limit. With the right timing and the appropriate set of people to pull it off, anything is possible."

"Investors, you mean."

"Money's important, but you have to have a group of supporters, willing participants. Sometimes that's the hardest part, especially in a small town. Sorry, I'm not more helpful."

Kate said, "You'll let me know if you hear anything. Right?"

"Yes, but I wouldn't count on someone confiding secrets to me."

"Can we discuss Bryan Porter before I go? We were interrupted earlier."

"Nothing more to discuss," Etta said with a shrug.

"Can you tell me what proof he wants from you?"

"Kate, I'm not sure how much you overheard, but as I told Bryan, even if I had the proof he thinks I have, it wouldn't matter," Etta said, sweeping her hands in front of her to emphasize her point. "He's hanging on to a grain of truth his father gave him and his mother nurtured. But he's wrong."

"It sounds mysterious. If I knew more, perhaps it would explain why he does some of the things he does."

"You mean like protesting against Larry when he ran for city council?"

"Yes, and now he's made an official claim against the city of Branson."

Etta furrowed her brow and said, "What kind of claim?"

"That the Building Department has shown favoritism with some of the contractors in town, in particular Fortune Enterprises."

"Anybody can *claim* anything," Etta said.

"But his complaint has caused a state audit."

"Missouri is pursuing his accusation?"

"They have no choice. They'll investigate and do a report and take whatever action is necessary. Do you know why he might hold a grudge against your company?"

"Bryan has had it in for the company since his father left abruptly more than fifty years ago. He believes Jack made Lex quit or fired him. When Lex's own business failed, he was forced to search out of town for work. Bryan blames Jack for that and all his father's, and his family's, problems, including his father not coming back to Branson."

"But Jack and Lex were good friends. Right?"

"Yes. And as far as I know that never changed. I don't recall an issue that might cause Lex to leave or not come back. It was a long time ago."

Kate questioned Etta's memory gap regarding her two childhood friends, even if it was fifty years ago. One thing was certain, the older woman didn't want to discuss it with a reporter. She turned off the recorder and dropped it in her bag and eased off the sofa. Etta followed her to the door.

"Kate, I'm sorry I was rude. I shouldn't take out my frustration with Bryan on you."

"Maybe I should stick to the subject of my articles and stay out of other people's business."

"Don't ever apologize for being curious. It makes you a good reporter. And speaking of that, wait here. I have something for you."

When Etta returned to the porch, she was holding the handcrafted cedar box Kate admired during their first session. "I want you to have this ... for being kind to me and doing a good job on all the articles."

Kate said, "That's very sweet of you, but I can't take a gift from someone I interview."

"Your articles about me are over. We're friends now. This is a gift to my friend."

"Seriously, I can't accept it," Kate said.

Etta raised the box higher and smiled. "Call it a loan. You can take a picture of it for a crafts fair article."

"A loan," Kate said, taking the box. "But I *will* bring it back."

"Don't try to out-stubborn me, Kate. I've had more time at it."

Chapter Fourteen

Kate scanned three gossip magazines cover-to-cover before becoming first in line at the grocery store. Her father's desperate pleas were the driving force behind the Saturday morning errand, something she would never do for herself. *Whatever he had planned for lunch better be worth it,* she mused.

Bryan Porter crossed the lot toward the entrance as she emerged. She saw no reason to let the opportunity go by. "Mr. Porter, do you have a moment?" she shouted and rushed toward him.

His head jerked around, and he squinted. "Kate Starling. Fancy meeting you here."

"May I ask you a question?"

"Not if it's the same one you asked at the press conference," he said and walked away.

Kate persisted. "What do you want from Etta Stupholds?"

He looked over his shoulder. "Why don't you ask her?"

"She wouldn't elaborate. Perhaps I could help you find what you're looking for."

"Why would you help *me*?"

"Does it have something to do with Riverside Mercantile? My father told me you helped out at the store when you were a young boy."

"Well, it has nothing to do with me."

"Mr. Porter, I'm a good investigative journalist. Let me try to help."

"Sorry, it's in Etta's hands."

"What about Jack Brighton or Randy? Maybe I could ask them about it?"

He rubbed the back of his neck, glanced at Kate, and stuffed his hands in his trouser pockets. As his cheeks blushed, she wasn't sure if he was going to answer her or explode in anger. Without a word he spun around and continued toward the entrance. Just as quickly he whirled back toward her and poked his index finger into the air several times. "Ask Jack about the agreement he had with my dad. Ask him why he reneged on that promise and destroyed my family."

"What agreement?" Kate shouted, but he was already in the store. She'd have to pursue his vague statement another time.

Kate's father scooted the table across the patio and onto the lawn. He pulled some weeds out of the cracks in the cement, then grabbed the broom and swept the dirt and dead foliage into the yard. Once he returned the table to its usual position close to the sliding glass doors, he arranged the chairs around the table and wiped everything down with a rag.

She put the grocery bag down on the table. "I'm going to take a wild guess and say you've invited Margie to join us for lunch."

"I distinctly remember your giving me your blessing to date Margie," Roger said.

"I suppose I did, not that my approval is needed."

"Your approval is important to me," he said, giving her a one-arm hug.

"Dinner rolls and potato salad. Right?"

"That should do it. And you're almost correct." He opened the lid to the grill and emptied the remainder of a bag of charcoal on the bed.

"Almost correct?"

"We'll have one more guest. Someone closer to your age."

"Why didn't you tell me you invited Tom?"

"Guess I wanted to surprise you."

"Lucky for you I consider it a good surprise these days. Two weeks ago, not so much."

Roger followed his daughter into the kitchen. He took an ear of corn from the pile on the counter and removed the shuck. Kate accepted his handoff and prepared the cob for cooking on the grill. Working with him, living at home again, reminded her of the happy family years. The toll of the last few years—his arrest, declining business—had changed her dad. With business returning and a new lady friend he was enjoying life again.

Tom tapped on the glass as he slid the patio door open. "Guess who I found lurking outside your house?"

"I wasn't lurking, officer. I promise," Marge said.

Roger smiled. "She was probably checking out my refurbished patio."

"Actually, it occurred to me I was at the wrong house," Marge said.

Kate chimed in, "Refurbished may be an exaggeration, but it is definitely an improvement."

Marge handed a large plastic container to Kate. "I brought the last of my tomatoes and some peppers."

"Great. That will make the meal complete."

Marge rolled up her sleeves and joined Kate at the sink. "Let me help you with those."

"What can I do, Roger?" Tom asked.

"Come out and help with the grill. I'm sure the coals need a little coaxing."

Kate finished wrapping the next ear. "I'm glad you could join us today."

"I appreciate your saying that," Marge said.

"I mean it. I haven't seen Dad this happy in years."

"Really?"

"Definitely. It may be a coincidence, but I noticed the difference as soon as he devoured that chicken soup you brought him."

A flush crept across her cheeks as she handed Kate another ear of corn. "That's nice to know," she whispered.

Tom crossed the room and removed the tray of steaks from the refrigerator. "How's the corn coming? We'll be ready for it in three minutes." He didn't wait for an answer.

"He made that up," Kate said.

"It did seem a bit precise."

"He's pretending he knows how to work the grill. I've seen this act before."

"I'm glad to see the rumors are true."

"About the reprise of the star-crossed lovers?"

"You were so cute together in high school."

Kate wasn't sure about cute, but they had fun. She stacked the corn on a tray and handed her guest a plate for the tomatoes and peppers. Marge pitched in without a word, comfortable in the kitchen, genuinely happy to be part of the action. Concerned at first about the twelve-year age difference between the realtor and her dad, Kate was beginning to consider it an advantage. Clearly her father was full of energy and on cloud nine.

Marge added the last dish to the lineup on the counter as Tom returned. "We're ready," he said, grabbing the plates and silverware.

The women put the food on the table and took seats opposite one another. Roger served the steaks as Tom gathered the corn from the grill.

"I forgot the tea," Kate said, heading to the kitchen.

Tom followed her and grabbed two beers from the refrigerator. "You forgot this plate," he said.

"That's dessert."

"My favorite cookies from the town bakery."

"They are also my father's favorite."

"I remember," Tom said.

Roger and Tom took turns topping one another's fishing stories for over thirty minutes.

Kate incorporated her version of a particular story on occasion. Marge hung on Roger's every word and managed a chuckle or two for Tom's stories too. It wasn't until Marge returned from the kitchen with the platter of cookies that Kate realized the other woman had been excluded from the conversation.

"Thanks for clearing the table, Margie. Apparently, I was mesmerized by the tall tales. I should have helped."

"No problem. The stories were great."

"So, what's happening in the real estate business?" Kate asked.

"I've sold some small residential and business properties. And I have a few rentals to keep me busy."

"I know the Building Department has been swamped with new projects, but I'm glad business in general is okay."

Roger said, "Tell them what you told me, Margie."

"They wouldn't be interested. It's not much more than town gossip."

"Hey, nothing wrong with good gossip," Tom said. "I'd love to hear it."

Kate agreed, "My journalist's creed is never pass up a good rumor, it might be true."

Marge smiled and shrugged. "Okay. Keep in mind, I haven't spoken to the owners directly, but my source is usually reliable."

Roger interrupted. "They'll be surprised."

"Dad, give her a chance."

"Sorry."

Marge continued, "Well, some big corporation has offered to buy the Sammy Lane Resort for big money."

Kate said. "I can't imagine they'd sell."

"It was put on the National Register of Historic Places last year," Roger added.

Marge said, "You're right, Kate, they refused the offer. So did the other owners approached by the company."

"How many others?" Kate repeated as her interest grew.

"Maybe a handful in that same area."

Roger beamed. "There's more. Tell them the rest."

"You're making too much of this," Marge said, frowning in her date's direction.

"You may as well spill it. If my father is that tickled with something, I'm sure it will be worth hearing."

"I called the state of Missouri and asked about the corporation. It's registered as a Foreign Limited Liability Company with a state agent, but the officers and owners are not listed. The LLC was created in Delaware."

"Did you call Delaware?"

"Yes, but the information they provide is about the same, LLC and the Delaware agent information. They also said the company was in good standing, which means they've paid their fees in a timely fashion."

"Did you call the agent?"

"No. By the time I finished all the calls and transfers, including time on hold, I was exhausted."

"I'll bet," Kate said, recalling her two hours to get a simple bio for Charles Fredericks.

"How about you provide me the information. Who knows, it might even lead to an interesting article."

"Your articles about Etta and the crafts fair have been great. I've worked on the fair for several years and even I learned things about it. I've always wondered about the relationship between Etta and Jack Brighton."

"Was that in the article?" Roger asked.

"Calm down, Dad. Etta and Jack are lifelong friends, nothing more. You'll have to forgive him, Margie. Etta was his first crush."

Roger cringed, and Tom patted him on the back.

"Weren't ready for that announcement, I bet," Tom said.

Marge laughed. "I've had a great time. Thanks for including me. Come on, Roger, that movie starts in twenty minutes. Katie, come to the office Monday for my notes."

As the older couple drove away Tom said, "Appears to be you and me, Katie."

Kate took his hand and pulled him toward the patio. Embers flickered in the white-hot coals in the grill. Tom scraped the grate with a wire brush, and then set it aside to cool. Kate put the remaining dishes on a large tray and carried them into the kitchen. Her friend followed shortly with the last of the condiments.

"That's it. I'll check the ashes later," Tom said.

"Thanks. Dad would be mad if we set the motel on fire."

"My thoughts exactly."

Tom helped her put the plates in the dishwasher and dried the items she washed and placed by the sink. Once she ensured everything was where it belonged, she motioned for him to follow her to the back porch.

"What did you think? Of Margie, I mean," Kate asked.

"I've always liked Margie. She helped me sell my folk's place when Dad died. Nice lady. Seems good for Roger."

"I agree."

"But?"

"No but. I like her. I'm still absorbing what she told us."

Tom chuckled. "About the big bad corporation?"

"It's not funny. I spent yesterday and much of last night going over logs from the Taney County recorder's office. The number of transactions dealing directly with Branson was staggering. Many of the change of ownership deeds were for property in the city itself."

"I'm not sure what you're getting at. Are you sure they weren't refinances?"

"I have the logs. I'll dig deeper."

"For what?"

"I don't know. I'll recognize it when I see it."

Tom smiled and sat next to Kate on the glider, putting his arm around her shoulders.

Kate pulled away and scooted forward on the bench. "Why are you smiling?" she asked.

"Because I like you. I like being with you."

"Seems more like a there-she-goes-again smile."

"Can you please take off that reporter hat and sit back and relax for a few minutes?"

She pretended to remove her hat and throw it on the lawn. Old habits were hard to break and Marge's story made Kate even more curious about what Fortune Enterprises or some other company was doing in Branson. But that could wait until Monday. For now, she wanted to settle into Tom's arms. She touched his chin with her forefinger and moved his lips close to hers.

Tom kissed her gently, like he was holding back. She snuggled close to his chest, her head resting against his shoulder. They had issues to resolve. Finding a good time to have a discussion was important. They sat silently for a few moments before they spoke.

"We need to talk," each said, responding in unison, "I know."

Kate got up from the glider and leaned forward against the banister. Tom stood by her side, the warmth of his hand on hers coursed up her arm and across her shoulders.

"We've never discussed what happened," he said.

"I'm not sure I know what happened."

"Maybe we can figure it out together."

They held each other close, a rush of memories filling her head. This is how she wanted to feel—not angry or frustrated or threatened. The warmth of his body next to hers, his hands pressing her back, bringing her closer. Kate couldn't deny her emotions, her longings. She turned her face toward his, their lips met, and she responded to his passion. As quickly as it happened, he pulled back and she reluctantly followed suit.

He kissed her forehead gently. "I want this, Katie. I want it to work. I've never stopped loving you."

"But you left."

"You left."

"Technically yes, I left first, but you knew I'd be back."

"After a while, it didn't seem like you wanted to come back ... at least not to me," he countered.

"But you stopped waiting for me."

He pulled her back to the glider facing one another and holding hands. "Honestly, I don't remember the sequence of events. You went off to college. I joined the police force. That seemed to work for a year or so."

"We had that huge argument. I don't even remember what it was about."

"Strawberries," he said.

She squinted in disbelief.

"You were home for spring break. It was your sophomore year. You wanted fresh strawberries for some stupid dessert you were going to fix."

"Yes. And you refused to get them for me."

"They weren't in season. It was early March. You wouldn't settle for frozen."

"But you refused to check the store."

"Can we agree, in retrospect, this was not a reasonable argument? We were both frustrated. You'd been talking about joining some newspaper in Columbia after graduation. I felt like you were moving on without me."

"We were young. We didn't have a clue."

"I met Linda."

"You married Linda."

"Not right away. I tried to speak to you ... to patch things up."

"But I wouldn't listen. I remember. I guess it was all my fault, that stubborn streak."

"Hard to place blame. Things happened. Like you said, we were young."

"Ironically, I came back and you had moved to Kansas City."

"We both had good reasons. But I returned and I've never explained what happened with Linda. Bottom line is the marriage didn't work despite both of our efforts. We split up. I stayed with the Kansas City PD for a few years. Then I heard about the open position at Branson PD."

"And we lived happily ever after."

"We might."

Kate leaned forward into his arms and snuggled close. Talking about it helped. Saying aloud what everyone knew happened helped. Maybe they could have a happily-ever-after. *He never stopped loving me.*

"I didn't stop either," she whispered.

Chapter Fifteen

A chilly October breeze swirled around Tom and Sid as they waited outside the coroner's office. None of the other offices or stores in the small strip mall were opened. Artie's preview of the report was succinct and somewhat interesting, but the detectives needed more than that to solve their case. Tom hoped the forensic anthropologist would earn his fee.

Sid pulled his jacket collar closer around his neck. "What time did Artie say?"

"I told you ... first thing," Tom grunted.

"Hey, my watch says half past first thing."

Ten minutes later, Artie arrived. "Sorry guys, got a call as I was about to leave home."

"No problem. Where's Fredericks?" Tom asked.

"That was the call. He's been delayed by a personal emergency. But I can start the briefing. Let's go in the lab. Fortunately, we set everything up before we left last night."

Several tables filled the largest room of the office suite. Displays of photographs and physical evidence taken from the site covered each work surface. Artie handed each man a written report.

Tom was impressed with its weight but would be more impressed with substance.

"Hot off the press, gentlemen. It includes a summary. Each topic is detailed in the subsequent pages. The corresponding material is shown on these evidence tables. Before we sit down, let me go over each exhibit and recap the findings. Keep in mind we started on this a week ago. Some additional analysis is ongoing and should be completed in about a month."

The detectives studied the first page, which contained the bulleted list. Not surprisingly, the first two—condition of skeleton and analysis of covering—intrigued them the most. The skeleton itself was stored in the morgue at the hospital, but numerous photos illustrated each point Artie made about the condition of the remains and what Fredericks had determined about the victim. Tom and Sid listened intently and made notes on the detailed portion of the report. When Artie moved to the next table, Tom raised his hand.

"Can I summarize what I've heard to make sure we're clear?"

"Sounds good," Artie said. "Start with the victim."

"Caucasian male, between thirty and fifty years old, about five-foot-seven-inches tall. He had good teeth, although a couple were missing. He had broken both arms during his life, including breaking his left arm when he was younger. His bones healed poorly and may have caused issues later. Some pieces of clothing remained, but other than suggesting work clothes, they offered no clues. Nothing else was found in the blanket or inside the grave. No wallet or wedding ring. You did determine, however, that he died from a severe blunt force trauma to the head."

"Causing a compound depressed skull fracture," Artie added.

"Whoever wielded the weapon had to be pretty strong," Sid said.

"That's one explanation, but there are other things to consider. Let me move to the next table before we talk about the weapon. This wool blanket was manufactured in Minnesota during World War II. As it turns out, after the war the company began blending synthetic fibers in the wool blankets. In any case, a product logo and lot number run along this edge."

"Amazing," Sid said, squinting to see the small lettering.

"The good news is that lot was manufactured and sold in the Midwestern United States beginning in 1941."

Tom said, "Let me guess that the bad news is there's no way to determine where or when it was purchased."

"The company has records, which are provided in the report, but the list is rather overwhelming. Still, you never know what might help. As you'll see in Chuck's summary, the condition of the skeleton, the clothing, the grave itself, and the invasion of the tree root suggest interment was somewhere in the 1940s."

"More good news ... our possible open cases have been cut significantly," Sid said.

Artie turned to the next table, covered with photos of the skull, including close-ups of the wound and the grave itself. Several photos had been placed face down.

Before Artie could begin, Charles Fredericks joined the group and offered to take over the presentation. "Sorry, I'm late. I see Artie has covered the victim and the blanket. Both held a great deal of information for your case. Although we can determine the general nature of the weapon, it was not ... exactly ... found at the scene."

"That sounds intriguing. Do we get to guess the murder weapon?" Sid asked.

Chuck smiled and moved to the opposite side of the table. He centered one of the larger photos of the skull wound directly in front of the detectives. Red circles highlighted areas of trauma—two deep indentations, about two inches long, and a third sharper slit, about an inch wide. The grouping reminded Tom of an equilateral triangle.

"The fracture indicates the victim was struck from behind, most probably while turning around to face his attacker. The position of the wound, close to and behind the left temple, resulted in death, but not necessarily immediate."

"You determined all that from this indentation?" Sid asked.

"It would be unusual for someone to come at another person face-to-face and get in such a solid strike. More likely, the victim heard the approach, turned to see the blow coming with his peripheral vision, maybe even took evasive action, but was too late."

"And the weapon?" Tom asked.

"These not-quite-parallel indentations created the compound fracture. As you can see the bone was pushed inward. The third notch was incidental. The weapon was metal, at least the portion striking the victim."

Tom and Sid studied the primary photo and others taken from different angles.

"Something with that weird pattern. Can't be a rod or a bar," Sid said.

"Kind of looks like the back of a shovel, where the handle fits in above the blade," Tom commented.

"Very good, Detective Collingwood," Chuck said. "What else?"

"The handle must have been fairly long if the attacker surprised him."

Artie turned over the remaining photos— several different views of a long-handled shovel and three enlargements of the grave wall. Chuck circled the triangular pattern shown on the rear view of the shovel, then several markings in the grave.

"Remember, Tom, I suggested there were two diggers because of the depth range?" Chuck asked.

"And you said there may have been different shovels."

"In fact, there were markings from a pickaxe and two types of shovels. The murder weapon, with a rounded wider blade, was used to dig the deeper end. That type of shovel, as shown in our sample photo, is consistent with the indentations made on our victim's skull."

"You say he didn't necessarily die immediately. Was he buried alive?"

"Doubtful, but possible. I'm sure the gravediggers assumed he was dead. The type of trauma he suffered would no doubt render him unconscious. A wound so deep would result in massive blood loss. We found traces of blood on the blanket."

"That's great," Sid said.

"I'm pretty sure they won't be able to type it or extract DNA. However, we sent samples to the lab at the University of North Texas, including clothing and blanket swatches plus the femur bones. They'll do the best they can to extract the mitochondrial DNA."

"This DNA thing is pretty new to us, Chuck. But I'm guessing we'll need matching samples," Tom said. "How do we do that if we don't know who he is?"

"It will be your job to narrow the possibilities. With the age of the remains, the mitochondrial DNA may be all the lab can extract. We'll need a DNA sample from the victim's mother or sister, or even his mother's sister, or the sister's daughter."

"If those people even exist," Sid said.

"I'm afraid that will be critical to confirming the identification," Artie said.

Tom paced the room from table to table, studying the evidence displays. He wasn't sure what he had expected. The information provided one picture of how the murder took place—

essentially Chuck's guess. Figuring out the method and the weapon and the motive was difficult enough with an actual crime scene and the identity of the victim. Without those, it was purely speculation.

"Any advice?" Sid asked.

"I suggest you both read the entire report, review the photos, and go to the scene. I wouldn't release the lot until you've been at least one more time. The reports from the lab will take several weeks. Until then, work your cases and develop your assumptions about what might have happened. I'll be available for any follow-up questions. Artie has my contact information. I can come back, if necessary."

Tom and Sid helped Artie pack the report and photos and other physical evidence into three large boxes. The detectives signed the chain of custody forms for Artie and proceeded back to their office.

"First thing we need to do is speak to Dan about the archives," Sid said.

"Way ahead of you. I asked ... actually I *begged* him to speak to the City Clerk or Mayor or whoever it took to have those files loaned to us for use in our office."

Sid cleared a table on one side of the room normally used as a catchall for stacking case evidence. He placed the photos and evidence from Artie's lab on the table and gave himself and Tom a copy of the full report.

"You want to give this other copy to Lieutenant Palmer?"

"Make sure he signs for it.," Tom said.

"Yes, sir. Right away, sir."

Sid was on his way to the door when the lieutenant came in. "On my way to bring you a copy of the consultant's report, sir. Lots of information, but we're still trying to digest it."

"Sid is being too subtle. We have no idea what it all means. We know the victim is a male and *maybe* how and when he died. We have a lot of work to do."

"We didn't expect the forensic anthropologist to fill in *all* the blanks," Dan Palmer said.

"True enough. But a wallet with a picture ID would have been nice."

"Maybe it will help that you have permission to bring whatever files you need from the archives into the office. Cindy will brief you on the procedure. Can we release the crime scene?"

"Fredericks says not yet."

"It better be soon. Allen has called two more times. Even the mayor asked me about it."

Palmer signed for the coroner's report and handed the form to Sid as he started to leave. "One more thing. I read your report on the Porter suit. Do you have anything to add?"

"I don't know if we could call his suit frivolous, but we found nothing illegal or even particularly questionable going on around town. Since Porter provided no witness names or specific details, we've investigated the general process for each job. Leatherman has made a lot of procedural changes and is stricter on the permit process than in the past. I'm sure if the state finds any issues during its investigation they will already have been remedied. We spoke to the City Attorney who is preparing his response point-by-point. He's satisfied the responses will quash the suit. Both Leatherman and the City Attorney's office have tried without success to get additional information from Porter."

"We still have our hot line open and will continue to follow any leads," Sid added.

"Consider the case tabled, at least until the audit is complete or you get a new lead."

Tom and Sid walked Palmer back to his office on the way to speak to Cindy and get the files they needed from the storeroom. They checked out the cases from the 1940s and 1950s. After they helped Cindy return files to boxes and boxes to shelves, they went to lunch, then stopped by the crime scene.

"Nothing out here we haven't seen," Sid said.

"I wanted to walk around before I read the detailed report. I'm sure Artie and Chuck were thorough, but I want to refresh my memory."

"Something keeps nagging at me."

"You've narrowed it to one thing?" Tom asked.

"One in particular. Why in the world would someone murder a person then bury them in the city?"

"I'm not sure if this was in the city in the 1940s."

"Still, why not take the body to some remote part of the county or, even better, to Arkansas?"

"Good question. I guess we'll need to start a list of those little nagging mysteries," Tom said.

"Except this one will have a longer list," Sid said.

"Here's another one. Why would they bury the body not fifty yards from the creek? Why not weigh it down and dump it downstream?"

"Like I said, a long list."

Chapter Sixteen

The list of recent property transactions provided by Kate's new friend Evan included refinances and transfers between individuals Marge knew—no mysterious corporations, no sinister plots.

Since neither the Missouri nor Delaware agents from Marge's notes had returned Kate's calls, she decided a stroll down to the Sammy Lane Resort was in order.

As she passed the cottages next to the pool area, she recognized a man carrying a large toolbox. "You're Darin Smith. Do you double as the maintenance man?" she asked.

"One of the perks of being an owner," he said. "I haven't seen you, Kate, since I was on the Planning and Zoning Commission a few years ago."

"Don't you wish you were on it now with all the development?"

"Not on your life."

"You know, when I was a young girl my family would spend a day or two here in that cottage by the pool. My mom called it our little vacation."

"Did you want to rent it for old time's sake? I just fixed the plumbing for the umpteenth time, but it's ready for occupancy."

Kate laughed, but considered the idea for a second—perhaps a romantic weekend for her and Tom. She shook off the idea as a bit impetuous.

"Thanks, maybe someday. I do have a few questions, if you have time."

"Depends. Am I going to read about it in the newspaper?"

"You never know," she said with the sweetest grin she could muster.

"Let's go to the office and get out of this blustery wind."

Kate followed for a short distance, then stopped and turned her attention across Lake Taneycomo. The Candlestick Inn, situated on top of the bluff, was her mother's favorite restaurant. *It seems impossible she's been gone almost twelve years.*

She pulled her sweater close against the cool breeze and caught up with Darin. "Must be amazing to own this resort," she said.

"Most of the time. It can be a challenge, but Dad's still around to come to my rescue."

"I'm writing a series of articles about Branson's history. Sammy Lane Resort is an important part of that. You should be proud."

"We are. We've been around for a while. We have many regular visitors, but new folks come all seasons."

"My parents brought us maybe twice a year, even though we lived in town."

"You probably don't remember, but I went to school with your brother. RJ was a year behind me, but we played baseball together in middle school. To be honest, I had a crush on his little sister."

Kate fidgeted in the chair and glanced out the window. She knew without a mirror that the freckles on her face were emphasized by a blush.

"I'm glad you didn't bring up that fact at the planning meetings. RJ took no prisoners when it came to teasing me about you."

"I'm sorry. I didn't mean to embarrass you."

"That's okay. Good memories. It was hard on our family when he was killed in the boating accident."

"I know your father blamed himself, but there was nothing he could have done."

"It was my mother who got us through that tragedy. But we're okay now, I suppose."

Darin smiled and said, "I'm sure that's not what you came to discuss with me."

"First of all, I wanted to see if the resort was still the same, still in good hands."

"What's your verdict?"

"Yes, on both counts. But I also wanted to ask you about a rumor I heard."

"Must be exhausting to check out all the rumors in a small town like Branson."

"I rather enjoy it. I hope this one isn't true."

"Sounds ominous," he said, widening his eyes and smirking.

"It is if you're planning to sell the resort."

Darin snickered. "That's the rumor? I can officially take that one off the circuit."

"But someone did approach you about selling. That's what I heard."

"Correct. But this resort has been our family business for decades. We won't sell."

"Can you tell me about the person who made the offer?"

"It was more of an inquiry to see if we'd be open to the idea. It was a short conversation. The man was from out of town ... *way* out of town. I'm talking big city. He gave me a card. I can see if I still have it."

"That would be great."

Darin rummaged through a side drawer on his desk then searched the drawer below it. "I know it's here. I've been called a packrat. Never throw anything away. The man was wearing a five-hundred-dollar suit. His nails were manicured. Around thirty-five years old, I'd say. Very not-Branson. He said he represented a potential buyer."

"Did he say who?"

Darin slammed the third drawer and shouted, "Found it."

Kate took the card and wrote the information down in her notebook. The company name—handwritten on the back—matched the name Marge had been given. The name on the front was a new one. It didn't match the agent listed with Missouri or Delaware.

"Thanks," she said, returning the card.

"To answer your question, no, he didn't say who the buyer was. He told me he represented some company. I asked him to write the name on the back. I guess that's the point of using an agent from out of town."

Darin walked Kate to the north side of the resort at Main Street. She thanked him for his time and asked him to contact her if anything else happened, and then walked toward the marina. The dock owner was tending one of the slips, helping a fisherman cast off.

"My father would say this is a great day to be out on the lake," she said.

"And he would be correct." The man in his late forties, Kate guessed, with an outgoing personality and warm smile, offered a strong Midwestern handshake. "Hi, I'm Jake Forester."

She handed him her card as she introduced herself and explained the series of articles she was writing.

"Nice to meet you. I'm not sure how much I can help. I've only been here a year."

"Let's start with why you chose a boat dock in Branson, Missouri."

"You might say it's been a dream of mine for a while. When this business became available, we grabbed it."

"How'd you hear about it?"

"Like a lot of people who've moved to Branson, we vacationed in the area for years."

"Timing's everything," Kate said. "Any plans to change the name?"

"Nope. Scotty's Trout Dock suits it."

"I don't suppose anyone has approached you about selling."

"Funny you mention that. Some big city lawyer-type spoke to my wife when I was out one afternoon several weeks ago. She told him it was no longer available."

"Do you remember his name? Maybe he left a card."

"If he did, we tossed it. Like I said, this has been a dream for a while. I don't intend to sell it any time soon."

Kate continued walking along the lakefront and spoke to several business owners. They told similar stories about turning down offers to sell. She considered knocking on doors of private residences but decided to discuss it with Marge first.

Commercial Street was bustling with tourists and locals, alike, visiting crafts fair booths. She stopped by Connarde Realty and was surprised to see a poster-size blowup of her first article, complete with Etta's picture. Etta and her volunteer friends were positioned in the entryway behind a display table covered with memorabilia. Small space heaters blazed at either end of the table.

"You ladies seem cozy," Kate said.

"Looks can be deceiving," one of the older women said.

"Lots of people milling around," Kate remarked.

"We've had lots of drop-ins who want to meet the famous lady you created in your articles," Etta said. "I told them she was run out of town on a rail."

One of the volunteers pointed her finger at Etta. "Now, don't be modest. You did after all have the idea. And you did nurture this event every year for many decades."

"Well, if this year is a success, we can thank Kate for all the publicity," Etta said.

"Amen to that," Marge said, emerging from the back room with a large thermos.

"Just doing my job, ladies. And speaking of that, do you have a minute, Margie?"

Margie's office was small but tastefully decorated, including several personal awards and family pictures. A framed photo of Roger and Marge at a recent Chamber of Commerce event sat next to the phone. It was good to see her father having such a good time. Marge smiled toward the photo, and then handed Kate a mug of coffee before sitting in a nearby chair.

"Great picture of your dad."

"You know, he whistles all the time now. I remember when I was a kid he was always whistling, and it really annoyed me. He resumed the habit when you two started dating. Now he's in this persistently happy mood."

A rosy blush bloomed across Marge's cheeks.

"Yes. It is all your fault. But I forgive you."

"So, what did you want to discuss?"

"I spoke to a few of the owners on the lakefront. None of them knew about others being approached. The mysterious out-of-towner ... his name is Kyle Henderson ... didn't press the issue, merely asked if they were interested in selling. He didn't reveal who the actual buyer was, although he did tell Darin Smith the name of the company he represented. It was the one that we checked out in Missouri and Delaware. Incidentally, neither registered agent has returned my call. I got Henderson's voicemail too."

"Maybe one of them will call you back."

"I didn't leave a message for Henderson. It occurred to me I might want to bend the truth a bit when I talk to him. You know, keep the newspaper out of the conversation."

"Sounds devious. Good idea though."

"I wanted to ask you about the residential owners in the area. Have you heard anything? What's the best approach to find out about offers?"

"I suppose that would be for me to do *my* job. Any good realtor is constantly looking for listings. The only way you find out if someone wants to sell is to ask. People will be much less suspicious of my inquiries. Nothing personal, dear. I'll see what I can find out."

"Something bothers me about Larry Allen," Kate confided.

"Jack Brighton's grandson?"

"He cleared that lot where the skeleton was found but won't say why. He claims his grandfather was going to replace some buildings for Etta. But when I asked Brighton about the lot, he was clueless, not to mention angry, about the clearing."

"Sounds like a bit of miscommunication. But I agree with your misgivings about Allen. I've had some bad experiences with him on previous sales. One was so ugly, I had to ask for Jack's help."

"Jack?"

"We're acquaintances."

"Very mysterious," Kate said.

"My former husband was involved."

Kate nodded, even though she had no idea what Marge meant—the subject of a future conversation, perhaps. "I'm not sure what's going on, but if folks are interested in buying lakefront property, there has to be a reason."

"Maybe they're simply checking things out," Marge offered. "Branson has been in the news lately. Most of the attention has been for the land on West 76 with all the new theaters and hotels. Could be some sharp real estate tycoon wants to see what else is available."

"You may be right, but I'm going to see what I can find out at City Hall in the morning, not that they'll tell me anything willingly. But the rumor mill is always abuzz with something."

Marge walked Kate to the front of the building. "This is exciting. You investigative reporters must be on a constant adrenalin high."

"It comes and goes, trust me."

Chapter Seventeen

Kate moved her finger down the agenda for next Monday's city council meeting. Nothing stood out–the same general topics the alderman discussed every two weeks. She tapped her finger on the seventh item. "Ah. Newest member of annexation-of-the-month club."

Mayor Kenneth Holt's admin assistant shrugged. "Job security. And at my age, I need it."

"Come on, Laura. You know this place would fold without you. Besides, if I remember correctly, you turned forty-seven last year. That's not so old."

The woman tucked an errant brown strand into the otherwise neatly packaged bun on top of her head. "Spoken like a true politician, and, I might add, an above average reporter."

"Thanks. My goal in life is to be above average."

"You know what I mean."

Kate bowed her head in mock modesty. "You're right about job security. Branson's growth pays the bills, for sure."

Laura leaned forward, resting forearms on the counter separating the administrative offices from the cavernous lobby. "And the city expects it to be a record year for building permits and rezoning applications. We haven't had an accurate city limits map in two years. We need more room for all the paperwork and additional staff. I swear it hasn't been this crazy since the city annexed everything on West 76."

Kate folded the agenda and filed it in the to-be-studied compartment of her portfolio. "Definitely bizarre but I love it."

"Speaking of bizarre." The woman nodded toward the building department office across the way. "There's an unlikely pair."

Kate's initial heart-skipping reaction upon seeing her newly reinstated boyfriend gave way quickly to her reporter's curiosity. "Wonder what Tom's doing with Bryan Porter," she said, not expecting an answer.

Laura leaned forward and whispered, "I'd wager it has something to do with yesterday's city council luncheon."

An edge of white outlined Porter's well-groomed auburn hair from the temples to behind the ears. Probably in his late fifties, his sunbaked face added years to his age. Tom, who at six foot two stood more than a head taller, placed a hand on Porter's shoulder. The older man shook his head, making gestures with both hands as he spoke, his voice low, his words inaudible.

"What happened?" Kate asked.

"Interrupted the session. Got in a squabble with Councilman Allen."

"He's been working toward a face-to-face confrontation for a while. I bet the youngest alderman was suitably embarrassed."

"Are you kidding? Allen's not one who likes public humiliation, even in small groups."

"I've noticed. Did they argue?"

"I'm not sure, but it was definitely loud. At least according to someone who attended. Allen responded to Porter in a way that ..."

"Spill it, Laura. You have to know more."

Laura straightened her back. "I've already said enough. City administrator's getting real uptight about the media, especially a certain noteworthy member of the press. You know, with everything that's going on."

Kate crinkled her brow. "Audit a headache?" she said, taking a guess at *everything*.

"Unfortunately, I'm three requests behind already."

"What a drag. Take up a lot of your time?"

"Mine and the entire ..." Laura squinted and shook her head. She pursed her lips and turned an invisible key.

"Okay. Maybe I should speak to the mayor about it."

"Won't be in today."

"How about Mark Orchard? Is the esteemed city administrator available?"

"Not to discuss what you want to discuss."

"Okay, I get it. Audit is off-limits. What about the city's own up-coming project?"

Kate knew she'd hit a chord when Laura's eyes glazed over. The reporter held her breath hoping for a deep dark secret. Instead, the other woman made the invisible key motion again.

"Come on, give a hungry reporter a break. I need to know the status of the project as of today. You can put that in one simple sentence."

"It's on track."

"You mean the plans for construction are on schedule?"

"You said one sentence."

"True, but I want to be accurate. The more specific, the more accurately I can report."

"You can't report this until the city makes an official announcement."

Kate knew the administrative assistant's position in city government exposed her to a great deal of information. But Laura had never provided Kate with more than rumors—albeit juicy ones. Goodness knows the lunch with Claire was a bust—the relatively new employee either knew very little or was terrified to say something and get herself fired. Prying more from Laura would require a bit of a push.

"Hopefully they'll release something before the ground-breaking ceremony," Kate said.

"I'm sure something will be published before they tear up the parking lot."

"What parking lot?"

Laura shook her head. "You're fishing."

"I meant *which* parking lot will be done first?"

"Adams Street. But that's all I'm saying. Now go away."

Kate crossed the room slowly, pretending to check her calendar as Tom and Bryan shook hands. She was close enough to see the anger in Porter's face and overhear the official warning.

Tom stared into Porter's eyes and said, "Give it some thought. Stay away from Allen, for your own good. You can get in a lot of trouble making accusations about someone, especially if you have no proof. "

Without a word, Porter turned and walked to the exit doors. He hesitated one moment then left the building.

"What was that all about?" Kate asked.

Tom wheeled around and replaced his frown with his familiar grin. "Hey, Katie. Saw you talking to Laura. What's up?"

"I asked you first," she said, checking out his police uniform.

"Nothing you need to be concerned about."

"I didn't know you were friends with Bryan Porter."

"That was more like an official conversation. Call it a warning."

Kate shrugged as if disinterested and changed the subject. "What's with the uniform?"

"I'm testifying on a case this morning. Prosecutor suggested my official attire might lend an air of credibility, whatever that means."

He stepped back as if to give her a better view. "What do you think?"

Credible maybe, definitely alluring. And the touch of gray in his dark brown waves gives him an air of maturity, which will probably come in handy for a thirty-four-year-old detective sergeant.

Tom persisted, "Will I convince the judge?"

"The judge will be impressed, believe me. Anyway, Laura and I were chatting about the big new construction project the city is about to announce."

"But Laura didn't give you any details, so you're pumping me."

"More like I'm curious"

"As far as I know the city project is a simple city hall expansion. Apparently, we have outgrown the building. Even I know about it, but the mayor prefers to control the publicity."

"Maybe something else is going on you don't know about," she said.

"I'll let you know when I get the next tidbit. I'm sure I'm on the need-to-know list."

Kate frowned at his sarcasm and moved on to the next topic. "Laura also told me about Porter's recent altercation with Larry Allen. Was that what you two were discussing? Does he have something against the councilman?"

"You mean, is it newsworthy?"

Kate took a deep breath. "Allen is a public official. We have a right to know about any grievances."

"In my opinion ... and this is not for publication ... Bryan has some serious anger issues."

"Etta said he's always been angry."

"Always?"

"He worked at her mercantile when he was a kid. She's known him all his life."

"Amazing."

"Which part?" Kate asked.

"That you know these things. You never cease to surprise me with some obtuse fact about this town or the people in it or how they all fit together."

"I ask questions for a living, remember?"

"Sometimes that slips my mind. But since you brought it up, I'd like to ask you a question about the day Sid and I saw you at Etta's. Bryan Porter drove away as we arrived."

"Wow, this is a switch. Usually, I'm the one digging for info."

"I'm not digging, I'm curious."

"Must be something in the air."

"So, do you know why Bryan visited Etta?"

"Since we are old friends, I'll tell you what I know. When I got there Bryan and Etta were arguing. He was shouting at her, but I was too far away to distinguish their words. He left before I could ask him any questions."

"But I bet you discussed his visit with Etta."

"I'm beginning to see how my interviewing techniques must annoy people."

"You forget, I'm a detective. I ask questions for a living too."

"Sometimes that slips my mind," she said with a smile. "Apparently Etta has some proof Bryan needs. He thinks that she *owes* him. It has something to do with why his father left the business they all ran. But she says she can't help him."

Tom stared ahead, not at Kate but through her. He seemed to be digesting what she told him, seeing how the data fit with other information he possessed.

"Where did you go?" she asked.

"Sorry, my mind wandered."

"Care to share?"

"I have to get to the courtroom," he said, turning to leave.

Kate said, "Don't forget dinner Saturday at my house six o'clock."

The drive to the county seat seemed unusually long. Kate had time to mull over both the lakefront and the skeleton issues. Unfortunately, neither story would pass Helen's inevitable fact-check-and-substance test. Even Kate would be hard pressed to draw any logical conclusions at this point. Hopefully Evan's update was not a tease to lure her to Forsyth.

She took her place behind two other customers, but Evan motioned for her to go to the far end of the counter where he handed her a manila envelope.

"Here are the pages you asked for," he said aloud before lowering his voice to a whisper. "These transfers will interest you."

Kate pulled out the sheets and glanced over the first pages of two recently recorded deeds. Both properties were in the lakefront residential area. Each now belonged to the same individual. The name seemed familiar, but it was not the company or either corporate agent. She hesitated to get too excited. Marge would know the significance of Evan's observation.

"Thanks, Evan. I appreciate your doing this for me. How much for the copies?"

"You prepaid. Remember?" he said with a wink. "I hope they help with your research."

"Time will tell."

Evan seemed pleased with himself. He blushed as he returned to his position at the counter. "I'll call you when the next batch is ready."

"I appreciate your help." She said sweetly and waved goodbye, deciding not to dwell on what Evan was hoping to get for his services. Perhaps he's a bit of an armchair detective himself and in it for the excitement.

Kate called Marge from her car phone to find out if the visit was worth her time.

"Margie, this is Kate. Who is Harold Wainright?"

"I'm not sure. What's he done?"

"Can I meet you at your office in about twenty minutes?"

"I'll be here. And I'll see what I can find out about Mr. Wainright."

Kate was beginning to enjoy this teamwork thing. Maybe Helen had the right idea. Having someone else's perspective and resources was refreshing, plus neither Evan nor her father's girlfriend would ask for a shared byline.

Marge met Kate at the entrance and started talking before they got settled at her desk. "I had to make several calls to find out about Harold Wainright. I'm afraid you'll be disappointed. He retired from some big company in Chicago and moved to the area about a year ago. Lives with his wife in a spectacular house on Table Rock Lake. I remember the listing. No one who contacted me had that kind of money, but I went out there for a gander. Great view, built about fifteen years ago."

"And so?" Kate interrupted.

"Just the facts, right?"

"Please."

"He closed on two rentals and has contracts on at least two others, all along the downtown lakefront."

"Interesting."

"Yes and no."

"Go ahead. Take the air out of my sail."

"First, it's not that unusual for rentals to change hands. These four properties were owned by four individuals. Rentals are hard, even for professionals. Second, these four houses are old and small. Consequently, the asking prices were low. And, by the way, all of them were listed well-before Mr. Wainright arrived in Branson. The owners were eager to sell. The locations are probably coincidental."

"Do you have notes?" Kate asked, trying–unsuccessfully–to hide her disappointment.

"Already made you a copy."

Chapter Eighteen

Tom parked as close to the house as possible, but still more than halfway toward the motel office. Roger's business had *definitely* recovered in the last year—good for him and Branson. And good for Tom that he didn't see Roger's truck. *Maybe Roger and Marge are out on a date.*

Kate—framed by the front picture window—directed him around to the patio. Two candles were centered on the table, which had been set with what Tom knew to be Kate's mother's best dishes.

"What did I do to deserve this?" he asked.

"I decided to take advantage of the warm evening. Oh, did I mention that Dad and Margie are in Springfield at a real estate thing. Won't be home until late."

"Sorry I missed them."

"Liar."

Tom leaned forward and kissed her on the cheek. "I confess. I'm not disappointed we are able to spend a little quality time alone."

Kate put her arms around his neck. "After dinner, I have a surprise for you."

He kissed her gently on the lips, pulling her closer. His heart pounded in his chest, or maybe it was hers. Welcoming her eager hug, he nuzzled his cheek against hers. He didn't want to let go, and he knew she felt the same as he welcomed her lips with his own. The depth of his obsession with Kate had never diminished. When they broke up and he moved away, he buried the feelings, tried to forget how special their relationship—their love—was. But that changed when he returned to Branson.

She pulled away and stepped back. "That was the pizza."

"What was the pizza?"

"Didn't you hear the timer?"

He followed her into the kitchen. "Perhaps you didn't notice, but I was seriously in another world."

She glanced over her shoulder and wrinkled her nose like the schoolgirl he remembered. He grabbed her arm and drew her to his chest. She pressed against him until the oven bell sounded again.

"Let me turn this off."

"Can you do that without moving?"

She shook her head. "Do you want to eat charcoal pizza?"

"My favorite."

"We have all evening. Remember?"

"Exactly how late will they be?"

She raised an eyebrow and pulled away to retrieve the pizza and slice it. "I'll take this out. Can you grab a couple beers?"

"Does this mean we're going to eat now?"

Tom had to admit, the evening was spectacular–a light southern breeze and a still bright waning moon. He leaned back in the chair and watched his companion slip a wedge of pizza on each plate. She poured her beer into a glass and took a sip.

"I love ice-cold beer, especially with pizza," she said.

"This looks great. Did you make it from scratch?"

"Okay. Either that was sarcasm, or you've forgotten who your date is."

"I made a little joke. I'm having a great time, that's all."

The first pieces disappeared in silence with Tom lost in his memories. Although Kate was quite a bit taller now, the five-year-old he met in school was still around–the long auburn hair, dazzling blue eyes, and glowing freckles. So much had happened. He was grateful for another chance at happiness.

"Why are you staring at me with that silly gaze on your face?" she asked.

"I was remembering this cute little girl I used to see during recess."

"The one you chased around the school yard?"

"That's the one."

Kate served each of them another slice. "Wonder what happened to that cute little gal."

Tom reached across the table and took her hand in his. "She grew into a beautiful, intelligent, lady. I lost touch with her for a while, but we've recently reunited."

"How's that going for you?"

"Seems pretty good so far." He came out of his chair at the same time pulling her toward him. They shared a passionate kiss, but he stopped. He didn't want to rush things. Stepping back, he let his fingers slide down her arms and squeeze her hands.

She returned the squeeze. "Too soon," she said—not quite a question.

"Part of me feels as though we've never been apart. The other part keeps remembering we reconciled ... once again ... less than two weeks ago."

"You do have a way with words, Detective Collingwood," Kate commented, rolling her eyes.

"I don't want to mess this up. This time it seems like we have a chance."

"We've been up and down on a few occasions. You're right about that."

"What's the surprise?"

"I almost forgot. I rented our favorite movie."

"Okay. Remind me again the name of it."

"You don't remember?" The wrinkle in her brow and the daggers coming from her eyes meant he was in serious trouble.

We saw a lot of movies in high school, he thought. *Our favorite, meaning her favorite, was probably a chick flick. Or maybe a special date. Think, man.*

Kate crossed her arms in front of her—time was running out.

There was one special night. He had to try it. "Heaven something. Warren Beatty, right?"

"You have no idea how close that was, detective."

"Uh, I'm pretty clear on that point."

"*Heaven Can Wait*. Pop it in the VCR and I'll get us another round."

He followed her orders and cued the tape. When she returned, she snuggled close to him and laid her head on his shoulder. Although he had hoped the evening would take a different turn, he was happy. In the months after her dad was cleared of the murder charge, the couple had tried several times to start dating again. Something always came up to sabotage the relationship. Perhaps this time would be different. Kate surprising him with the movie they saw the summer before his senior year was a good sign—a good place to start fresh.

Tom relaxed and enjoyed the movie. He'd forgotten how funny it was. What he did remember was the time afterward with Kate. They were celebrating her seventeenth birthday early because his family would be out of town on the actual date. It was a special evening.

Kate brushed a tear from her cheek and sat forward on the sofa as the final titles rolled on the small screen. She sighed deeply and walked to the VCR. "I love that ending," she said, putting the tape in the rewinder.

"It brings back good memories," he said.

"You do remember."

"Yeah, I remember a lot about that night."

"I hate to say this, but Dad will be home soon."

"What happened to later?"

"We spent it watching a movie."

They walked through the living room into the small foyer by the front door. He leaned against the wall next to the bookshelf, trying to stretch out the goodbye.

"Thanks for coming over. I had a great time," she said, taking his hands.

"Me too. I enjoyed seeing our favorite movie again."

"Even if you didn't know it was our favorite?"

"Hey, is this a new bookshelf?"

"Okay. I'm not sure we voted it our favorite movie, but it was fun to see again. And *all* the furniture in this house has been in exactly the same place for thirty years."

"But this box hasn't. Is it one of Etta's?"

"Very observant, detective. It was a gift from her for my incredibly kind and extremely professional job of writing about the creator of the Branson crafts fair."

"I'm impressed."

"It was a thoughtful present from a lady who lives a simple life."

"Right."

"What does that tone mean?"

"Don't get me wrong. I'm sure the gift was sincere. But don't for a second feel sorry for Etta Stupholds. She is most likely one of the richest women in town. Remember she's a full partner with Jack Brighton in Fortune Enterprises. He established a trust fund for her in the 1940s. She wants for nothing."

"Technically their partnership is in Riverside Mercantile."

"Which owns Fortune Enterprises."

Her hurt expression caught him off-guard. When it turned to a sweet pout, then the Katie-has-you grin, he relaxed. She smiled and moved close. Relieved that his weak attempt at banter had not backfired, he returned the hug and kissed her. He hesitated briefly before letting her go.

"To be honest, I didn't know about the trust fund. How'd you find out?"

"I know people who know people," he said before changing the subject. "So, what do you keep in the box?"

"That is somewhere between nosy and curious."

"Ah, secrets. Not a good start for a long-term romance."

She put her arms around his waist. "Long-term?"

"We should definitely give it a try and see how it goes."

"Etta didn't have a key, but she says the box is empty."

"That will not slow down a good detective."

"Maybe Sid could unlock it for me."

He squinted and frowned, then took her hand as they walked across the lot to his vehicle.

"I'll see you soon," she said.

"Count on it."

When he arrived at his apartment, Tom stayed in his car for several minutes. He stared at the building, but all he could see was Kate's face. It was almost one in the morning when he finally lay down. Only a couple of hours later, he sat straight up in bed. The dream—more like a nightmare—was elusive, but it had something to do with Kate breaking up with him in the middle of the city hall lobby. He couldn't go back to sleep, so he got up and walked around his apartment for several minutes. Unable to calm himself down, he gave up and went to work. He'd been going over the stack of cold cases for a while when Sid arrived.

"What are you doing here on a Sunday? Didn't you have a date with Kate last night?"

Tom walked to the coffee stand and filled two mugs.

Sid said, "No comment. Now I get it."

"You get what?"

"The date went better than you expected it would. But when you went home ... *bingo!*"

"Bingo?"

"You questioned the greatness of the date itself. You were afraid she'd dump you again. You couldn't sleep."

"How can you know all that?"

"Been there."

"So, what are *you* doing here on a Sunday?"

"Couldn't sleep. This skeleton case gives me insomnia. Did you solve it without me?"

"I wish. But a couple of things interest me. First, let's discuss the crime itself. We know the victim was approached from behind. He heard or saw the killer and turned to face him and was struck in the side of his head. The weapon was most likely a long-handled shovel and the blow was fatal."

Sid interrupted, "But he may not have died immediately."

"Right," Tom said, shrugging. "There had to be more than one killer. At the very least, someone had to help transport the body to the lot."

"We know the buildings on the lot were not occupied at the time. The murder could still have taken place on site."

"Could, but probably not," Tom said, pouring himself another cup of coffee.

"Because?"

"Brighton's records show the buildings were vacant, meaning no furnishings and no electricity, from late 1942, when Etta moved out, until early 1949, when they started renting the property."

"Unlikely a shovel happened to be available for a spontaneous murder."

"Exactly. This was not planned. If it was, it was a dumb plan. If you want to kill someone, do it away from civilization, with an appropriate weapon, and dispose of the body where it will never be found."

"Unfortunately, that means the murder took place anywhere in the city of Branson."

"That's true, but let's assume it was in the place where a shovel similar to the one Chuck likes for the weapon would be found," Tom said.

"A farm. A business. Anywhere."

"But probably not far from St. Limas Street. The body was carried or transported manually or at best in some simple hand cart. If a car or truck had been available, the killer would have used it to take the bundle farther out of town."

"I hate to be the devil's advocate, but you're counting on our perps being logical, even smart. What if they were stupid or wanted to frame someone in the city?"

"Let's go down the logical path for now. If that doesn't work, we'll retrace our steps."

"Okay, if the murder wasn't planned, something happened to provoke the attack."

Tom said, "I see a couple of options, but one makes more sense. The guy with the shovel was trying to stop the victim from hurting someone else. I know you're skeptical, but hear me out. Let's say our victim was arguing with someone. The argument heats up. Our victim attacks someone, knocks him down or pushes him. The fight continues and eventually gets out of hand. The shovel guy grabs the conveniently located weapon and strikes our victim. Maybe he knew it would kill him, maybe he didn't."

Tom handed Sid a large black marker and motioned toward the three-foot square pad of plain paper resting on an easel beside the worktable. Sid made notes as his partner recapped the scenario. When he filled a sheet, he ripped it off the pad and taped it to the wall. When they finished, they leaned back and stared at the five sheets.

"Let me guess," Sid said picking up the cold case folders, "all we have to do is see which of these missing persons fits neatly into our crime scene."

"Three good fits are on top, all from your review of the 1940 cases."

Sid opened the first file. "John Newsom. Age fits. Went missing in November 1948. Lived in Omaha, Arkansas, but worked in Branson at the lumber company. According to his wife, he stayed in Branson during the week and came home most weekends. When he failed to come home the second Friday in a row, she tried to find him. Eventually a report was filed in the city. Branson police worked with the Taney County Sheriff's office to check out several leads. Found nothing."

Tom said, "However, several reports concerned Mr. Newsom's possible relationship with a local woman. Both of them seemed to disappear at the same time. All the department could do was wait for another lead."

Sid shrugged and took the next folder from the pile. "I remember this one. Robert Jeffries. One problem with him."

'Too old?"

"Right, but everything else fits. Missing in 1947. Lived a couple miles north of the city. Had a hard time adjusting after returning from the war. His only living relative, a sister, made the report when she hadn't heard from him in several months."

"Not much to go on, so the case was quickly tabled. Still we could follow up with the sister or her children."

"Last one. Alexander Porter. Wife reported him missing in 1945. He'd been living and working in some factory in Kansas City, Missouri. Hadn't been home to see her in a while but corresponded regularly. Last letter she received was in September 1945. He said he hoped to be home soon. Branson PD followed up with Kansas City and the surrounding area. The fleabag hotel where he was staying hadn't seen him in a while, but ... being a fleabag ... they didn't care. When his prepaid rent ran out, they removed and stored his belongings, including personal letters, his toiletries, and some clothes. Eventually they returned the property to the wife."

"Branson PD found no other leads, no indication he had returned to Branson. He did not match any Kansas City-area John Doe. In fact they checked as far north as St. Joseph, Omaha and Cedar Rapids, and the rest of Missouri for unidentified bodies matching his description."

Sid walked to the easel and wrote down the three names with a few key words under each. Then in large letters under the three lists he wrote and circled: NEED DNA LINK.

"We need to see if any of these victims have living relatives and hope one of them is a maternal link. I'll start by speaking to the old-timers ... I mean long-term residents," Tom said.

Sid stepped to the board and put a large arrow next to the third name and shook his head.

"Spit it out," Tom said.

"Two things. One, we went through a lot of files. Fredericks said the murder could have happened anywhere in the 1940s or 50s. We've selected three files out of maybe two dozen from that time period. What if our victim had no kin or friend or whatever to report his absence? What if his kin didn't care or did the deed?"

"We have to do this step by step. My gut tells me someone buried in Branson was probably killed close by. I'm going to assume his absence was reported in the city. We have to eliminate those possibilities before we resume the what-ifs."

"Fair enough," Sid said.

"You said two things."

"Yeah. Do you suppose this Mr. Porter is related to our favorite complainer, Bryan? You have to admit that would be quite a coincidence."

"My thought exactly."

Chapter Nineteen

Kate's father peered over his newspaper. "There you are. I was beginning to think you moved out of the old homestead."

"Why would you say that?"

"You haven't been around much. I don't think I've seen you since you and Tom were lingering in the parking lot on Saturday."

"I went to the office while you were at church yesterday. But I was home and in bed before you drifted in last night. How was the real estate thing with Margie on Saturday?"

"It was okay. I have a feeling you had a more interesting evening with Tom. How'd Margie's pizza recipe work out?"

"I decided to use one of my own."

"You called Domino's?"

"Good guess, but I bought a fresh one at the store and baked it myself."

"So, you two managed to get along for a few hours. That's progress."

She shrugged and poured a glass of orange juice.

"Katie? Is everything okay with you and Tom?"

She glanced over her shoulder. "We've tried so many times to make it work. I suppose I'm afraid I'll blow it again."

"Take it from me, you and Tom are meant for each other. I knew that when you were nine years old and the two of you vowed to be "best friends forever." You've had a bumpy ride, sure, but you seem to be on track this time. Of course, that's from the point of view of a third, almost impartial, observer."

She shrugged and took a sip of coffee. "What's for breakfast?" she asked.

"Considering the time, it will have to be brunch."

"Oh no. Helen will kill me." She raced to the phone. One of the reporters answered on the third ring. The good news was Helen had taken the day off. The bad news was she called to make sure Kate was working on the Branson history article for the weekend edition.

"Don't worry, I covered for you. She said for you to call when you returned to the office. By the way, that's four you owe me."

"Whatever you want. Thanks."

By the time she scurried around and raced to the office it was almost noon. A message from Tom was posted on the reporter's check-in board. The warm feeling of Saturday evening overwhelmed her. She pulled down the note and rushed to her desk. She started to call his office but noticed the number on the message was for police dispatch. The joy of hearing from him turned to anxiety. Tom's message was almost an hour old. By the time the dispatcher forwarded her call to Tom's radio her heart was pounding.

The line clicked and he said, "Katie, I need your help. Can you come to Etta's house?"

"Is she okay?"

"She's shaken, but unhurt. Maybe you can help her and me at the same time."

She made the ten-minute drive in less than six, turning into the drive a few moments after an ambulance pulled out. The absence of lights and siren helped to reduce her concern for Etta. Tom met her car as she made the final turn. Two patrol cars were parked in the yard. He motioned for her to pull over, then opened her door.

"Etta's fine. Her friend Sarah picked her up at the crafts fair. When they pulled up here the front door was open. One of the intruders knocked Sarah down as they fled. The EMTs transported her to the hospital to be checked out."

"Knocked her down? Why in the world did she get out of the car?"

"We've been unable to get that answer. Sarah was quite shaken. Etta refuses to speak to us. I was hoping you could calm her down and maybe get answers."

"Where is she?"

"In Sarah's car with Sid."

"Considering her age, maybe she should go to the hospital too," Kate said.

"Going to the hospital was not an option she would consider. We're doing our thing in the house, which is a mess. Try to talk to her. Maybe if she calms down, she'll help us."

Kate opened the driver's side door. Sid was in the back tapping the blank pad with his pen. He raised his eyebrows and gazed desperately in the reporter's direction.

"Are you okay, Etta?" Kate asked. "Sid, maybe a glass of water, please?"

The detective said, "Be back in a few minutes."

The older woman took a deep breath and exhaled, placing her hand on her chest. "I'll be okay. Give me a moment."

"Etta, you're as white as a sheet. You should go to the hospital to have them look you over. Maybe you could call your doctor. I'll take you, if you like."

"The young man in the ambulance checked me."

Etta rested her head against the seat as the color gradually returned to her cheeks.

"Were you able to tell Sergeant Greene anything?"

"I don't know anything, but he doesn't believe me."

"They're trying to get a time-line, Etta. What time did Sarah take you to the crafts fair this morning?"

"She picked me up at eight-thirty, as usual."

"But you normally stay until noon. What changed?"

"I'd been there a half hour or so when Sarah called to say she had to go somewhere. I could go home early or wait until she returned around three. I didn't want to stay downtown that long, especially with the rain coming."

"What time did she pick you up?"

Etta sighed, shaking her head. "It had to be around ten, maybe quarter after. Margie might know."

"And you came directly home?"

"We stopped at the grocery store. It took about twenty minutes."

"Good. This will help Tom."

"Why? What difference does it make when we got here?"

"Because your schedule is set during the fair. You go downtown, entertain the fairgoers for a few hours, leave at noon and generally come directly home."

"I wouldn't say I entertain anyone."

"But the rest is true. Right?"

"Maybe you should join the police department."

"Somehow, I doubt that would work out. You know how I am about rules."

Etta smiled and relaxed into the seat.

Kate said, "Can you remember exactly what happened when you got home?"

"Nothing unusual when we drove up. I was fiddling with my purse, still trying to put the change away from the grocery store. Sarah got out of the car and grabbed the bag from the back seat. When she got to the foot of the steps she stopped."

Etta paused, her focus on the stairs leading to the veranda.

"Was she waiting for you?"

"No, she was staring at the open front door. Before I could think, two young men came barreling out of the house. One of them pushed Sarah out of his way as they came down the stairs. She fell down and I just stared at her," Etta said, her brow furrowed.

"I'm sure she'll be okay. They weren't even running the siren when they left."

"I know. But I couldn't move. Several minutes passed before I got to her. What if she'd been seriously hurt?"

"Your reaction was normal."

"Not for me. I've never felt that terrified. *Ever.*"

"Did you recognize the two men?"

"No, but they were traveling pretty fast. They were in their late teens, maybe early twenties."

"Tom said the house was really ransacked. They had to be searching for money or valuables."

"I suppose it's possible, but all of my money is with me." She tapped her purse in the seat next to her. "I have nothing of value to anyone but me."

"Someone may think you have something of value."

Etta squinted and shook her head, staring directly at Kate. "Bryan would not do this. For sure he wouldn't hire someone else to do it."

"You know him better than I do."

Without acknowledging Kate's remark, Etta got out of the car and picked up the groceries strewn at the bottom of the stairs. She sat down on the top step next to the collection.

Tom opened the driver's door and took Kate's hand, squeezing it gently.

Kate said, "I asked her a few questions. Maybe her answers will help."

"Etta seems calmer now. Thanks for speaking to her. I don't suppose you took notes."

Kate handed him her pocket recorder and smiled.

"Thanks," Tom said. "Maybe you can help her put things back together. It would be good if she can give us a list of anything that's missing. A patrolman will drive by at least once an hour for the next few days. But make sure she locks things up tight."

"Will do."

He took a few steps, then turned around. "I'll be in touch."

Kate joined Etta on the stairs and watched as each police vehicle drove away. "What can I do to help you?"

"I'd like to go see Sarah, or at least find out what's happening."

"We can do that. Would you like to go inside first?"

"How about we lock the door and go to the hospital?"

The two women spent almost thirty minutes trying to get information about Sarah's condition. Kicking herself for not doing so sooner, Kate finally enlisted Shirley's help.

"Strictly speaking, you didn't get this from me," her best friend said. "Nothing is broken. Her shoulder is bothering her. They are concerned about a concussion. She has a serious bruise on her forehead. They're waiting until her husband arrives to decide about keeping her overnight."

Etta said, "Thank you so much. They wouldn't tell us anything."

"You are most welcome. See you tomorrow for lunch, Katie."

"Thanks again. I owe you," Kate said.

"Lunch will do."

Kate convinced Etta to go home and check with Sarah's husband later. They stopped at the grocery store to get a couple items which didn't survive the rain. The reporter put the bags on the hall table, and then joined the older woman at the archway.

"I'm not sure where to begin," Etta said, bracing against the wall.

Every shelf in the living room had been emptied, including the mantel over the hearth. Fingerprint dust was everywhere. From where the women stood it was hard to tell how many of the boxes—now lying on the floor—were damaged. Restoring order seemed insurmountable.

Kate said, "Why don't we sit down and make a plan."

"Can we plan order out of chaos?"

"I'm ready if you are."

Getting comfortable on the sofa, Kate took Etta's hand in hers. They both sighed, unable to process the mess on the floor. Despite her qualms about seeing more damage, Kate ventured into the kitchen to brew some tea. *Nothing like a nice warm cup of chamomile to calm one's nerves.* At least she hoped that would be the case.

Everything seemed to be in place in the small room. The chamomile was in the first cabinet she tried—where her mother would have kept it given the layout of the cabinets. The third door was the charm in finding the kettle. It was a gas stove, which wasn't surprising. At *least I don't need a match like at Grandma's house.* While the tea was steeping, Kate found two mugs, then peeked into the living room to make sure Etta was okay.

She was not surprised to see the octogenarian sitting cross-legged next to one of the large bookshelves. Apparently, she'd already dusted each shelf. As she selected a box from the floor, she cleaned it, and returned it to the appropriate location. No doubt Etta knew where every item was displayed and would soon know which, if any, were missing.

The reporter placed one of the mugs on the table by the sofa and handed the other to Etta. Since she was halfway to the bedroom, she decided to see if the intruders went that far.

An old mahogany chest sat against the wall next to the closet. Every drawer and its contents were strewn on the bed or floor. A jewelry box had been emptied on top and tossed to the side of the room. The mattress was askew, and the closet door was open. All the hangers, many of which held nothing, had been moved to the sides. She suspected some of the clothes were in the pile on the floor.

Two places had not been touched, probably because of the resident's unexpected arrival. One was the nightstand by the bed. Three drawers remained shut. The items on the top—among which were two small boxes—were neatly arranged. The other area which seemed undisturbed were the two shelves in the closet over the hanger rod. Each held a couple of medium-sized storage boxes. A small suitcase was on the far left of the top shelf. A metal letter-sized file box lay empty on the floor, sheets of paper and folders strewn under and around it.

"Oh, my," Etta said, her hand covering her heart as she caught her breath at the bedroom door. In a moment, she moved to the bed and sat down, slowly taking in the turmoil.

"Are you okay? Maybe we've done enough today," Kate said.

Spying the discarded jewelry box, Etta crossed the room and returned it to the dresser. She replaced the contents, then paused to evaluate the arrangement. "Clay's wedding ring," she said, quickly examining the floor.

Kate joined the search and discovered a man's ring buried under several scarves. "Is this it?"

"Thank you." Etta took the ring and placed it carefully. She closed the top of the jewelry box and centered it on the dresser. After arranging some pictures and other items around it, she returned to the bed and sighed deeply.

Kate went back to the living room to get Etta's mug of tea. Two of the five shelves on the largest display case were back to normal. Most of the keepsakes were still in the center of the floor. The framed pictures had been returned to the mantelpiece, but the whatnots previously displayed with them were not. Kate scanned the floor and selected one of the items she remembered seeing—the one next to Clay and Etta's marriage photo.

As Kate returned to the bedroom she said, "You left your tea. And I found this. Can you help me put it in the correct spot on the mantel?" Etta accepted the mug and stared at the carved piece of wood in Kate's other hand. "Do you mind if I lay down for a while?" "No, that's a good idea. How about I grab a quilt and get you settled on the sofa."

Kate helped Etta into the living room and arranged the throw pillows at one end. She covered her with the quilt, then sat down in the chair by the window and finished her tea. "I'll try to put your things away in the closet and drawers. I may not get them in the right place, but they'll be off the floor."

Etta made a little sound, her eyes closed, the quilt nuzzled against her chin—tacit approval.

Before starting in the bedroom, Kate called Helen and explained the situation. Her boss understood but reminded her she had a deadline to meet for the weekend edition. She took a blouse from the floor, trying to remember how far she'd gotten on the history article. Somehow, it didn't seem important.

Most of the items were easily divided into the drawer or closet categories. The process took less time than expected. A pile of miscellaneous non-clothing items remained, which Kate allocated to the two small catch-all drawers at the top of the dresser. *Etta will have to divvy the items to the correct spot later.*

One square metal container was behind the dresser trapped between the bottom and the wall. She rocked the chest forward slightly and reached behind to recover the tin. With some difficulty she freed the top from the bottom's rusty hold. Fifty or so small keys–suitable for use in opening the collection of boxes–were inside. She took it with her to the living room, where Etta had resumed the task of restoring order to her shelves.

"Look what I found," Kate said, handing the metal box to Etta.

"Where was it?"

"Behind the dresser, for a long time by the look of it."

"I haven't seen it for a while. You're welcome to try to find the key for your box."

"I'm borrowing it, remember?"

"Yes, and it needs to have a key."

Kate accepted the proffered box and dropped it into her jacket pocket. Clearly that was the end of the discussion, at least for now. She called the hospital and was connected to Sarah's room. She had been admitted for observation and her husband suggested postponing a visit until the next day.

"Thank you for doing that," Etta said.

"How about I pick you up in the morning to go to the hospital. Is nine too early?"

"That would be fine."

"Don't forget to lock up everything when I leave."

Chapter Twenty

Helen's "see me" note was in the middle of Kate's desk. The reporter decided to make the corrections she'd marked on the draft so she'd be more prepared for the meeting. The last page was printing when her boss appeared in the doorway.

"Perfect timing. The draft is ready for you. If it's okay, I'd like to do one a week maybe putting more than one profile in each article."

"Sounds like a good approach," Helen said. "I recommend you start with people who are still alive, perhaps work in others who were contemporaries."

"Good idea," Kate said even though she already planned that approach.

"How's Etta?" Helen asked, accepting the pages. "Are you helping her again today?"

"I dropped her at the hospital. She'll stay with Sarah for a while and call me later. She's doing much better, moving into the angry stage. Her friend is doing okay too."

"That's good news."

Helen remained, but did not sit down. At the risk of a long conversation, Kate said, "Something else we need to discuss?"

"I've gotten a call. A complaint."

"About me?" Kate asked, trying to imagine what she'd done recently to offend someone.

"To be honest the complaint sounds like you were doing your job. But I want you to be aware so you can smooth things over. Maybe you can try a more subtle investigative technique."

Kate chuckled, then noticed her boss wasn't laughing. "I'm sorry, Helen. Smoothing things over and being subtle are not skills I have fully developed."

A whisper of movement in Helen's lips, then a full-out smile.

"Who made the complaint?" Kate asked.

"A city councilman."

"Let me guess. Larry Allen."

"Yes. He says that you've agitated ... he actually used that word ... his grandfather. And that you've interfered in his business. And last, certainly not least, that you have been snooping at City Hall."

"Snooping?"

"You have obviously made an impact on his life."

"He doesn't like me."

"Since he wouldn't give me specifics, I'll say go easy with him. See what you can do about developing those people skills."

Well, Helen's attitude toward me has certainly changed. Maybe mine has too. Either way, working with her has been much more enjoyable lately.

Kate rounded up photographer Barry Turner and headed toward Table Rock Lake and her appointment with Harold Wainright. The new area-resident had agreed to what Kate told him was a customary profile on interesting transplants to the Ozarks. Fortunately, he enjoyed her articles on Etta and Branson in general, so he agreed. She decided it would be more productive—if not easier—to go to the source. Sitting on hold for ever or trying to figure out what an internet was and what it could do for a journalist did not appeal to her.

Barry, a willowy brown-haired twenty-one-year-old, joined the part-timers at *Tri-Lakes News* last spring. He primarily helped the staff with research but had been pressed into service more recently to take photos for various articles. Besides, Barry wouldn't lend her the camera, which he had owned since being on the high school yearbook staff—not too long ago.

Getting to the lake road turn-off was a cinch, after that Marge's directions became a challenge. The looping roads and hidden turns weren't unusual for the area around Table Rock. The lake itself was created in the late 1950s when the White River was dammed not too far south of Branson. It served as a major tourist attraction with all the fishing and camping, enhanced by the beautiful, still rustic, scenery.

The final turn led to an asphalt road which curved in front of a simple log structure perhaps forty feet wide. A separate two-car wooden garage sat at the far end of the curve, which headed back to the main road. A matching wooden covered walkway spanned the distance from the garage to the house.

Kate continued on to a cleared area so as not to obstruct the photography. Barry snapped several shots from various angles as the two approached the entrance. The clear sky and fall foliage made for a breathtaking view.

Harold Wainright greeted them almost immediately and ushered them inside. He was at least two inches shy of Barry's six-foot-one height. His well-groomed thick dark hair somehow made him seem taller. But the most disarming aspect of her subject was his ear-to-ear warm smile and cordial demeanor.

The foyer ran the entire length of the building. Across from the door, the largest picture window Kate had ever seen provided a panoramic view of the lake and surrounding hills. Hallways exited the entryway to the left and right. Although the wood paneling was impressive and the entry spectacular, the place had been grossly overpriced.

But first impressions can be deceiving. Their host turned left and down a short hallway, at the end of which a curved stairway descended into the main—and previously hidden—part of the house. Barry started clicking at the top of the stairs and didn't stop until he reached the bottom. He continued, as if mesmerized, to the center of the lakeside wall, a series of glass doors framed in oak.

"My wife fixed some iced tea and lemonade," Wainright said, motioning toward the bar at the back of the fifty-by-fifty-foot room. "Help yourself."

Barry took some shots of the view, including one with Wainright posed next to the center door. The width of the deck beyond the glass wall matched the room, with L-shaped extensions on either side. A relatively small hot tub occupied one of the extensions. Three separate conversation areas took up the rest of the deck area.

"This is amazing," Kate said.

"We were pleased to find it," Wainright said.

"I'd love to include your wife in the interview."

"Rachel planned to be here, but something came up with the volunteer work she's doing. It was unavoidable."

"I'll leave my card. If she'd like to meet me somewhere to chat, that would be great."

He took the card and placed it on the table next to the sofa, then sat down across from Kate in an oversized chair next to the hearth that dominated one wall.

"If it's okay, Barry will take a few pictures while we talk. Then he'll probably go out on the deck and gawk at the lake."

Wainright chuckled. "You're welcome to wander around, Barry. That stairway on the left goes down to a path below the deck leading to our dock."

"Of course it does," the photographer mumbled.

Once Kate cleared the use of the recorder, she asked a few introductory questions.

Wainright and his wife, as many before them, had come to the area to retire after spending several vacations over the years. He loved to fish and they both loved boating and hiking. It was an easy and natural choice for them. His wife had jumped in quickly to do volunteer work at the hospital. She'd been a nurse when they met and for a brief time after they married in the 1960s. He spent twelve years in the United States Air Force with his final tour in Southeast Asia.

"You got out after twelve years?" Kate asked.

"I was too old to risk another tour in that war. Rachel and I were married four months before I left for Vietnam. She begged me not to reenlist. To be honest, I was easily convinced."

"And after the air force?"

"When we separated from the service, we went to Evanston, Illinois, close to Rachel's family. Living near my family was not a good option. I used the GI Bill to finish my degree at Northwestern University. Eventually we moved to Chicago."

Wainright told of how they struggled as a couple with three young children in a Chicago suburb during the 1970s. He commuted to his entry level position at a real estate development company in the city. He got his big break by impressing the CEO of a rival firm with his expertise. That company—Illinois Land Futures Inc.—offered him a promotion, a corner office, and more money.

"And you'd found a home."

"For over twenty-five years."

"Still, you were young when you retired."

"The time was right."

"Fair enough. But you've been here for a year or so and recently purchased some residential properties."

"You've done your research."

"I have a few sources. So, are you going to expand that new venture?"

"Anything is possible. But I'm basically a frustrated retired workaholic. I tried some volunteer work, thanks to Rachel's urging, but it wasn't enough. I'm not embarrassed to admit I like to make money."

"Not much remuneration in volunteer work. You should join the area Chamber of Commerce."

"Started attending meetings last spring. Branson is a charming town that's expanding at an exponential rate. It would be dishonest to say I'm not interested in taking that ride."

"Plenty of contacts at the chamber. I'm not sure how many big players we have, but they care about the city and the area."

"I met a couple of players."

"Jack Brighton was one," she guessed.

"I'm impressed."

"Don't be. He's one of the few in town who are in your league."

"Smart and blunt too."

"Sorry, I'm told I need to tone it down some."

"Don't listen to that advice."

"Well, I'm sure you and Mr. Brighton got along. Did you meet his grandson?"

"I've spoken to his son, Randy, and his grandson. Larry Allen, right?"

"You all will make a good team," she said, fishing a bit.

"You may be jumping the gun on that collaboration, Kate. I've purchased a half dozen rentals, nothing more."

"This area, especially Branson, is breaking loose, Mr. Wainright. Anything is possible."

"That's what Larry tells me."

She decided not to press her luck regarding other gems Larry imparted.

The spicy smell of fall filled the air, damp leaves covering the path, as Wainright walked her down to the dock. Barry was sitting next to his boots at the end, his bare feet dangling in the water.

"Time to head back, Barry," Kate shouted.

"Sorry, can't hear you," came the reply.

In fact, she also hated to leave. Something about the water and the bucolic atmosphere relaxed her. Maybe she and Tom could live on the lake.

When she returned to the newspaper office, she drafted a piece without reviewing the tape. She'd listen to it later and expand the article for Helen's review. Maybe the Branson transplant series is a good idea after all.

A message from Marge requested Kate to call, but she walked up the street to Connarde Realty instead. One of the best things about being a reporter was not staying in the stuffy office all day. With that in mind, she invited Marge to take a walk to the lakefront to discuss their mutual progress.

"I interviewed Wainright at his home this morning," Kate began. "You were right about the house and the setting. He seemed like a nice man. I'm doing an article for the paper, so I won't spoil it for you. But he knows both Brightons and Larry Allen."

"Lots of people know them. It doesn't mean they're in cahoots," Marge said.

"I know. Something about how coy he was when we discussed them. I wouldn't be surprised to see them join forces someday."

"We'll see, I suppose. This is a list of the lakefront owners who've been approached to sell. As you can see, I'm a frustrated spreadsheet creator."

"No kidding. Name of owner and/or resident, address of property, sale/no sale, who approached each owner. This is great."

"Thanks. I'll keep my eyes and ears open for more activity."

Kate tucked the pages into her pocket. "I'm afraid I didn't find out anything at Branson City Hall. My contacts are limited, and the city administrator has warned people not to speak to the media. I've asked my dad to check with some of his old planning commission contacts to see if anything is cooking. The city can't do anything in secret, but I was hoping to find out about long-term plans. Turns out the only thing going on is the city hall expansion, which is slated to begin in two or three years."

Marge said, "The Chamber has undertaken something interesting. But don't get your hopes up. It may not be a big deal. I only wish I participated in the committees."

"Because ..."

"One of the groups is doing a big survey. They've sent out hundreds of questionnaires to small, medium, and large companies nationwide. The majority are in the Midwest, but the committee figured it was worth the price of postage to ask."

"And they were asking?"

"What would make you bring your company meetings to Branson? You know, things like how big would the meeting rooms need to be, how many would you use, how many hotel rooms, what other activities would be of interest? It goes on and on."

"I don't suppose you have a copy."

"I have one in my office ... just for you ... including a list of the companies."

"Great," Kate said. "When was it sent out?"

"Several months ago."

"Which means they've been working on it for a while."

"A company developed the questionnaire, but certainly members of the committee provided input and review. A list of members is on the contact page by the way."

"It does sound interesting."

"I suppose, but this is what chambers of commerce do. They hope to encourage people with money to come to the area."

"Knowing what will get them to come is clearly important. Can you find out the status of responses? They should have some preliminary data by now."

"I'll give it a try. Can't hurt to seem interested."

Kate waited in the chairs not far from the nurses' station while Etta wrapped up her visit with Sarah. She was reviewing her notes on Wainright when a familiar voice stopped to speak to a nurse. By the time the butterflies in her tummy stopped fluttering, Tom was next to her chair.

"Hi, Katie. Thanks again. The tape of your interrogation was a big help."

"Interview. You interrogate. I interview. And you are welcome. I hope you can arrest whoever trashed Etta's house."

"Did she say anything else?"

"It was a pretty traumatic afternoon putting everything back together."

"I'll bet. I'd like to ask her a couple more questions."

"Etta's in with Sarah now."

Tom motioned to Sid, who tapped the door jamb as the two detectives disappeared into the room.

Kate was finishing her notes when the policemen and Etta stopped in front of her. "All set to go home?" Kate asked.

"This nice young man of yours is going to take me."

Kate grinned in Tom's direction. "That's very sweet of you, Detective Collingwood."

She took Etta by the arm and walked her to the elevator, Sid and Tom following closely behind. They rode silently down to the lobby level. The police vehicle was parked close to the door, so Kate said her goodbyes as they exited the building. She smiled all the way to her car thinking about that *nice young man* of hers.

Chapter Twenty-One

Tom and Sid's discussion with Etta took less than twenty minutes, including the seven silent ones between her house and the hospital. Gathering no case information beyond that on Kate's recording, the senior detective learned more about the victim herself.

"Something's off," he said, after the two men were summarily ushered out of the octogenarian's house.

Sid said, "Other than your interrogation skills?"

"Her frustration has nothing to do with me. Look, she may simply be an angry victim of an assault on her privacy and safety. But in my opinion, there's a lot more beneath the surface."

Tory's Treasures were closer to old junk, at least from Tom's vantage point by the entrance. Nevertheless, the parking lot was full—three tourist busses and a dozen or so automobiles—and so was the store.

The thirty-something man at the register put down his comic book when the officers entered.

"Where can I direct you gentlemen? Looking for anything specific?"

"Bryan Porter," Sid said.

"Sorry, he's not working today."

"Any idea where we might find him?"

"I just watch the counter. Check with the office lady. Take aisle four all the way back."

"Thanks," Tom said.

A picture window on the back wall revealed the tiny office. A woman, probably in her late fifties, sat at the desk with the view of the store. Smoke from a cigarette encircled her head, blending in with her mostly gray disheveled hair. The pungent odor hung in the short hallway by the door. She gazed at her visitors as she crushed the butt in the already overfilled ashtray.

Tom introduced himself and his partner as he showed the woman his badge. "Man up front said you might know where Bryan Porter is today."

"At home, I'd guess."

"We checked there," Sid said.

"City Hall maybe. He likes to go and stir things up sometimes."

"Any other guesses?"

"To be honest, Bryan hasn't been in the store for a while."

She stood up and extended her hand to each man. Her petite stature, belied by the raspy, deep voice. "I'm his cousin, Sylvia. I do the books and keep an eye on things."

"Your last name?" Sid asked, taking out his notepad.

"Lockhart."

"Does your husband help with the store too?"

"Never been married. My mother was Bryan's aunt."

"When was the last time you saw your cousin?" Tom asked.

She shuffled some papers scattered across the desk and held one so Tom could read it. "I filled this out for him to review and sign two weeks ago. It's due to the state of Missouri by the end of next month, so I haven't pressed it, but I did leave a message."

"Did he say when he'd be in?"

"Never returned my call."

"Aren't you worried about him?"

"This is not unusual for Bryan. But, yeah, I sent one of the kids who work for us to check on him. He was sitting on his porch."

"And that was when?"

"Five days ago, three days ago, and yesterday. The kid said Bryan had different clothes on, so I figured he was still alive."

Tom stifled a snicker as he handed her his card. "Please tell him to contact us as soon as possible. He can come to our office in City Hall or phone that number."

She pinned the card to a small bulletin board close to the door and returned to her desk. When Tom glanced back halfway down aisle four, Sylvia was on the phone having an animated conversation, the newly lit cigarette hanging from her lips.

"Charming family," Sid said.

"Explains a lot," Tom commented. "I think she called him when we left. Let's drop by his house on the way back to the office. Maybe he ignored our knock before."

As they pulled out of the parking lot, dispatch radioed for them to see Larry Allen at his job site. No additional information was provided by Palmer when he requested the relay.

"I wager Allen has been chewing Dan about releasing the lot again," Tom said.

"No bet."

Allen wasn't in his office trailer when the detectives arrived, but he came charging out of the building before they could find someone to ask about his location. His face was flush and his jaw taut when he met them halfway across the still unfinished lot. Tom knew the man had a temper, but he'd never seen him this upset.

"Where have you been? I spoke to Lieutenant Palmer hours ago."

"We came as soon as possible," Tom said, glancing at Sid.

"Good thing Porter didn't do anything worse than rant and rave at me."

"Porter was here?" Tom asked.

"Tell me you're surprised he violated the restraining order."

"This happened today?"

"No. Last week, and then last night."

"Why did you wait to call Lieutenant Palmer?"

"Last week I reminded Porter about the protection order. He left in a huff but didn't make much of a scene, so I was going to ignore it. But last night he went crazy. It took me and another guy to get him off the lot."

"Can we go somewhere to discuss what happened?" Tom asked.

"I don't want to discuss it. I want you to take care of it. I've got a business to run and have lost enough time trying to fend off this lunatic."

Tom said, "Mr. Allen, I understand you're upset, but we need specifics to file an official complaint. How about your office?"

Allen's brow furrowed, his face now a light pink. He turned sharply and made a beeline to the trailer. Opening the door, he waited at the bottom of the two steps for the detectives to enter. When he joined them, he motioned to the office toward the back of the unit. He leaned against his worktable and bowed his head.

"I shouldn't take my anger out on you guys," he said with a sincere smile. "But the man gets more and more erratic with every attack."

"Tell us about the times he's approached you. How does he act? What does he say?"

"How much time do you have?"

"Whatever it takes," Tom said.

Allen spent the next several minutes criticizing Porter's suit against the city. His voice became louder and more enraged with each point as he denied the veracity of the accusations. He then recounted each time Porter visited the job site or City Hall to accost the councilman. In the end, he stopped in midsentence and shook his head.

"What I've told you is summarized in the request for the restraining order. I'm not sure what can be accomplished by going over the details."

Tom glanced over the notes he'd been taking. "One thing is missing in both your complaint and what you've told us today. Give us specifics about what you call Porter's ravings. You've mainly identified accusations he made in his suit against Branson. Has he raised additional claims, demands, or threats toward you or your company?"

"The truth is what he says, the words, don't make sense. He's like a gnat flying around your head but really loud and in your face."

Sid chimed in with a different approach. "Mr. Allen, if we know more about Porter's beef with you, it may help us talk to him and call him off."

"That's the weird thing. He attacks my family in general, like *you all* ruined my life. Last night he went on about how the truth will come out. More than once he's said we took what was rightfully his."

"Have you discussed this with your family?" Sid asked.

"Numerous times."

"How did they respond?"

"Uncle Randy says Porter was a troubled boy and has grown into a troubled man."

"That's it?" Tom asked.

"Neither my uncle, nor my grandfather, comprehend the rants any more than I do."

⟡

"Light's on. Maybe he's home," Tom said as Sid parked in front of Porter's house.

Sid said, "The least he could do is leave his truck outside the garage, so we'd know."

"We can mention that next time we see him."

Several knocks brought no response, so Sid wrote a note on the back of his card and slipped it between the door and the jamb. Before Sid could start the car, Porter drove by the house, speeding up as he passed.

"He can't seriously be avoiding us," Sid said.

"All evidence to the contrary. Let's follow him. He'll probably pull over."

"And if he doesn't?"

"I guess we'll have something else to talk to him about."

They caught up with him at a stop sign at the intersection of his road and Highway 76. He was two cars in front of them. When he turned onto a side road into an old residential area, they followed. Tom put the emergency light on the dash and turned on the red beacon. Porter sped up for a couple blocks, but Sid closed the gap without effort. Tom flicked the siren on and off, causing one shrill bleep. One more block and Porter pulled to the right and parked.

Tom walked to the driver's side of Porter's truck. The window came down slowly. "Guess you didn't see us at your house."

"Didn't notice. I remembered I had to be somewhere. Then I saw someone tailing me and I panicked."

"Maybe you missed the light and siren too."

"To be fair, Tom, that's when I pulled over, as soon as I saw it was you."

"We need to talk, Bryan."

"Like I said, I'm on my way some place right now."

"Not back to Councilman Allen's construction site, I hope."

Porter shook his head.

"Okay. It's getting late. Come by the station nine o'clock tomorrow morning and be prepared for a long talk."

Chapter Twenty-Two

Kate punched redial for one final try and was taken aback when a real person—not the message system—came on the line. "Hi, I'm calling Kyle Henderson. Is he available?"

"Sorry, I thought this was my call. Let me see if I can find Kyle."

Several minutes went by and Kate was about to hang up when the line clicked.

"This is Kyle Henderson."

"Mr. Henderson, I've been given your name as someone who might be interested in purchasing property in Branson, Missouri."

"Depends. May I ask your name?"

"Margaret Carson," Kate said, using her mother's maiden name.

"Are you interested in selling your land in Branson, Miss Carson?"

"I'd like to explore the possibility. Are you representing a buyer or yourself?"

"Would that make a difference?"

"Branson is a small town, Mr. Henderson. I would want to know who the actual purchaser is."

"Certainly. Let's start by your telling me the location."

Kate included the address and phone number for her father's motel. She knew Henderson would check it out, so she said she was calling for Roger Duane Starling, the current owner and a close friend. The broker said he'd do some research, speak to appropriate clients, and get back to her within forty-eight hours. They could move forward with an on-site inspection at that time. She gave him her home phone number for future contacts. As soon as she hung up, she called her father to tell him what she had done and ask him to play along.

"You know, I was hurt because you were using Margie as your investigative assistant. I finally feel like part of the team."

"Cute, Dad. Thanks."

Shirley was already at the restaurant. Kate never beat her friend to a meeting place, even when it was down the street from the newspaper. Shirley waved as Kate made her way across the room, weaving around the closely arranged tables.

"I suppose you've already ordered for me," Kate said, sitting across the table.

"No, I just arrived."

"So close," Kate whispered, picking up the menu.

The lunch crowd of about thirty filled the small restaurant's dozen or so tables. The small staff had no trouble keeping up. One of the three waitresses took Kate and Shirley's orders then brought their iced teas. Kate was making mental notes about her conversation with Henderson and hadn't noticed the patrons standing by the door.

"So, how's it going with Tom?" Shirley asked.

"Great. Absolutely great."

"Is that why he followed you to the restaurant?"

Kate turned toward the entrance where Sid and Tom were speaking to one of the staff. The waitress nodded and the two detectives crossed the room and stood next to Kate's table.

"Do you want to join us?" she asked, glancing at Shirley who shrugged her approval.

"Our table will be ready in a couple minutes, but I wanted to say hello," Tom said, pulling out one of the empty chairs.

"Sid, this is my best friend Shirley Barrens. She works at the hospital in the administrator's office," Kate said.

Shirley and Sid said, "Nice to meet you," simultaneously, and then started laughing.

"Thanks again for helping out with Etta," Tom said. "She can be a handful."

"She definitely is strong-willed," Kate said.

"That sweet lady you brought to the hospital yesterday was the woman you wrote about in your articles?" Shirley asked.

Before Kate could respond, Sid smiled at Shirley and said, "She nearly bit my head off when I tried to question her."

The waitress returned to the table with two menus. "Do you boys want to stay here?"

Tom poked Sid's arm and responded, "No. Lead the way."

Shirley, who had been staring in the direction of the departing detectives, turned her head and blushed.

Kate said, "You are truly smitten."

"I am not *smitten*. But he is kind of cute. Too young for me, though."

"*Au contraire*, my friend. He's only three years younger than us."

"Hmm."

"Does that mean you're interested?"

"We were talking about you and Tom," Shirley said.

"We're making progress. All I have to do is keep my reporter hat and my girlfriend hat in separate closets."

"How hard can that be?"

Kate shrugged. "By the way, thank you for getting that info for Etta yesterday. She was beside herself worrying about her friend."

"I didn't tell her much."

"Enough to calm her down. We were able to return to her house and put everything back together."

"How bad was it? I haven't heard anything about the break-in."

"Someone trashed a couple rooms. Apparently, Etta and Sarah surprised them."

"Any idea who?"

"One, but Etta doesn't agree."

"Someone she knows?"

"Bryan Porter. His father was one of her best friends."

"The guy who owns that flea market we went to a couple months ago? Somebody's Treasures?"

"*Tory's* Treasures. That's him."

"I seem to recall my dad helping him out once. It was a while ago, before I went to college. No big deal."

"If your dad helped him, it is a big deal. Bryan feels like he's been shafted most of his life. He blames the world for ruining his family and his life."

"The world of Fortune Enterprises?"

"Mostly," Kate agreed. "How did your dad help him?"

"I'm not sure about the details. Porter was getting a divorce and was in some kind of bind. I'm not even sure why Dad got involved."

"Bryan Porter was married?"

"Why not? Many people get married."

"I've spoken to quite a few people about the guy lately and no one has mentioned a former wife."

"It would have been in the 70s. Why do you care?"

"I don't. I'm naturally curious, I suppose."

"You are *nosy*," Shirley corrected as the waitress placed their meals on the table.

"It is part of my job description. And speaking of nosy, let's talk about you and Sid."

Shirley scowled mid-bite and said, "I'm not quite over that little marriage of mine."

"The divorce was final seven years ago," Kate said.

"Six years and eight months," Shirley said.

"Long enough to move on."

"You may have forgotten, I've tried to move on with several charming fellows, none of which survived more than three months and the last of which took a hike only five months ago."

"All I can say is you never eyed any of those charming dudes like you did Sid. Maybe he's worth a try. And, lucky you, I have a way to make that happen."

"Is this my payback for encouraging you to get back together with Tom?"

"Yes, but consider it a reward."

Shirley made no other comment regarding Sid Green, which Kate interpreted as a go-ahead to set them up for a double date with her and Tom—a little surprise for her friend.

Kate walked the short distance to City Hall to speak to Libby who went to school and graduated with Shirley and Kate. Since becoming the city engineer's secretary Libby had proven to be a willing and usually reliable source at City Hall.

Claire was mumbling to herself as she organized a large pile of blueprints at the table behind the customer counter.

"Hi, Claire," Kate said, causing the woman to turn around.

"Good morning. Sorry, I was trying to vanquish this chaos."

"Always a noble gesture."

"Thanks again, for lunch."

"It was fun. We'll have to make it a monthly thing," Kate said. "Do you happen to know where your office mate is?"

"Right behind you," Libby said, making a grand entrance. "I was at the copier. I seem to spend a lot of time at the copier." She stacked a huge pile of paper on the counter and slapped the top page. "And this is for one meeting."

"Sounds like fun," Kate said. "Can you squeeze me in? I have a few questions for the real manager of engineering."

"You do know how to grease those skids. Have a seat."

Kate retrieved the project list from her bag and placed it in front of her friend. "Something is missing from this list," she said.

"I can't imagine we have an error on our log," Libby said with a smile. "Tell me what's missing and maybe Claire or I can solve the mystery."

"There's no project development listed for the St. Limas lot where the skeleton was discovered. From what I understand, it's unusual for a lot to be cleared without a plan in place for use of the land. The clearing permit submitted by Councilman Allen is on file, but nothing else has been done."

"Well, you're correct in your assumption. Maybe this is one of those things that slipped through the cracks in the system, which is full of large cracks, as you know. Have you spoken to the councilman about this?"

"He gave me a couple of answers to pick from. I wondered if your boss had discussed the lot with Allen."

"I'm not sure. He visits Calvin on occasion regarding official city business. I'm not aware of any meetings concerning this lot. Do you want to set up an appointment?"

"I'd rather avoid the traditional response to a reporter. Would you be able to casually approach the subject?"

Libby furrowed her brow slightly and smiled. "You want me to snoop around for you?"

"Like you said, your system has cracks. I'm thinking he'd be more receptive to your inquiring about a possible oversight. At best, Calvin is aware of specific development and everything is fine."

"Let me see what I can find," she said.

"Thanks. Anything you can share would be super."

Chapter Twenty-Three

When Kate returned Jack Brighton's "urgent" phone call, she reached his secretary, who said Mr. Brighton wanted to see her immediately about the article she'd sent for him to review. Kate wasn't sure why he wanted to meet in person and could not imagine an urgency applied to the article contents. A simple phone call with changes would have sufficed, unless he hated the article beyond imagining. The reporter shook off the silly notion as she entered the office suite, where she was immediately taken to Brighton's office.

"Kate, come in. You remember my son, Randy," Jack said.

"Nice to see you again, Kate," Randy said. "I'm off to St. Louis, but I wanted to compliment you on your article about Riverside Mercantile."

Jack nodded toward his son and said, "Keep me posted on your progress."

As soon as Randy left, Kate said. "Your secretary said you wanted to discuss the article. Did you hate it?"

"Absolutely not. As Randy said we wanted to tell you in person how much we enjoyed it. It was accurate and made the time seem more interesting than I remember."

Although Brighton wouldn't hurt her—at least not in his own office—she was beginning to feel a little nervous. Complimenting her profusely couldn't be the only reason he wanted to see her. She wished he'd say what he needed to say or ask what he wanted to ask and let her move on.

Taking a chair close to Kate's, he leaned forward as if preparing to tell her a secret. "I'm sorry, I don't mean to seem mysterious," he said, apparently reading her puzzled expression. "To be blunt, I'm concerned about Etta."

Now she was totally baffled. Why would he want to discuss Etta with a reporter? The woman seemed genuinely fond of Kate, but nothing more. Certainly, their newly formed relationship was trumped by an indisputably loyal friendship of over seventy years. Something told her Brighton was fishing so she waited for him to continue.

"I know you've spent a good bit of time with my friend these last few weeks. Has she said anything about a problem with Bryan Porter?"

"Not specifically," Kate said.

"You know who he is?"

"He owns the Tory's Treasures flea market on West 76."

Brighton moved close to the edge of his chair. "I gather he's been threatening Etta."

"Did *she* tell you that?"

"She told Randy and me that Bryan came to her house demanding her help."

"That happened two weeks ago," Kate said.

"But now his behavior has become more radical. He's been harassing Larry at the job site and has called Etta several times regarding his demands."

"But Etta said Bryan had nothing to do with the break-in at her house."

He came off the chair and moved to the center of the room. When he turned back toward Kate his face was flushed. "I'm sorry. I've heard nothing about this."

Kate said, "Etta's okay. Nothing has been released by the police."

"But you know about it."

"Detective Collingwood called me. He knew I wrote the articles about the crafts fair. Etta was upset and he hoped I could help."

"Porter's not a suspect?"

Kate shook her head and decided it was time for her to do a little fishing of her own. "I know Porter has a thing about Fortune Enterprises. He's been in Larry's face on more than one occasion."

"His attacks have escalated to an intolerable level. He's even tried to get past my receptionist and secretary to see me."

"Good luck with that," Kate said with a smile.

"Unfortunately for Larry, he's accessible. He doesn't have anything to do with Porter's beef against the company."

"What is his beef?"

Brighton stared intently into Kate's eyes. She suspected he was considering the wisdom of revealing family secrets to a reporter so she threw him a little more bait.

"Etta told me it has to do with Bryan's father."

"Did she elaborate?"

"Only that Bryan was wrong about what happened and that she couldn't help him."

Kate decided against bringing up what Porter ranted toward her in the grocery store parking lot about the deal going sour between his father and Brighton. "Clearly something has bugged him for a long time," she said. "I assume the success of your company and the relative failure of his own has intensified the grudge."

"I'd say you're correct. So much so that Larry has taken legal action to keep the lunatic off company property."

"And that's why you're concerned about Etta?"

"I wanted to make sure she was not being harassed by Porter. I've spoken to her, but she says everything is okay. I wanted your take on the situation and I appreciate your input. I'm looking forward to seeing our story in the paper."

"It will be in the weekend edition."

"Let me know what I can do to help you. In exchange, I'll ask you to keep me posted about my friend."

Kate wasn't sure what that meant exactly. But becoming an agent for Jack Brighton, no matter the cause, did not sound like a good idea. She walked back to her office, still mulling over the strange exchange. As usual, she was greeted by a note from Helen requesting a meeting. Her boss was on the phone, so Kate tapped the door jamb and waited for a motion to enter.

"You're back," Helen said, hanging up the phone. "How did it go with Brighton?"

"Rather interesting if somewhat unnerving," Kate said. "He asked me about Etta. Specifically, if she's been harassed by Bryan Porter."

"Seems a bit bizarre he'd ask you, since they're lifelong friends."

"The topper is he wants me to keep him posted," Kate said, using air quotes. "Another interesting tidbit ... Allen has apparently taken out a protection order against Porter who, according to Jack, has been escalating his attacks."

"Better Porter than you, I suppose."

"No doubt. Is that what you wanted, or do you have an extremely exciting new assignment for me?"

"Maybe more exciting than a crafts fair. I'm sure you've seen Barry's photos of the recent fires by the lakefront. So far, we've run them with extensive captions."

"You want me to see if we have a serial arsonist loose in Branson?"

"If that's what the evidence shows, yes. In any case, three fires in the last two months are worth your time to investigate and do a comprehensive article."

"Will do. By the way, I forwarded the Riverside Mercantile article to you. Brighton loved it. The next in the series, about the first country music group in Branson, is finished. The current members of the family are reviewing it."

"Keep the articles coming. I've enjoyed getting accolades rather than complaints."

"We are working on our people skills," Kate said, turning to head back to her desk.

Before meeting with the Branson Fire Chief, Kate called Harold Wainright, who had–according to Marge's list–been modest about his Chamber involvement. "I understand you're on a chamber committee that is doing a nationwide survey for the Branson area."

"That's correct," he said after a moment's hesitation.

"I'd be interested in hearing about any responses you've received and how the committee plans to proceed with the project."

Another pause. "Kate, your best bet would be to contact the chamber president."

"Why? Is the committee's activity a secret?"

"No, of course not. The truth is we don't expect to see the survey analysis report for months. Beyond that, I'm not sure what the protocol is for releasing information. I'm sure the survey responses will be shared, but not by a phone call with a committee member."

"I see your point. I guess coming from a big city, you aren't familiar with how information is distributed in a small town. We may not use as much caution as we should."

"Right," he said, a slight chuckle in his voice.

"It seemed like it might be an interesting addition to my article about you. I've mentioned your chamber membership, but this committee sounds so proactive for the area. Folks should know you've become a contributing citizen of the community."

"That's nice, but–"

"I heard the survey was your idea," she lied.

"I was part of a committee."

"I'd want to make sure everyone involved gets credit."

When he didn't respond, she read the committee member names from the list on the survey to refresh his memory.

After a pause, he said, "I'm not sure who brought up a survey first. Your best bet is to contact the chamber for an official statement."

Wainright's hesitation to share harmless, public information triggered her cynicism, but she stopped pushing. "I'll do that. By the way, your article will be faxed to you by the end of the week. Let me know, if you have any questions or comments."

"I'll give you a call when I've read it."

"Thanks for your time today," she said.

"No problem. Sorry I couldn't be of more help."

Kate doubted that. Maybe it was a cultural difference, but he seemed unnecessarily tight-lipped about a business survey. She decided to have Helen approach the chamber president at the next meeting. Too bad her boss wasn't on the survey committee.

Branson Fire Chief Theodore Scherington—Theo to his friends and co-workers—was in his small office in City Hall. He ran his fingers through his graying hair and spoke to the computer monitor taking up much of his desk.

"When are you going to get a real office?" Kate said.

He greeted her with a hug then pulled back. "This *is* a real office, which, I might add, you don't visit often enough. How's old Roger doing?"

"Dad's fine."

"I bet he's more than fine. Margie Connarde is a sweet lady."

"Yeah. I was a little freaked out at first, but she's been good for him."

"I was a little jealous when I found out they were dating."

"Like you don't have the best wife ever?"

"You're right. Forty years last July. But I'm guessing you want to talk about the recent fires by the lakefront not the love lives of two doddering old fools."

"How'd you know?"

"A good investigative journalist can smell a story. Look, I'm not saying we found anything definite in our investigation. You could call it a gut feeling."

"You mean the intuition of a man who's been Chief of the Branson Fire Department for over twenty years?"

"That's what I mean."

"Can I get copies of the reports?"

"You bet. They're public record, after all," he said moving to the file cabinet.

As he copied the report pages and accompanying photos, he summarized each incident from damage to cause. When he offered to take her on a tour of the three houses, she jumped at the chance.

Each building was a small residential unit not far from the park at the north edge of the lakefront. The fires had been extinguished quickly. In one case, only the porch was burned. In another, a window and part of the roof were gone. They were all rentals, still unrepaired and standing vacant. The relatively minor damage nevertheless put each owner out of business at least temporarily.

"The Fire Marshall declared them all accidental," Theo said. "And I couldn't find any reason to disagree with his findings."

"But you have your doubts," Kate said.

"Somehow, it's too neat, too easy. They are all separate with different owners, different circumstances, different causes, and definitely no proof of anything approaching arson."

"Just a gut feeling," Kate said before the two parted company. She hadn't told Theo, but she recognized the three owners as individuals who were on Marge's approached-to-sell list. That may mean something or nothing, but in her reporter's opinion it was an unlikely coincidence.

Chapter Twenty-Four

Tom and Sid waited as the duty watchman escorted Porter to the interrogation room not far from the jail holding cells, hoping the formality would convey the importance of the questioning. The detectives' soft approach during the last few weeks had fallen on deaf ears.

Sid motioned toward a chair when the visitor arrived and closed the door.

Tom said, "Thanks for coming in."

"Like I had a choice," Porter whispered.

"You have a choice," Sid said.

"And you can have a lawyer present, if you want," Tom added.

Porter pushed the chair back and headed for the door.

"But answering a few questions and taking a little advice might be your best bet."

"Or else?"

"No threat. We're simply trying to mitigate a situation," Tom said.

The older man returned to the chair, leaned back, and folded his arms across his chest. His lips tightly pursed, he stared straight ahead, avoiding eye contact with both officers.

Tom leaned toward him, hands outstretched as if pleading a case. "Bryan, we've known each other since I was a kid. I remember you as a nice man who gave me odd jobs on the weekends and during the summer."

"What happened to that nice man?" Sid asked.

Porter shrugged.

"Something happened," Tom began. "Something made you angry enough to assault an alderman. Something made you escalate your attacks to a point warranting an order of protection against you. If Councilman Allen has done something to you, revenge is not the answer."

"Allen isn't my problem," Porter said.

"You *made* him your problem," Sid countered, pacing the room.

"His family ruined my father's life. They took everything from him."

"Jack Brighton?"

"And his worthless son."

"You say they took everything from your father. Explain." Tom said.

Porter shook his head. "It doesn't matter."

Tom said, "Obviously it matters to you. But why now? Your father hasn't lived in this town for a long time. What made you start this vendetta now?"

"My therapist says I have baggage," Porter said, looking directly at Tom.

"You've been seeing a therapist?" Sid asked, leaning on the table.

"My mother died six months ago. Things seemed to bubble to the surface. I couldn't sleep.

My doctor recommended a guy in Springfield. I quit going after a few sessions."

"No kidding," Sid said not quietly enough, provoking a scowl from Tom.

"They chased my dad out of town and broke my mother's heart. She never recovered."

"Is that why you sued the city of Branson ... to get even with Jack Brighton?"

"No."

"But Fortune Enterprises takes the brunt of your accusations," Tom said.

"Maybe."

"Speaking of your accusations, how did you come up with them? The suit doesn't contain many details," Sid said.

"I didn't make anything up, if that's what you mean. Everything is true."

"Okay, let's move on to the break-in at Etta Stupholds' house," Tom said.

"What break-in?"

"Where were you two days ago?"

"I suppose I was at the flea market. I sure wasn't breaking into Etta's."

"According to your accountant, you haven't been in the store for at least two weeks. You argued with Etta recently about something she had that belonged to you. Is that what you were searching for when you tore her house apart?"

"Absolutely not," Porter shouted.

"Maybe you hired someone to do it."

Porter slammed both palms on the table and stood up. "I would never do anything to hurt Etta. She was like a second mother to me as a child. At least before ..."

"Go on," Sid said. "Before the Brighton's chased your father out of town?"

"Something like that," Porter said, resuming his seat.

Tom filled a glass with water from the cooler in the corner of the room and placed it in front of the visitor, who locked his fingers around the glass but did not drink. After a moment he pushed it a way and leaned back in the chair.

"Where did your father go?" Sid asked.

"Up north."

"Iowa? Minnesota?"

"I don't know. Somewhere around Kansas City. Maybe St. Joseph. He tried to make a go of it in Branson first, even opened a small grocery store."

"You said Brighton chased him out of town," Tom said.

"No, he fired him," Porter said with a shrug. "Can you fire a partner?"

"When did this happen?" Sid asked.

"Early 1940s."

"Your father was a partner with Jack Brighton and Etta Stupholds at Riverside Mercantile?" Tom asked, doubt in his voice.

"Why is that hard to believe?"

"I guess, because no one's mentioned it."

"They were childhood friends. At least that's what I was told."

"But you couldn't have been more than ten years old at the time."

"Eight. I was almost ten when Dad left to find work."

"Why didn't you and your mother go with him?"

"He wanted us to keep the store opened. He was trying to make extra money, that's all. I helped out when I could. After a while, my mom closed the store and went to work somewhere else. I don't remember where."

"And your father?"

"Never came back. She got letters saying he would be home soon, but it didn't happen."

"So, he abandoned the two of you," Sid said.

"My mother never accepted that. We even went to the address where she sent her letters."

"And?"

"And nothing. No one knew where he had gone."

Tom glanced at Sid, silently motioning for his partner to take a seat. They both pulled up to the table and leaned forward. Tom felt sorry for Porter, but the past did not justify his current behavior. "It had to be tough as a kid without a father. We understand what you've said. But you may be wrong about Jack Brighton. You don't know what happened. You were a young boy. No one tells a kid the whole truth."

The older man furrowed his brow and stared at his clenched hands. "Are we finished?"

"One more thing. You need to do whatever you have to do to stay away from Allen and the Brightons. See a lawyer and sue them, if you have a case against them. But do not go near them. If you do, our next meeting may be when we arrest you. Do you understand?"

Porter walked to the door and waited for Sid to open it.

Tom called out, "Last warning, Bryan," as Sid took the man to the jail exit. The detective wasn't sure if Bryan heard the message, but the conversation was worth the trouble, providing a lead in the skeleton case.

Sylvia Lockhart met the detectives at Artie Richards' office as soon as she got off work from Tory's Treasures. As Lex's niece by his sister, Sylvia could be a match to the mitochondrial DNA of the skeleton. Tom wasn't sure what all that meant, but he had confidence in Fredericks' conclusions and expertise.

The woman was eager to help them with an ongoing case even though they provided no details. Artie took the sample with cryptic comments about collecting evidence for an old case.

"I've never heard of this DNA thing," Sylvia said.

Artie explained, "It's a scientific method for identifying a particular person,"

"You mean like fingerprints?"

"Yes, but also useful in making a family connection," Tom said.

"But you don't think I did something wrong."

"No, we're trying to identify remains," Sid said, immediately biting his lip.

"Like a human body?" she gasped.

"One deceased many years ago," Tom assured her.

"Good. I mean, not good, but ... you know what I mean."

"Yes, we know," Sid said.

Artie walked her to the door. "Thanks for your help."

"No problem."

"One more thing, Sylvia," Tom said. "This is an ongoing investigation, so please don't discuss this with anyone."

"Who would I tell?" she said with a Cheshire cat grin.

Once the woman was out of sight, Sid remarked, "She could tell any number of people."

"She won't say anything," Tom said. "Besides, if we're right and clear this up soon, it won't matter."

"What about the other two victims? Have you found any relatives?" Artie asked.

"We're supposed to get samples this week, assuming they show up," Sid said.

"But don't wait for those to get Sylvia's sample to the lab," Tom said.

Artie said. "I'll send it FedEx priority first thing tomorrow."

＊

Tom dropped Sid at the police department entrance and headed home for a quick shower and change. He didn't want to be late for his big date with Kate. He was beginning to enjoy feeling like a sixteen-year-old again. And this date would be a great surprise—or so he hoped.

She was waiting in her living room, framed in the big picture window. When he parked, she waved and rushed to the front door. He didn't get a chance to knock. *Plenty of those teen hormones going around,* he guessed. The smile on her face warmed his heart, but the twinkle in her eye set his blood on fire.

"You're ready," he said.

She whirled around and stopped in the middle of the room. Her baggy jeans and his old football jersey transformed her into the young teenager he remembered.

"Am I dressed appropriately for your surprise? You said late-seventies-casual."

"You are *perfect.*"

"Well, that's good then," she said, taking hold of his hands.

He pulled her close and gave her a peck on the cheek. The scent in her hair–shampoo she'd used so long ago–resurrected good memories. He breathed it in and sighed quietly.

Kate said, "Do you like it? I found a bottle of that lilac conditioner I used in high school. I figured it would go with the outfit."

"Maybe we should stay here and order pizza."

"No way. You promised a great surprise date and you are going to deliver."

She grabbed her purse from the sofa and headed for the door.

"You may need a coat. It's breezy and damp outside."

"I'm not sure I still have one old enough."

"Suit yourself, but don't complain later," he said with a shrug.

She turned on her heel and rushed to her room, coming back in less than a minute in one of her father's old coats. Tom was sitting on the sofa waiting.

"Isn't this that box Etta gave you?" he asked pointing to the end table.

"Yes, I'm searching her key stash for the one to open it."

"I tell you; it would be easier to let an expert crack this lock."

"Give me the name of an expert. I'll call if I can't find the match."

"Very hurtful," Tom said. "Seriously, you haven't opened it yet?"

"We found the box of keys last Wednesday, cleaning up after the break-in. I've been busy. Right now, we have a date to enjoy." Halfway to the door, she glanced back at her companion and said, "Race you to the car."

"No fair. You started without me," he said, catching up with her nonetheless.

They rode in silence down the Strip toward the city proper. He was a little disappointed she wasn't pumping him for information. As they approached the bridge crossing over Lake Taneycomo to the east, he was about to give her a clue.

"I knew it," she shouted.

"What do you know?"

"We're going *bowling*."

"You sound happy," he said, pleased with the glee in her voice.

"Despite the fact that we haven't been bowling since before I graduated from high school in 1980, I'm thrilled."

"Seriously? I was ready to settle for happy. Thrilled is much better. But hold on to that feeling, because I'm going to trounce you like I did in those olden times."

"Fat chance."

The passage of time had not improved the couple's bowling skills. Kate accused her date of sabotaging her game by failing to bring her old shoes and ball. Tom, who lugged his high school ball along for the contest, claimed he was "a bit rusty." In the end, they agreed they were never that good. The important thing was to have fun. And, for Tom, beating the sox off his girlfriend was the ultimate in fun.

"Another game?" he asked.

"Are you kidding? Three major losses is enough humiliation for me."

"At least you can admit defeat."

"Winner buys dinner. Right?"

"The least I can do," Tom said, placing their shoes on the counter.

"We'll have a large pepperoni, extra cheese, and two beers," Kate told the attendant.

"Coming right up," the young man said before disappearing into the kitchen.

By the time the two would-be bowlers were settled at the table, the girl working behind the counter brought the drinks. Tom clasped the cold glass between his hands and marveled at his good fortune. It seemed real this time, like his relationship with Kate would last. He'd never been happier, and she seemed happy too. Maybe he should have let her win at least one game.

Kate took a sip of beer. She smiled and tilted her head to the side. "You know, you don't have to be so happy you walloped me at bowling."

"Why would you say that?"

"Your ear-to-ear smirk."

He reached for her hand and squeezed it slightly. "Being a champion bowler did not cause my glee. Spending the evening with my best-friend-forever is what makes me joyous."

She placed her free hand on top of his. "I understand the feeling."

"You know, I'm not that hungry," he said.

Kate snickered. "Not a chance. You owe me dinner at least."

"We could take the pizza with us."

"Where are we going?"

"Perhaps you'd like to see my small but really nice apartment."

The young man placed the pizza between them. "Can I get you anything else?"

Kate stared at Tom, then the attendant. "We need a to-go box, please."

The drive to his apartment seemed like a lifetime. At first, he babbled caveats about the condition of the apartment, warning her not to expect it to be as clean as her house. With her silence, he was afraid she would change her mind.

Once inside, he took the pizza box from her and placed it on the counter in the small kitchen. When he turned around, Kate was directly in front of him. She put her arms around his neck and moved close enough that her lilac-scented hair overshadowed the pizza. When he couldn't stand it any longer, he kissed her again and again. He placed his hand in the small of her back and pulled her as close as he possibly could. Her physical responses allayed his earlier fears. He led her down a short hallway to his bedroom.

Kate took his hands and pulled him gently onto the edge of the bed, seemingly oblivious to its rumpled condition. She caressed his cheek, then kissed him gently on the lips. He laid back on the bed and pulled her down beside him. He regretted losing her in the first place and wouldn't let that happen again. His heart erupted with an overwhelming feeling of contentment—of oneness with the only woman he had ever truly loved. Everything seemed so right, so good, so meant to be. They made love for the first time since his return to Branson, then fell asleep in each other's arms.

The soft breeze brushed lightly across his face, tickling the end of his nose. Something touched his lips. He eased his eyes open.

Kate's finger made another circle around his mouth, then stroked his cheek. "Good morning," she whispered.

"It is now."

Kate leaned her head on his shoulder and cuddled her body closer to his. His mind reeled with feelings he couldn't describe, let alone explain.

"What's going on behind those gorgeous eyes?" she said.

"That I'm not interested in ever leaving this bed."

"Ever is an extremely long time."

He smiled and gave her a peck on the tip of her nose.

"I probably should call my dad, let him know I haven't been kidnapped," she said.

"Does that mean you'll be hanging around for a while?"

"It's Saturday, our day off, and I can't imagine a better place to be."

Chapter Twenty-Five

Kate poured herself a mugful of fresh coffee and sat across from her father at the kitchen table. "Are you going to tease me without mercy?" she asked.

"Why would I do that? You don't tease me when I linger at Margie's."

"You haven't lingered for a day and a half. Not yet anyway."

"I did have in mind to say I told you so. And I'll add I'm happy for you."

"It might last this time, Dad. He took me bowling Friday night."

"A sure sign of commitment."

"It feels like when we were teenagers and fell in love. Please don't tell me this buzz will fade. I'm not interested in hearing anything negative."

"I was not going to say anything about the buzz. I was going to say life has its ups and downs and in-betweens. Your job is to stay buckled in and ride that ride."

"That sounds really wise, Dad." She reached for the front section of the paper. "Wow, Helen put me on the first page, below the fold, but who cares."

"It was a good piece, Katie. Jack Brighton never seemed that community-minded to me, but maybe I overlooked those characteristics."

"The series is about Branson's history and Jack played a big part. Even today he holds a lot of power and influence. But the article was not meant to be a biography of him or his family."

"Perhaps an exposé would be appropriate someday."

"Not a bad idea, but I'd rather do one on Larry Allen."

"You're right, he is smarmier than his grandfather."

"Speaking of smarmy, I'm expecting a phone call from a Kyle Henderson. He's the one I used mother's maiden name to contact about selling the motel property."

"Called yesterday evening. I told him you'd be out of town for a day or so. He left a direct number for you to call back."

"Why didn't you say something?"

"Hey, I'm happy to be one of your investigative team members, but I'm not a very good secretary. The note's by the phone next to your key project."

Kate ran to the living room. Her father had shoved the note under the pile of rejected keys. The gift box from Etta and the metal container with the remaining keys were close by. The note said call anytime, so she dialed the number and hoped for an answer.

"I'm returning a call from Kyle Henderson," Kate said, when the woman answered.

Sitting on hold, Kate stirred the keys in the metal box, then selected one and inserted it in the lock. Like other rejects, it didn't budge. She tried another. No movement. Maybe Tom would get a chance to show his lock-picking skills after all. She tried several more keys and had chosen the next when Henderson came to the phone. She gave her mother's name as she inserted the key in the cedar box.

He paused. She detected a faint sound of paper shuffling before he said, "Ah, yes. Miss Carson. I researched the motel and spoke to the owner. Frankly, this location is not what we're interested in at this time."

"May I ask why?"

"We're looking for something closer to downtown Branson."

"The action in Branson is along the Strip, Mr. Henderson. Downtown Branson is not much of an attraction."

"Perhaps not at this time, Miss Carson. But we have an eye on the future."

"Really? What's in old downtown Branson's future?"

"One never knows. Perhaps a facelift of sorts. In any case, we are not interested in buying the land you proposed."

Kate was still sitting on the sofa staring at Etta's box and pondering Henderson's words—specifically his use of the plural pronoun and the facelift in Branson's future—when someone knocked on the front door. A reflexive twist of her wrist initiated the key's smooth rotation in the lock. "Whoa," she whispered as she raised the lid slightly.

A second knock reminded Kate of the visitor. She locked the box and slipped the successful key in her jeans on her way to the door.

"Katie, I was hoping you were home," Marge said.

Kate furrowed her brow and stepped back to let the woman enter. "Dad already mentioned I lingered more than usual."

Marge chuckled. "I'm glad you called him. He seemed worried for a moment or two. But what I mean is, I have some information for you."

Kate led the way to the kitchen and was taken aback when Marge leaned down to peck Roger on the cheek with her greeting.

The realtor poured herself a cup of coffee and removed a hefty stack of papers from a large manila envelope. "As it turns out the Chamber already has a preliminary report prepared by the survey company. The return on the mail-out was seventy-two percent, which is truly incredible, and most companies responded immediately even though they were given a six-month window to reply."

"That's impressive," Kate said, adding "By the way, Dad has joined our little team."

"Oh, I thought he was already a part of it. Can I spread this stuff out here?"

"You bet," Roger said with a gleam in his eye.

It took the woman several minutes to get the piles of paper in an acceptable order. All the pages were facing so Roger and Kate could read them. Marge sat behind the array, her fingers clasped in front of her on the table.

Kate said, "Wainright indicated the responses weren't expected for months."

Marge clarified, "Only the committee members have it. They're still compiling data to be discussed in a general meeting, or so I was told."

"Why wouldn't they simply turn over the report to all chamber members, including the city government?" Kate asked.

"Very good question," Roger commented.

"Before we discuss that, let me give you a quick summary."

Marge explained that, the four stacks represented the four parts of the questionnaire–company demographics, facility requirements, services and features, and desired activities. Surveyed companies ranged from small, with less than fifty employees, to medium with up to three-hundred employees, to large with between three-hundred to a thousand employees, indicative of the sample selected. Most of the responding companies had between three-hundred to six-hundred employees, with a few in the upper end of the large category or greater. Respondents were based nationwide, although most of the surveys were sent to and received from companies headquartered in the Midwest.

Overwhelmingly, the preferences involved centralized facilities, with sleeping and meeting accommodations for up to two-hundred individuals in the same hotel or hotel campus. A few respondents specified higher capacities.

Required amenities included access to three meals per day, with some meals—as well as beverage services—provided in the meeting areas. Extra-curricular activities, such as visiting area attractions, should be close or easily reached and prepared for large groups. Most of the activities or attractions were in-line with what the Branson area could provide, with some notable exceptions. Meeting rooms should accommodate various numbers of attendees, ranging from twenty-five to two-hundred, and should be equipped with a comprehensive audio-video system, including recording features. Full-service copying, faxing, and phone services should be available close to meeting areas.

Marge paused as Roger and Kate scanned the draft report sections. She poured each of them a cup of coffee and started another pot.

Roger was the first to comment. "You know, in my conversations with former and current planning and zoning members, nothing like this has been proposed."

Marge offered, "But chamber members have been promoting a convention center for a couple of years now. We've been competing with Springfield for large meetings for a while."

"The convention center that folks around town are picturing is not the sophisticated facility described by the survey responses," Roger said.

Kate added, "I agree. These companies want something John Q. Hammons can build, like the large hotel complex on Table Rock Lake he's supposedly planning. Certainly, that would help

Branson compete with Springfield, but it won't be within city limits."

"And the size of the hotel is only part of it," Roger said.

"Right," Marge agreed. "Although Silver Dollar City is a popular attraction, the companies expressed the need for a menu of activities for their members."

"What about the lakes themselves? Those are big attractions with both boating and fishing," Kate said. "And we have the new Tanger Outlet and other shopping areas."

Marge said, "Remember a big issue is proximity to the hotel or easy transport for large groups. We do not have a transportation system in Branson. Commercial busses are okay for small tourist groups, but not practical ... or even available ... for these large corporate clients we want to attract. Don't forget, wives will come too. And although outlet shopping is popular, not everyone wants factory-overflow or irregular items, name brand or not. Boutiques and small specialty or novelty shops were specifically noted in the responses."

"Okay, so we need a facelift," Kate said, using Henderson's term.

"I'd call it more like major reconstructive surgery," Roger said with a snicker.

Marge said, "You asked before, Katie, why the chamber hasn't released this report and the detailed responses to the members. I don't have an official answer and, since I acquired this draft *prematurely*, I couldn't ask the question of the board or the committee. But I will say fulfilling the requirements summarized in the report would be monumental and way beyond the loose structure of the chamber."

"Like Katie said it will take a major developer to address these needs," Roger agreed.

"No developer in town comes close to Hammons' caliber," Marge said.

"True, but there may be one who aspires to that standard," Kate said, drumming her index finger on the stack in front of her.

When her dad and Marge left for a seniors' miniature golf tournament, Kate gathered up the papers and went to her room. She sifted through the summaries, her head spinning with excitement. She fell asleep speculating about what Allen and Wainright had in mind and if Henderson was involved with them or someone else or no one.

Chapter Twenty-Six

Kate usually enjoyed covering the Board of Aldermen meeting every other Tuesday, but public comments about the new sign ordinance were less than stimulating. Her mind drifted from one topic to another finally landing on the key that unlocked Etta's box. An almost unbearable hour and thirty minutes later the adjournment gavel rang down and she was out the door.

Breezing into the living room and ignoring her father, she came to an abrupt halt by the table next to the sofa. Both the cedar box and its metal companion were missing.

"Are you okay," her dad asked.

She spun around and plopped down on the couch, shaking her head.

"If you're searching for that box, I moved it to the shelf in the foyer. I needed the table space yesterday when I was sorting pamphlets for Margie."

"You couldn't sort them in the kitchen?" Kate said, immediately regretting her tone.

"Hey, I tried to find you to ask your permission, but you were at work."

"I'm sorry, but the other night I found the key that opens the box. Then I got distracted and forgot about it. But tonight, I remembered."

"That explains everything," Roger said, shaking his head.

The metal container was on top of the wooden box, but the pile of rejected keys was not on the shelf. Worse than that, the working key was not in the lock. *Calm down.*

Kate picked up and shook the key case. She took a deep breath and stepped back into the living room. "Dad? What did you do with the pile of keys? And the one in the lock?"

"The little bowl on the second shelf, but there wasn't a key in the lock."

Kate examined the keys in the dish but didn't remember what the successful one looked like. She sat down on the sofa, one hand cupping the small container, the other hand massaging her throbbing temple. She searched the floor next to the arm of the sofa then around and under it.

"Did you drop it in the pile?" she said.

"No key in the lock," her father repeated slowly. "You need to relax and try to remember what *you* did with it."

She had to admit the moment was a blur. She tried it and it turned. What did she do next? Marge knocked. Kate let her in. "I put it in my jeans pocket."

"See? Relax and remember. Works every time."

She grabbed Etta's gift and the metal box and headed for her room. The jeans she'd worn Sunday were in the clothes basket in her closet.

And the key was safe and sound in the right-hand pocket. Hoping she had not imagined it unlocking two days ago, she turned the key clockwise. As before, it rotated without effort.

Placing the box squarely in the middle of her bed, she raised the lid a crack and peeked inside. *Etta was wrong. It's not empty.* Kate gently lifted a folded piece of paper, revealing more below. She laid the first on her bed and dumped the remaining contents on top to maintain the order. She stared at the items, suddenly overcome by an unsettling realization that she was invading Etta's privacy, but shook it off and proceeded.

The oldest of the sheets, quite yellow and creased with age, was now on top. It appeared to be an official document. The paper was heavier. Even folded, the dark lettering revealed a structured form design. She smoothed open the creases to reveal a marriage license application, requested and signed by Claymore Phillip Stupholds and Henrietta Jo Freehman. The form was approved and certified at the bottom by a judge in Taney County Missouri on October 23, 1924—the day Etta turned sixteen.

One down.

Still concerned about reading the other keepsakes, she considered taking them to Etta. Certainly, they had nothing to do with Kate.

She returned them to the box and locked it, placing it on her bedside table. She stared at the object as if it would convince her it was okay to open and read the pages. In a few moments her reporter's curiosity outvoted her sentiment.

Maintaining the order of the box, she lifted the middle sheet and spread it out carefully. The penmanship reminded her of her mother's cursive, the style taught long ago in grade schools. At the top of the page, the date was also written in long hand—September 2, 1942. One glance at Clay's signature and she knew what it was. She read it anyway.

"My Darling Wife," the note began. "My true regret is that I failed to provide you all that you want and deserve in this life. Please know I tried. I hope you can forgive me. Eternally yours, Clay."

Putting aside the uneasy feeling of reading such an intimate confession, Kate agreed with Etta—the note made no sense. Etta seemed to treasure memories of their life together. Yet in his mind, he failed her. *How truly sad.*

The final document consisted of two hand-written pages. "An Agreement" was in the top left corner of each page-numbered sheet. In the top right corner was the date—October 23, 1942, Etta's 34th birthday. The agreement itself seemed official, but not in legalese. It spelled out an "arrangement for life" among the three old friends: Randall John Brighton, Alexander Benjamin Porter, and Henrietta Jo Stupholds. The last paragraph stated that the three, with the names listed again, had sworn solemn oaths on "this Friday, the 23rd of October in this year of Our Lord 1942," by signing at the bottom of the second page.

"Bryan Porter was right," Kate said aloud. "But is it valid?"

She found her father in the kitchen, having a short and neat whiskey, something he was prone to do on bill day. He lifted his glass in a mock toast and downed it quickly.

"All the checks written?" Kate asked.

"Mercifully, yes. Too bad this happens every month."

"At least we have money in the bank to pay them now. It was touch and go for a while."

"Would you care for a relaxer?" Roger asked.

"No, but I have a question. Do you think Phil Bingham would help me with something?"

"That's not the best thing to ask your old dad on bill day."

"Seriously. I need a lawyer to examine an agreement to see if it's binding."

"I imagine Phil's up to the task and he has an office in Branson now."

"Yes, close to the newspaper office. I'll check him out."

"Aren't you going to let me read it? I'm a team member after all."

"Sorry. I'll have to invoke the need-to-know clause."

Kate overslept the next morning after a restless night of mulling over the survey report and Etta's agreement—first one, then the other, then back and forth. It seemed likely Allen had either directly or indirectly orchestrated the Chamber's questionnaire. But so what?

She dragged herself to the newspaper office and plopped down at her desk. She was several minutes into reviewing her appointments for the day when she realized someone was lurking at her doorway.

"Nice of you to make it in," Helen said.

"I had a rough night," Kate retorted.

"What have you found on the series of fires? Anything worth a feature article?"

"I spoke to Chief Scherington. He was helpful. I'm still following up with owners and residents. Can I get you something in a day or so?"

"Sounds good. Keep me posted," the editor said as she started to leave.

"Uh, Helen? Do you have a minute to discuss something else I've been investigating?"

The editor pulled a spare chair closer to Kate's desk. "Does this have something to do with the skeleton case?"

"Sort of. Allen clearing the lot without his grandfather's permission caused me to speculate about other things and now I'm not sure how ... or if ... it all fits."

"Maybe we can sort it out together."

Kate told Helen about the owners who were approached to sell their property by the lakefront, the Chamber's survey, the preliminary report, and her theory about Allen's involvement. She concluded with her list of what-ifs and what-if-nots, which was followed by several moments of silence.

"I can see why you couldn't sleep," Helen said, preparing to leave the room.

"Aren't you going to tell me what to do?"

"Let me speak to some Chamber members, including your favorite, to check out the purpose and ultimate intention for this survey. If Allen plays dumb, I'll see if he's still having problems with my star reporter. My advice, however, is to stick to the facts. Throw away your what-if list and any other list of opinions, guesses, and rumors. Find out what has happened, not what may happen. Perhaps that will clarify the article."

"Thanks, Helen," Kate said as her boss walked down the hall.

Kate stopped at the front desk to copy Etta's agreement. She wasn't ready to give up the original, and the lawyer would need time to review it. She smiled as she left the building, recalling Helen's "star reporter" comment.

Located on the second floor of one of the oldest buildings in town, Bingham's office was accessible from an entrance off the alley. A sign on the heavy metal door read "Phil Bingham Esquire" in bold, red letters with Attorney-at-Law underneath in smaller, but still bold, black letters. On the third line in parentheses, it said Suite 201. She was halfway up the flight when the door slammed shut behind her. A smaller version of the outer sign hung on the door to number 201–a room rather than a suite.

Two desks took up most of the space in the office. A small desk near the door was unoccupied with only an empty pencil holder and blank pad of paper on top. Phil Bingham sat at the back desk next to a file cabinet and a small table holding a coffee pot. Stacks of papers covered his desk except for the space in front of him where a huge law book rested. He combed his fingers through his thinning gray hair. In his late fifties, his hair had been shades of gray for as long as she could remember.

"Is this a good time?" Kate asked, tapping on the door frame.

"Katie, good to see you," the lawyer said, coming to his feet.

She crossed the room to receive his usual warm greeting—an almost-hug with a brief pat on her back. She returned the gesture and stepped back with a smile.

"How's your dad? I haven't seen him for a month or so. When we finished the taxes, he said he didn't want to see me ever again."

"You may not know about his new lady friend."

"Marge Connarde? You can't have an office on this street, even for only two days a week, without knowing about Margie and Roger. I'm happy for him."

"They seem to get along."

"So, what did you want to discuss?" he asked.

She took the copy of the agreement from her purse and handed it to Phil, then waited for him to scan it. "I found it in an old cedar box that Etta Stupholds gave me," she said.

"Why did you bring it to me?"

"I wanted to know if it's a valid legal contract."

"I can give you my opinion, but I'm due at a client's by eleven, and, as you can see, I'm stuck on a point of law," he said waving a hand across the opened book.

"I'm sorry, I should have known you'd be busy."

"Don't be silly. I'm never too busy for my favorite red head. How about you check with me tomorrow late afternoon?"

"That will be great," Kate said, making a quick exit.

She had a few minutes before her scheduled follow up interview with Jack Brighton. Although the meeting was supposed to be about the more recent years and future prospects for Fortune Enterprises, she hoped for an opening to discuss Bryan Porter's accusation that Jack reneged on a deal with Bryan's father.

As usual, Ellen was alone in the large oval anteroom. She was smoothing her nails with an emery board when Kate opened the door.

"Oops, you caught me," the young girl said.

"Hey, an emergency nail repair is critical," Kate said.

"Absolutely," Ellen agreed with a smile.

"I have an appointment with Jack Brighton."

"Right. His assistant had an emergency at home. She told me to let you go on back. Mr. Brighton is expecting you."

Kate walked across the room but hesitated for a second at the door. She felt odd without an escort, but—as Ellen said—he was expecting her. When she passed his assistant's desk, she heard the voices and realized Jack was not alone. Once she entered the hallway between the two offices, the voices were clear and loud. Jack's comments were softer and more controlled. No surprise to

Kate, his visitor—Larry Allen—did not inherit his grandfather's restraint.

Allen shouted, "I don't know, and I don't want to know the details of the problem between you and Porter. But it better not bite us in the butt as far as the city project goes."

"Or what?" Jack's control was loosening. "What will you do, Larry? Sue me?"

Torn between the terror of being caught and the desire to hear more, Kate froze momentarily. The two men were silent, and she feared the meeting would end and Allen would burst into the hallway any second. She turned and rushed through the assistant's office and into the reception area.

Ellen was not at her desk. Kate knew she had to tell her something. Jack would probably ask if she'd called or come by. She needed a good excuse for leaving abruptly. Before Kate crossed to the desk, Ellen returned from the outer hall.

"Wow, that was a quick meeting," she said.

"You know, I felt a little queasy at work, but I came anyway. All of a sudden I felt like I was going to faint."

"Did you see Mr. Brighton?"

"No, I didn't make it past his assistant's office. I had to sit down. I'm okay now, but I better go. I wouldn't want to spread my germs."

"Do you want to rest for a moment? Maybe it will pass. I can call him and explain."

"Please don't. I feel like an idiot. In fact, don't tell him I came by. Can you tell him I called to reschedule, that something came up?"

"I suppose I can do that."

"I really appreciate your understanding."

"No problem. I hope you feel better soon."

"Thanks. I'm sure I'll be fine. Please, tell his assistant I'll call for a new time."

Kate wasted no time getting to the end of the hall and down the steps to the street and back to her office. What was she doing—lurking in the hallway like that? But she was glad she did. Now all she needed to figure out was the reason for the argument.

Chapter Twenty-Seven

The police dispatcher woke Tom at five-thirty a.m. with an apology and a new call from the construction report hot line. The not-quite-awake detective told her to put the call through. He sat on the edge of the bed waiting for the telltale click and hoping perhaps this tip would have more substance than the hundreds of others they'd received.

"Sorry, Sergeant Collingwood, the caller hung up," the dispatcher said.

"No problem. Did he say anything or give you a name?"

"It was a female. She insisted on speaking to you but wouldn't tell me her name."

"Okay. Thanks for trying."

Tom hung up and leaned back, propping his pillow against the headboard. He was nodding off when the phone rang again.

"Detective Collingwood," he said, knowing the dispatcher would connect the informant immediately on a callback.

A quick low gasp, as if surprised by his voice, then silence. He waited for a moment then repeated his name. Music, probably a radio, played in the background.

"This is a mistake," the female said.

"Wait, how do you know? Tell me why you called," he said without hesitating.

The radio deejay announced the next tune, but the caller remained silent.

"Anything you say will be confidential. Obviously, you feel you know something that will help our case. You've gone this far. You called back. Please tell me what you have."

"Probably nothing."

"Every piece matters. Can you give me your name?"

"You said it would be confidential."

"Right, right. I'll call you Mary. That's my mother's name," he lied, hoping to develop some trust. He added, "You can call me Tom."

"Okay," she said, but fell silent again.

"So, Mary, do you work in the construction business in Branson?"

"My boyfriend does. We moved here when he heard about available work."

"I see. When was that, Mary?"

"Almost three years ago. And he's worked steady. But things changed this past year ... became more difficult."

"Longer hours? Too many bosses?"

"No, he's used to the demands of the business. But part of the reason we left home was the big city corruption."

"Big cities can be complicated."

"No kidding," she said, her tone becoming less stressed. "Don't get me wrong," she continued.

"We love Branson. It was so friendly, so different at first."

"But that changed?" Tom asked, hoping to reach a relevant point in her story.

"Yes."

"Where does your boyfriend work, Mary."

"I'm not sure I want to say."

"That's okay. Can you tell me the name of the project?"

"I may as well tell you the company."

"Any one project has many companies involved, some large, some small. Wasn't it like that in the big city, Mary?"

"Julie. My name is Julie."

"Thanks, Julie. Do you remember the project name?"

"Yes, but. I'd rather not say."

"Okay, tell me whatever you can. We'll take it from there."

A new song played in the distance. Julie hadn't hung up. Tom waited, not wanting to push too hard.

"My boyfriend saw someone give the city inspector an envelope."

"A building inspector?"

"Yes."

"Does he know what was in the envelope?"

"Yes. He saw the person put a bunch of cash in the envelope."

"Is he sure it was cash?"

"Yes. He worried about it for over a month. I knew something had happened, but he wouldn't tell me what. Finally, the other night he blurted out that we needed to go back to Chicago. He said jobs were scarce in Branson. I knew that wasn't true. It took a while to make him tell me what was bothering him."

"Okay. Now, Julie, I want you to listen carefully. We can protect your boyfriend. And you. But we'll need to have him make a statement regarding what he saw. It can still be confidential, but we need to have it in writing, if possible. We need to find out what other information he might have."

The radio music was replaced by a dial tone. He called the nonemergency number for the police dispatcher. "Please tell me I can pick up a recording of that call in an hour."

"Did you have any doubt, Sergeant Collingwood?"

"Not for a second," he said, uncrossing his fingers. "What about a trace?"

"Pay phone at a gas station about two miles north of the Arkansas-Missouri line."

"Better than nothing, I guess. See you in a bit."

The dispatcher seemed impressed when Tom tapped on the glass behind her less than thirty minutes later. She gave him the cassette and a note with the name and location of the pay phone. As he flipped on the light in the police detective suite, he was still hoping Julie would help them. It would be a lot easier.

He put on a pot of coffee and sat at his desk to listen to the tape. The woman went from very cautious to more-or-less comfortable during the conversation. Convincing her boyfriend to trust the police would be a different story.

"Burning the midnight oil again, partner?" Sid asked, grabbing his mug and heading for the fresh brew.

"Not exactly," Tom said, brandishing the small cassette in the air.

"Recording those 900-number calls again?"

"Even better."

Sid placed the mug on his desk and sat down. "Do I have to guess?"

"Give it a shot," Tom snickered.

"I'll go for door number one. Someone called on our hot line and had a certifiable tip about construction ethics ... or lack thereof ... in Branson."

Tom nodded and slipped the tape into the player. When Julie hung up, Sid shrugged. Tom came to his feet and leaned forward across Sid's desk. "Hey, this was a banner call," he said.

"Sorry, but the woman, who claims her name is Julie, said nothing we can use."

"I know that."

"And yet?"

"If she talks her boyfriend into making a statement, we might have something."

"Okay. Two words: if and might."

"We can start at the gas station. Either she works there, or someone saw her use the phone at that ungodly early hour."

"Hey, maybe we could check with every construction-related firm in Branson to see who relocated from Chicago with a girlfriend named Julie."

"Did you speak to Artie?" Tom asked, ignoring Sid's sarcasm and tossing the tape into the Porter complaint box.

"The lab received Sylvia's sample Monday. We should have a report later this week. The other samples will be on the way today."

"I want to move forward as if Lex Porter is our victim," Tom said.

"I agree. What do you have in mind?"

"Let's speak to Etta. See what she knows about Lex's disappearance."

"Then we can visit Jack Brighton and compare their stories," Sid said.

"Now you're getting the idea."

The detectives caught up on paperwork until the department secretary arrived. They asked her to call and make an appointment with Brighton, knowing he didn't like surprises. They stopped for breakfast before heading–unannounced–to Etta's place.

The older woman seemed small, cocooned in a colorful quilt, rocking on the far end of her veranda. They were almost to the bottom of the steps before she noticed, or at least acknowledged, their arrival. She unwrapped the blanket and hung it over the railing.

"Hope this isn't a bad time," Tom said.

"Enjoying the fall colors. They're so vibrant this year."

"If you don't mind, we have a few questions for you."

"You're always welcome," Etta said, motioning toward the glider. She moved her rocker so that she faced the detectives. "Is it about the break-in?"

"No, we want to discuss Lex Porter. We understand you were good friends and business partners," Sid said.

Etta furrowed her brow and stared at the two men. "Does this have something to do with Bryan?" she asked.

Tom took a small notebook from his jacket pocket and opened it to a blank page. "We're trying to close the case on Lex Porter's disappearance," he said, ignoring her question.

"He left Branson to find work in the Kansas City area."

"Did he find it?"

"I assume so, he didn't come back, but I wouldn't call that a disappearance."

"You'd know if he returned, right? You were best friends as children, had been close all your lives. Did you find it odd when he left his family behind?"

"Tory stayed to run their business."

"Did she tell you he stopped communicating with her?"

"I don't remember. Is that what Bryan says?"

"We haven't discussed this with Bryan yet."

"He'd remember more than I would."

Tom made some notes, cuing his partner to ask the next question.

"What happened to cause Lex to leave Riverside Mercantile? He'd worked with Jack from the beginning, right? You three were partners."

"I know Bryan believes we were partners. But we were just close friends."

"But you and Jack are partners now," Tom interjected.

"Yes."

"So, when did that happen?"

"I'm not sure of the exact date."

"We could check the date on your contract," Tom said.

"I'm not sure when he and I first spoke of the partnership."

Sid said, "Back to why Lex left Riverside. Do you remember the circumstances?"

"He started his own store shortly afterward. Maybe that's why he left."

"You're saying he quit Riverside to start his own store?"

"I guess that's what happened."

"You know, it seems like a person would speak to a best friend to see if leaving and going out on his own was a good idea. Did Lex consult you about quitting?"

Etta rocked forward and stood up. "You're getting me all confused, putting words in my mouth. I tell you I don't remember exactly what happened. That's not a crime, as far as I know, especially if you're eighty-something years old."

The men hesitated briefly, but Tom shrugged and signaled Sid. When they reached the stairs, Tom turned and said, "Thanks for your time. If you think of anything else, give either one of us a call."

The detectives returned to their vehicle and pulled out of Etta's driveway. As Sid turned onto the main road he said, "That lady was lying."

Tom snickered. "What was your first clue?"

"Hey, I sat in the back of her car with her for thirty minutes, remember? And I finally read Kate's articles. And neither of those Etta Stupholds was on that porch."

"I agree. Unfortunately, I'm not sure what that means or, more important, what we can do about it. The questions are: Is she protecting someone? Is she in denial? Or even worse, has she forgotten?"

"Probably. Maybe. And I doubt it," Sid said.

"It isn't likely she has forgotten something as serious as the departure of a lifelong friend ... partner or otherwise ... from a business he had been a part of for many years," Tom said. "And she would have been concerned that he didn't return to Branson."

Sid said, "Odds are Brighton has a similar story."

"What time is he expecting us?"

"In about thirty minutes. Maybe, on our way, we could see what Bryan remembers."

"Worth a try, but remember he was eleven years old when his mother filed the missing person report, even younger when his dad left Riverside. Most of what he remembers is what his mother told him."

"Not necessarily a bad thing."

"No, but most likely a softer, romanticized version. Let's talk to Jack Brighton first."

The receptionist told them to have a seat while she called Brighton's assistant. As expected, they waited several minutes before being escorted to his office. The detectives did not expect to see Randy Brighton and Jack's personal lawyer, Keith Hawthorne, at the meeting as well.

Tom had dealt with the lawyer many times in court. The man had a knack for getting his clients off the hook when it came to minor offenses and civil suits. His success could be attributed, at least in part, to his professional–almost sleek–appearance. At a modest five foot eight inches tall, maybe one hundred sixty pounds, he dressed for success and wore his charm like it was part of his wardrobe.

Jack came to his feet and walked, hand extended, to greet the policemen. "Tom, Sid, nice to see you again. I hope you don't mind, I asked Randy and Keith to stick around for our little chat. We were in an early-morning meeting when your secretary called."

"No problem," Tom said, nodding in the direction of the other men.

Once they were seated, Jack asked, "What's the topic for today, gentlemen?"

"We have questions about the disappearance of Alexander Porter," Tom said.

"Seriously?" Randy said, drawing the attention of all present and an unspoken censure from his father.

Keith said, "Sorry, if you'll indulge me, who is Alexander Porter?"

Jack explained before the detectives had a chance. "He was a dear friend from childhood, Keith, but I haven't seen him for over fifty years."

Tom injected, "And you wonder why we're interested now."

Jack said, "As a matter of fact ..."

"We are examining old missing person cases. One was filed by your friend's wife in 1945. At the time, all leads were followed, but nothing led to Porter's whereabouts."

"I know crime is low in Branson, but it would seem more productive to concentrate on today's issues," Randy said.

"Point taken," Tom said.

Jack asked, "What is it you want to know about Lex?"

"We understand he and you were good friends and had been in business together at Riverside Mercantile for many years when he abruptly left the company," Sid said.

"To be accurate, the store didn't become Riverside Mercantile until Etta merged her store with ours in 1942. Nevertheless, Lex, Etta, and I were close school chums and the friendships continued into adulthood."

"Why did Porter leave the store?" Sid asked.

"He wasn't happy with the direction we were taking."

"Excuse me," Tom interrupted, "by we you mean you and Etta?"

"Yes. Lex wanted to run the store one way. We had other ideas. Although we tried to compromise with him, he decided to go it alone. He opened his own store."

"But he couldn't compete with us," Randy added.

Tom glanced at Jack for confirmation.

"That's correct," the elder Brighton said. "They did okay, but he decided to find work up north, in Kansas City, I think."

"Why didn't his wife and son go with him?" Sid asked.

"I couldn't answer that question."

"When did Lex come back to Branson?" Sid asked.

Jack shook his head. "He didn't. I'm sure I would have known if he had come back."

"You don't know what happened to him after he left for Kansas City?"

"Exactly," Jack said, glancing at his attorney.

"That takes care of it then," Keith said, coming to his feet. "Are there other issues to discuss today?"

Tom and Sid spent the remainder of the day trying to run down Julie's boyfriend and reviewing building department personnel files for potential bribery candidates. As Sid speculated, many workers left Chicago for Branson in the early nineties.

At four o'clock, Tom stacked everything neatly on his desk. "My eight hours were up several hours ago. No more phone calls. I'm going to go pick up Katie and we'll meet you and Shirley at the pizza place in one hour."

When Tom pulled into the motel parking lot, Kate was already waiting by the office. He figured her day had probably gone like his and she was ready for a night out. He would prefer to test drive Sid and Shirley's relationship another time, but the commitment had been made. He would not be able to convince Kate otherwise.

"Did some perp beat you up?" she asked, scooting into the passenger seat.

"Thanks. You look pretty great yourself."

"I'm sorry, I didn't mean you weren't your usual incredibly handsome self. But I detect a bit of tiredness in those sexy blue eyes of yours."

"Good recovery. I could have used some of that finesse today."

"Bad day in cop city, huh?"

"Like every day since that stupid oak stump flipped up those remains."

"I bet you've met all kinds of interesting people. And you get to interrogate them without making a lot of excuses or manipulating your way into their lives."

"You mean like the lady who smoked like a chimney and nearly bit our heads off because she didn't know where her boss was?"

"Sounds charming. Where was that?"

"Some flea market. But I don't want to talk about any of the interesting people I've met in my line of work. I want to have a special evening with my newly reestablished girlfriend on a double date with my partner and his new girl. No. I'm lying. I wish we were going to my place or your place for a quiet evening alone together. But I know how much matchmaking means to you."

"Are you finished?"

"Yes."

"So, you don't want to talk about work?"

"Right."

"Why didn't you say that?"

Chapter Twenty-Eight

Kate lingered in bed and tried to attach Tom's description of the lady from the flea market to a woman she had seen recently. She couldn't quite remember where or why she had run into the smoking chimney. Ordinarily she wouldn't worry about it, but she was curious why Tom encountered the woman and felt compelled to satisfy that curiosity. She considered her natural inquisitiveness an asset rather than a neurosis, given her current occupation.

Answering the phone in the living room, she was pleased to hear Shirley's voice. "I'm glad you called," Kate said.

"Before you tell me why, I have to thank you from the bottom of my heart for setting me up with Sid," Shirley said.

"You must have had a good time after the movie."

"Don't get too excited. We talked for a while and he left."

"That's it?"

"He did kiss me goodnight."

"Sounds exciting to me. I knew you two had something going in the restaurant."

"And you're glad I called because?"

"Where did we see that crazy old woman who was smoking one cigarette after another?"

"What?"

"I seem to remember you were with me, but I can't remember where."

"What brought this up?"

"Tom mentioned this woman that worked in a flea market that smoked like a chimney. I was trying to figure out the connection."

"Tory's Treasures. She was yelling at the clerk at the counter about something as we arrived. She didn't stop smoking the entire time, even lit a couple cigarettes during the lecture."

"Bryan Porter's place?"

"So, is Tom having an affair with this lady?"

"Very funny. He said he was trying to find her boss. I guess he meant Bryan. Anyway, it doesn't matter."

"That does not sound like the Lois Lane of *Tri-Lakes Newspapers*."

"I'm sure Tom wanted to speak to Bryan about that suit or something."

"Oh, by the way, I spoke to my dad about Bryan. Apparently, the marriage had been of the shotgun variety. As it turned out, the not quite 20-year-old bride lost the baby."

"Good lord, Bryan had to be in his thirties."

"Yes. And, in the spirit of the decade, he tried to make a go of the marriage. It did not work out. In other words, she dumped him."

"What did your father have to do with it?"

"He intervened with the bride's family, who insisted on ... shall we say ... a settlement."

"Ah. Curious, but not relevant to the events of this decade."

"Probably not. Well, I have to go. Thanks again for Sid."

Kate hung up and tapped her index finger on the receiver. *Bryan's marriage isn't important, but why Tom drove out to the flea market to speak to the man might be.*

Bryan's building was larger and the merchandise less treasured than Kate remembered. As she recalled, she and her old friend may have indulged in a glass or two of wine before going on the flea market binge tour that afternoon.

"Is the manager available?" Kate asked.

"Not today," the young girl at the counter said with a snicker.

"Does he have a second in command?"

"I guess his cousin Sylvia. She's in the back office. Take aisle four."

Kate made her way beyond the ten or so rented stalls along either side of the aisle. At the end of the row the large picture window framed a small office and its occupant—a gray-haired smoking chimney. The reporter tapped on the glass and waited for the seated woman to wave her to the door.

Kate entered, then took an involuntary step backward, overwhelmed by the stench of stale smoke. "My name is Kate Starling, *Tri-Lakes Newspapers*," she said, offering her card.

Sylvia crushed out her current cigarette– forcing several butts to overflow the large ash tray–and accepted the business card.

"You wrote those articles about the crafts fair. They were interesting. Brought back memories for me. I'm not that old but I've been around for a few."

"I'm glad you enjoyed them. Maybe you can help me with some information."

"What about?"

"As a follow-up to the articles, I would like to do a series on the antique stores in Branson. They're crafts fair cousins, after all," Kate said.

"I think they're the central attraction for tourism in this town."

"Exactly," Kate said with a smile. She stole a breath of air from the hallway and eased into the room. "May I sit here?"

"You bet."

"I understand from the clerk that you are the owner's cousin."

"Correct. But I've been involved with flea markets, I mean, antique stores, for lots longer than Bryan."

Kate made the mistake of asking how the stores worked and Sylvia was off and running with every aspect of the flea market business. She continued the occasionally interesting diatribe for several minutes as Kate took notes. The reporter waited for Sylvia to pause and light a cigarette before interrupting.

"Wow. This is great. You've given me a lot for my articles."

"When will they be in the paper?"

"First, I have to convince the editor to do them. I'm still accumulating information for my proposal," Kate said moving toward the door. "How long have you been working with Bryan?"

"A little over fifteen years. I worked at several other places, but Bryan needed a manager so I agreed to help him out. Didn't hurt having my accounting skills, either."

"I'll bet. The reason I ask is my boyfriend used to work for Bryan when he was a kid. It would have been before you started, though."

"What's his name?"

"Tom Collingwood."

"Detective Tom Collingwood?"

"Yes. You know him?"

"Met him a week or so ago. He came to see Bryan."

"Hmm. Small world. We don't discuss work. It leads to too many arguments, if you know what I mean."

"I can imagine. Anyway, your boyfriend is a nice man. He explained everything to me about the test. Made me feel okay about doing it."

"Test?"

"Some new thing to help with an old case they're trying to close. I'm not sure how I can help, but I guess I've been around long enough to qualify."

"Did it have something to do with Bryan?"

"I don't think so," Sylvia said.

"But you said Tom was looking for Bryan, right?"

"No, the test thing happened later. He called me about that separately."

"I'm glad he took care of you."

Sylvia smiled.

"Thanks for your help. I'll let you know about the articles," Kate said, not wanting to push Sylvia about the test. Maybe a subtle question to Tom about old open cases, would be an exception to the off-limits-topic rule. But she doubted it would be that easy.

Helen's staff meeting went on longer than usual. It was more of a pep talk to stimulate ideas for articles during the upcoming winter months when the town would be in off-season shut down mode. All the young and eager part-time reporters chimed in with ideas for feature stories. Helen, to her credit, was gentle with her comments and encouraged everyone to bring her proposals as soon as possible. Kate drifted in and out of daydreams in which she scored major points for exposing Allen's unethical, maybe even illegal, shortcomings.

"Something humorous to share, Kate," Helen asked.

Kate scanned the room to see who was laughing loudest. She scooted forward in her chair and straightened her back. "Turns out I'm planning an article revealing the long-unnoticed crimes of a prominent Branson businessman."

More laughter.

Helen said, "In that case, I'm sorry I disturbed you." She paused for effect then said, "Okay, everyone, get to work."

"Can I have a moment?" Kate asked, following Helen to her office.

"I have a couple items to discuss with you also."

Helen closed the door and sat in the chair next to Kate. "I attended a small group of area business owners last night. The attendees were a strange combination, including Larry Allen and Harold Wainright."

"That is a bit odd," Kate commented.

"I managed to speak to Wainright before the activities began. He said you weren't a real problem. He understands you need to follow up."

"How nice."

"I asked him about working with the chamber and, as with you, he claimed he enjoyed the meetings, but hadn't developed any real business relationships. He was enjoying his retirement far more than he expected he would."

"So, what was the meeting about?"

"The announced purpose was to discuss Branson's future, which is innocuous enough. But the conversation quickly pinpointed the findings of the survey. Keep in mind, I would not have known that fact if you hadn't shared the preliminary report with me."

"What was said?"

"Nothing specific in terms of plans. Mainly ideas about making Branson a viable location for large corporate meetings. But the give and take between Allen and Wainright was more interesting than the discussion in general. The smooth way they ping-ponged the conversation and manipulated the rest of us to bring up certain suggestions was impressive. Even I was drawn into this rather exciting think tank atmosphere."

"What game are they playing?" Kate asked.

"Maybe it's not a game. Maybe they want to stimulate the debate and do what's best for the town."

"You're right. That's got to be it," Kate said, not trying to stifle her sarcasm.

Helen raised an eyebrow. "In any case, they were tight at the meeting. I've checked around with some contacts in town who confirm that the two are on the same wavelength ... whatever that means."

"It means they are both in it for the big bucks and I don't mean for the city."

"We know they're playing coy about their relationship at least to the press."

Kate smiled. "I'm still hoping for the big exposé."

"What's happening with the article about the fires?" Helen asked.

"Not much. I have a draft ready, but unfortunately there's no consistent pattern. The properties, all residential, belong to several different individuals or companies. Although many of the houses were located on the downtown lakefront, others have been vandalized throughout the county. None of the damage was particularly serious, all was covered by insurance."

"Had the owners been approached to sell?"

"Some."

"Okay, send me the draft and any other info and we'll decide what to do."

As soon as Kate got back to her cubicle, she sent the files to Helen. She was almost ready to leave for her appointment with Phil Bingham when the phone rang. It was her friend Libby from the city engineer's office.

"Hey, good to hear from you," Kate said.

"Thanks, but I don't have anything earth-shattering to report," Libby said.

"But you do have something."

"I spoke to Calvin about the lot and a lack of a follow-up plan," Libby said. "He told me not to worry about it."

"Isn't part of your job worrying about details and loose ends?"

Libby didn't respond so Kate asked, "So I'm guessing that's not all you have for me."

The secretary cleared her throat. "It seemed uncharacteristic for Calvin. So, I ..."

"Go ahead," Kate urged.

"I reviewed his meeting calendar and noticed something. Larry Allen and Calvin have had several meetings over the last five or six months. What is unusual is that the meetings had no purpose. I mean, they weren't scheduled through me with a particular topic. That's how official meetings are handled and those are generally group sessions. These were simply penciled in by Calvin on his personal calendar, which indicates to me that they were last minute."

"So, what do you make of it?" Kate asked.

"I think I've caught your overactive imagination."

"Sorry, there's no cure for that."

Libby chuckled. "Look, Kate. I have no idea what this means, but this is all I have. It's probably nothing."

"You're right. Don't worry about it."

Kate rushed out of the office and headed down the street to see Phil. "Sorry I'm late," she said as she tapped on his open door.

"No problem. Pull up a chair. This won't take long."

Phil shoved some papers and a book to the side of his desk and took a file from the cabinet beside his chair. He placed the copy of the agreement in front of Kate.

The margins were full of words with arrows pointing to various paragraphs or phrases in the document. Although the words didn't make sense to Kate, she assumed they referred to cases, or laws, or something. She squinted to read some of the smaller handwriting.

"Sorry. I got carried away with my notes. Let me bottom line it for you."

"That would be great. I don't want to take up too much of your time."

"In my opinion this partnership agreement is a valid contract, written in straightforward terms ... not necessarily legal jargon or format ... but clearly stated. It specifies that the agreement includes the three individuals and their heirs. As with any contract, verbal or otherwise, the identification of the participants must be validated. In the case of this written document, it would be necessary to validate signatures and to verify the age of the paper and ink."

"Could an heir make a case for a share of the partnership?" Kate asked.

"The validated document would be a good start. If someone has a superseding document or if any party denies the agreement's authenticity, the case becomes more complicated."

"I understand," Kate said.

"You'll want to keep this copy with my notes, just in case."

"Thanks, Phil. I appreciate your checking this out for me. Send your bill to the newspaper to my attention."

"I never charge red-headed reporters for a simple legal opinion," he said with a wink.

Chapter Twenty-Nine

All of Kate's notes about the skeleton lot, the property fires, and the lakefront offers-to-purchase were spread across the kitchen table. The survey report and interview notes with Libby, Henderson, Wainright, and Brighton were stacked beside her on a chair.

"None of this makes sense," she shouted to the empty kitchen.

"I can hear you," her dad called from the back porch.

She let the screen door slam behind her and sat down on the glider. "Do you think I have an overactive imagination?"

Roger leaned forward, stopping the movement of the glider, and scratched his head.

Kate stood up, spun around, and eased onto the banister across from her dad. "I'm serious. I want to know your honest opinion."

"How about you tell me what makes you ask."

"There are some strange things going on in Branson," Kate said, pacing the width of the porch.

"The lakefront stuff?"

"Yes, but the problem *is* the stuff. I know something is happening, but the picture is out of focus. Now I'm wondering if it's me. And my imagination."

"Look, honey, I know you want to uncover a big conspiracy in Branson, preferably led by Councilman Allen, or at least someone at Fortune Enterprises. But you may be disappointed."

Kate stared at her father and sighed deeply as she sunk down on the glider.

Roger said, "Okay. What else do you have?"

"Including my reporter's intuition?"

Her father shrugged.

"Allen and a new guy in town, Harold Wainright, are working together. They seem to have convinced the Chamber of Commerce to do this massive questionnaire."

"That's not even interesting."

"Okay, what about Henderson, the man who called you? He's been trying to buy property on the lakefront. And he wouldn't even consider buying your motel."

"Yeah. Hard to imagine he'd pass it up," Roger said, his words drenched in sarcasm.

"Hey, this place may not be pretty, but the location is primo."

"Good point," Roger said with a smile.

"And, how about all the suspicious fires in town?" Kate asked

"I've read about a few, but they didn't seem significant to me."

"The owners are all on the list Margie compiled."

"What else?"

"I'll admit a few pieces are missing," Kate said.

"You mean like proof of a conspiracy?"

"I agree. I'm an investigative journalist run amok."

"It's a shame you don't have someone who can help you put this all together. Not that Margie and I aren't crack investigators."

"Helen has helped me a little. Maybe she can assign another reporter to the story."

"I was thinking someone with more experience. Too bad you don't have access to someone like, I don't know, a police detective."

Kate pushed off the glider, not sure if she should thank her father for his suggestion or be furious with him for beating her to the idea.

Before driving to Etta's, Kate made another copy of the partnership agreement, and stuck the original in her bag. Etta was raking leaves away from her porch toward the large stand of trees in front of her house.

"You make me feel tired. And lazy," Kate shouted as she approached.

Etta laughed. "You're too busy for yard work."

"I'll try that excuse on my dad," Kate said, holding the papers over her head. "I have something for you."

Etta met Kate halfway and accepted the pages, which were in chronological order. She studied the top sheet as she walked toward the porch. Sitting down on her rocker, she moved the marriage application to the back, revealing the note from Clay.

"Where did you find these?" she asked Kate, who had eased onto the glider.

"They were in the box you gave me. I found the key."

Etta reread Clay's words. She touched his signature, then wiped a stray tear from her cheek. "I thought I put these with my important papers in my file box."

Kate said, "I didn't mean to upset you."

"I appreciate this more than you know."

"There's one more document," Kate said.

Etta moved Clay's note to the bottom and read the partnership agreement.

Kate asked. "Is this what Bryan Porter is looking for?"

The older woman furrowed her brow. "It means nothing."

"It seems important."

"It was a lark."

"I'm pretty sure Bryan would disagree with you."

"Jack and Lex were trying to make me feel welcome. Clay had just died. I felt pretty guilty about everything. After the funeral I came home and withdrew. For many weeks after Clay's death, I couldn't deal with anything. Jack and Lex helped me through that period."

"They were good friends," Kate offered when Etta paused.

"Eventually, I went back to Clay's store. I tried to get the word out that I was opened for business. No one showed up but Jack and it took him a couple of days. Anyway, that's when he offered to merge our stores. I knew it was a good idea. No one related to a woman store owner. They were nice enough, but it was a man's world back then."

"So, you accepted his offer."

"Yes. It took a few more weeks to get everything ironed out. The day of our official opening as Riverside Mercantile, the whole town showed up. I knew I'd done the right thing. Anyway, that night we had a private celebration for the families. It was then that Jack and Lex showed me this paper. It was the sweetest thing. We all signed it, but that was it."

"The papers weren't filed?"

"No. They gave it to me as a gesture of everlasting friendship. I tucked it away and forgot about it."

Kate decided to make one more go at the councilman. She found Allen in the middle of the newly grated parking lot for his office complex. He was chewing out a man about the quality of the asphalt he planned to pour. When the councilman spotted Kate, he turned his back on her and gave the contractor a few more instructions. After he finished his conversation, he went inside the building and emerged several minutes later, visibly disappointed to find her waiting by his office trailer.

"Sorry to keep you waiting," he said with his usual ear-to-ear smile.

"No problem. I was admiring the beautiful landscaping."

"Thanks. I hope we can say the same about the parking lot when those idiots finish."

"Subcontractors can be a challenge," she said.

"Sorry. I'm losing my patience, I guess."

"I understand, and I won't take too much of your time. I have a few questions about your new project in Branson."

"We have three finishing up, but the only new site is in Stone County, over by Kimberling City."

"Larry, I know you have something planned for Branson itself. I don't know what it is exactly, but I know it's big. All I'm asking is for a little information about the project and an exclusive on the announcement."

"Sounds fair. But I can't help you out on this one."

"You've promised the story to someone else?"

"Look, I don't know who your source is, but you've been misinformed. We have nothing going on or planned for Branson. End of story."

"Maybe I am confused. I could have mis-understood Mr. Wainright when I interviewed him. I usually take pretty clear notes, but I'm not infallible."

"Harold Wainright?"

"Yes, your new best buddy at the Chamber of Commerce."

Allen furrowed his brow then replaced the frown with his stock grin. "I know Harold. He's new in town. I've been nice to him. That *does not* mean we are best buddies. Nor does it mean he knows anything about my business."

"What about the business you share with him?"

"Okay, now I know you're fishing. Harold Wainright is a retired businessman from Chicago. He and I are acquaintances at the chamber. That's it."

"I suppose you aren't associated with Kyle Henderson either."

"All I know about him is he is interested in purchasing land in Branson."

"Specifically, along the downtown lakefront."

"I didn't know he was particular."

"Do you have anything to do with his approaching the owners?"

"I give up. You're relentless," he said, opening the door to his trailer.

"You didn't answer my question."

"Thanks for dropping by, Kate. Always a pleasure." He let the door slam behind him.

Chapter Thirty

The spaces in front of the building were full as was the side lot. Missouri's low gas prices and a full-service coffee bar—not to mention alcoholic beverages—attracted many commuters to the convenience store located on US 65 a couple miles north of the Arkansas border.

Sid walked toward the small attached garage where a mechanic worked on an old pickup. Tom went inside, fixed two large coffees, and waited by the register until a slightly scruffy man in his late twenties emerged from the back room.

"Anything else for you this morning?" the man asked, adjusting his ball cap.

"Not unless you have some glazed doughnuts hidden somewhere," Tom said.

"Sorry, two truckers heading to Kansas City made off with the entire stash."

"Timing is everything," the detective said.

"True enough. It'll be two dollars and fifty-six cents for the coffees."

When Tom put the change in his pocket, he pulled back his jacket to reveal his badge. "Detective Tom Collingwood, Branson PD. I have a few questions for the owner."

"He won't be in for another thirty minutes or so."

"Maybe you can help. We're looking for a young woman who may be an employee. Her name is Julie."

"Honestly, I don't know everyone's name. But you're welcome to hang around for the owner, Chet Avery."

Tom nodded and joined Sid outside on a bench close to the double glass doors.

Sid took the coffee and said, "No doughnuts?"

"Sorry. We should have come sooner."

"Like that could happen. Man, this place is swamped. Every pump. The mechanic has two oil changes waiting and he's working on an oil leak in that old Chevy."

"Owner's name is Chet Avery. He'll be in soon. The clerk didn't know, or wouldn't say, much on his own."

"Maybe old Chet would be interested in selling this place. We could retire in style with a business like this."

"My grandpa would respond by telling you the grass always looks greener on the other side of the fence," Tom said.

"You have a grandpa who talks like that?"

"Did you get anything from the mechanic?"

"Believe it or not he *does* come in at five every weekday morning. However, he said he is too busy to pay attention to who uses the pay phone, which is located on the far side of the building."

"Good to know," Tom said.

Twenty minutes and—by Sid's count—sixty fill-ups later a man in his late forties walked up to the bench. Considering his expensive cowboy boots, logo T-shirt, and tailored jeans, maybe Sid was right about changing careers.

"Chet Avery," he said extending his hand. "Understand you fellas have some questions for me. We can go into what I call my office, if you like."

The two men followed the owner to a small area carved out of the large storeroom in the back of the structure.

"Pull up a crate," Avery said.

"We're looking for a young woman named Julie. She may be the person who made a call from your payphone to one of our hotlines early last Wednesday."

"Sounds like Julie Hill. She quit on Wednesday. I hated to see her go. Some kind of family emergency in Chicago."

"She moved here from Chicago?" Sid asked.

"Yeah, probably two, maybe three years ago. Let me pull her file."

"Did she give any notice?"

"She hung around for a couple of hours for me to find someone to cover the rest of her shift. I'm convinced the family emergency was her boyfriend, Frankie."

"Why do you say that?" Tom asked.

"He was pressuring her to go back to Chicago."

"Did she say something?"

"Nothing specific, a few little comments, but she wasn't a complainer."

"I don't suppose you have a forwarding address for Julie."

"Turns out she gave me her mother's address, so I could send her final check. She didn't want to wait for payday."

Sid copied the address into his notebook. "How about the boyfriend. Do you know where he worked?"

"Some construction company in Ozark. They have numerous projects in Branson. I'll remember the name in a minute or two."

"Do you know what type of work he did?"

"He was a finisher, mostly with tile, but also woodwork. I know because Julie showed me pictures. She's very proud of him."

"You've been helpful, Mr. Avery. Thanks for your time," Tom said.

"Meacham and Company," Avery shouted as the detectives left the storage area. "The name of the company Frankie worked for in Ozark is Meacham and Company."

Tom stopped at the coffee bar on the way out. It would be a long drive to Ozark.

Sid met him at the register, waving a ten-dollar bill. "My treat," he said.

"What's the occasion?"

"You want me to say it?"

"I want you to admit this lead may actually pay off."

"Wait until we finish in Ozark before you get too cocky, partner. We still have nothing."

Tom shook his head. "You are so wrong. We have Julie Hill. We have Frankie. We have a forwarding address. And we have Meacham and Company."

The medium-sized metal building sat about fifty yards off the main road through Ozark. Two men were loading supplies from a raised dock into a cargo van. A magnetic sign with the company's name, address, and phone number was attached to either side of the van. One car was parked in front of the office door.

The attractive lady in her late forties greeted the officers when they entered. She said her name was Vivian, but please call her Viv. Tom explained who they were and asked if she would be able to help with personnel information.

"You have found the Jill-of-all-jobs in this place. I'm the receptionist, the accountant, the payroll lady, and the typing pool."

"Well, Viv, sounds like you run this place," Sid said.

"I leave that up to my husband. He's the owner, manager, and shop foreman."

"Your last name is Meacham?" Tom asked.

"Sam Meacham was the original owner. My husband is Lincoln Stoddard. We bought the place almost twenty years ago. Kept the name and all the goodwill that went with it."

"Sounds like a good business," Sid said.

"What brings you two detectives twenty miles north of Branson?"

"We understand you had a young man named Frankie working for you until this week."

"That's right. He came in Monday when he finished his last job and quit. Really odd, if you ask me."

"Had he been with the company long?"

"We don't work that way. We have one shop employee, the overall supervisor. Individuals hire on per job as contractors. Being a small business, we couldn't afford to carry folks between jobs. We're busy now, but we've had many thin months in previous years."

"So, when you say he quit, he basically took himself off the roster?"

"We tapped him for another job in Branson and he declined. But you have the right idea."

"Did he give a reason?"

"Told Linc it wasn't working out, which seemed strange. He's been in our tech pool for almost three years. He's a topnotch installer, both tile and woodwork. Linc and I hired him to redo *our own* kitchen tile."

"What project was he working?"

"The last one was the new office complex, but it was outside Branson."

"Do you have a forwarding address for him?"

"Do you have a warrant?" Viv smiled, fingering some files in her desk drawer, adding quickly, "Always wanted to say that."

"You're not alone," Sid said.

She opened the folder and wrote down Frankie's full name and an address for future contact. She handed the slip to Tom.

"Let me get you a printout of all the jobs he's done for us."

"That would be great," Sid said.

"Hope he's not in any trouble. He's a nice kid."

Sid said, "Not at all. We hope he can help us with an ongoing case."

"Thanks for your hospitality, Viv," Tom said. "We appreciate it."

He handed the note to Sid as they crossed the lot. "Same address Julie gave to Chet. And we have Frankie's last name with all his work in Branson."

"What's next?" Sid asked.

"We need to get clearance from the lieutenant to go to Chicago, try to get a statement from Frankie Martin. But right now, we need to get back to Branson for our meeting with Artie on the DNA analysis report."

Artie's van was already parked near the police department entrance. Tom glanced at his watch to confirm they weren't late. "He's early. I hope he has good news," he said.

They found the coroner in Lieutenant Palmer's office discussing DNA evidence in a case making national headlines.

Tom said, "You didn't start without us, did you?"

"We're debating the use of DNA findings in court cases," Palmer said.

"Hey, use of DNA has been around for decades in identifying remains," Artie said.

"Like our case?" Sid asked.

Palmer shrugged. "Problem is it's difficult to explain to a jury."

Tom and Sid pulled a couple of chairs closer to the lieutenant's desk. Artie handed each of the others the two-page report.

"Brief and to the point," the coroner said. "By the way a copy of the report was sent to Fredericks. He called me earlier to make some recommendations."

"These odds sound pretty hard to beat," Sid said.

"The results of the comparison between Sylvia's DNA sample and that from the victim's femur is definitive. For legal identification purposes they match. None of the DNA from the other potential victims' relatives came close. The lab and Dr. Fredericks concur that our victim is Alexander Porter."

Tom reviewed the brief report before asking, "Is this enough?"

Artie said, "The pieces of clothing and blanket included in the grave can be used to pinpoint the timeframe. No other missing person fits in that equation. I know the DNA evidence will need to be explained carefully by at least one expert in the field. Fredericks is well-known and respected as a forensic anthropologist. He has years of experience in precisely this type of investigation."

Palmer commented, "But the real question is who killed Porter? After you convince the jury you know who the victim is, you must convince them you know who did the deed."

"We're working on that," Tom said.

"Artie, you said Fredericks made recommendations. What exactly?" Palmer asked.

"He cautioned against telling anyone what we've found until you've made a firm case against someone. Relatives, in particular tend to go off half-cocked."

Tom agreed, "Bryan's pretty close to the edge already. If whoever killed his father is still alive, we don't want the individual to see us coming."

"Precisely," Artie said.

"We plan on questioning Bryan about an issue related to the case. We've already discussed his father's disappearance. He brought it up when we questioned him about his accusations against Fortune Enterprises. Can we ask a few more questions on that subject?"

"Use caution. As you said, Bryan's a fragile guy," Artie said, leaving the office.

"Lieutenant, can we speak to you about another issue?" Tom asked.

"What's up?"

Tom explained the hotline call and the detectives' follow-up activities, then waited for his boss to ask questions or—even better—suggest someone go to Chicago.

Palmer said, "Which one of you needs to go?"

Tom said, "I would. Julie contacted me specifically. This is a good lead."

"Don't oversell it, Tom. I'm all for it. I know someone who works at Chicago PD. I'll make some calls and find a contact for you. Check with me when you finish with Porter."

Tom and Sid found Bryan Porter on the porch of his house. When they parked behind his truck, he didn't move, but his stare acknowledged their arrival.

"Taking the day off, Bryan?" Tom asked.

"I'll probably go in later. The place pretty much runs itself," Bryan said.

"Do you mind if we ask you a few questions?"

"My lawyer says I shouldn't discuss my suit against the city."

"Fair enough. We've been working some old open cases, trying to tie up loose ends. Turns out one of the cases is about your father."

"What about him?"

"After we talked before, we checked to see if your mother had filed a missing person's case when your father didn't return as expected. Remember you said she tried to find him at the address where she sent letters?"

"I'm still not following you."

"She filed the report in 1945. The investigators had a few leads, but eventually hit the dead end in Kansas City. The case was never closed," Tom said.

"Did anything come up after that?" Sid asked.

"I don't remember anything except that she cried constantly and eventually we had to close the store."

"Seems strange ... your dad opening that store. Why did he strike out on his own?"

"I told you. Brighton ran him off."

"Are you saying Jack Brighton fired him?"

"I told you that."

"I'm sorry, I guess I misunderstood," Sid said.

"Did your father tell you he was fired?" Tom asked.

"He didn't have to. I was in the store when it happened. I heard them arguing. Then Uncle Jack ... I called him that when I was young and naïve ...

he yelled for my dad to get out and never come back."

"You're sure that's what was said?"

"Don't tell me I was too young to know what I heard. And don't tell me it was a long time ago and I may not be remembering it as it happened."

Tom said, "I didn't mean that. I guess I'm surprised you haven't been this specific before about why your dad left Brighton's store."

"Did Etta know about the argument?" Sid asked.

"She did after I went running straight to her crying my eyes out."

"And what did she say?"

"That she couldn't help my dad. She said he'd have to live with what he'd done."

"What did she mean?"

"She wouldn't tell me. My dad wouldn't tell me. As you said before, no one tells a kid what's going on, at least not in the 1940s."

"And you were how old?"

"I remember exactly. It was a month before my ninth birthday."

Sid started to say something, but Tom shook his head and stepped off the porch.

"I'm sorry to bring all this up. I didn't realize what happened. We have enough to close the case without bothering you again."

By the time Tom and Sid returned to City Hall, Lieutenant Palmer was gone for the day, but he had left an envelope for Tom at the police department entrance. "Forgot about big date with wife. Had to go. See inside for instructions. DP."

"Great. I guess you're all set," Sid said.

"Let me open it before we get too excited. Flight itinerary, hotel information, contact name and precinct. Now all I have to do is explain to Katie why we aren't going to Silver Dollar City on Sunday or bowling on Monday."

Sid shrugged and said, "How hard can that be?"

Tom's flight arrived in Chicago on time Sunday afternoon, much to the amazement of several regular travelers. A tall man in jeans and a sports coat, arms folded across his chest, waited outside the gate area. When he made eye contact with Tom, he held up a sign with "Collingwood" hand-printed in thick felt-tipped capital letters.

"You must be Sergeant Cross," Tom said.

"Call me Eddie."

"Thanks for picking me up."

"No problem. Your boss said you'd take a cab and call me in the morning. But my wife took the kids to her mother's in Cincinnati, so what the heck."

"Great. I'm all set. Everything's in my carry-on bag."

"Traveling light," Eddie said.

"I'm hoping for a quick trip."

"We'll get you checked in and go somewhere for a bite."

The drive to the hotel took longer than Tom expected. Eddie explained it was located near the precinct. Tom registered at the front desk and took his bag to his room while Eddie waited in his car.

"Beer and pizza okay," Eddie asked when Tom slid into the passenger seat.

"Sounds great. I'm guessing your precinct was chosen because of proximity to the address we have on our witness."

"Bingo. Which reminds me. Your lieutenant spent over two hours trying to get this all set up. No telling how many people he spoke to. I got the impression he doesn't know how big Chicago, or Chicago PD, is."

"Branson's a small town. Lieutenant Palmer is from Springfield, which is larger, but still doesn't compare."

"I understand you were in the Kansas City PD for about ten years."

"Still nothing like Chicago."

Eddie parked in the precinct lot and the two men walked a few blocks, mingling with the crowds on the busy sidewalk. Distracted momentarily, Tom lost track of his guide.

"I'll try harder to keep up," he said as he caught up several doors later.

"No problem, this is it."

A neon sign on the brick wall next to the plain wooden entrance proclaimed "pizza" in bright red letters. Eddie pulled the door open and motioned Tom inside. Once they ordered the two detectives continued to exchange career information until the beers arrived.

"So, let me tell you what I've done already," Eddie said, redirecting the conversation.

Tom nodded and sipped his beer.

"The address is one half of a duplex a few miles from here. Owners are Lionel and Beverly Frieden. They own the whole building, live on one side, rent out the other half. Not sure who the current tenant is. Could be your witness. I have a request submitted to see who's paying the utilities. We should know tomorrow."

"You've been busy."

Eddie shrugged. "The Friedens are exemplary citizens, meaning they have no priors, no wants, and no warrants. Daughter Julie Hill was married at eighteen for a grand total of twenty-seven months. No children, former husband arrested a couple times for petty stuff, no convictions. Julie is squeaky clean like Mom and Dad."

"Which leaves Frankie Martin," Tom said motioning to the waiter for another round.

"Yes. He's not quite squeaky, but close. He was a gang member when he was in middle and high school. Got in a bit of trouble, but somehow managed to outgrow and outrun the gangs. I know this because, when I couldn't find anything current, I asked a few people I know at his high school. Otherwise, nothing. He's been a union guy since he got out of trade school."

"All this background is great. I appreciate your doing my job for me."

"No problem. I expect the same in return when I come to Branson someday."

Chapter Thirty-One

Jack Brighton's assistant showed Kate into a small conference room close to his office suite. The meeting, rescheduled from last week, was a follow-up for the Branson history series, which had proven to be popular with readers. She hoped to get information from Brighton about some individuals he knew and worked with in the early days as Riverside Mercantile evolved into Fortune Enterprises. Her ultimate goal was to maneuver the discussion to the "city project" his grandson confronted him about during their argument.

"Great view," Jack said, joining Kate by the large picture window. "You know Randy. And this is my lawyer, Keith Hawthorne. I hope you don't mind if they sit in on the interview."

"No problem." She took out her recorder, turned it on, and placed it in the middle of the table, following the if-you-don't-want-to-know-don't-ask rule of journalism. When no one made a comment, she started with her first in a series of questions about the first decade of Jack's company. The questions were innocuous and straightforward, preliminary inquiries to make the interviewee comfortable and begin to tell his story. His responses were complete and accurate, according to research Kate had done in preparation for the discussion.

Hawthorne chimed in about thirty minutes later, "I might make a suggestion, Kate. Jack could probably use a break. I'd like to get up and stretch my legs myself."

"That's a good idea," she said, turning off the recorder.

During the break, Randy excused himself to go to a meeting in Springfield. Kate, impatient to finish the interview, waited five more minutes before switching on the recorder.

"I'd like to move on to more specifics about Fortune Enterprises during the 1960s up to the present. Our research department made a list of major projects, in particular ones that were turning points for the Branson community." She handed Jack and his lawyer a copy of the list and asked Jack to discuss the impact of each on the city and him personally. Jack described each project thoroughly.

"One final question," Kate said an hour later.

"It seems like you have enough for several articles," Hawthorne commented.

"You're right. The stories have been so interesting, I didn't want to stop. But I have one more question and this will be the last session for the series. I promise."

"I'm fine, Keith. What's your question, Kate?"

"I've heard rumors that your company has a big project in the early planning stage for Branson. Specifically, the project involves a major renovation of old downtown and a significant development along the lakefront."

"And your question?" Hawthorne said when she paused.

"Can you tell me more about the project, including specifics and a timeframe? I'd like to give the readers a little teaser for the future."

"Specifics and a timeframe would be a lot more than a teaser," the lawyer said.

"But you can confirm there is a project in the works?" Kate asked.

Hawthorne started to respond, but Jack held up his hand and shook his head. "You are very clever, Kate. But we had this conversation weeks ago. As I told you then, Larry will keep you in the loop for any announcements, which we will make at an appropriate time."

Kate turned off the recorder, securing the latch on her portfolio before she rose to leave. "I'll have a draft of the article to you in a few days," she said.

Jack said, "Before you go, I would like to chat about the papers you gave to Etta. I'm interested in one of the documents."

"The partnership agreement?" Kate asked, pushing her luck a bit.

Jack took a step closer to the reporter. "You gave Etta a copy. Where's the original?"

Hawthorne touched Brighton's arm and said, "We don't want copies to be circulating that may confuse the issue. The fact is, the document is not a legal contract that would stand the test in a court of law."

"Why would I test it in a court of law? I prefer the court of public opinion," she said, immediately regretting her words.

"Etta would appreciate your giving us the original document and any copies you have made," Hawthorne said.

Kate said, "She told me the document was a lark, the act of two good friends trying to cheer her up during an incredibly sad time in her life. She didn't ask if I had copies. You are the ones placing importance on an invalid document."

"You have no reason to keep the original. You have nothing to gain by sharing it with anyone," Hawthorne said, speaking slowly and more sternly.

"You're right. I have nothing to gain by doing that." She paused at the door with one parting shot. "But I thought perhaps Bryan Porter would be interested in seeing a document signed by his father."

Kate couldn't get out of the building fast enough. Her people skills—not to mention her common sense—had taken one giant step backward. She rushed to her office and removed the original partnership agreement from her case. She took a deep breath and tapped on Helen's door.

"You have a safe in your office, don't you?"

Helen looked over her computer screen and sighed. "I'm afraid to ask ..."

"I need to use it for a few days."

"Sit down. Sounds like we need to talk. You first."

"I finished my final interview with Brighton for the history series."

"Did you plan two more articles about him, his family, and company?"

"Yes, but that may not be possible now."

"Explain, please."

"You know I'm doing research on Larry Allen. Well, I am now convinced he has some big project in mind for Branson. How bad can that be, right? But what if he is setting himself up to make a lot of money?"

"I hate to point out the obvious, but Allen is a businessman. His family has been extremely successful in this town. I can't say it would be surprising for him to make lots of money. But what does this have to do with putting something in the safe?"

"The interview cruised along for two hours and everything was fine. But I was trying to find out about Allen's project. His grandfather has to know about it. But that's another story. Anyway, Brighton got defensive and clammed up."

"You didn't push him at all, right?" Helen asked.

Kate shrugged and then said, "I was about to leave, but he stopped me. He wanted the original copy of an agreement I found in one of Etta's keepsake boxes."

"And that is the document you are gripping in your hands as if it were attached?"

"This is an agreement between Jack Brighton, Etta Stupholds, and Lex Porter, which sets up the three dear friends, and their heirs, in a partnership for life in Riverside Mercantile."

"Which owns Fortune Enterprises," Helen said. "And, let me guess the rest. Since you were out on the limb, you decided to jump up and down on it."

"That would be a good description of my next move. Brighton and his lawyer insisted the agreement was not valid, so I asked why they wanted the original document. And then the conversation went downhill."

"How far downhill?"

"I may have implied I would give the document to Bryan Porter."

Helen closed her eyes and rubbed her temples. "I'm not seeing how this fits in with any of your current assignments. You found this document in one of *Etta's* boxes?"

"Don't worry, I showed her what I found. I gave her a copy of the agreement, but I returned the originals of the other two."

"Good. More or less. Why did you keep the original of the contract?"

"I'm not sure. Maybe because Bryan deserves to know about it. Etta and Jack might not be eager to share it with their partner's son."

"I would suggest that you put it somewhere other than the newspaper's safe until you decide who to give it to."

"Speaking of turning things over. I know my investigation on Allen and this big project hasn't turned up anything more than my curiosity. My dad encouraged me to confide in Tom. He hasn't said anything, but the police have to be checking on Porter's lawsuit, hoping to prove or disprove his allegations. Maybe what I've collected can help."

"I agree with you. It seems so sensible, maybe even wise."

"And out of character?"

"You have to admit, this is not your usual way of completing an investigation."

"Trust me, I haven't finished with Allen. Or the Brightons for that matter. But I realize I need help."

"I'm proud of you, Kate."

"Don't be too hasty. I plan to blackmail Tom into giving me an exclusive on the councilman's arrest."

"Do his activities warrant criminal charges?"

"Maybe not. But whatever it is, I'll have the story."

"That sounds more like my ace reporter."

Kate concealed the partnership agreement in her mother's recipe box between spaghetti marinara and squash soufflé—no one would look there. The note by the phone indicated her father planned to "linger" at Marge's after dinner and a movie. Kate smiled, then frowned and blocked the mental picture.

Tom hadn't elaborated about his unexpected trip to Chicago. He was sorry they'd have to reschedule the Silver Dollar City outing and bowling date for next week and the surprise she had planned for tonight.

She had no choice—she'd take a nice hot bubble bath.

An hour later she gathered the left-over tuna surprise casserole and a half bag of potato chips and snuggled down on the sofa. She watched a marathon featuring the last six episodes of *Cheers* followed by cast interviews, recording the last two hours to share with Tom when he returned from the windy city.

Her arms full of dishes, she couldn't quite flip the light-switch in the kitchen. As she set the load on the counter, she saw the councilman standing outside under the patio lamp. Without thinking, she slid open the glass door.

Allen said, "I rang the bell, but you didn't answer. Your car was out front, and I saw the light on the patio, so I came around."

She didn't respond, trying to figure out why he'd come to her house and why he lied about ringing the bell.

"Can I come in?" he asked, but he was already brushing past her.

He continued down the short hall to the living room. Her first instinct was to leave the house, go to the hotel office, and call the police. But it occurred to her he couldn't be stupid enough to hurt her in her own home. Nevertheless, she scooped up the paring knife from the dish drain, slid it into to her robe pocket, and proceeded down the hallway.

"What do you want?" she asked.

"My grandfather is unusually upset."

"I'm sorry to hear that."

"You have something he wants."

"Councilman Allen, you'll have to contact me tomorrow at the paper. This is my home. I'm expecting my boyfriend any minute. He's returning from a business trip. You know my boyfriend, don't you?"

"I know Detective Collingwood is still in Chicago. He won't be back until tomorrow or the next day."

"I spoke to him a couple hours ago before he boarded the flight to Springfield."

"Nice try. And don't even bother to say your father will be home soon. He's still at the movie with that realtor girlfriend of his. I'm sure they'll go to her place afterward."

"Okay. How about I don't want you here. Please leave."

"It will take you less than five minutes to retrieve Etta's original document from whatever clever place you've stowed it and bring it to me. That's all I want, and I'll be gone."

Kate put her hand in the pocket containing the knife and walked to the front door. Her pounding heart echoed in her temples. She wasn't sure if her adrenalin was pumping out of fear or anger. She turned on the porch light, opened the door, and then turned to stare at her visitor.

Allen shook his head and took a step backward. "Okay. I'll search for it myself," he said, opening several drawers in the living room tables.

She approached him, even though her twitching muscles argued for her to stay put. After taking a shallow breath, she said, "You know, according to your grandfather's lawyer, the document is a useless piece of paper. Why do you think it's so important?"

"We have no doubt it will be invalidated, but don't want to create any confusion."

"You mean, if I give it to Bryan Porter."

Allen stepped closer and crouched down to stare directly into her eyes. Pushing his pointed index finger into her shoulder with each word, he said, "Very bad idea. Understand?"

She glared at his hand until he withdrew it, straightened up, and stepped away—assessing her reaction to his obvious threat. Taking a deep, calm breath through her nose to quell the anger welling in her gut, she counted to ten as her mother would have insisted.

"You have forced your way into my house and assaulted me. You are essentially holding me a prisoner in my own home. The question is, Councilman Allen, do you understand?"

Careful not to touch her as he headed to the door, he made a beeline to his car and drove off the motel lot. She engaged the front dead bolt, pulled down the safety bar on the patio entrance, and double locked the back door. Then she checked all the windows to be sure they were closed and secure.

Once in her room, she crawled into bed and—still shaking—cried herself to sleep.

Chapter Thirty-Two

Eddie promised a traditional Chicago PD breakfast when he picked up Tom at seven in the morning. It turned out to be a doughnut and coffee at the precinct. A fax from the utility department arrived about eight-thirty indicating the Friedens paid the utilities for both sides of the duplex.

"Guess we'll have to find out where Julie and Frankie are the hard way," Eddie said.

"When will the parents be home?"

"Lionel works full-time, but Beverly works mornings at the local library branch not far from the house. I'd say we could drift over after lunch."

"In the meantime, I'm going to check in with my boss and partner," Tom said.

"And don't forget that girlfriend of yours."

"Not likely."

Lunch consisted of a quick hotdog—fully loaded in Chicago style—and a soda. They parked as close as they could to the duplex and walked to the small porch. When a middle-aged woman answered the door, Eddie confirmed she was Mrs. Frieden and introduced himself and Tom.

"Is my husband okay?" she asked.

"He's fine. I mean, it's not about your husband," Eddie said.

"You scared me for a moment."

"I'm sorry, Ma'am. No one's in trouble or hurt. We just have a few questions."

"Let's sit on the porch, if you don't mind. My daughter is visiting. The house is a lot messier than I'd like to share with strangers."

"We understand. This is fine."

The three settled into some metal chairs in front of the left side of the duplex.

"Mrs. Frieden, I'm from Branson, Missouri," Tom said. "Your daughter Julie and her friend Frankie may be able to help me with a case. She called on a tip-line we set up."

The woman frowned but remained silent.

"We'd like to speak to Frankie. Do you know where he is?" Eddie said.

"I'm not sure. You need to ask Julie, but she's at work. She takes care of several children in an afterschool program at the grade school up the street. But please don't go there."

"No, we wouldn't do that," Eddie said.

Tom asked, "When will she be home?"

"About six, when all the kids have gone home."

Mrs. Frieden wasn't too keen on Eddie and Tom sitting on the porch—or in their car in front of the porch—until Julie came home.

Consequently, the detectives drove around the block, garnered some snacks at the convenience store, and parked a good distance down the street so Julie's mother wouldn't see them. A couple of hours later, Tom was wishing he'd been able to get in touch with Kate, who had been in meetings all day.

Eddie straightened in his seat. "Frankie Martin, I presume," he said, smiling.

"Are you sure?"

"No, but I'm hopeful."

They watched as the young man continued toward them then turned and ran up the steps at the Frieden duplex. Tom didn't budge a muscle as he waited for the inevitable door selection.

"Bingo. Frieden side. Has to be him," Eddie said, already exiting the car.

"Let me take point on this," Tom said.

"No problem."

Tom used the door knocker.

"I'll get it, Bev," the young male voice said.

Tom explained why he tracked Frankie as a possible witness for a Branson case.

Frankie paced to a side window in the small living room. "I told Julie not to get involved. I don't know anything."

Eddie asked, "Can we speak to you on the porch? Just a few questions."

Tom sat across from Frankie. "The fact is, Julie was worried about you. She did get involved. She said you witnessed a bribe exchange. Would you be willing to give me a statement about what you saw and any other information you may have regarding the construction industry in Branson?"

"No way. And you have no jurisdiction in Chicago."

"But I do," Eddie said.

Frankie shook his head. "It's too dangerous."

"Did someone threaten you or Julie?"

The young man peered over the railing toward a passing vehicle.

"We can protect you," Tom said.

"Maybe so, but what I say doesn't mean anything. I'm one guy from out of town."

"If you help us, give us everything you know, maybe other guys who've seen stuff or heard stuff will come forward. They're probably afraid like you, but together you can build the proof we need to stop the corruption."

"I'll think about it."

Eddie scooted to the end of his chair. He leaned forward so he was even closer to Frankie. "How about you come down to the station with us now. You can tell your story. Then decide to sign it or not. It won't be an official statement unless you want it to be. Would that be okay with you?"

"And if I decide not to sign, you'll tear it up?"

"Hey, no problem," Eddie said with a smile.

Tom sat in the back with his witness to explain the process at the station, hoping to make Frankie comfortable. Eddie escorted the young man into an interrogation room while Tom picked up sodas from the vending machine.

Frankie took the Dr. Pepper, popped the top, and swallowed a long swig. "I want to make something clear," he said, wrapping his knuckles on the table. "I've done nothing wrong and I will not return to Branson. If my written statement isn't enough, you're wasting my time and yours."

"Good enough," Tom said. "Let's start with the event Julie told me about."

Frankie described the circumstances leading to the payoff, including the general contractor's man putting money—a stack of at least fifty bills—in an envelope. Before Frankie, could back out of the area, the inspector arrived and took the envelope from the contractor.

"Do you know the names of these two men?" Tom asked.

"No. I'd dealt with them, but don't remember their names," he said.

"It will be important to include a description in addition to a name and other details," Tom said, moving quickly to another question. "What happened next?"

"They shook hands and left the room. I went back to work. I don't even remember why I went to that area of the site to begin with. I know I shouldn't have been shocked, but I didn't expect it in Branson."

"This was your first encounter of a possible bribe?" Eddie asked.

Frankie said, "Yes, but not the first time I had suspicions about stuff."

"Can you be specific?" Tom asked.

"I'm a finisher, which means I do the tile and woodwork toward the end of a construction project. Usually, I arrive and leave and don't mingle much. But this project was full of loose talk about how permits and inspections were expedited. I only paid attention because there was so much discussion."

"We'll need details, including who made the comments," Eddie said.

"Look, if I tell you everything I know or suspect or heard and then have to write it down again later, I'll be here all night and most of tomorrow."

"You're right," Tom said. "Eddie, can a stenographer take all this down so—"

But Eddie was already out the door. Just as quickly, a police stenographer with her machine was seated and ready to go. Before he would say another word, Frankie insisted on calling Julie. The detectives stepped out while he made the call.

"Before you begin," Tom said, returning to the room, "I want to thank you and Julie again for your help. If you'll start with the details you remember from the office complex job that would be great."

"Like I said, the guys were always whispering about stuff. The project manager was really hyper about getting everything done on time. The workers said he was into every detail but hadn't been able to get the building permit issued. That's really unusual when the finishers are showing up."

"What did the workers think about it?"

"Same as me. They blamed the project manager."

"Did you know him?"

"I met Allen, but I dealt with the guy who managed the finish work. That's what I do. I go in, do my thing, and get out. I rarely have to coordinate with anyone or wait for something to be done."

Eddie said, "So things went along even though the permit hadn't been issued."

"Oh, they went along. Even when some piece of the job failed an inspection, it took no time ... and I mean a couple of hours ... to fix it, pass the inspection, and move along."

"Did you experience that with your work?" Tom asked.

"No, but I overheard guys talking about it lots of times."

"What else?" Eddie asked when the witness fell silent.

"More of the same on other projects."

Frankie related what he had heard and seen for several projects, giving the name or a description of individuals who made comments or were involved. The detectives listened, asking occasionally for clarifications. Eddie ordered in burgers and fries for dinner and let Frankie call Julie again while the stenographer transcribed the statement.

When she brought in the completed pages, Tom's witness read, then reread, the document. It was almost ten p.m. when he laid the last sheet face down on the others for the fourth time. He folded his hands on the table, fingers intertwined, and closed his eyes.

Tom and Eddie exchanged glances but said nothing.

"Do you have a pen?" the young man asked after a long thirty seconds.

Tom managed to get a reservation for the ten-a.m. flight to Branson. Eddie pulled up and stopped at the departure area about eight-thirty.

"Does this mean you aren't walking me to the gate?"

"That would be correct," Eddie said, smiling.

"I cannot tell you how much I appreciate your help. I almost hate to leave."

"I'm sure you'll be over that feeling as soon as the plane takes off. Hey, you're welcome. But don't forget you owe me the return favor if I come to Branson."

"No problem!"

As luck would have it the flight departure was delayed for thirty minutes while someone replaced the windshield wipers on the plane. Given the heavy downpour at the time, it seemed like a good idea. But nothing could upset him. He had his witness statement and he was headed home to Kate.

Tom briefed Sid on the drive to Branson from the airport. They spent the next couple of hours developing a list and calling individuals they needed to interview, starting with Ben Leatherman first thing Wednesday morning.

"Will we have enough?" Sid asked.

"You mean without in person testimony? I'm not sure. Maybe having what Frankie told us will help convince others to speak up as well."

"Brad Fortner, the inspector Frankie described, quit a couple of weeks ago. What are the odds we can compel him to return and testify?"

"As good as the odds are of finding him, which we'll know better after our chat with Leatherman."

Sid said, "It's almost five, do you want to hit some of the bars the constructions crews frequent? Maybe see what we can find out?"

"You know, that sounds like a fun time, but I have somewhere I need to be."

"I can't imagine," Sid said, but his partner was already halfway to the door.

Chapter Thirty-Three

Kate had heard her father come home about three a.m. He opened her door, probably to ask why she had locked everything so securely. She had pretended to be asleep even when he called her name, so he gave up. Waking again after another few hours, Kate had decided to go to the office early and work on the scathing exposé she'd like to release about Larry Allen. She wanted to pour every ounce of anger she still felt into the article. The first draft was finished at about nine o'clock when Marge called asking her to come to the real estate office as soon as she could.

As Kate headed down the street, she could swear she saw Bryan Porter duck inside the small flea market on the other side. The man was beginning to get on her nerves. What did he hope to see or find out by following her? *Stop being paranoid*, she thought. *He's probably checking on his competition.*

Marge was in her office reviewing hundreds of sticky notes attached to a formerly blank area of the wall by her window. Sheets of paper were spread across her desk and the table the crafts fair ladies had used.

"You've been busy," Kate said.

"I told you I wouldn't be able to bring all this to your office," the realtor said, smiling while admiring her handiwork.

Kate read a few of the notes and shrugged. "You'll have to decipher these for me. I don't understand your shorthand."

"Right. Sit down, this is important."

"I haven't seen you this excited since you brought that soup to my dad."

"This is almost as good," she said, pacing back and forth next to the notes.

"Calm down and start from the beginning."

Marge took a deep breath. "Remember when I brought you the survey results? I said the responses had come so fast and with an unusually high percentage of return." When Kate acknowledged with a nod, Marge continued, "Something bothered me about the whole thing. I kept bugging Roger with it, and he suggested I either get over it or do something about it."

"Sounds like his sage advice," Kate said with a smile.

"I started making calls to the companies who didn't respond and the ones who did and to the survey company itself. I won't go into all the details. Now keep in mind this is my opinion, but the bottom line is I'm convinced the whole thing was a sham."

Kate stared at the realtor, then the sticky note wall. *This must be how Helen feels when reporters take giant leaps to conclusions*, she mused. "Okay, Margie, I may need a few more of those details."

"I guess I left out a few things. I was going to practice on Roger, but I couldn't wait to share this with you."

The reporter waited, letting Marge sit down and gather her wits.

"Of the hundreds of companies on the mailing list, the first ten or so I called had not received the survey. That included three who supposedly returned responses. I assumed I'd gotten in touch with the wrong department, but each company said that was not the case. So, I called a few more. Quite a few more. Actually, *all* of them. None of the companies had received the original mailing and, consequently, none had responded. On the good news side, many were eager to answer the questions and embraced coming to Branson for meetings. I confirmed the addresses from the original mailing list. All were correct."

"Why would the Chamber of Commerce lie about the survey?"

"I called the survey company to find out. I was told that the person who handled our particular mailing was out of the office but would call me back. That was almost a week ago. So, this morning I called the Better Business Bureau in Chicago where the company is located."

"Don't tell me it doesn't exist."

"It exists, but no physical address, only a phone number and post office box. Numerous complaints have been filed against the company, all answered in the same manner. The work was subcontracted, and any complaints will be forwarded to the appropriate party."

"What kind of complaints?" Kate asked.

"Mostly overcharging and poor reporting."

"I must be missing something. If the surveys weren't mailed to anyone, how were the reports compiled? Who made up the responses?"

"That was another thing that bothered me about the results. The report said companies overwhelmingly requested large conference facilities and activities for large groups."

"Like someone manufactured the data to produce a desired result," Kate said.

Marge grinned, leaned toward Kate, and said, "That's not all I found out. I checked the survey company with the state of Illinois. It was incorporated in Delaware, which is fairly common, and is treated as a trusted out-of-state entity in Illinois. The last update for the registration was a couple years ago. Guess who the Illinois agent of record was."

Evaluating Marge's expression, the reporter whispered, "Harold Wainright," and waited for confirmation.

Marge nodded. "And for the life of me I can't figure out the point of the whole thing. It seems to be an elaborate way to say what everyone in this town already thinks. Branson needs a convention center."

Kate said, "Maybe, but I hesitate to point out that nothing has come of this somewhat complex hoax, not yet anyway. However, it does add to all the other odd things that are taking place. I'd be willing to bet that slimy Larry Allen is in on this."

"You don't like him very much."

"He's an arrogant, selfish and hateful man."

"Sounds like you've seen him in action," Marge said.

"He came to our house last night. It had nothing to do with this issue, at least not directly. He can be a bully, but his brazen and foolish attack on me was out of character."

"He attacked you?"

"Not physically. Well, he did poke my shoulder, but that's it."

Marge said, "Arrogant describes him all right. At a minimum he lacks civil decorum."

"Among other things."

Kate spent the rest of the day preparing for her evening with Tom. She wanted to fix him a nice dinner at his apartment before she tried to convince him that all the little things she knew about Allen and others would add up to some devious conspiracy worth the police department's attention. Marge's information about Wainright would be helpful. But so far nothing seemed illegal—unethical maybe and definitely strange but no more.

Tom arrived as she was putting the final touch on dinner. She ran to meet him, throwing her arms around his neck. He picked her up and hugged her tightly.

"I missed you," she said.

"Me too."

She kissed him and he returned the passion. He placed her gently on the sofa, her arms still clinging to his neck. She pulled him down next to her and leaned her head on his shoulder.

Tom said, "I don't mean to seem unappreciative of this attention, but is something wrong?"

"Can't a girl be happy to see her fella?"

"Sure, but I can tell when you're happy, mad, or sad. And I am particularly good at assessing your I-am-going-to-punch-someone posture."

"Are you saying I look like I'm going to punch someone?"

"Those dazzling eyes do not lie."

"I would argue with you, but you're right. I had a run-in with someone."

"Councilman Allen?"

"Why would you say that?"

"Because you like almost everyone else."

"Before I tell you, you have to promise me something."

"What must I promise?"

"Not to do something rash."

"See. Now that's a problem. You absolutely cannot say something like that to a boyfriend who's been away for three days."

"And you have to promise not to tell Dad."

"I'm going to promise to do as you ask to the best of my ability. Will that work?"

Kate shook her head.

"Sorry, that's my best offer. You can't expect more," Tom said, stroking her hands.

"He came to our house last night. Dad and Margie were out for dinner and a movie. And it was sort of creepy. He knew they were out. He knew you were still in Chicago."

"Why would he come to your house? What did he want?"

"This is sort of a long story. Can it wait till after dinner?"

"I already have plans for after dinner," Tom said, moving closer.

She slipped her hands around his and said, "I'll try to make it brief. I found the key to the box Etta gave me. Inside I found her marriage certificate, Clay's suicide note, and a partnership agreement for Riverside Mercantile."

"The company formed when Etta merged her store with Jack Brighton's?"

"Yes. The agreement, which was signed in October of 1942, named the three partners and any heirs: Jack Brighton, Etta Stupholds, and Lex Porter."

"Are you serious? A partnership in perpetuity?"

"According to Phil Bingham, if the document can be authenticated as far as age and signatures, the contract is valid."

"What does this have to do with Allen coming to your house?"

"I gave the papers I found to Etta, but I gave her a copy of the agreement and kept the original. And, before you ask, I'm not sure why. But Bryan has a right to know about it. Anyway, Etta told Jack and apparently he said something to the councilman."

"Who came to retrieve the original from his friend Kate."

"Precisely. But he wasn't exactly friendly."

"This is where I may do something rash, I suspect."

"He was rather abrasive, especially when he poked his index finger in my shoulder and threatened me. Not only that, he refused to leave and started searching for the agreement."

Tom's silence surprised Kate, who expected some reaction that more-resembled anger. Instead, her boyfriend stared blankly at her, his brow furrowed. She let go of his hands and pushed off the sofa and stormed into the kitchen. *Apparently, poking someone with one finger was not cause for alarm—unless, of course, you are on the receiving end.*

He followed her and eased up behind her, caressing her shoulders and kissing the nape of her neck. "I'm sorry," he whispered.

"That I was poked or that you don't care?"

He twisted her around to face him. "It occurred to me the partnership agreement may help a case I'm working. I guess I sort of drifted off."

"Drifted off? You could at least pretend to listen. Wait a minute. Are you saying that the skeleton is Lex Porter?"

"I did not say that."

"I knew it," Kate shouted.

Tom grabbed her shoulders and put on his most serious expression. "You can't know."

"Maybe I didn't know it *exactly*, but I was getting close."

"That makes even less sense. And you're still guessing."

"But—"

He placed his index finger on her lips. "I'm serious, Katie. You can't put your suspicions in your paper. When the identity is confirmed, you will be notified. I'll make sure you are notified before anyone in the entire universe."

"Maybe we shouldn't get too excited," Kate said.

"We are not excited."

"The problem is Jack Brighton, his lawyer, and Allen say the agreement is not valid. Even Etta told me it was done as a lark and she didn't take it seriously."

"And yet she placed it in a box with other valuable documents and gave it to you for safe-keeping."

"I hadn't considered that," Kate said, mulling the possibility. "But she didn't have a key."

"Or so she said."

"Anyway, the agreement was more of a memento than a contract from her point of view. But both Jack and Larry said it would be misunderstood creating unnecessary problems."

"Yeah, for them and the company. Where's the original?"

"In a safe place."

"You have to turn that over to me. I'll also need a statement explaining how, when, and where you found it. And throw in whatever discussions you've had about it, including this one with me and the one with Allen."

"Yes, Sir, Your Detectiveness Sir."

He reached behind her and lifted the lid of the pot on the stove. "Smells wonderful. Can we eat now?"

"You cannot drop this conversation after barking all those instructions. We have more to discuss," she said, replacing the lid and pulling him to the living room.

He sat down next to her and said, "I'm sorry I barked. I suppose I am a little excited about the agreement. I'm not sure how important it will be, but I want to make sure we document everything properly. I agree Bryan should be aware of it and I'll take care of that in due time."

"Okay, I forgive you."

"Great. Can we eat now?"

"I told you we have more to discuss. I fixed your favorite dinner to butter you up."

"Not because you love me?"

"That too, but I don't want you to be mad."

"About?" Tom said slowly.

"I've sort of been investigating the construction situation in Branson."

"Sort of?"

"It all started with Bryan's suit against the city. Then other things happened."

"You know I've been researching the claims Bryan made," Tom said.

"I didn't know for a fact, because we don't discuss work things. Remember?"

"Okay, where is this conversation going?"

"I've put together a notebook containing a lot of little things. My dad thinks since I can't prove anything with all my pieces, I should turn everything over to a real detective. I picked you."

"Ah, Sid is no longer your favorite?"

"Not anymore."

"Where is this notebook?" he asked, scanning the apartment.

"At my house. Do you want to see it?"

"Are you going to make me ask for it?"

"If you don't mind."

"Can I please review the information you've collected? And would you mind throwing in the original partnership agreement and associated documentation I previously requested?"

"I would be happy to have your help."

"Uh, you misunderstand. Didn't your encounter with Allen last evening make it obvious you must turn everything over to the authorities?"

"I was joking. I did the notebook *for you*. And I prepared it while you were in Chicago. Allen simply convinced me I was on the right track."

Tom smiled and pulled her closer.

Kate placed her hands on his shoulders and said, "All of my work for only one favor."

"Ah-ha. Here's the catch."

"I want the hometown advantage on any information to be released regarding whatever Allen is up to. Oh, and the skeleton case resolution too."

"Is that going to do it for you?"

"That's it. And I won't even ask you to put it in writing."

"Can we eat now?"

Chapter Thirty-Four

Waking up to breakfast in bed with Kate delayed Tom's departure for work on Wednesday. Fortunately, she had gotten up early to document the information he requested about the partnership agreement. He arrived in time to see Sid crossing the police department lobby toward the stairs leading up to the building department suite.

Sid said, "Hey, partner. I was beginning to think I'd have to go solo with Leatherman."

"We need to postpone the meeting for a bit," Tom said, tapping the notebook he'd picked up from Kate's house.

"What's that?"

"Research Katie's been doing regarding Porter's suit and other things. I'm not sure what's in this binder, but I want to review it before we talk to anyone about anything."

"You get the coffee," Sid said, heading back to their office, "I'll call Ben to reschedule."

Tom scanned Kate's documentation, which was topically organized and separated by index tab sheets. He put the notebook in the center of the worktable and added a stack of information the detectives had assembled and a stack for statements by witnesses, including those by Frankie and other tip-line callers.

Sid slid his chair over to the table. "You didn't say why Kate gave you all this stuff."

"Trying to organize what she gathered, I suppose."

"Or maybe she found out a lot of little bitty things that she believes in her newspaper reporter's heart will prove something somehow to someone."

"Excellent summation. The good news is she has promised ... more or less ... to stay out of the investigation for the time being."

"That is good news. By the way, Leatherman says he'll be free all day, we can drop by any time. But if we want to speak to his inspectors we'll have to wait until later this afternoon when they return to the office."

"Good. Also, one document Katie gave me isn't in the notebook. She found it by accident and showed it to me this morning. I made her turn it over to me."

"You *made* her? Sorry I missed that."

"Let's say I convinced her it was a good idea," Tom said, handing his partner the agreement and Kate's statement.

As he read the document, Sid's *what-now* facial expression progressed to keen interest followed by alarm. "He went to Kate's house? Is he crazy?"

"More arrogant than crazy. Don't worry. Kate knocked him down a notch or two."

"This agreement could speak to motive," Sid said.

"I agree. I'm not sure what happened between Jack and Lex, but something caused Porter to go out on his own. Maybe he changed his mind, wanted to come back. Maybe he realized he had a right to one-third of the business."

"They argued, it got ugly. Sounds plausible," Sid said.

"We need to go over the scenario some more. Right now, log it as evidence in the skeleton case and put it somewhere safe. I'll get started on Katie's tome."

The detectives each reviewed the notebook, which included the reporter's interview transcripts and her take-away opinions from the meetings. Another part documented the Chamber of Commerce survey, including Marge's findings. In addition, Kate provided information from the Fire Chief and others regarding more recent residential fires and offers to purchase property on the lakefront. The next to last section, titled "pure speculation," lived up to the name. In it she outlined her conspiracy theory involving Allen, Henderson, and Wainright. The final portion of the notebook included biographies of all "conspirators" and information about every business included in her research, linking individuals and businesses and locations in a complex relationship chart.

Tom finished his review and pushed away from the table before returning the last pages to the binder. His admiration for the really cute red-haired girl he met in grade school and grew to love deeply had taken on a new dimension. For one thing, her incredibly convoluted train of thought both horrified and amused him.

"You know what terrifies me?" he asked.

Sid shook his head.

"I see her point."

"That is frightening, but I know what you mean."

"If we consider this circumstantial evidence in conjunction with what we have already, we might have a case," Tom said.

Sid poured himself another cup of coffee and topped off his partner's. "But a case for what? I see the bribery angle, but can that be tied to her band of conspirators? What are they guilty of? Wanting prosperity for the city? Even wanting personal wealth isn't against the law."

Tom countered, "Unless you achieve success by *breaking* the law."

After going around a few more times and getting nowhere in particular, the detectives agreed to visit Leatherman, who was surprised to hear about the hotline lead regarding Fortner.

"Brad was one of my best inspectors. Unfortunately, he quit two weeks ago."

"We found that out when we called your office," Sid said. "What reason did he give during his exit interview?"

"No interview. His letter of resignation was waiting for me on my desk that Monday morning. It was pretty vague, so I boiled it down to personal reasons."

"Did you have any issues with him?" Tom asked.

"When I was hired, he'd been with the department for a while, which was a good-news-bad-news thing. Took me a few months to get him used to the different rules and processes."

"Did he resent that?" Sid asked.

"He seemed to be okay with it. What's this about? Did Fortner call the tip-line with some claim against the department?"

"We received the information from a subcontractor on one of the jobs Fortner inspected," Tom said. "The informant claims to have witnessed your inspector taking a bribe from one of the general contractor's men."

Leatherman jerked his head up, and his brow furrowed as he rolled his chair back from the desk. He pulled a file from the cabinet and handed it to Tom. "I haven't even had time to process this. I was hoping he'd call and change his mind. He was a good man."

"Like you said, it's pretty vague," Tom said after reading the hand-written note.

"I take it this accusation against him surprises you," Sid said.

"Absolutely. Have you substantiated the claim?"

"We're still investigating," Tom said. "Had you noticed anything unusual about Fortner's attitude or performance in the last few months? Did he have any personal problems?"

"I'll have to admit I've been distracted with this building code update and review of Branson ordinances relating to construction. I personally have not seen anything unusual. I'm not aware of any financial issues, although he was divorced a little over a year ago. The rest of the staff may be able to help with more information."

"Can you list the jobs Fortner inspected?" Sid asked.

"He's probably had occasion to inspect all of them, but I can get you a list with the number of inspections per job. Is that good?"

"Perfect. And I'd like to take his file," Tom said.

Sid added, "Please send your staff down to our office, one at a time."

Leatherman walked the detectives to the customer counter close to Claire's desk. He leaned toward his secretary and spoke in a low tone. "These gentlemen need a list of inspections performed in the last year. Sort it by project name, please. And another sorted by inspector."

Tom extended his hand to the department manager and said, "Thanks, Ben. We appreciate your cooperation."

"Let me know if you need anything else. Claire can be your first interview when she brings you the reports. I'll send the others as soon as they return from the job sites."

Claire spent less than thirty minutes with the detectives. She had barely met Fortner or anyone else in the department. From her point of view, they were all hardworking and honest guys. Ben Leatherman was a good boss, although it had taken her a couple weeks to get used to his no-nonsense management style. Fortunately, the reports she brought proved to be more interesting.

Sid handed Tom the printout ordered by inspectors, which he had studied while Tom spoke to the secretary. "Fortner worked primarily on Fortune Enterprises projects," he said.

"Including the one Frankie told us about," Tom commented.

"It could be a coincidence, but Fortner didn't do as many reinspections as the other men in the department, especially on Allen's projects."

Before Tom could comment one of the building inspectors knocked on the detectives' door. He extended his hand and crossed the room when Sid motioned him in. "Harry Pine," he said. "I work for Ben Leatherman. Claire said you need to ask me some questions."

Sid said, "Have a seat, Harry. This shouldn't take too long."

"What's this all about? Am I in trouble?" Pine asked. His forced smile twitched before disappearing.

Tom shook his head. "Today we are interested in Brad Fortner. You worked with him for several years. Correct?"

Pine seemed puzzled, but relieved. "Yeah, I guess."

"How would you describe his performance?" Sid asked.

"He did his job okay. I sat in on one of his preemployment interviews. He knew the building codes, but he'd been in the field for less than two years as an apprentice. I felt we needed someone with more experience, but management out-voted me. Still, he came onboard pretty quickly."

"Seemed like a competent, honest inspector?"

"From where I stood, yes. I've never heard a bad thing about him. But, to be honest, I don't pay much attention to how other inspectors do their jobs. That's why they pay Leatherman the big bucks. Right?"

Sid chuckled. "Would you know why Fortner quit a couple weeks ago?"

"Complete surprise to me, especially not giving notice. You can burn bridges that way. And I was under the impression he needed the job. I hope he found another good one."

"Does that mean you don't know where he went?"

"Not a clue."

Tom asked, "What do you mean he needed the job?"

"The divorce. I heard his wife took the credit cards with her. Word is the cards were maxed out before Brad could even pick up the phone to cancel them. I know he worked another job in the evenings for a while to pay them off, but it was a temporary part-time thing."

"Does he have friends or relatives who might know how to locate him?"

"I'm afraid you've gotten everything I know about Brad Fortner."

"Okay," Tom said, standing up. He patted Pine on the back as they moved toward the door. "You can tell Claire we're ready for the next interview."

The second inspector confirmed what Pine had said but offered also that Fortner hung around with a fellow gun enthusiast called Stevey or Stoney, but he didn't know a last name. Each of the two part-time apprentices hired by Leatherman in the past year echoed Claire's general statement.

Sid volunteered to check out the Stevey-Stoney lead by speaking to a guy he knew at the shooting range east of town.

Tom contacted his friend Gary Wyler to pin down who may have given Fortner the bribe. The detective did not specify a company or project, nor did he tell his friend why he was asking. Based on Frankie's description alone, Gary gave Tom the names of three men. Two of the men were fairly low-level employees at a couple of the contractors working Branson jobs. However, one was a site manager for Fortune Enterprises. According to the inspection reports provided by Leatherman, the man had worked several projects in town over the past year, including the one at which Frankie witnessed the payoff. Gary said the guy was Allen's assistant.

Tom was hanging up from speaking to Fortner's credit card company when Sid returned to the office. "I hit pay dirt," Tom said.

"I did pretty well myself," Sid said, taking his notepad from his pocket and slamming it on his desk.

"Did you find Stevey?"

"Brad and *Stoney* were regulars at the shooting range on JJ Highway near Kirbyville. They haven't come around for a few weeks. My contact said it isn't particularly unusual for the two to miss a couple weeks occasionally.

Apparently the two frequent the little bar on JJ in the Pinetop area not far from the range."

"That's it?"

"Hey, this is the Ozarks. We don't keep track of our fellow man."

"What about an address or phone for Stoney?"

"I'm afraid the bar is as close as my friend could get. Like a lot of people, including Fortner, Stoney has a post office box. If the bar doesn't pan out, we can try the range on the weekend when more members are around. Maybe someone will have better information."

"We can try the bar tonight. What did you get from the landlord?"

"Land*lady* is Evelyn Hartman. Her office is in Ozark. Runs several low-end rentals in the area, mostly south of Branson. She had nothing on the ex-wife Sharon who moved out a while ago. Evelyn didn't care because Brad paid the rent on time."

"Does Evelyn know he moved out?"

"She does now."

"Does she have a forwarding for him?"

"The post office box we already know about. None of the neighbors saw anything strange, like a moving van. The place is furnished so Fortner probably didn't have much."

Tom said, "I did a bit better than you. I was able to verify our guy paid off his extensive credit card debt. Didn't take long as it turns out."

"Hmm," Sid said.

"Also, I may have a lead on the person who bribed Brad. We can take a ride out to the job site and check him out."

"Let me guess. The new office complex?"

Based on Frankie's description, Tom spotted Paul Andrews immediately. The detective observed the man from a distance, then approached a small circle of workers and asked to speak to the site manager. The group simultaneously turned in Paul's direction. One of the men shouted, "Hey, Paul, someone to see you."

Andrews waved, then finished his conversation with a crew delivering a load of gravel. Tom waited for Paul to walk toward him, hoping Sid could get a clear photo from the car.

"How can I help you, Detective Collingwood?"

"You know who I am?"

"I've seen your picture in the paper a few times. What's up?"

"We're trying to find a former city employee, Brad Fortner."

Andrews glanced down and kicked a rock with the side of his work boot. "Can't say the name sounds familiar. Frankly, I don't deal with inspectors much other than to resolve an issue of some kind. You should speak to the job foreman."

The Site Manager turned and walked toward the unfinished building. Within two minutes the foreman emerged. It took him another two minutes to tell Tom that he knew Fortner and was sorry to see him quit and move away. Brad was one of the few competent inspectors the construction boss had worked with in his fifteen years in the business. Tom handed him a card and asked him to call if he remembered anything else or if he saw Fortner anywhere.

Tom scooted into the passenger side and said, "Let's go see what Stoney's up to."

The detectives were quiet for several minutes, but apparently Sid couldn't stand it. "What did Andrews say?" he asked.

"He said he didn't deal with inspectors much, didn't remember Fortner."

"That's probably reasonable. Is that why you talked to the other man?"

"That was the job foreman. He said Brad was a good inspector and he enjoyed working with him. He didn't know why the guy left town or where he went."

"Dead end."

"Maybe not," Tom said.

"How so?"

"I didn't tell Andrews that Fortner was a city building inspector. I said he was a city employee."

The bar was larger than Tom expected. A metal and wooden building was sheltered by tall cedars on three sides. The gravel parking lot extended from the front wall to the road and currently accommodated a dozen vehicles—all pickup trucks. "Cold Beer" in red neon lettering dominated the large window next to the door.

When Tom and Sid crossed the threshold, the barkeeper glanced around the room. As if warned by a secret alarm, the customers turned toward the door.

Tom said, "We need to talk to Herman Stonebridge."

Everyone laughed except the man sitting on the end bar stool. "I didn't do it," the man shouted and loud cackles filled the room.

"Are you Stonebridge?" Sid asked.

"Stoney."

"Can we go somewhere more private?"

Stoney swiveled off the stool and moved to a table. "You fellas want a beer?"

"Maybe later," Tom said.

"You must be the one who went to the range today," Stoney said, pointing toward Sid.

"News travels fast."

"It does in this neighborhood." He took a drink of his beer, then continued. "I'm afraid I can't help you much. Brad and I have been friends for quite a while and he said nothing to me, just disappeared. I didn't know he'd taken off until I saw his house was up for rent."

Tom asked, "You hadn't noticed anything odd in his behavior? Anything bothering him? Problems with the ex-wife?"

"Sharon will always be a problem, but I doubt he heard from her once she moved back to her mother's in Harrison."

"When was that?" Sid asked.

"Two, maybe three months. She went traveling after the divorce. Brad said she charged things as far away as New Orleans before he could get those cards cancelled. I guess when the ex-husband-well dried up, she returned to Momma."

"Anything else?"

"I wouldn't say his behavior was odd exactly, but a few weeks ago he seemed spooked by something. When I asked him about it, he said I was imagining things, so I let it go. Next thing I know, he was gone."

"When you say spooked, do you mean frightened?"

"More like antsy, like something was out of his hands."

Sid said, "Maybe it was the credit card debt."

"No, he paid those off pretty quick. Had an extra job for several months to make sure he took care of it."

"Do you have any guess where he might've gone? Somewhere he used to live or wanted to move? Any friends he might have asked for help?"

"Nope. He was born in Taney County. I don't remember him discussing any other place he wanted to see, let alone live in."

Tom pushed away from the table and Sid followed suit.

"Thanks for your help, Stoney," Sid said, handing him a card. "If you think of anything or see Brad, give us a call."

"I have to say, you fellas have me worried. I'll ask around, see if anyone else might know something."

As they drove back to the office, Tom said, "Let's see if we can find the ex-wife or her mother in Harrison. And put out a bulletin on Fortner. Start with an identify-and-report. We don't want him to run any farther than he has already."

Chapter Thirty-Five

By the time Kate removed all the vitriol from her first draft nothing remained about Allen. She clasped her hands and cracked her knuckles—a habit her mother could never get her to break. When she started the new draft, she envisioned the least charge or accusation which could be brought against the councilman. Two immediately came to mind, so she led with those points and provided background for the offences. She sailed to the end paragraph, which provided some biographical information about the Fortune Enterprises executive. Usually, she would work an article more before sending to Helen, but she wanted to make sure she was on the right track. An hour after the upload, Helen knocked on Kate's cubicle wall.

"This needs a bit of tweaking," the editor said, pulling a chair close to the reporter's desk.

Kate said, "Is it worthless or worth fixing?"

"Given that we have no idea what, if anything, will be brought against Allen, your article is a good template. My suggestion would be to put stronger information about each charge. You would want to confirm with the police or prosecutor what can be released. For example, I know you have more about the relationship with Wainright and what happened with the survey."

"I'm probably doing this too early."

"Keep in mind, the police may have a lot more than you do. It would be better to let their investigation come to a conclusion and let the prosecutor decide what the charges are."

"I know you're right, and I appreciate your reading my cathartic piece. You should have seen the first draft."

Helen snickered. "I hesitate to imagine."

"Honestly, my greatest fear is that nothing will come of it. That he'll get away with what may turn out to be making a huge profit for himself and bolstering Branson's tourist industry."

"Don't forget, you can probably have him charged with assault. It might be a stretch, he might get away with it, but nevertheless he threatened you."

"He was so desperate when he came to our house. It was so out of character, at least his public persona. More than that, it was careless."

"And it was all about the agreement between his grandfather and Etta Stupholds?"

"And Lex Porter. The three were best of friends."

"Right," Helen acknowledged in a whisper.

"Best of friends," Kate repeated, remembering her conversation with Etta about the three childhood companions.

"Kate, I need you to focus on the article about the local fires. Do a follow-up based on the new information you've gathered. Check with Chief

Scherington to verify before we print it. Let's run it past your detective friend too, as a courtesy."

Helen's reference to Tom created a warm bubble in Kate's tummy which quickly spread to her arms. She smiled as the editor walked away. But before Helen made it down the hall to her office, the reporter returned to the nagging question she had about Etta.

Kate knocked on the screen door still mulling over the best approach to a follow-up interview. Although surprised, Etta nodded, turned, and ushered the reporter into the living room.

"So, tell me what has confused you," the older woman said once they were settled.

"The partnership agreement," Kate said. "First, let me confess I gave you a copy. Call it my reporter's instinct or paranoia, perhaps."

"I realized later it was a copy."

"You didn't contact me to request the original or to ask what I intended to do with it. But you must have mentioned it to Jack, because his grandson came to my house to retrieve it."

"I didn't know," she whispered. She sat forward in her chair, her expression somewhere between embarrassed and concerned.

Kate said, "He took me by surprise and was quite rude, even threatening."

"I understand why you'd be upset and maybe even confused, but, as you pointed out when you returned the documents, they belong to me. They are *my* keepsakes. I don't believe I have to explain my motives or my actions regarding them to you."

Taken aback by Etta's sudden frankness and, even more so, by the controlled low tone of her voice, Kate hesitated before responding, then chose the direct approach.

"I would agree with you except for one thing. The partnership agreement is potential evidence in a criminal investigation."

"That's pretty far-fetched even for you."

"As a matter of fact, it brings up another point of my confusion. It seems to me you would have to know details about Lex leaving the company, since you were not only longtime friends, but partners."

"I told you he wanted to start his own store."

"Why go it alone? Why not open another location for Riverside? And you had to know when he returned to Branson."

"You'll have to leave, Kate. I don't intend to defend myself against your fantasies."

Before Kate could react or respond, the front screen slammed and Bryan Porter stormed into the room, his face flushed, his tearing eyes focused on Etta.

Kate came off the sofa and stepped back toward the window, not sure what the clearly troubled man might do.

"I'd like to hear your answers to Kate's questions. And don't forget I witnessed Jack kicking my dad out of Riverside. And, I might add, you did nothing to help him."

Etta said, "You don't know what you're saying. You were a boy. You're remembering your mother's version of events."

"I may have bought that once, Aunt Etta, but I'm beginning to question what you've told me. So I want the truth. You owe me the truth. Like you owed me the partnership agreement, the one you said didn't exist, but you had all along."

"I'd forgotten about it."

"You're lying," Bryan said, wiping his damp cheeks.

"Your father lied to you, then abandoned you and your mother. You're trying to push his guilt off on me." Etta walked toward Bryan slowly, stopping about two feet from him. "I don't blame you, Bryan. I understand how much your father meant to you."

He hung his head. Etta took a step toward him and the sobbing man responded to her offered hug. Kate couldn't hear their exchange as they prolonged the cathartic embrace.

Etta took a step back, gently releasing her hold. She steadied herself against the chair, then sat down.

Kate said, "Can I get you some water, Etta?"

"I'll be okay, but I probably should lie down."

Bryan slowly guided Etta to her bedroom.

Mesmerized by the strange encounter, Kate sunk to the sofa. She understood the impact of losing a parent, but the additional complications of Lex Porter's betrayal and disappearance had devastated his son's life.

Bryan returned to the room and said, "Can we talk for a moment?"

The reporter came to her feet but wasn't sure how to respond.

"Don't worry, I'm okay," he said, his demeanor more relaxed. "All I want is to hear about the partnership agreement you found. It's between Jack, Etta, and my dad. Right?"

"The document is informal and handwritten, but my father's lawyer says, if authenticated, the contract is legal."

"And she had it in one of her boxes?"

Kate asked, "Is that what you were searching for?"

"I told you before, I had nothing to do with that break-in. But from what I heard about the aftermath, I can't believe whoever did it wasn't able to find the agreement."

"She had given me the box on loan for one of my crafts fair articles."

"Seems like a strange coincidence."

"I suppose," Kate said.

He stuffed his hands in his pockets and stared at the floor.

"Bryan, what did you mean Etta didn't help your father when Jack kicked him out?"

"I was on my way to my after-school job at the store. I heard the loud voices, a terrible argument. I knew better than to go inside. I ducked behind a big barrel on the porch."

He bowed his head and closed his eyes, forcing a tear down his cheek. After a moment, he wiped his face and shook his head as if to chase out the memories. "Sorry," he said.

"Could you make out details of the argument?"

"My dad was defending himself, saying he had no idea what Jack was talking about. Jack called Dad a liar. The louder Uncle Jack got the quieter Dad became. Ultimately, Jack shouted for Dad to get out and never come back. I didn't know what to do so I watched my dad walk off the porch and away from the store."

"And Etta was there?"

"No. I ran to the back entrance. I knew she'd be in her office. I begged her to do something. To smooth things over between them. She said it was my dad's fault and he would have to live with the consequences. She wouldn't tell me more."

"What did you do?"

"What would any eight-year-old do? I ran as fast and as far away from that office as I could. I never returned."

"Did you tell your dad you heard the argument?"

"Nope. Not my mom either. But she knew about it."

Kate said, "Your anger makes more sense now."

"My therapist would disagree with you," he said, managing a half-smile. "Can I ask you something?" When she nodded, he said, "Why are you so sure my dad came back to Branson?"

Reluctant to tell him the truth, Kate said, "What makes you think I'm sure?"

"You told Etta she should have known *when* ... not *if* ... he came back to town."

"Wouldn't you and your mother have seen him if he had?"

"You're trying not to answer my question," he said.

"How could I know for sure?"

"For one thing, you're a good investigative journalist. And I suspect dating a cop helps."

"Tom and I don't discuss work."

"Never mind, I already know the skeleton is my dad."

Chapter Thirty-Six

Sid stared at the status board, his feet propped on the desk. He shook his head and took a sip of lukewarm coffee. "We're not ready," he said.

"Despite that fact, the lieutenant wants a briefing," Tom said.

"Fine. But why with the City Attorney?"

"Consider it a brainstorming session and, more to the point, something we must do."

Sid shrugged and collected some papers from the worktable along with the pad and easel. Tom took down the summary pages from the wall, rolled them, and grabbed some large clips and two black markers.

"I hope the lieutenant made fresh coffee," Sid said, walking into the common area.

The detectives set up their briefing materials on one side of the conference room as they acknowledged Palmer and City Attorney Mortimer Dunlap. The coffee pot in the corner was sitting half-empty with a non-illuminated ready light. Sid sighed as he sat down next to his partner.

Lieutenant Palmer said, "I know we're still in the middle of both cases, but I want to get Mort in on the conversation. Give us the high-points and the direction you're taking."

Tom pushed his chair away from the table and moved to the pad, flipping the cover to reveal a summary sheet for Porter's construction complaint. "We've talked to almost a hundred individuals in the construction business in Branson and Taney County. Although we found a clear indication that a good-old-boy culture is still in place, we saw no evidence of criminal activity until recently. Keep in mind this is one incident, which we haven't completely verified, in a town with millions of dollars of active construction projects."

Sid arranged some papers in front of the other men. "This is a sworn statement from a witness to an apparent bribery of a city inspector by an employee of Fortune Enterprises."

Dunlap said, "But you haven't verified the accusation?"

"We haven't been able to find the inspector. His name is Brad Fortner and he quit abruptly a couple weeks ago. Ben Leatherman, who said the guy was a good inspector, did some analysis of the man's inspection records."

"Did Leatherman suspect anything?" Palmer asked.

"No, but after we spoke to Ben and filled him in on our witness, he decided to check it out. Over the last six to eight months, Fortner completed follow-up inspections that did not seem right. In Ben's words, the initial rejection was followed up too quickly. The items being redone or corrected should have taken longer than a return trip on the same day."

Sid said, "All of these anomalies were on Fortune Enterprises projects."

Dunlap asked, "What about other companies?"

"None," Tom said.

"Pretty weak without being able to talk to the inspector. Anything else on that case?" Palmer asked.

Tom glanced at his partner who shrugged and folded his hands in his lap. "We noted some tangential issues, which seem to indicate Larry Allen, the grandson of company founder Jack Brighton, may be up to no good," he said.

Mort said, "I'm afraid you have way too many hedges in that statement, Detective Collingwood. Not much up-to-no-good case law on the books, I'm afraid. Do you have anything specific in these *tangential* issues?"

Tom shook his head, realizing any link to the suspicious fires by the lake was speculative at this point.

Palmer said, "You're still working the bribery angle and hope to find the inspector?"

"Yes, sir," Tom responded.

Dunlap said, "You can't take what you have to the County Prosecutor. Let's hope you learn more. A confession would be great."

"Maybe that's not a bad idea," Palmer said. "Why don't we have a meeting with Allen, ask him some questions, and see how he reacts."

"Can't hurt, but you'd have to be careful not to make flimsy allegations," Dunlap said, glancing at Tom. "I'd be available for later today, if you can arrange it."

Palmer asked, "Can you two put together some questions, including about the other suspicious activity?"

"Sure," Tom said, but his heart wasn't in it. Allen was not stupid enough to admit to anything based solely on innuendo or unsubstantiated information. Tom flipped the page on the pad to the summary sheet for the skeleton case. "We have DNA confirmation that the skeletal remains belong to Alexander Porter. He was reported missing by his wife in 1945."

"Any relation to our complaint guy, Bryan?" Dunlap asked.

"His father."

Dunlap raised an eyebrow but did not comment.

"We are still investigating his last-known activities and why someone would want him dead. Unfortunately, the only person talking is Bryan Porter, who was eleven years old in 1945. We do have a partnership agreement between Lex, as everyone called him, Jack Brighton, and Etta Stupholds."

When the men finished reading the agreement, Tom said, "As you can see this could point to motive."

"But?" Palmer asked.

"The agreement was created in 1942. These three were close childhood friends and it doesn't make sense that the agreement itself would be a reason to kill him."

Dunlap said, "I can tell you this document qualifies as a legal contract, in perpetuity, I might add. Bryan Porter would stand to benefit. First, we'd have to prove it is a document signed by these three individuals over fifty years ago."

"Etta, admitted as much," Tom said.

"To you?"

"To Kate Starling, a reporter at *Tri-Lakes Newspapers*."

This time it was Palmer's turn to raise an eyebrow and remain silent.

Dunlap said, "Sounds like you need to wrap up a few loose ends on that case before going to the County Prosecutor."

Tom and Sid spent an hour or so developing a list of questions to put to the councilman. Each question had an introductory narrative to make it seem like they had evidence for each item presented. Once the detectives finished a third draft, they took it to the lieutenant for his approval.

"Looks good to me," Palmer said. "By the way Allen was all too happy to cooperate with us. He said he appreciated the opportunity to clear up any misinformation."

"I'll bet," Tom said.

Mort Dunlap and Dan Palmer were alone in the conference room when the detectives arrived. Sid headed directly for the freshly brewed coffee and carried two cups back to the table.

"Thanks, partner," Tom said.

Sid asked Palmer, "Don't suppose we've been stood up by any chance?"

At that point the department secretary showed Councilman Allen into the room. Keith Hawthorne was close behind.

"This is our company attorney," Allen said. "Granddad insisted. I hope you understand and don't read anything into his coming along."

"No problem," Palmer said. "The idea here is to clear up some issues before we go further with our investigation."

Tom took everyone's silence as a cue to begin. He set up the first question with a brief summary of Porter's suit against the city and complaint to the state of Missouri. After a couple of sentences, Hawthorne waved his hand above the table and said they were familiar with Porter's claims.

"Good," Tom said. "Are you also familiar with our construction tip-line?"

Allen and the lawyer said they were not.

"We set up the hotline primarily to allow construction workers to provide anonymous tips regarding issues in the trade around Branson. We received over a thousand calls, most of which reported what we knew ... that a strong good-old-boy network exists in Taney County."

"No kidding," Allen said with a snicker.

Tom continued, "But we did get several calls reporting more serious abuses at current job sites. The most serious involved a construction worker witnessing what appeared to be an exchange of funds between a general contractor employee and a city official."

Hawthorne said, "Presumably the general contractor was Fortune Enterprises, since we are the company being questioned."

Palmer said, "That's correct."

Allen squirmed in his chair and sat forward laying his hands in front of him. "First of all, we have no reason to pay a city inspector *anything*. We follow all codes. We cooperate in all plan reviews. We defer to all inspections. And before you bring up beginning construction before the permit is issued, I would suggest you consult with Leatherman, who gave us the verbal go-ahead."

"Slow down," Tom said. "The reason for this meeting is to inform you of this accusation and to see what you might do to clarify what was seen by our witness."

"I'd say your witness was mistaken about what he saw or who he saw."

Hawthorne glanced at Allen then addressed the lieutenant. "Has your staff verified this witness account with the city official? Have you identified the alleged company employee?"

Despite being excluded from the question, Tom responded, "The description of the employee matches your site manager, Paul Andrews. We did speak to him and he denies dealing with the city employee. Another gentleman on your team remembers the employee, who definitely inspected your project."

"And the city official himself?" Hawthorne asked.

"Unfortunately, he quit. We're trying to locate him."

Allen started to say something, but Hawthorne placed his hand on the younger man's arm and said, "We've responded to that issue. Do you have more questions?"

Tom brought up the visit to Kate's house and suggested Allen entered without invitation and remained when asked to leave and acted in a threatening way toward the reporter.

Hawthorne said, "And are those the formal charges Miss Starling made against Larry?"

"She hasn't filed an official complaint," Palmer offered.

"Let us know when that happens," the lawyer said. "Anything else?"

Tom decided against going into most of the questions he had prepared. Hawthorne's presence clearly kept Allen's temper in check. The young executive would not make a mistake—let alone a confession—today. Still, the detective felt one topic might be worth mentioning.

"A gentleman named Kyle Henderson, an out-of-state realtor-broker, has been making offers to purchase various properties in Branson."

Hawthorne stood up. "That's it. We are not interested in more fairytales."

Palmer said, "Please, have a seat. This will be the last topic."

Tom continued, "Henderson has closed on several residential sites over the last year or so.

Those properties were sold to a holding company registered in Delaware."

"This is Kate's doing, isn't it?" Allen asked. "Sure, I know about Henderson. Who doesn't? He's been calling or visiting folks for a while. But he has nothing to do with us."

"And what if he did?" Hawthorne said. "Buying property is not against the law."

"Maybe not," Tom said. "Quite a coincidence that at least six of the owners who sold to Henderson were victims of rental-house fires. Perhaps you've noticed how many more fires we've experienced in the last year compared to a normal year. According to Fire Chief Scherington a couple of them were questionable, but not enough to suspect arson."

"Are you coming to a conclusion soon?" Hawthorne asked.

"Here's the strange thing," Tom said with a smile. "The purchased properties are all along the Taneycomo lakefront in old downtown Branson. Henderson is listed as purchaser for twenty percent of the recent sales. If you add that to Fortune Enterprises' current holdings in the area, the total climbs to thirty percent."

"Are you saying Henderson is torching structures to make the purchase?" Allen asked.

"Possibly."

"I'm afraid I don't see how this concerns us," Hawthorne said.

"Did I forget to say that Henderson named Councilman Allen as his primary contact in all his dealings in Branson?"

"Why would he do that?" Hawthorne said with a shrug.

"Probably didn't want to take the wrap himself. After we discussed the suspicious fires, he decided to give us more information about his involvement in the land purchase activities."

"We've addressed all your questions," Hawthorne said, pushing away from the table and motioning for Allen to follow suit.

Tom returned to his office thirty minutes later when he, Sid, and Lieutenant Palmer determined they had only one course of action—to wait until something broke in the case. On his way in, the department secretary handed him an urgent message from Kate.

"I'd return it soon, if I were you. That was her sixth try to get you."

"Did you explain that I was in meetings?"

"All six times. And she understood completely."

"Right."

He tried her car phone and office first, then her house, and finally found her in the motel office with her dad. When she came to the phone, he skipped the amenities. "For the record, you are not too easy to get in touch with either."

"Where have you been?" Kate asked.

"I'm a cop, remember? I've been doing cop things, having cop meetings."

"I have important information for you."

"Can't it wait? We're having dinner this evening." As soon as the words came out, Tom regretted them and his tone. The silence on the other end of the line told him his girlfriend wasn't too pleased either. He said, "I'm sorry. Bad day."

After a beat or two, Kate said, "I shouldn't have yelled at you. I'm sorry too. And you're right it can wait. But since we're talking now, can I tell you?"

He shook his head, but said, "What did you find out?"

"Please don't say anything until I finish. Promise?"

"Katie, you know how I hate when you say things like that."

"Promise?"

"I'll give it my best."

"I saw Bryan Porter today. He followed me to Etta's. I can fill you in later. The most important thing is that Bryan knows the skeleton is his father."

Kate paused, which Tom took as the cue to respond.

"Over the course of our investigation we've talked to Bryan a couple of times. He may or may not know we tested his cousin's DNA. But he's a smart man. I wouldn't be surprised that he put everything together and came to a logical conclusion. I might add that a certain reporter made the same inference."

The department secretary dropped a piece of paper directly in front of Tom. "Urgent" was circled at the top and "Boone County Arkansas Sheriff line 3" was underlined three times.

Kate said, "Did you hear me? That's not all Bryan said."

"I have another call."

He punched line three before realizing he had forgotten to put Kate on hold. He cringed and shook his head, knowing he'd pay later and may never know what Bryan said.

"Lenny, what's up?" Tom asked.

Lenny Harper had been Sheriff of Boone County Arkansas for over fifteen years. When Tom was in his teens the lawman, Roger Starling, and Tom were hunting buddies every November. The Branson detective had coordinated with the Sheriff on a couple cases since returning to the area. He hoped Lenny had good news, because the day could not get much worse.

"Got that notice on your Brad Fortner," Lenny said.

"Have you seen him down your way?"

"Turns out we have. We got a call late last night from his ex-wife. Sorry to tell you, the man is dead. Shot twice. We finished at the crime scene about thirty minutes ago. I didn't see your locate request until I got back to the office."

"I was hoping for better news," Tom said.

"Sorry, buddy. You're welcome to come down and see what we took from the scene. Or I could send you my report when I complete it."

"Sid and I will be down in a couple of hours."

By the time the detectives spoke to Lieutenant Palmer about Lenny's news, made a few calls, and drove to the Boone County Sheriff's Office, it was almost six-thirty. The sheriff briefed the two men and showed them the crime scene photos.

Fortner had been shot twice in the back—once in the torso and once in the neck.

"Maybe I'm missing something. Doesn't Sharon Fortner live in Harrison with her mother?" Tom asked.

"Correct. I haven't been able to talk to her yet. According to the dispatcher, she was pretty upset when she called. She met the first responders at the location but left before I arrived. Told the deputy she'd be at her mother's if we needed to speak to her. By the way, the house where he was found belongs to her family."

"Do you have a time of death?" Sid asked.

"Best guess, based on the condition of the body and the blood pool, is sometime Tuesday, maybe Wednesday. We're talking to neighbors and local businesses to see when he might have been spotted. Unfortunately, the nearest neighbor is about a thousand feet."

"Maybe Sharon can help," Sid said.

"Possibly. I'd say she or her mother gave him permission to stay at the location."

"We'd like to go with you when you interview her," Tom said.

"Figured as much," Lenny said. "But she asked that I wait until tomorrow. You can either come back first thing in the morning or stay at a local motel."

Sid shrugged and Tom said, "We'll be at that little motel down the road."

Lenny said, "One of Harrison's finest."

"Give us a call if anything comes up. Otherwise, we'll see you at eight."

Chapter Thirty-Seven

When her dad slammed the screen door, Kate jerked around, setting the glider in motion. She slid her feet down and planted them firmly on the porch, sloshing her coffee on her robe.

"A little tense this morning, are we?" Roger asked.

She frowned and scooted over so he could join her.

He put his cup on the railing and made himself comfortable on the now stable bench. "How long have you been out here?"

"A while. I couldn't sleep."

"This has something to do with Detective Collingwood going to Harrison, Arkansas, at the last minute, cancelling your dinner plans, and spoiling your evening."

"I need to talk to him about our case."

"*Our* case?"

"Okay, *his* case. But I have important information for him."

"Let me try to catch up," Roger said, reaching for his coffee. "The plan was to turn over everything to Tom. You promised to sit back and wait for him to finish his job, at which time, you'd be given an exclusive to the outcome."

"Yes, that's true. But I had to modify the plan."

"Ah. Do you want to put me out of my misery or shall I try to guess what you did during the plan modification activity?"

"For a parent who is usually supportive, you can be extremely sarcastic at times."

"Don't forget I shared those genes with you."

"I went to Etta's yesterday. You could say I started having my doubts about her forthrightness." Kate moved to the railing so she could check her dad's reaction. His furrowed brow said as much as his lack of comment.

"Anyway, I was trying to clarify some things, I wasn't investigating anything."

"Clearing up your confusion, so to speak."

"Exactly. My confusion about the partnership and Lex and what Etta knew. When we'd discussed Lex leaving the business before, she had said he wanted to open his own store. When I asked why he left Branson, she repeated what Bryan told her."

"What is confusing about that?" Roger asked, his tone approaching defensive.

"Jack, Etta, and Lex had been friends for a long time. They had been in business together, one way or another, for years. All of this Etta told me during our interviews. She had to know more about Lex's motives."

"I guess I'm not seeing why this matters."

"I wanted to see her reaction to the questions so I pressed a little bit. She was in the process of throwing me out when Bryan Porter showed up.

It doesn't matter why. But based on their conversation and what he said to me later, I'm convinced Etta knew Jack fired Lex, apparently for something unforgivable."

Roger came off the glider and walked to the screen door.

Kate said, "Don't you want to know the rest?"

He opened the door, then let it slam shut as he took a couple steps toward his daughter. "Katie, I can see you're trying to put all the pieces together. That's in your nature. But I'm not sure you have all the facts. What you see as suspicious behavior can be explained. Etta's in her eighties. She has one friend she trusts and protects," Roger said, holding up his index finger to emphasize his point, and then added, "Jack Brighton."

As her father turned and retreated through the screen door, Kate weighed his words but her doubts about Etta's honesty remained.

⁓

Cassie handed Kate her messages, none of which were from Tom. The reporter walked past the counter and was surprised to see Ellen at the reception desk filling out some paperwork.

"I didn't know interns could have interns," Kate said, smiling at Cassie.

The young girl laughed nervously.

Ellen said, "I'm filling out a job application, Miss Starling."

"You lost your job? I'm sorry," Kate said, making a mental note. *No inside contact at Fortune Enterprises.*

"I didn't lose my job, at least I don't think I did. But I may be quitting. Sometimes it can be a little stressful."

Kate stared at the young woman for a moment wondering how a job where you did virtually nothing all day could be stressful. "Good luck with your job search, Ellen," she said heading toward her cubicle.

Cassie said, "Kate, do you have a minute? You may be interested in the strange activity at Ellen's office today."

"It's no big deal," Ellen said. "Not a lot different than other days."

"I'm not following you," Kate said, her impatience building.

"Well, the arguing and yelling are not new. But this is the first time I've been told to connect the phone to the answering service and leave immediately. Even Mr. Brighton's assistant went home early."

"No one's in the suite?" Kate said.

"Just Jack and Randy Brighton and that lawyer who visits all the time," Ellen said.

"Keith Hawthorne," Kate whispered, her mind racing.

Ellen nodded and handed Cassie the application. "I told you it was no big deal. Probably needed to discuss something without interruptions."

"I'm sure you're right," Kate said, forming a plan in her mind.

Kate tiptoed up the stairs. The hallway light seemed dimmer, like it was in "night mode." She eyed the plaque on the entrance and took a deep breath. Not expecting the door to be unlocked, she was grateful, if a bit stunned, when it opened. A single spotlight above Ellen's desk illuminated the empty reception area. She tapped lightly on the door to Allen's suite and opened it slowly. No lights at all in the area normally occupied by his secretary. A nightlight glowed close to the floor in the short hall leading to his office. She knocked and waited, then peeked inside.

Empty and dark.

Kate returned to the reception area, crossed through the conference room, and paused in the anteroom normally occupied by the company's executive assistant. The hallways leading to Jack's office straight ahead and Randy's office to the right were also illumined close to the floor. Voices were coming from the younger Brighton's office. She moved closer to the door but stayed in the shadows of the short hallway.

"Everything ... *everything* ... will come out," Randy said, his tone now louder and more dramatic, but she couldn't distinguish the response. She moved again, straining to hear the conversation. Without warning the lights in the executive assistant's area came on, reaching a foot or so into the hallway. She held her breath and slipped into the darkness.

Chapter Thirty-Eight

A thick morning fog covered the gorge behind the motel next door as Tom and Sid emerged from the diner after breakfast. The air was cool and damp following last night's brief rain. Tom popped the trunk to retrieve their jackets. The detectives were settling into the front seat when the Sheriff drove up and suggested they go to the widow's residence in his car.

Sharon Fortner's house was about six miles from the motel in an older part of Harrison. Lenny parked in the drive behind an old blue mini-van. A young woman appeared on the porch as soon as the men exited the vehicle. They followed her into a small living room.

Lenny removed his hat. "We're sorry for your loss, Mrs. Fortner. If possible, we'd like to ask a few questions to help us with our investigation."

Tears welled in her red eyes as she eased into the chair next to the sofa and placed another used tissue on the pile next to the lamp on the end table.

"This is Detective Tom Collinwood and his partner Detective Sid Green with the Branson

Police Department. They were trying to locate Mr. Fortner for an ongoing case."

"I didn't believe him at first," she said. "I hadn't seen Brad in almost a year when he showed up asking for help. I told him to go away," she said, tears starting down her cheeks.

Tom asked, "When was that?"

"A couple weeks ago."

"Did he say why he needed help?" Lenny asked.

"Something about important people trying to find him and it would be better if they didn't. I told him I wanted no part of any trouble he was in." She paused, blotting away the tears with a fresh tissue. "He said he didn't have anywhere else to go."

"So, you let him stay here?"

"No. He said they'd know where I lived. That house where I ..." Sharon leaned forward, burying her face in her hands, and started to sob.

Tom reached across the table and slid the tissue box toward the distraught woman.

Lenny said, "We understand it's family-owned."

She took a deep breath, regaining her composure. "My parents tried to sell it for years, long before my father died."

"Is it still on the market?" Sid asked.

"I'm not sure. The listing broker died last year. Anyway, Brad knew about the house."

"And you gave him permission to stay there."

"He said it would be a few weeks, no more than a month. I offered to have the electricity turned on, but he said that wouldn't be necessary."

Tom asked, "Did you talk to him after that?"

"About four days later I drove up to make sure everything was okay. He warned me not to come back. He was afraid someone could follow me and find him. This is all my fault."

Sid asked, "Were you followed?"

"You don't understand. I was unhappy in our marriage. When I left Brad, I wanted to celebrate, but I wanted to make him as miserable as I was. I took a trip to New Orleans, first class all the way. New wardrobe, good hotel, good food. When both of our credit cards were maxed out, I came home and moved in with my mother."

"Did Brad contact you about the credit cards?" Sid asked.

"We didn't talk, not from the time I left him until the time he showed up asking me for help. Like I said, I told him I wanted no part of it. He said I was the reason he was in the mess in the first place. I was the reason he needed the extra money to pay off those cards."

Tom said, "Mrs. Fortner, Brad made a few bad choices. You didn't put him in the mess. He did."

She started sobbing again.

Tom said, "Can I ask what caused you to go up there Thursday night?"

"Brad called me every few days after my first visit to let me know he was still okay. But I hadn't heard from him for a while. I was worried. I waited another day, then drove to the house."

"Did you see anyone near the property?"

"I saw a few trucks on the highway, nothing on the road that goes by the house."

"What about Brad's truck?"

"I didn't see it. I figured he parked it out of sight down the road like on that first night."

"So, you went in the house," Lenny coaxed.

The tears started again, but she quickly wiped them away. "I called his name as I went through the hall, but he didn't answer. It took my eyes a couple moments to adjust to the darkness in the kitchen. That's when I saw him."

Lenny took Tom and Sid back to the diner to pick up their car and they followed him north to the crime scene, located about halfway to Branson. The Sheriff made a left turn on a dirt road and parked on the far-side of the road from a picket fence that had seen happier times. The yard had been mowed, but not recently. Although the house itself was in disrepair, it seemed—at least from a distance—to be structurally solid. The crime scene tape encompassed the yard and drive.

"Have you located Brad's truck?" Sid asked as they followed Lenny into the house.

"Nowhere around here. We have an all-points out on it and we're continuing our search in this area. Nothing so far."

"How did they find him?" Sid asked.

"We're questioning the local businesses to see if anyone saw Fortner or if anyone was asking about him."

The dried pool of blood and the chalk outline of the body in front of the kitchen sink were the only suggestions of a crime. Everything else in the house seemed to be in place, with the exception of the sheet and pillow on the living room sofa.

Tom said, "I bet he didn't even know what hit him."

"Crossed my mind he didn't see his killer," Lenny said. "No conversation. No threats. Bang-bang, you're dead."

Tom let that vision hang in his mind for a second or two, and then asked Lenny, "What's out back?"

"Mostly trees. We've searched it but found nothing interesting," the Sheriff said.

"I'll meet you by the car," Tom said, nodding toward Sid. He paused on the rickety back deck and then walked down the stairs. He needed some fresh air, but there was none to be found.

Sid and Lenny were waiting by the front fence.

"We appreciate your showing us the murder scene," Tom said. "Please, keep us posted."

"No problem. But you know that goes both ways. Hell, you may get a confession from someone in Branson about killing Fortner."

"Could happen," Tom said, adding in a whisper to his partner, "but I wouldn't bet on it."

The drive back to Branson allowed Tom and Sid to plan what they would say to Lieutenant Palmer to persuade him that they should confront Larry Allen about Fortner's death. As it turned out, the lieutenant didn't require much convincing. When the detectives pulled up at the office building site, they spotted Paul Andrews and asked him where they could find his boss.

"Left in a hurry not ten minutes ago," Andrews said. "Got an emergency phone call from his granddad. Apparently, he was late for a big family meeting back at HQ."

"Do you know when he'll be back?" Sid asked.

"I'm pretty sure it won't be today."

"Incidentally, where were you every day this week?" Tom asked.

Andrews gave the detective a what-business-is-it-of-yours stare before he shrugged and said, "I was on this site, like every day, twelve hours or more each day, for the last several months. We're working like crazy to get this job done on time and within budget."

"Others working with you?" Sid asked.

"Yes, including Larry."

Sid smiled and asked, "You sleep on site?"

"I've been known to take a nap on the boss's cot, but not these last few days. I spent evenings and nights at home with my wife."

"You don't mind if we confirm that," Sid said.

"Not at all," Andrews said, reeling off his home number.

Fortune Enterprises was shut down for the day. Although the door was unlocked, the lights were either off or dimmed and no one was in the reception area. Tom glanced at his watch to see if it was past quitting time. "Maybe they closed early for the big family meeting," he said.

"Maybe the big meeting is at Brighton's house."

"Andrews said headquarters. Besides, the door to the suite was open. Let's see if we can find the councilman."

Sid knocked then slowly opened the door to Allen's portion of the suite. He peeked inside and disappeared into the dark area. "Lights off in the secretary's area and his office."

Tom led the way into the hallway going to Jack and Randy's offices. The detectives were entering the secretary's area when Sid stopped and held his index finger to his lips. Tom heard the voices too—some faint, others louder. He waved his thumb toward the door and Sid followed him out of the suite and down to their vehicle.

"What was that all about?" Sid asked.

"They're having a family meeting alright, and it sounds like someone may be very angry. We better contact Allen through his lawyer."

Tom radioed dispatch and requested a patch to Keith Hawthorne's office.

"I'm sorry, he's out for the rest of the day," his assistant said.

"Do you have a way to contact him?"

"Only for an emergency."

"Good. This is an emergency. Please have him contact me as soon as possible. He has my number."

Chapter Thirty-Nine

The councilman mumbled something about all the lights being out as he stormed past the hidden reporter and opened the door to his uncle's office.

"What's going on?" he shouted.

Jack said, "We sent the staff home."

"And they left you in the dark?"

"I'd say you are the reason we're in the dark, Larry. What was so urgent about having this meeting?" Jack said.

Randy added, "And since you called it, why are you late?"

Weighing the open door against being exposed, Kate made her way to Jack's office hoping the Brighton's adjoining door was not open and that she could distinguish words through the ancient walls. Finding both conditions to be true, she made one final wish—to remain undiscovered. Unfortunately, everyone was speaking at once blaming each other for numerous catastrophes. Jack's usual calm voice was the loudest, at least until his grandson took charge.

"All I know," Larry shouted twice, causing the others to be silent. "All I know," he repeated slowly with his voice lowered, "is that I had a plan. We *all* had a plan. Everything was going smoothly. Everything was handled."

Randy snickered and said, "You know what they say about best laid plans."

"Hey, I'm not the one who dragged the reporter into the mix," Allen sniped. "Thanks to you, Granddad, Kate's snooping may destroy the whole thing."

Jack countered, "You think your late-night visit to her home didn't raise a red flag?"

Randy chimed in, "This downfall started with Porter's accusations."

"Nothing has come of his suit," Jack said.

Randy countered, "That may change soon."

Larry shouted, "Porter's claim is bogus as far as our company's concerned. We may be a little loose on certain procedures, but we build to code. I guarantee you those topnotch detectives have found nothing to the contrary."

Jack said, "Save your defensive posture for the courtroom. I'm more interested in what change Randy sees coming."

His son responded, "I've been told by individuals who are reliable that the PD is making progress on the Porter suit. They have a tip-line. Even worse, people are calling in. Sooner or later, something will surface."

Larry said, "Keith, you were there when Collingwood grilled me yesterday. I don't know how he put it together, but it had nothing to do with Porter's suit."

Hawthorne confirmed, "Their suspicions are vague and unsubstantiated. They are nowhere near to making charges against this company or any other."

Randy interjected, "Larry, if what you say about your projects is true, why are you worried?"

"Who knows what someone might have manufactured? Even Porter. He hates us. Hell it may be someone close to us," Larry said. After several seconds, he added, "Uncle Randy, *what have you done?*"

"I've fixed something you should have fixed," Randy said.

Kate visualized Allen strangling his uncle through the long silence.

"What did you fix?" Jack asked, his voice almost inaudible.

"Issues at the office complex, mainly failed inspections."

Larry interrupted, "You're lying!"

"How would you know? You won't listen to Paul Andrews. He was frantic. He came to me for help. I took care of the problem."

"You took care of it? I swear, if you've done something that puts the lakefront project in jeopardy, I'll—"

"What? Thrash about demanding we put everything back in place and start fresh so your big plan succeeds?"

Hawthorne chimed in, "Let's not get too far afield. Maybe something will come of the Porter accusations, maybe not."

"Easy for you to say," Larry shouted.

Jack raised his voice. "Keith's right. The suit is not the most important issue."

"Tell me you're not referring to the item found on Etta's land," Larry said.

"The property belongs to the company, to us, not just Etta," Jack corrected.

A chair bounced across the wood floor, possibly tipping over. Kate guessed Allen was up and flailing his arms above his head. Her image amused her, especially when the councilman confirmed it by shouting. "You swore to me that skeleton meant nothing to us. You swore to me that everything was a go for the Branson riverfront project."

Jack said, "And everything is a go, but—"

The response was interrupted by the annoying and persistent sound of someone's pager alert. The alarm was silenced and its owner revealed when Hawthorne spoke. "I'd better call the office. My secretary doesn't use her emergency code without a good reason."

Hawthorne must have moved to Randy's desk to use the phone. The room was silent until the lawyer returned to the group. "Detective Collingwood wants to speak to Larry."

Jack asked, "That was your secretary's emergency?"

"Apparently he made it seem like an urgent request."

Again, the room became quiet.

After a moment, Larry said, "Why are you all looking at me? I've done nothing illegal. I have cooperated one hundred percent with the good detective."

"I can call him for specifics," Hawthorne said.

"No. Let's wait." Jack said. "We need to get a few things ironed out first."

Larry offered, "How about we start with that skeleton. Or, even better, the partnership agreement. You made it clear Bryan Porter would believe he was entitled to part of the company. You manipulated me by making me angry enough to confront Kate."

"I did not trick you. I merely pointed out an obvious problem. I certainly did not suggest that you confront the reporter at her house," Jack said, his frustration building.

"But that's not the real problem, is it?" Larry asked.

"I'm not sure what you mean," his grandfather said.

"The real problem is that partnership agreement was a problem long before now."

"You have no idea what you're talking about," Randy shouted.

Larry shot back, "That's true. No one discusses what happened. In fact, nothing happened. Right? An employee quit, moved out of town, and never came back. Hell, he deserted his family. Happens all the time."

Randy said, "Calm down, Larry."

"I'll calm down when you assure me they won't prove the skeleton is Lex Porter."

Jack said, "Lex Porter worked for our company. Whether he was a partner or not is irrelevant. What must be remembered is that only three living people know the facts of Lex Porter's last few years and none of those three are going to say anything to the authorities."

Hawthorne said, "We better continue this discussion another time. The good detective is not going to wait much longer for a return call."

Jack said, "Make it."

Kate couldn't hear anything but the faint sound of Hawthorne on the phone with Tom. She wished she could see Allen's face. Surely, he wasn't smiling.

"Collingwood and his partner will be over as soon as possible," Hawthorne said. "He wouldn't give me any details about what they want to discuss."

Kate didn't intend to be in the building, hidden or not, when Tom arrived. But she couldn't chance running into him on the stairs or in the reception area. She decided to stay put and leave quietly once the detectives were speaking to the group.

Unfortunately, Jack had something else in mind. "Keith, wait for the men at the entrance and take them to Larry's office for the interview. I'm sure Collingwood will not allow the grandfather and uncle to participate, so we'll wait in our offices until the detectives leave."

Before Kate could move, Jack turned the knob on the adjoining door. Opening it a crack, he said, "And, Larry, make sure you display that self-control you're always bragging ..."

Kate was across his assistant's area before Jack finished his sentence. She ducked into the empty conference room and waited by the door to the reception area.

Within five minutes Hawthorne said, "Sergeant Collingwood, welcome. You must have been waiting in the parking lot."

"We were close by," Tom said. "I appreciate your allowing us to interrupt your meeting. Would it be possible to speak to Mr. Allen privately?"

Hawthorne said, "Already arranged. I'd like to sit in."

When she was sure they were in Allen's office, Kate cracked open the door. She was in and out of the vacant area and down the stairs as fast as possible. She wouldn't be able to share what she heard with Tom or anyone else for that matter. The detective would be at best furious and at worst unforgiving.

Chapter Forty

Tom and Sid followed Hawthorne into Allen's office. The councilman was seated at a small conference table on one side of the room. The lawyer sat down next to Allen and motioned for the detectives to take chairs across the table.

"I don't mean to seem critical," Allen began with a smirk on his face, "but we spoke to you not twenty-four hours ago. You asked all your questions."

"As I told you yesterday, we have a witness who described and subsequently identified your site foreman, Paul Andrews, as the individual who gave the funds to a building inspector."

Hawthorne asked, "You didn't mention the inspector's name."

"Brad Fortner."

Allen said, "I know him. He's worked on several of our projects. He's been with the department for many years. I'd say he's above reproach."

"I'd agree with you except he got in a bind and needed quick cash."

"So what? It doesn't mean he took a bribe," Larry said.

"We have a witness. And he took care of his cash flow problem."

"Sounds circumstantial too me," Hawthorne said.

"We're still working the case."

"It wouldn't make sense for Paul or anyone working for the project to bribe an inspector," Allen said, his voice growing louder. "We've never had a safety issue on *any* job. We abide by the building codes. What would be gained?"

Tom said, "Let me give you a general answer from our point of view. Sometimes the motive for doing a crime is not logical or even understood. It could be much more than completing a project on time and within budget. Perhaps the goal is to lay the foundation for a much larger, more ambitious project. Or even to eliminate an issue which might threaten that future development."

Hawthorne asked, "Are you referring to your fantasy lakefront project?"

"I'd say the project is far from a fantasy. A good bit of work has been done to place your company in a key role for a huge project, at least by Branson standards."

The lawyer said, "We are right where we were yesterday. Unless you can bring up something more interesting than your opinion, we are done."

Tom observed the councilman and said, "Brad Fortner was murdered in Arkansas this week. We're here today to ask you to detail your activity for the last seven days."

Allen came out of his chair, his face turning light pink. "You're asking *me* for an alibi? Like I would go to Arkansas and kill a man?"

"We are checking the alibis for all individuals of interest," Sid said. "As a matter of fact, Mr. Andrews verified you were on site each day this week, but he could not verify every hour. Nor did he know how you spent your evenings. We're trying to fill in the gaps."

Allen walked away from the table, turning his back to the others. He lowered his head and shook it in disbelief or perhaps denial. After a few moments, he returned to the table, his arms folded across his chest. When he spoke, his tone was calm and measured. "I've been at the job site every day this week. I'll have to check with my secretary to see when I had meetings somewhere else. One notable exception is when I visited your friend Kate on Monday evening. My wife has been visiting relatives in Florida, but you can check with my neighbors to see if they noticed my comings and goings. That's all I can tell you other than I did not kill Brad Fortner. Nor did I have the man killed."

The detectives returned to City Hall and spent thirty minutes documenting the interview and discussing how to proceed with the Fortner bribery-murder case. Neither one could decide if the councilman was telling the truth about his involvement. They were hoping Lenny would find a suspect on his end, preferably someone who would identify Allen. They were about to head out of the office when the phone rang.

"I'm already late for dinner at Katie's. Can you take that?"

Sid shook his head and said, "Not if it might be an angry Kate."

Fortunately, it was Lenny Harper. His men stopped an individual driving Brad Fortner's truck. The man claimed a friend had sold it to him, fake invoice and all. The friend was identified as one of a pair asking about Fortner in the Lead Hill area.

Lenny said, "Once we convinced the two slimeballs we had them cold for first degree murder, they were happy to finger the man who hired them."

"You've had a busy couple of days," Tom said.

"Don't get too excited," Lenny said. "These guys don't have a name, but they gave me a description. I'd say it fits about twenty-five percent of the men in Taney County."

"Swell. How about I send you photos of some possibilities. I'll throw in a few more to complete the line-up."

"Fax them tonight, but messenger them ASAP, in case the faxes aren't clear."

"Better yet, Sid can bring them down right away."

"We'll be waiting," Lenny said.

Sid said, "You better get to Kate's. I'll take care of this and call you with any news."

Tom leaned against the banister and breathed in the cool night air. Kate slipped up beside him and massaged his back with both her palms. He relaxed his neck and allowed his head to ease forward.

"You have no idea how good that feels," he whispered.

"One of my many valued talents."

"But not the most valued."

"Careful, you'll turn my head," she said, scooting onto the glider and setting it in motion.

"Is this seat taken?"

"I was saving it for someone special."

"How special? Maybe I can qualify."

She reached up and took his hand, pulling him down beside her. "You definitely can."

Kate nuzzled closer, resting her head on his shoulder. A stray thought about Sid taking the photos to Lenny tried to distract him, but he brushed it aside.

"Tommy?"

"Uh-oh. You haven't called me that for a couple decades."

She sat up straight on the glider and the faraway gaze she'd had several times during dinner reappeared. "I need to tell you what I did today," she said.

"I knew something was bothering you."

"I guess I've been a little quiet. I've been trying to decide what to do."

"That's not what tipped me off. First, you didn't even mention I was almost an hour late for dinner. Then, you didn't want to discuss your conspiracy theories when Margie brought them up. Next, you didn't comment when your dad winked and said he and Margie would be going out for a while so don't wait up. But I knew it was serious when you didn't want me to clear the table or help with the dishes."

"Has anyone ever told you what a great detective you are?"

"Not lately. So let me have it. What did you do today that you aren't sure you want to discuss with me?"

"I was in the Riverside Mercantile building today. I happened to be in Jack Brighton's office when Jack, Randy, Larry, and their lawyer Keith Hawthorne were meeting in Randy's adjoining office."

"You *happened* to be in Jack Brighton's office?"

"Please, let me finish. I know it was a bad idea."

Tom pushed off the glider. "What time?"

"It was late afternoon, maybe three-thirty or four o'clock. But don't worry, I left before you and Sid arrived."

He rolled his eyes and looked toward the sky.

Kate paced the width of the porch. Her speech resumed, slowly at first and with several more caveats. As she relayed what she heard she became more animated and provided her analysis of each statement. Tom's head was beginning to spin, it was like reading one of her articles—full of hearsay and innuendo. The difference being he was privy to information which made her report—and consequently the men's discussion—make sense. He was still trying to sort it all out when he realized she was silent and again sitting on the glider.

"Say something," she demanded, looking at him with those beautiful blue eyes.

"I won't bother to tell you how your story would end had you been discovered by Jack Brighton. I will admit what you've reported is interesting. But unfortunately, it is no more than that. I can't tell the prosecutor that Randy Brighton confessed to doing something bad when a reporter I know overheard him while hiding in the office next door. And, by the way, I'm not sure what it was that he did."

"You're angry."

He sat down next to her and took her hands in his. "Not at you. I'm angry because I am so close to solving two murder cases I can taste it, but I don't have nearly enough proof."

"Two murder cases?"

"Oops."

"You may as well tell me."

"We got a tip about a possible bribery at one of the job sites. The tip led to a man who witnessed Paul Andrews allegedly provide an envelope full of cash to a building inspector."

"Andrews is Larry Allen's go-to-guy at all his job sites," Kate interrupted. "But you said another murder not bribery."

"Brad Fortner is the inspector in question. He was found dead in Arkansas several days ago. The sheriff has a suspect in custody who will name the man who hired him and his buddy in exchange for a plea deal."

"Maybe that's what Randy did to fix the problem at the office complex job."

"We believe Allen is the actual culprit, despite his protestations. Randy's only the accountant."

"I hope you're right, but in the meeting, Allen swore he'd done nothing, that all his jobs are clean. Randy's the one who said he took care of a problem."

"We'll have to see what Sid finds out tonight. He's taken some photos to Arkansas for the suspect to review. Maybe he'll ID someone. Or maybe whoever hired him is an intermediary. We may never tie the Brighton family to the crime."

"What about Lex Porter's murder?"

"We know the victim is Lex Porter. We have an idea what happened. But unless someone confesses or something else comes up that shows a strong motive, we have an unresolved case."

"You never know, what might happen," Kate said.

As Tom was taking in the suspicious gleam in her eye, his radio sounded off and the dispatcher patched in a call from Sid in Arkansas.

"Hey, Tom, sorry to interrupt, but I figured you'd be happy to know we have a positive ID on the individual who hired these two dudes to kill Fortner."

Chapter Forty-One

Kate got up early, fixed a pot of coffee and parked herself on the sofa in the living room. She was sure Tom would call with an update about his trip to Arkansas soon. She still didn't understand why Sid couldn't take care of everything with the Sheriff. Since the murder charge would be made by Boone County Arkansas, it wouldn't even be Tom's case. Her head ached with a thousand questions about who hired the men and who was involved with the bribery. She sipped from her third cup of coffee and stared impatiently at the phone.

"You haven't moved for over thirty minutes," her dad said on his way to the kitchen.

"You missed the first four hours of my vigil."

Roger returned shortly with a steaming mug of coffee. He made himself comfortable in his recliner and cleared his throat. "I hate to ask, but did you and Tom have a fight? Margie and I both noticed things were a bit strained during dinner."

"We're okay. He went to Arkansas about a case not long after you and Margie went out."

"And he was supposed to call, I take it."

"Don't you think he should? I mean, we were having a serious conversation."

Roger smiled and took another sip.

She said, "You think I'm being selfish."

"I didn't say that."

"I'm worried that's all."

He raised a fatherly eyebrow.

"Okay. I confess. I wanted to discuss an idea with him about the skeleton case. I was about to run it past him when Sid called."

"I would offer my advice, but I don't want to know what your idea is. I have a feeling Tom would be skittish too."

Kate got up and huffed toward the kitchen, throwing her parting comment over her shoulder. "You have no sense of adventure."

The swing moved with the southern wind, but the veranda was deserted—no warm welcome from Etta today. Kate opened the screen door and started to knock, but let it close quietly and pressed the rusty doorbell.

"I didn't expect you for another few minutes," Etta said, her hand on her chest and slightly out of breath.

Kate took her usual position on the end of the sofa next to Etta's chair and placed her recorder on the end table.

"Is this an official interview?" Etta asked pointing to the small device. "You said you had important news to tell *me*."

"Force of habit," Kate said picking up the recorder and dropping into her bag. "Have you spoken to Jack in the last few days?"

"I'm supposed to have dinner with him and Randy later this week."

"For your birthday," Kate said. "I forgot."

"That's okay. You don't have to keep track of my birthday."

"This wasn't a good idea. I better go," Kate said.

"You can't ask me about Jack and not tell me why. Should I call him?"

Kate regretted the obvious concern showing in Etta's eyes. "I didn't mean to alarm you. It's just that the police have identified the remains found on your lot as Lex Porter."

Etta said, "That's not possible."

"I'm afraid there's no doubt."

The octogenarian shook her head, coming out of her chair and walking to the mantel. She touched the picture of Clay.

"I'm not sure of details, but the investigation has shown Porter was murdered. As you know the detectives have questioned those close to Porter, yourself included. I guess they were in the process of interviewing Jack again, laying out all the evidence they have, when apparently Jack confessed," Kate lied.

Etta turned, took a few steps, and leaned on one arm of her chair. She lowered her head and squeezed her eyes shut, then eased onto the seat.

"Are you okay?" Kate asked.

Etta shook her head, then rested it on the chair back, her eyes searching the ceiling as if for clarification. "It was my fault," she whispered. "If I had told Jack when I found out, he would have begged Lex to come back. Once I knew Lex wasn't the one who stole the money and stock items from the store, I should have gone to Jack."

"That's why he broke up the partnership?"

Etta nodded and said, "But Lex did nothing wrong. When the stealing resumed, I realized Randy was the guilty party. When I confronted him, he promised to stop and begged me not to tell his father. Before long Lex left town. In time I assumed he wouldn't come back. But I was wrong."

"You saw him?" Kate said out loud, more a realization than a question.

"I was in my office, but I heard them arguing, so much anger between them, and each friend thinking he'd been betrayed by the other. The fight escalated. By the time I went up front, Lex was choking Jack. I don't know why I pointed to the shovel. He took it out of the display. Lex let go of Jack's throat, but it was too late."

Etta buried her face in her hands and sobbed.

Kate tried to process the woman's declaration, but it didn't make sense. As the reporter visualized Etta's description of the event, something—or someone—was missing. "Who took the shovel from the display?" she asked.

Tears flowing down her cheeks, Etta raised her head. "He was so young. I only wanted him to help his father. I didn't mean for him to kill Lex. He didn't know his own strength."

Kate paused in the entranceway. Tom and Sid didn't notice her at first. They were busy sorting papers at the conference table. Occasionally they reviewed the notes on a large pad attached to an easel in the corner of the room. She wasn't sure she knew where to begin to explain what happened, unsure if it would help or hurt the case. She stared at the two detectives until a passing patrolman greeted her by name and Tom turned around.

"Katie. I didn't see you," he said. "What's wrong?"

"I need to speak to you," she said.

"Can it wait? I'm in the middle of getting stuff ready for an indictment. We're on a tight schedule to get the package to Arkansas."

"I understand, but you should listen to this first." She held out her hand and revealed the small recorder in her palm. "It was in my purse, so I'm not sure how clear it will be."

Tom accepted the device and said, "Let's go in the office."

The three listened to Etta's version of what happened the night of the murder. By the end Tom was massaging his temples and Sid was leaning back in his chair shaking his head.

Kate lowered her chin and said, "I know it's lame to say I wanted to help. I was convinced Etta had information she was hiding. And now you know who killed Lex."

Tom said, "I'll have to admit this is one notch above listening to a private meeting from the office next door. Unfortunately, it has the same impact. You tricked Etta into telling you her account of the events."

Sid said, "And, to be precise, we know only what Etta says about Lex's death. I'm sure Hawthorne will have a good time with this."

"I don't know what to say. I'm sorry seems a little shallow."

Sid pushed away from his desk and said, "I need a refill."

"I'll be out in a minute," Tom told him.

He took her hands in his. "I'm not saying I'm not furious with you. I know you were trying to help, but I wish you had discussed the plan with me first."

"I was about to when you ran off to Arkansas."

"We'll discuss this later. I have to get back to work."

Chapter Forty-Two

The three police officers walked silently to Sid's vehicle as the last sliver of sunlight sunk behind the clouds. Tom took the backseat and laid his head against the cushion. The long day had been filled with meetings, capping a week's worth of conference calls, brainstorming, and interviews to prepare two cases for two prosecutors—one in Arkansas and one in Missouri.

Dan Palmer said, "Good job, both of you. The bribery case is solid."

"Let's hope the prosecutor agrees," Sid said.

"He seemed a little unsure of Frankie's statement," Tom commented.

"Don't forget Paul Andrews' testimony against Randy Brighton. His plea deal was a significant turning point. And we have the additional circumstantial evidence."

Tom asked, "Will there be a problem trying Brighton in Missouri before releasing him to Arkansas for the murder case?"

"That will be up to the prosecutor to figure out, but probably not an issue."

Tom knew the Arkansas case against Randy depended on the testimony of the thug he hired to kill Fortner. Fortunately, Sid chose a picture of Larry Allen surrounded by his coworkers, grandfather, and uncle to include in the photo lineup. And, if Randy is found guilty of the bribery charge in Missouri, it will go a long way to balance the scales of justice in Arkansas.

The men rode the remainder of the trip between Forsyth and Branson in silence. Sid pulled up to the police entrance and stopped.

"You're not going in?" Tom asked.

"Already dangerously close to being late for my date with Shirley. Unless you need me for something tonight," he added glancing at the lieutenant.

"Nothing more we can do this evening. Have a good time tonight," Palmer said. "I'm going to take my own advice and I suggest you do the same," he added in Tom's direction.

"I want to finish up a couple things. See you Monday."

Tom hadn't called Kate all week. At first, he was angry she disregarded his request to stay out of the skeleton case. Her meddling diminished hope of determining for sure what happened that night with Lex Porter, let alone proving who killed him. As the week dragged on, he focused on preparing for the Fortner-related charges, which seemed more straightforward and which were undamaged by Kate's curiosity.

Ultimately, missing her softened Tom's anger. He reached for the phone, but paused, tapped the receiver, and withdrew his hand. He wasn't quite sure what to say to that little red-haired girl inside that beautiful annoying woman. He gripped the receiver but left it in place.

"So, are you going to call me or not?" Kate asked.

Tom smiled, hoping he wasn't imagining her voice, and slowly turned toward the door.

"To call or not to call? Tough dilemma," she said.

"I'm leaning toward *to call.*"

He came out of his chair and welcomed her into his arms. Pressing his cheek against hers, he embraced the soft lilac scent of her hair. "How did you know I'd be here?"

"You weren't everywhere else," she said with a grin.

Tom opened his eyes. A trail of discarded clothing led from the living room to the bedroom. *It wasn't a dream.* He rolled over and studied Kate's face and the slight raising and lowering of her chest with each resting breath. As he drifted back to sleep, he marveled at his fortune in recapturing this perfect love.

"Breakfast is ready," Kate whispered in his ear.

"Did you order in?"

"Very funny. Come to the table and feast your eyes on my creations."

Tom got dressed and met Kate in the dining area.

"This looks great," Tom said, helping himself to eggs and sausage.

Kate asked, "Did you hear Ward I needs a new alderman?"

"Allen resigned?"

"Friday morning. Personal reasons according to his resignation letter."

"Hmm, I'd say that fits."

"How's the bribery case going?"

"You're not going for the Porter suit?"

"I'm trying to make conversation, not pump you for information!" She gathered the empty plates and silverware and took them to the sink.

"Sit down. I'll tell you what I can," he said with a smile.

She pulled her knees close to her chest. "I'm ready. And I won't print a word."

"We'll be able to take care of the bribery case in Missouri before Randy is extradited to Arkansas to face murder charges. We've received more tips and Leatherman is helping with the investigation."

"What about Lex's murder?"

"That's another issue."

"I tainted the evidence," she said, a sincere apology in her eyes.

"Nevertheless, Jack Brighton has confessed. Hawthorne says his client is ready to turn himself in. Jack claims he and Lex were alone, they argued, and Jack lost his temper."

"I suppose it could have happened that way, but it's not what Etta told me."

"More to the point, it doesn't jive with the forensic evidence. Frankly, Etta's story makes more sense. But with all the confusion and the time that has passed who knows?"

"Jack's trying to protect his son and Etta," Kate said.

"No doubt. But we continue to work the case. You will probably be happy to hear that Bryan Porter has hired a hotshot lawyer from Springfield to handle the inheritance issue. Thanks to you, he has a fighting chance with the partnership agreement."

"That's good, I suppose," she said. "You know, I've been thinking it may have been Randy who hired those boys to break into Etta's to find that document."

Tom said, "Didn't I mention? We nabbed the two young men who trashed her house. Randy did hire them, but that may not be enough."

Kate shrugged and furrowed her brow.

Tom said, "Hey, at least you can be happy about Allen's resignation."

"To some extent, but he was cleared of bribery. He'll probably end up running his grandfather's company. And he, Wainright, and Henderson are free to go ahead with the mysterious lakefront project, which Allen still disavows by the way."

"I wouldn't be too sure. Your article put folks on notice. They're going to think twice about selling land to those guys. Besides, as you suggested in the piece, I wouldn't be surprised if Branson has plans of its own regarding the lakefront."

"Nevertheless, I'm keeping my eye on the former councilman," she said with determination. "So, you actually read my article?"

"Of course, I did. Best-friends-forever, remember?"

Beth Urich

After almost twenty-five years working in and for the Federal Government, Beth moved to Southwestern Missouri. Her goal: to find peace and quiet and begin a new career as an author.

Originally from Kansas City, Kansas, Beth moved to Florida when she was thirteen and graduated from high school in Tampa. After eight years in the United States Air Force, she went to work as a computer programmer for a Federal contractor in Washington, D.C. Sixteen years later, she sold everything, bought an RV, and hit the road with her mother. They decided to settle in Branson, Missouri, fifteen months after leaving D.C. and about a year shy of the 1991 CBS 60 *Minutes* broadcast that brought national attention to the small tourist town.

Branson's evolution to a major entertainment center surprised everyone. Famous-named entertainers built theaters. National-chain motels sprung up everywhere. The dynamics of that accelerated growth inspired Beth to write her Kate Starling Mysteries series.

As for most struggling authors, the road to publication was long and often discouraging. Although she actively pursued a career throughout the 1990s, her efforts decreased in this century. As her day job took over her life, beginning in 2003, her writing career took a back seat until her retirement in 2014.

In addition to writing Beth enjoys bowling, hiking, volunteering, and taking care of her Miniature Pinscher, Lilly, who shares her home in Branson.

1. The author has set the novel in Branson, Missouri, in the mid-1990s. What part does the city's expansive growth period play in the different storylines in the novel?

2. One of the two major storylines is set in the present, the other in the distant past. How does the mystery of the past reflect the activities of the novel's present-day Branson? Were the outcomes of those stories as you expected? Was justice served?

3. What drives Kate's pursuit of her conspiracy theory about Larry Allen? Is it her disdain for the arrogant, young Councilman or a reporter's intuition?

4. Kate often seems to push the envelope in her search for a story. What is the most careless impulse she follows in the novel to acquire information? Have you ever gone close to a line to accomplish your goal? Were you successful? Did you learn a lesson?

5. Tom and Kate have been struggling to hold onto their high school romance. Who do you think is trying the hardest? What is necessary for them to succeed?

6. During the novel Kate's father begins a new romantic relationship, several years after his wife's death. Do you think Kate approves? Are he and Margie a good match?

7. Of Kate's three close relationship, who is the one with whom Kate is most the candid and self-revealing–Tom, Shirley, or Roger? Which one

seems to measure Kate's motives more accurately?

8. The bond between Etta Stupholds and Jack Brighton seems unbreakable. Do you think it's a genuinely strong friendship or simply two people suppressing a crime from the past?

9. Do you think Jack Brighton has, or ever had, any intention of rebuilding Clay's store on the St. Limas Street property? Does Etta believe he will?

10. What lessons did Kate learn during the novel about herself and her "people skills"? Will she change her behavior going forward? Will her investigative journalism skills improve?

11. What do you hope will happen in the future regarding Tom and Kate's relationship? Will they be able to overcome the conflicting professions?

12. *Connections* is the second book in the Kate Starling Mysteries series. What challenges would you like to see in Kate's future?

Turn the page for a sneak peek of Book Three in
the *Kate Starling Mysteries Series* ...

Family
Matters

Chapter One

Kate Starling slapped the customer service counter, startling the *Branson Tri-Lakes Daily News* part-time receptionist Cassie Yeats. The young woman's golden tresses glided across her back in thick waves as she raised her head, swirled around, and lifted out of her chair. "You're here!" she said, surprising the reporter with an uncharacteristic enthusiasm.

"My early-morning interview with the souvenir shop owner lasted longer than I anticipated. Anyone ... meaning Helen ... notice I was late?"

Cassie shook her head, still grinning ear-to-ear. "Here's your copy. It came over the fax machine about twenty minutes ago. It's not very long. Read it," she said without taking a breath.

"Wow. I haven't seen you this excited since you were officially hired last year."

Kate turned the page right side up, and immediately spotted the police department logo in the upper left corner, sending an involuntary tingle up her spine and down to her fingertips.

Unidentified body discovered early this morning on Marvin Way. Police investigation is ongoing. If you believe you have information regarding this issue, please contact the Branson Police Department immediately.

More information will follow when available.

Leonard Daniels, Chief of Police

"This is why Tom was called to work early this morning," she whispered.

"So cool," Cassie offered.

Kate withheld comment regarding the young girl's excitement over a dead body as she pivoted toward the hallway leading to her boss's office. Looking back over her shoulder, she shouted, "Find Barry. Tell him to meet me by the back door in five minutes."

Helen met her in the hall. "I heard you coming. I've seen the fax."

"Please don't tell me someone else has already gone out there."

"No. But I want you to take a couple of deep breaths before you leave."

"I'll breathe in the car. I promise. And I won't interfere with the police investigation," Kate added, anticipating her boss's next ... and somewhat warranted ... admonition.

Following a long pause, Helen nodded her approval, and Kate headed for the alley entrance close to where she had parked her car. On their way to the scene, she briefed the photographer Barry, whose assignments usually involved city council and rotary meetings and the annual 5K run for charity.

"Are we assuming this is a murder?" Barry asked.

"Could be someone simply collapsed and died, I suppose, but Tom was called really early this morning. The police haven't made an update since the eight-thirty a.m. fax, so, I would say yes, we have our first murder in almost exactly three years."

"So, you're not counting the skeleton by the lake?"

"That was an *old* murder."

"Right. In any case, it must be handy to be a reporter dating a cop."

She glanced in his direction and said, "Not so much. Detective Collingwood and I have a complicated professional relationship."

"Check that out ... the patrolmen in that parking lot," Barry said, motioning to the small strip mall at the intersection of Marvin Way and Highway 165.

"I know those two officers."

"Looks like they're cordoning off an area around that incredibly ugly little car. I've never seen one that color before," Barry snickered.

"Yeah, chartreuse is pretty rare," Kate said, recognizing the vehicle in question, by the bumper stickers and its neon color. She had first interviewed the owner of the car two years ago in his condo, maybe three miles from the lot. The man claimed that the color was his favorite, but she suspected it was a company vehicle from the group he worked for in Kansas City.

Marvin Way took a couple of sharp turns into a small residential community on the south-western edge of Branson. Sandwiched between the growing number of commercial businesses along Highway 165 and a massive undeveloped wooded area stretching westward outside the city limits, the houses went largely unnoticed.

Two police officers stood between their vehicles, essentially blocking the street at its last sharp turn. Kate and Barry walked the short distance to the guarded access after she parked her Focus along the roadside.

"Hey Skip. Pete," she said with a nod and warm smile. She had met Patrol Corporal Harold "Skip" Rogers long before her high school sweetheart, now roommate, Tom Collingwood returned to the Branson PD three years ago. Skip had been in the first article of her police recruit series, which began in 1992 as the department expanded to meet the needs of the growing city. Patrolman Pete Sims, newer to the department, seemed very young when she interviewed him for the ongoing column two years later.

"We know nothing," Skip said with a grin.

"That goes without saying," Kate retorted, positioning herself so she could observe the activity toward the end of Marvin Way. She turned to say something to Barry, but he was already standing on an old tree stump taking pictures.

"You two can't go any further, Kate," Skip said.

"I understand. We're just responding to the police department fax. A reporter never knows what they might see or who might make a statement," Kate said.

"I suppose," Skip said, surveying the area behind him as if trying to determine her and

Barry's line of sight. "My suggestion, however, would be to head on back to the newspaper and wait for the next fax from the Chief."

Kate laughed. After a moment, she said, "Oh, I'm sorry. I didn't know you were serious."

Pete whispered, "Coroner's finally here, Skip."

Taney County Coroner Artie Richards rolled up beside Kate, his driver's side window opened. "Nice to see you Kate," he said, adding, "But not surprised you're here."

"Thanks, Artie. You're a little late to the party though," she said with a smile.

"Engrossed in a three-day medical examiner's seminar out in Springfield when I got the notification."

Kate said, "That explains why the body's still here."

"You can go on through, Mr. Richards," Pete said.

The reporter sidled up to Skip and said, "Saw the two patrolmen marking an area around a really bright yellow-green Plymouth Neon in the strip mall parking lot on 165. Does it have something to do with the victim?"

"Victim?" Skip said, raising an eyebrow. "It would be premature at this time to call the deceased a crime victim."

"Since Artie just got here, I'm guessing the detectives assume the corpse is a murder victim until shown to be otherwise."

Skip turned to Pete and said, "Have you noticed how some folks who date policemen think they know a lot about police investigations?"

Pete grinned widely and stared at the reporter.

Kate returned a smile and then walked nonchalantly between the two patrol cars. She stopped as soon as she caught a glimpse of Tom and his partner Detective Sergeant Sid Greene leading Artie to the body, which was in a narrow empty space between two houses close to the street's dead end.

Satisfied that she'd seen what there was to see from her position, she reversed her course and said, "Okay, Barry, I guess we'll take this young man's advice and head back to the office." She tossed a perfunctory wave toward Skip and Pete and said, "Thanks guys. We look forward to the next police fax."

"Got some good photos," Barry reported, struggling with his seat belt.

"I'll have to come back later to see if the neighbors saw anything," Kate said.

"Too bad Tom won't fill you in."

"Yes, very inconvenient," she agreed, turning the Focus around to leave.

Sharon Thompson served as Kate's police department contact for the crime statistics data used for the paper's weekly report. The forty-something woman had been Chief Daniels' secretary since he rose to the position more than a decade ago. She was very protective of him, his time, and his information, and only moderately tolerant of inquiries by the media.

The secretary was more than cordial when Kate picked up the weekly crime info, but the odds of learning anything about the police activity surrounding the dead body on Marvin Way were slim. Of course, low odds never slowed down a good reporter. *May as well go for broke.*

"Good morning, Kate," Sharon said, peering over her computer monitor. "I knew you couldn't wait until next Tuesday to pump me about the murder."

"So, you're saying I'm predictable?" Kate said, not surprised Sharon had her pegged.

The secretary shrugged with a smile, causing an errant brunette curl to fall across her forehead. Her new cut and hairdo had revealed a sprinkle of white beginning to creep into her thick now shoulder-length hair. Kate resisted offering a compliment knowing that Sharon would categorize it as flattery.

"I was hoping there might be a more complete press release by now. The patrol officers at the scene wouldn't let me past the perimeter. They wouldn't even admit it was a murder, as you apparently just did."

"Oops," Sharon said.

"Don't worry, that wasn't too hard to guess. Any other tidbits for an old friend?"

"There will be a fax sent out later today, but you shouldn't get too excited. It's will still be a preliminary and, therefore, boring announcement. After all, the victim was hardly a major contributor to the community." Sharon furrowed her brow and pursed her lips.

"Too late," Kate said. "So, the victim was not a local. Interesting."

"I didn't say that."

"Don't worry, I won't quote you ... directly."

"Good to know. But I really don't know anything. It's too early."

"Is that part of the PD mantra ... *it's too early to say*? Never mind, let's move on to another topic. Since I'm here, I'll pick up last week's crime stats if they're ready."

"We won't have anything for you this week."

Kate raised her eyebrows. "Because ...?"

"The city administration wants to review the policy."

"You mean the *City Administrator* wants to *suppress* the information?"

"I wouldn't put it that way and the decision to rethink the policy was a group effort."

"You mean Mark Orchard and a few of his cronies in the Chamber of Commerce?"

Sharon smirked and then proceeded to straighten piles of paper on her desk.

"Okay," Kate said after a few moments. "Can I speak to the Chief about this?"

"You'd be better off going to Orchard or Mayor Holt." After a moment, she looked at Kate and said, "Chief Daniels *did not* participate in the discussion regarding the crime statistics."

Sharon's last sentence propelled Kate directly to the mayor's office to speak with Laura Abbott, her friend and chief city grapevine monitor. Although her primary responsibilities involved the mayor and city administrator, Laura had held every post in the administration and still had influence within each city department.

The reporter found the executive assistant at her desk, positioned strategically between Holt and Orchard's offices. Unlike the metal items found in most city offices, the mayor's suite contained only wooden furniture, still stately but slightly tarnished by time. The secretary's desk, centered between the men's office doors, housed the access control center for the executives and guarded three four-drawer file cabinets. A small round conference table, surrounded by four executive armchairs, occupied the area close but off-center to the suite's archway entrance.

"I know nothing about the dead body," Laura said before Kate had a chance to finish her greeting.

"Why would I ask the mayor's assistant about a dead body? I'm here to complain to the mayor about the crime statistics," Kate said, feigning outrage.

"He's not here today. But if he were here, he'd tell you he's not responsible for crime in the city or providing crime statistics to the press."

"How about the City Administrator?"

"He's with the mayor in Jefferson City. What do you want to know? Perhaps I can find someone else to assist you."

"The police department refused to provide the information for next week's crime report column."

"Refused?"

"Sharon told me the policy was under review."

"*That* is correct. The topic was discussed at the last staff meeting."

"Can I have a copy of the minutes?"

"Really?"

"How about just telling me why?" Kate asked, letting her friend off for doing her job.

"How about I make an appointment for you to discuss the subject with Mark Orchard next week? Or Mayor Holt, if you prefer."

"I'll have one with each, please."

As Kate walked out of City Hall, she took her phone off vibrate. She was halfway to her vehicle when her best friend Shirley Barrens called. "Good timing," Kate said, "What's up?"

"You're not going to believe this," Shirley said, clearly upset.

"Are you okay?"

"I'm fine. It's Ginger. Carl's done it again. Can you come to the hospital? She's on the fourth floor. I'll meet you there."

Shirley greeted Kate in the hall outside Ginger's room. "They're examining her injuries," she said, motioning toward the closed door.

"Injuries? When did this happen?" Kate asked.

"Tuesday evening. She spent some time in the ER. They decided to keep her overnight."

"So, she's been here two nights already? How bad?"

"Apparently they were concerned about a concussion. She took a bad fall into the kitchen counter. The x-ray revealed a hairline fracture. I'm not sure when she'll be released."

"Thanks for calling me. I can't believe this happened again."

"Actually, I'm not surprised. Some of her remarks in the last several months have made me wonder if he was regressing."

The three friends had been close since elementary school, although Ginger had drifted away from the relationship occasionally. But the trio had always supported each other through life events—good and bad—regardless of what else was happening in their lives.

A doctor and two nurses exited the room, leaving the door propped open behind them. One of the nurses said, "She can have visitors now."

"Thanks," Shirley said.

Ginger sat propped up in bed, holding an icepack to her left cheek.

Kate found no words to express her thoughts.

"Don't worry, I'm on some good pain pills. But it feels just as bad as it looks," Ginger said, trying to smile. "Somebody say something."

Shirley said, "I'm sorry this happened. I know you wanted things to work out with Carl."

Ginger shrugged, tears forming in her eyes. "Sorry, I'm a little weepy. I guess I'm a little overwhelmed. The other times were bad enough, but not like this. I thought he'd changed."

"Will you be able to go home today?" Shirley asked.

"They're going to do another x-ray. The doctor wants to see how things look now that the swelling has gone down."

"Have you called your mother?" Kate asked.

"No. I'm not ready for that lecture again."

"Do you want me to speak to her?" Kate said.

"I'll deal with it later, but I appreciate your offer. I really can't think clearly right now. Once I go home—"

"You can't go home," Kate said. "You have to go somewhere safe. You can contact the crisis center. I'm sure they'll help you with temporary housing."

"Carl's in jail. They picked him up this morning at his cousin's house."

"Robbie helped him?" Shirley said.

"They're close." Ginger said. "In any case, I'll be able to go home. The prosecutor wants to press charges. I'm not sure what that means. I know this is my fault. I should never have taken him back after he got out of jail."

"For the third assault ... I might add," Kate said.

"It's not your fault," Shirley said.

"That's what they tell me in my group sessions at the crisis center," Ginger said. "But the truth is, I stayed with him. I made that decision. Obviously, we're not good together."

Kate looked at her watch. "I've got to get back to work."

"You both do," Ginger said. "I'll be fine. Thanks for coming by. I'll keep you posted."

"I'm going to come back after work," Kate said. "Maybe you'll know more about getting released. If you can leave sooner, call one of us and we'll get you home."

"In the meantime, call the crisis center hotline and tell them what's happened," Shirley said. "Ask them what options you have through them."

"Will do," Ginger said, pushing through another smile.

A Note from the Publisher

Dear Reader,

Thank you for reading Beth Urich's second novel of the Kate Starling Mysteries, *Connections*.

   We feel the best way to show appreciation for an author is by leaving a review. You may do so on any of the following sites:

www.ZimbellHousePublishing.com
Goodreads.com
or your favorite retailer

Join our mailing list to receive updates on new releases, discounts, bonus content, and other great books from Beth Urich and